NET

By the same author
MAKING WAVES

ACKNOWLEDGEMENTS

Thank you to Elizabeth Rectanus for her invaluable insider's view of New York; to Dave Austin for help with TV technicalities; and last but not least, to Jill Dearlove for her unique brand of encouragement and support.

NETWORK

Liz Allen

ARROW BOOKS

To Malcolm and Sam
with my love
always

Arrow Books Limited
20 Vauxhall Bridge Road, London SW1V 2SA

An imprint of the Random Century Group

London Melbourne Sydney Auckland Johannesburg
and agencies throughout the world

First published in Great Britain by Century 1989
Arrow edition 1991

© Liz Allen 1989

The right of Liz Allen to be identified as the author of
this work has been asserted by her in accordance
with the Copyright, Designs and Patents Act, 1988

This book is sold subject to the condition that it shall
not, by way of trade or otherwise, be lent, resold,
hired out, or otherwise circulated without the
publisher's prior consent in any form of binding or
cover other than that in which it is published and
without a similar condition including this condition
being imposed on the subsequent purchaser

Printed and bound in Great Britain by
Courier International Ltd, Tiptree, Essex

ISBN 0 09 953680 3

Chapter One

She wasn't supposed to suffer from nerves, stage fright, call it what you will. Try 'sheer terror'. So how come her stomach felt like it had molten lead glopping around in its murky little pit?

And she wasn't supposed to be ugly. But look at that face! It would stun a police dog at fifty paces. Definitely past its sell-by date.

That was hardly the ice-cool Kate O'Connell gawking blearily out at her from the bathroom mirror – the Beautiful Bitch, the Lady of the Lance, or whatever nickname the reviewers might think up for her this week. Nope. That face belonged to plain old Katy, (this morning, oh so very plain, if not so very old,) who looked about as sharp and glamorous as a leftover soggy dumpling.

She hadn't felt like this yesterday morning, and probably wouldn't tomorrow, so why today of all days? Just when she could do with being her most confident, optimistic, self-assured, elegant, dazzling, charming, witty, attractive . . .

She gave a hefty yawn, turned the shower mixer to full force, cold, then shuddered, took a deep breath and stepped under the spray. She yelped out loud. It can't be worth it, she told herself, soaping her body vigorously in an effort to resuscitate her shocked circulation. All this agony just for the sake of a simple lunch date. But one could hardly describe the invitation for her and Julian to dine with Ed Franklin – and at Lacey's, no less – as a simple lunch date. Not since 'dear old Ed' had been transformed into Head of Programming, the man with the brief to pull the ratings up by their socks or else.

TV7's pyramid of power had a double pinnacle. At the very top, so high up that it was above the clouds and therefore never seen and rarely remembered by the workers, was the Board of Directors – the financial backers, entrepreneurs, businessmen, people who collected directorships instead of old age pensions. They had little to do with the nitty gritty or the ethics of broadcasting. For them, TV7 was nothing more or less than a financial investment. Below them, just beneath the cloud blanket, was the Board of Management whose members actually *ran* the company. They were broadcasters and media people all, who'd climbed their way up the TV7 or some other broadcasting pyramid.

However, the one power the Board of Directors did have – and it was a pretty significant one – was that they decided just who was going to be *on* the Board of Management. Normally it was a straightforward issue. When one of the management team either retired or moved on to pastures new – rarely was he pushed out – his deputy, being the obvious successor, would be rubber-stamped on to the Board of Management.

Until recently, that is. Falling ratings and consequent falling advertising revenue had resulted in the erstwhile Head of Programming being given the *sack*! And his deputy – the effrontery of the man! – had gone off to join the BBC in protest. So there was no longer an obvious successor and the Board of Directors had to hold many meetings behind closed doors before the new appointment was finally decided on the casting vote of the Chairman of the Board, Sir Arnold Bickerdyke. Ed Franklin was to be the new Head of Programming and Ed Franklin was determined to make his mark.

That's why Kate couldn't allow herself to regard the invitation as a simple social lunch. Not on the day after the quarterly Programme Planning Board, not when rumours of programme cuts had been pelting back and forth with the speed of Japanese ping-pong all yesterday afternoon. And especially not when her ratings were still hovering stubbornly just *below* the top ten. Kate O'Connell might fool a lot of the people a lot of the time but she rarely, if ever, fooled herself. The Katy part of her saw to that. So, for lunch at Lacey's with her producer and the newly elevated Head of Programming, read 'execution in a public place so she can't throw a wobbly on us'.

She shivered at the thought. Or it might just have been the icy water. Either way, she turned on the hot tap for consolation. It warmed her a little but didn't do much to ease that nagging sense of impending doom.

After that it was downhill all the way, a morning of self-indulgence. All the little comfort rituals that she hadn't needed or thought of for months were dragged out of the cupboard. A cigarette *before* breakfast. Sugar on the cornflakes. Cream in the coffee. Butter *and* honey on the usual dry toast and so what if she got fat and spotty and wheezed all day long? She munched her way through a third slice. The condemned TV personality had as much right to a hearty breakfast as the next character on Death Row. She didn't spend much time wondering what other programmes might be up for the chop. All she cared about was her own. *Kate In Company*. Her baby. Almost literally.

She'd spent nearly a decade watching from the sidelines while her contemporaries from school, and after a token show of resistance her fellow graduates too, produced the regulation, human, variety of infants, having succumbed first to the lure of husbands (usually) and security (sometimes). Kate had looked on smugly, offering the expected cheers, albeit a little half-heartedly, at the appropriate moments, while firmly convinced that it was they, not she, stuck on the sidelines. She was the one in the thick of the real game, right in there amongst the shoulder pads and helmets, tackling, butting and eventually scoring for all she was worth. Television was the name of the game. Her own programme, devised and presented by Kate O'Connell, the ultimate, winning goal. Her baby.

It had taken her eight years. Years of bowing and scraping, and being helpful and enthusiastic, and starting early and staying late, and being patted on the head like a good little girl for her efforts. Until the pats began to feel more like collisions with a brick wall. And it was one hell of a brick wall. She should have realised it the day she first set foot inside the glass and concrete monolith that housed TV7, a naïve and sassy optimist going for a job interview. But she'd realised it soon enough and in the process of dismantling the wall, first painstakingly, brick by brick, and then impatiently, going at it with a sledge-hammer, she'd rapidly lost the naïvety. The sassy optimism hadn't so much disappeared as undergone a subtle trans-formation into something harder and more brittle, an assertive opportunism, perhaps. Though this morning there didn't seem to be much of that left either.

She went back upstairs and surveyed the devastation of her bedroom. The almost empty shoe-rack glared accusingly from the open wardrobe at the heaped jumble of footwear spilling across the creamy, pure wool shag-pile. The laundry basket, an Ali Baba wickerwork affair, had a definite Leaning Tower of Pisa aspect with the precarious column of unwashed miscellania growing steadily above the rim. A pair of escapee French knickers and three odd stockings peeked out at her from under the bed. And the bed itself looked as if it hadn't been made for days – which it hadn't, as her cleaning lady had been on holiday.

It was at times like this that Kate thought wistfully how wonderful it must be to have one of those old-fashioned household fixtures that used to be the God-given right of every upwardly mobile young executive – the 'housewife'. But there weren't too many of those around these days, especially if you wanted the model which came ready equipped with all male fittings. But how lovely it must be to have someone wave you off to work in the morning with a kiss and a cuddle and a reassuring, 'There, there, darling, don't worry.'

Forty-five minutes later she studied her reflection with reasonable satisfaction. Face in place and dressed for battle she quickly tidied round the room, gathered up the overflow from the laundry bin into a towel, took it down to the kitchen and hid it inside the washing machine. She didn't think to switch it on. She swilled out the breakfast dishes and stacked them in the dishwasher along with yesterday's culinary debris then scribbled a note for Mrs Pickles, satisfied that the place looked lived in but not overwhelmingly so. Good cleaning ladies are hard to find and even harder to hang on to. Finding Mrs Pickles a year ago – a whole year and the woman was still coming back for more, bless her – had been like coming across a diamond ring on the costume jewellery counter at Woolworth's. She cosseted her like mad.

'*Dear Mrs P.*,' she wrote, '*Hope you've had a splendid hol. New box of tea bags next to Jaffa Cakes. Money in microwave. Please ignore downstairs today – bedroom and bathroom are more needy. Love, K.*'

Actually, the rest of the house was pretty messy too but it could wait. Alex was coming round this evening and he might not be aware of it yet but he wasn't going to be allowed much time for relaxing downstairs . . .

She propped the note up against the kettle which was always Mrs Pickles' first port of call then took a final check in the mirror. Vanilla crêpe de Chine shirt, putty-pink wool crêpe trousers pleated into the waistband, with the whole deal nicely clinched by a taupe suede belt. Understated, stylish, expensive yet practical and above all comfortable for work . . . 'Overalls by Armani' she thought wryly before turning from the mirror confident that she could forget about her appearance for the rest of the day.

A glance at the slim gold Rolex on her wrist told her it was time to leave so she briskly gathered up her survival kit – cigarettes, Dunhill lighter, money wallet, credit card wallet, mini-atomizer of Shalimar – and dropped them into a suede Gucci shoulder bag. She threw her Burberry trenchcoat over her shoulders and jingling the car keys in her hand Kate O'Connell headed in the direction of a bound-to-be-stormy day, determined that if her ship was going to be scuttled she'd be damned if she'd go down with it gracefully.

She paused briefly on the doorstep to survey her patch of garden – her very own little piece of England. She'd bought the place a few months ago, riding high on the tide of a rapidly rising salary, but today she felt a stab of fear as she looked almost longingly at her domain. It was the realisation of a dream she'd had for years, moving from a single room to a tiny basement with shared bath to a self-contained, one-bedroomed affair and finally, this. A real house, by the river, with a private bit of outdoors and *her* name on the title deeds.

A high brick wall covered in honeysuckle and clematis enclosed a space about twenty feet square beyond which was a footpath, a road, a weedy bit of embankment and then the Thames. From the doorstep she could just see over the garden wall to the river surface. The sun was warm on her face and its light glinted like lots of little silver petals floating on top of the water. She took one more deep breath then closed the garden gate firmly behind her, climbed into her bright orange Volkswagen, turned the ignition and gunned the engine into life. She set off through the snarling traffic of Chiswick with a snarl inside her to equal whatever the rush hour could throw at her. And any suicidal pedestrians had better keep well out of her way, too – she might just let them have their death wish.

She arrived at TV7 just before ten. Her allotted space in the underground car park was still labelled with her car's registration number. The security man on duty at the doors smiled at her and said, 'Good morning, Miss O'Connell,' without even glancing at the laminated ID card she held out. Joyce, who ran the third floor tea trolley thrust a lidded polystyrene cup at her as she passed, with the words, 'Here you are, ducks, you can pay for it later,' and as she opened the door to her office with a look of grim determination on her face she was met with an unusually cheery, 'Morning, Kate! Thought I'd surprise you and get here early for a change,' from Linda, her PA/researcher, who was already halfway through opening today's pile of mail. Frizzy, pale ginger hair already escaping from its rubber band, jade corduroy dungarees slightly balding at the knee, polythene shopping bag from Tesco's nestling by her desk with a pair of knitting needles poking out, Adelle Davis vitamin book on the shelf next to Linda's dictionary and phone directories . . .

It was all so incredibly normal!

Kate summoned up a smile but it felt a little weak round the edges as she said 'hello' and hung her coat on the hook behind the door. She felt Linda's eyes on her as she crossed to her desk and sat down. Now that she was actually at TV7 the nerves were worse rather than better and it annoyed her. And it was still only ten o'clock. If it was like this now what the hell was she going to feel like in another three hours? She'd be totally incapacitated. Butterflies in the tummy would have mutated into a plague of locusts by then. There'd be nothing left in her veins but the purest of pure H_2O. It was pathetic. And pointless.

'Anything the matter?' Linda was looking at her oddly, paperknife poised in mid-air.

'No,' came the glaringly white lie. 'Should there be?'

Linda shrugged and resumed wielding the plastic knife.

'Sorry,' Kate said. 'Just got a bit of a headache, that's all,' the lie turning murkily grey.

Linda quickly rummaged about in the Tesco bag then straightened in triumph and tossed a brown plastic bottle at her. 'Here, take a couple of these.'

'Aspirin?'

'No way. The last thing you want to do when you've got a headache is add more toxins to your system. That's vitamin C. Thousand milligrams. I should take two.'

Kate unscrewed the cap and shook a couple of fawn coloured half-inch long torpedoes on to her palm. 'Must I?' the way her throat was constricting she'd probably choke.

'Yes, you must. They'll do you good, honestly.'

Kate followed her secretary's orders as every good boss should, then with a determined effort to get her act together she said, 'Oh, by the way, I'm having lunch with Ed Franklin at one so I'll probably be a bit late back this afternoon.' Or very early. How long does it take to say 'You're fired' or almost worse, 'We're axing *Kate In*

11

Company, would you like to present *Jack in the Box* instead? Are you any good at wriggling around on the floor pretending to be a caterpillar?'

'Fantastic!'

'What?' Kate looked up, shocked by Linda's obvious enthusiasm.

'Lunch with the Big Boss? They must be giving us a new series then, or maybe even making it daily instead of twice a week or . . .'

Kate laughed in spite of herself. 'God, the optimism of youth! Hasn't it crossed your mind that we could be in for the chop?' She was amazed that she could actually say the words out loud and with a passable imitation of levity.

'Rubbish.' Linda picked up a fistful of letters and waved them at her. 'Testimonials from Joe Public. Read 'em and smile.' She thumped them down on Kate's desk.

As she glanced her way through the correspondence Kate did indeed begin to smile. Mostly they were complimentary. Only four insults. One death threat – she'd send that one off to Security. Seventeen asking for a signed photo. One request for an item of her underwear, preferably used. This letter was promptly disposed of in what the two women referred to as 'the round file' i.e. the rubbish bin. And one marked *Personal* with Snoopy on the envelope which Linda had left for her to open. But mostly, very nice. Maybe Linda was right, maybe a posh lunch with Julian and the HP meant a pat on the back rather than a slash at the jugular. All she had to go on was a phone call late yesterday afternoon from Ed Franklin's assistant. No reason to have spent the night in such a stew over it, immediately assuming that it was a harbinger of doom. A stupid, instinctive response, that's all, nothing more concrete than that. She mentally took her emotions by the shoulders and gave them a good shake. But a sneaky little voice from somewhere deep inside her head insisted on whispering, 'Don't get your hopes up, O'Connell. Your instincts have been right before, remember.'

She ignored the voice, reached for the pile of letters and

began to sort through them properly, saving the Snoopy one as a little treat for when the task was completed.

Kate In Company attracted more mail than the usual run of the mill chat shows in spite of the fact that Wednesday and Friday lunchtimes were hardly prime time. The secret of its success was its presenter, Kate herself, who after an initial few programmes bumbling around trying to be nice, polite, the friendly interviewer, had lost patience with one of the guests of the day, an eminent Civil Servant who was the world's expert on evasion. She hadn't quite lost her temper but she'd figuratively taken him by the scruff of the neck, dug her teeth in and shaken him around until a straight answer fell out. The audience loved it. After that she'd stopped pussyfooting around and started asking the sort of questions that everybody would really like to ask – but up until now had never had the nerve, at least not on British television. Questions like, 'Are you gay?' or 'Have you had a face lift?' She didn't necessarily always get the answers but the viewing public loved the questions.

The pre-production workload was fairly heavy. Two intimately researched guests were invited on to each programme with the specific hope that they'd get right up each other's noses. Or at least provide enough kindling for Kate to apply the match and get a few sparks flying. The subjects (victims) were varied, from film stars and pop musicians to writers, politicians and even, on a couple of memorable occasions, royalty. It was taped in front of a studio audience and Kate had pushed and pushed to get the executives to let them do it live, but the seventh-floor moguls hadn't the nerve. The show was controversial enough as it was. Given the reputation that it had gradually built up she often wondered why on earth anyone ever accepted an invitation to be on it. She certainly never would if the situation were reversed. But it all boiled down to 'any publicity is good publicity' and a lot of people seemed to enjoy rising to her challenge, trying to turn the tables on her and make her lose her cool. No one had quite managed it yet but the frisson was there – that one day someone would – and that was another thing that made for compulsive viewing.

She rapidly divided the mail into separate piles, scrawling brief instructions at the top of each letter. It was a job that Linda could have done perfectly well on her own but Kate still made a point of reading each and every one that came in simply because she enjoyed it – she still got a kick out of counting them. And on days like today they provided a very therapeutic massage to the ego.

'Tea round? Doughnut? Sticky bun?' she asked as she put the letters back into Linda's in-tray.

A shuddering 'No thank you!' was the reply. The words were delivered separately and with vehemence. 'I'll have a carton of pure apple juice and a Nutty Crunch bar, seeing as you're offering. You ought to try it sometime, Kate, it's much better than poisoning your system with all that tannin and sugar.'

'Maybe. But a little of what you fancy does you good, that's my health philosophy. And right now I fancy something . . . sticky!' She delivered the last word with a gleeful relish that made Linda grimace, then wandered along the corridor to see Joyce from whom she purchased not one, but two, warm doughnuts.

She settled herself back at her desk and bit into the mouthwateringly crunchy sugar coating. Reading the fan mail couldn't have been quite as therapeutic as she'd thought. She reached for the research notes for Friday's programme then pushed the folder to one side again. 'Linda, when you have a minute, could you chase up that profile video on Sullivan for me, please?' She pulled the doctor's latest bestselling diet book out from under a heap of new hardback publications that were awaiting her attention and looked at the author's introduction . . . hell, she could do all that this afternoon. What she *should* be doing right now was thinking up her counter-attack strategy for lunchtime.

She gazed around the room but the air might as well be a thick, grey fog for all the inspiration it offered. She lit a cigarette, something she tried not to do too often in the office out of consideration for Linda. The action was met with a glare and a tut tut and a, 'You must be feeling more nervous about this lunch thing than I thought,' as the girl crossed the room and opened a window. 'Hey, cheer up.' She pointed to the unopened envelope on Kate's desk. 'Snoopy loves you. So things can't be all that bad now, can they?'

'This is true.' Kate picked up the envelope, turning it over in her hand and studying the outside with renewed interest. It was addressed in large, childlike print. She opened it and as she read the contents a slow smile crept across her face and her body began to relax back into the chair.

'*Dear Auntie Katy*,' it began. '*Mummy said I had to rite this becaus its my folt she hasnt got your adress or phone number anymore. I have to apola . . .* ' The last word was scored out and '*say sorry*' written in its place with '*love from Sammy*' and '*PtO.*' to finish it off.

Kate laughed. 'Wonderful!' she exclaimed as she turned over the sheet. The rest of the letter was from Mo (Maureen), a room-mate from college days and soul-mate ever since in spite of the differences in their lifestyles. Kate, single and single-minded career woman. Mo, most extraordinary creature, still in love with her husband after eight years of marriage, six of which had been shared by a third party, Sammy-The-Boy-Wonder – the unbiased maternal description.

Kate felt a pang of guilt that she hadn't been in touch with Mo for ages, not since she'd moved to the house in Chiswick now she thought about it, but time seemed to whoosh down life's plughole and . . . and she had a million excuses but none of them mattered because Mo was her friend, time didn't matter, Mo was there for Kate just as she was for Mo and who gave a damn that it was weeks – or in this case quite a few months – between get-togethers?

It appeared that Mo did. '*So just what do you think you are?*' read Kate, '*some kind of star or something? Blood out of a stone would be easier than wringing your private address and phone number out of that tight-arsed*

TV station you work for! I know you're ex-directory, but really!' The letter went on to explain that the page with Kate on it had gone missing when Sammy had decided to practise his alphabet by rearranging Mummy's loose-leaf address book and as Mo wasn't much good at sending out thought waves, or Kate didn't seem much good at receiving them, she'd had to resort to the good old GPO and work address, and just hope that Kate wasn't too much of a megastar to read her own mail.

'*There! Okay, lecture over,*' wrote Mo. '*And now to the point of all this. The Dreaded Thirtieth Birthday looms on my horizon – as it does on yours, my dear, even if a few months later than mine so don't think you're immune. I'm having a wake on Sunday afternoon, rounding up a few old friends and old faces (getting older by the minute!). I know it's short notice but please come if you can. Bring your man of the moment. Call me. Love and Kisses, Mo.*'

Kate grinned across at her assistant. 'Give me a direct line, would you, Linda?' she said as she picked up her phone. Linda pressed a button on her extension and Kate got the dialling tone. She dialled. It rang. She began counting. She normally hung up on thirteen but this time she decided to give it a couple more. It clicked and a rather breathless but familiar voice said, 'Hello, can you ring back?'

'Hold it, Mo, it's Kate!'

'Hi! Terrific. Look, lovey, I'm up to my elbows in the middle of an ongoing crappy nappy situation here – give me two minutes, can you?'

Kate laughed. 'The joys of motherhood? I'll hang on. Take your time. TV7's paying the bill.'

'Great. Don't go away. 'Bye.'

Kate listened to the faint background noises at the other end of the phone and thought: *nappy*? My God, she's produced another one!

A couple of minutes later their conversation was resumed, with Mo sounding a little bit contorted as if she had the phone jammed between chin and shoulder which, she soon explained, she had. 'And that disgusting slurping noise you can probably hear is Rebecca, whom you haven't met yet. She's eleven weeks old and absolutely beautiful, wildly intelligent and ... Oh God, I *adore* breastfeeding! It's so sexy!'

Kate listened with half an ear while Mo brought her up to date on *Life with the Levys*. On this particular morning it all sounded very attractive. Kate was almost envious. Almost. They nattered for a good half-hour and by the time she put down the phone Kate felt positively refreshed. Darling Mo. Intellectual turned Earth Mother. Far better than any amount of vitamin C. They'd talked as if they'd only seen each other yesterday, apart from an incidental incongruity like the production of a brand new human being. And yes, Mo must've already been pregnant when they saw each other last, and no, she hadn't realised it at the time. And yes, Kate would be there on Sunday at two, and no, she didn't know who she'd be bringing with her yet and oh, by the way, she'd been summoned to lunch with the new Mr Big which could well mean she'd be an ex-megastar by then and what should she do?

'At Lacey's, you said? Then order caviar and lobster, my girl, what else?' declared her friend.

Kate was ushered through the doors of Lacey's at two minutes to one. The head waiter conducted her to a table right in the middle of the dimly-lit interior where Ed Franklin and Julian Howard rose to their feet to greet her. She found it rather ominous that Julian was already there, for punctuality wasn't one of his virtues, but his expression gave nothing away. She wanted to kill them both with a look, particularly Julian for sucking up to Management instead of forming a united front with her, but for now she just put on her best smile and wished she were back at TV7 with a ham sandwich and a glass of plonk in the club bar. She also wished, as she scanned the extravagant menu, that she hadn't spent so much of the morning stuffing her face with comfort food. She settled for a Planter's Punch and the Caribbean Salad, handed the menu back to the waiter, then looked silently at her two companions.

Ed Franklin was a large man, tall and broad with an impressive musculature that was only now, in his mid-fifties, showing signs of tending towards middle-age spread. His hair was thick and silver-white. Julian seemed almost flimsy beside him. He too was a six-footer, but he was lanky rather than tall, thin rather than lean, the type of person who had obtrusive elbows and knees, as if stuck in the middle of an adolescent growth spurt. Though he was still only in his thirties, a shiny scalp was much in evidence, as if his head had kept on growing upwards ignoring the treeline of pale brown hair.

She watched them and waited. It was their game. She was damned if she was going to be the one to start the ball rolling.

'Well, darlings, this is very nice, isn't it?' said Julian, glancing at their surroundings.

Kate nodded.

'And discreet,' Ed whispered, leaning across the table to pat the back of her hand. 'Thought you'd prefer the sort of place where they take celebrity guests as a matter of course.'

Kate smiled. Which course, she wondered? Appetiser or entrée?

Julian cleared his throat. 'Well,' he said.

'Yes. Well, er . . .' said Franklin.

Kate and Julian shot a glance at each other. It was like being summoned to the headmaster's study when you don't know if you're in for a caning or a gold stick-on star. It was unbearable.

'Well?' Kate echoed. She couldn't keep it up any longer. She had to know the worst so she gave in. 'To what do I owe this pleasure, gentlemen?'

Chapter Two

As Kate O'Connell sat in the muted lighting of one of London's top restaurants steeling herself for the reply that might or might not put her career on the line, another meal was taking place in another capital city and things weren't running too smoothly there, either. Three thousand miles across the water, in the upper Westside area of New York City, Jeff Coolidge found the daylight blasting through his kitchen window a little too loud for his liking. For Jeff, five hours behind Greenwich Mean Time, the day was just beginning. And so far he didn't think much of it.

He'd woken up with his mouth tasting as though a camel had spent the night in it. The lower half of his face was rough with stubble as if someone has spread his skin with wet rock-salt which had dried while he slept until it was caked on stiff. He still hadn't shaved and it was nearly eight already. Danny was in one of his whining moods and complaining of a belly ache while Nancy was ostentatiously going from room to room flinging those of her possessions that had migrated from her apartment to his into a large zip-up carryall. Jeff's carryall. 'Don't worry,' she'd said, oozing sarcasm from every pore, 'I'll mail it back to you.'

He ran his fingers through his hair, in urgent need of a trim, and yawned as he methodically denuded the refrigerator of its meagre contents. According to his housekeeping régime it should still have been at least half-full. Damn Nancy and her appetite. Somehow he'd have to fit in another trip to the supermarket before he got home again tonight. But when? Lunchtime was out. He'd promised that to Laura Babski for the fourth time this month and the rainchecks were running out. After work then. He could come back and pick up Danny first

19

and they could make an expedition of it. Poor kid. It was hardly a substitute for a father and son outing to see the Mets in action at the Shea.

'Oh, Christ!' He cursed loudly as he dropped the one remaining egg on the floor. It didn't bounce. Why is it that mornings always have to come so early in the day when your resistance is at its lowest, he wondered? Life would be so much sweeter if they just strolled along after lunch when you stand a better chance of coping with them. 'Danny?' he yelled. 'You dressed yet?' He took a long slow breath and concentrated on taking the edge off his voice. It wasn't the kid's fault that his father's co-ordination was working half-assed. 'Come on, Chief, get your butt in here and help your old man with the breakfast, huh?'

'Okay, okay, I'm coming.' The little voice didn't sound very enthusiastic and Jeff's heart suddenly constricted with concern. And love. So much love. He turned, leaving the broken egg on the floor staring stickily after him with its big yellow eye, and went through into his son's small, bright bedroom. The boy was sitting on the edge of his bed concentrating hard on doing up the laces on his trainers. Jeff sat down next to him and put his arm round the vulnerable seven year old shoulders. 'Hey,' he said gently, kissing the top of Danny's sleep-tousled fair head. 'You okay, Chief? You really got a tummy ache? Is it a real kind of tummy ache or is it a math-quiz-at-school-this-morning kind of tummy ache?'

'Aw, Dad, do I really gotta go to school today?'

'So it's the math quiz, huh?'

Danny nodded. 'I guess.'

He gave the little shoulders a comforting squeeze. 'Did I ever tell you that President Lincoln, Jesse James *and* Superman all flunked at math?'

Danny looked up at him, eyes widening with amazement. 'Honest? Did they really, Dad?'

Jeff grinned. 'I dunno. They might've. Just wondered if I ever told you that, that's all.'

Danny smiled reluctantly and they walked back to the

20

kitchen together where they found Nancy, who wasn't smiling at all.

Even stony-faced, as she was now, she was an attractive woman. Not exactly pretty, certainly not beautiful, but she had an urchin-like appeal with her short-cropped blonde curls and five-foot-one stature. She was a little on the plump side but it didn't bother her. She had a self-confident awareness of her own sexuality which made male observers think pocket Venus not excess poundage. But at this moment the signals were definitely of the 'hands off' variety. She was determinedly jamming an almost empty pack of Earl Grey tea down into one of the side pockets of the zippered carryall.

Jeff looked pointedly at the pack and said, 'Sure you've got everything?'

'Yes.'

'Cup of coffee before you go?'. His voice was friendly enough, unconcerned. A perfectly civilised question for an imperfectly managed situation. He'd been seeing Nancy for nearly six months and she'd been near as dammit moved in with them for the last two. It had been a bad idea from the start. As close to a disaster as you could get. One man, thoroughly domesticated out of necessity, organised down to the last detail and trying to do three full-time jobs – father, breadwinner, writer. One small boy, hero-worshipping his only parent and very politely resentful of the intruding rival presence. And one woman, funny, volatile, sexy, selfish, lazy, delightful, with a passion for English tea, food and Jeff, and not necessarily in that order. He hated to admit it but he'd be damned glad to see the back of her.

She put the bag on the floor, carefully avoiding the broken egg, then pulled out a chair and sat down. 'Might as well,' she said. 'Any toast?'

Jeff put the coffee on the table, Danny put two slices of bread in the toaster, Jeff reached for a cloth and wiped up the egg, Danny set three places and got the cereal carton out of the cupboard. Nancy sat with her back to the window nonchalantly studying the fried tomato stain

21

on the wallpaper just above head height. Jeff threw the floorcloth into the sink then sat down opposite her. Danny took the seat along the side like a tennis umpire in miniature waiting for play to commence. Except he didn't think that breakfast was going to be particularly playful and the thought of his imminent escape to school, even with a math quiz ahead, was becoming quite attractive. It was Jake Rascovich's mom's turn at doing the neighbourhood school run this week and he hoped she wasn't going to be long.

Jeff had calmly entrenched himself behind the battlements of the *New York Times* whilst Nancy looked as if she was gathering up her reserves, barricaded by the coffeepot and bumper family-sized box of Crispy Cornies. The tension between the two adults was like a thin wire stretched taut, and it was obvious that it wouldn't take much for it to snap. And if the past couple of months were anything to go by, the backlash might not just sting, either. It could whip and cut.

The breakfast conversation started in terse monosyllables. 'Juice please.' 'Toast.' 'Pass the milk.' The pouring, scraping and eating noises that accompanied the words sounded much louder than usual and very detailed. Danny noticed it. He thought it was like hearing sounds through a telescope and he didn't like it much. He wanted out. He quickly wiped the back of his hand across his mouth and got down from the table. 'I'll go wait for Mrs Rascovich down in the lobby,' he said. 'Don't wanna be late.'

Jeff grabbed for his arm as he passed and pulled him close for a hug. 'Tummy feeling better now, huh?'

'I'm fine, Dad. Honest.'

'Okay. Now you wait inside the lobby for her, you hear?'

'Sure, Dad.'

'And Danny?'

'Yes?'

'Good luck with the math.'

'Thanks. I'm sure gonna need it.'

Another brief hug and a playful punch on the shoulder and Jeff watched his son walk to the apartment door. Danny seemed so small sometimes, and the world which surrounded him so tall and threatening, designed by and for big people who were harder, tougher, stronger. He was often struck as he was now by the innate courage of the very young, yet fearful for their vulnerability. Danny's vulnerability. His son. 'Hey, and make sure you stay with Mrs Rascovich after school till I come for you. No kidding around. You wait for me there.'

Danny sighed as if he'd heard it all before, which he had. Nearly every weekday. 'Yeah, okay Dad. See you later.'

'Take care, Chief. I love you,' he added to the closing door.

With Danny's leaving, a silence seemed to descend over the apartment like a shroud until Nancy tore at it with, 'You smother that boy, Jeff. You'll make him soft. And he has no manners. He could at least have said goodbye to me.'

It was the signal to resume hostilities, let the previous night's unfinished battle be rejoined. Jeff bristled. 'Well, I'll say it for him then, shall I? Goodbye Nancy. There. Better? Now why don't you just go on back to your place and leave me and my son in peace to get on with our lives. The way we like it.' He stood up suddenly, pushing his chair back so it screeched against the floor setting his teeth on edge. With brisk, economic movements he cleared his own and Danny's breakfast things from the table while Nancy poured herself another coffee.

She was determined to stay calm this time, cool and unprovoked. She was annoyed with herself for last night, the way she'd let him needle her until she'd blown her top and thrown the tomato – only to miss him. But this morning she'd decided to retain her dignity, to leave with style. 'Don't be silly, Jeff.' She used the tone of voice that she normally reserved for Danny when he was being tiresome – which for Nancy was most of the time.

Jeff gritted his teeth. 'Look. I said "goodbye", Nancy.

I'm pushed for time already and I got to go shave yet and . . . oh, forget it. Just let yourself out, will you?' At the kitchen doorway he turned back. 'And don't forget to wash out your coffee cup before you go.' He ducked round the door just in time to escape the flying shards of crockery which ricocheted off the frame. Her aim was improving.

He went into the bathroom and locked the door. Things were certainly going to be tidier round the place with Nancy gone. Cheaper too. And he'd be able to repossess his evenings, those precious few hours at the end of the day when Danny was in bed, the apartment was quiet and he could get down to his own work, his real work. He heard the apartment door slam and with it a coil of tension suddenly unwound itself from his body and he leaned against the sink, head down, eyes closed, and breathed a long sigh of relief.

Forty-five minutes later, a not very immaculately suited Jeff Coolidge emerged from the second-hand air of the subway system into the claustrophobic atmosphere that was Lexington Avenue on a muggy New York day. He hurried along the sidewalk cursing himself for not taking a cab this morning and wondering why it was that whenever he was running late every other office worker in the city seemed intent on scurrying in the opposite direction to him. He felt like a pebble in the face of an oncoming tide. It was slow headway. He stood impatiently, jammed in the middle of a crowd on the corner of Lexington and East 42nd, waiting for the flashing red 'Don't Walk' signal to change to a green 'Walk' command. Eventually it did and a couple of minutes later he entered the lobby of the Matteson Building. The cool conditioned air slammed against him like a wall. By the time the elevator had regurgitated him on to the eleventh floor, the middle one of the five occupied by the Sherman Whitney Agency, he was beginning to feel a little less like a sweaty and harassed refugee from domesticity and more like the Vice-President, Creative Director, office furniture and equipment, plus the addition, now, of micro computer and software accounts.

He walked briskly along the corridor, the plush grey carpet completely absorbing the sound of his footsteps, past the chrome-framed ads on the walls and the chrome and glass cabinets displaying the products of their top clients. The concept of the décor was supposed to be clean, sharp and thrusting – to echo, they hoped, the direct and to the point spirit behind their style of ads. It reminded Jeff of a dentist's waiting room. His office was at the end of the corridor next door to the Senior VP's corner office – the one he was supposed to hanker after, being an up and coming young executive with the Board of Directors' eyes fixed benignly on him. And in the early days, it was true, he had coveted that office and the title that went with it. But that was in the days when one of his personal labels had read 'husband'. Somehow, when Jennifer died, his ambition had died along with her. No, that wasn't quite true. He still had ambitions but they had shifted direction, turned inwards. He'd always thought there was plenty of time. Time to build a home, raise a family, establish a firm foundation, climb to the top of the tree and *then* sit back and do your own thing. Which in his case was to write novels. But Jennifer proved that time was a finite commodity and its container was completely opaque with no gauge for its contents. You could just never tell whether it was nearly full or struggling along on its last drop. So if you wanted something, better go for it, do it *now*.

Jeff had tried to do just that. The novel which he was going to start tomorrow, next week, next year, became a part of the present, today. He started it. More important, he finished it. In a way it was his private therapy. It helped him, not to forget Jennifer but to absorb her into himself so that the pain of losing her gradually changed into gratitude for having known her. He called the book *Losing Time*, and himself C. J. Warren, (Warren being his middle name) and sent it off to a publisher. It came back three months later, dog-eared and with a coffee stain on the back page. At least that meant they'd read it. 'Interesting,' said the accompanying letter but, 'Too personal, self-indulgent, not right for our list.' At first the criticism had hurt, but when he calmed down he could see the justice in it. Losing Time was supposed to be a novel, preferably a commercial one. It was not a diary. He altered bits of it here and there, re-wrote seven whole chapters, retyped it and sent it off to another publisher. It came back again, cleaner this time and with the encouraging comment, 'We did enjoy reading your novel but . . . ' Always the 'but'. Nearly six months and two more publishers later he decided on a last-ditch attempt and a change of tactics, and sent the now almost hated manuscript, along with his collection of rejection letters, to a small literary agency which had been mentioned by a friend of a colleague as being interested in finding new writers. The agent was Laura Babski.

It had taken five years from that first daunting day when he'd typed 'Chapter One' at the top of a virgin sheet of paper to the day (last week) when he made a special trip to the bookstore and stood there for a full hour, staring at his newborn baby on the shelf, hoping desperately that someone would pick it up and buy it, terrified that someone actually might. Publication. As in 'going public'. Open to general scrutiny. And judgement.

He took off his jacket, loosened his necktie, undid the top two buttons of his shirt, rolled up the sleeves. He ignored the pile of work on the desk and walked lethargically to the wide sheet of glass which took up half a wall. He leaned his forehead against the window and gazed down at the teeming crowds on Lexington Avenue eleven storeys below him. Office workers, shoppers, tourists, streetvendors, the place was always crawling with anonymous humanity. Anonymous being the key word, Jeff thought. People had a God-given right to their anonymity, privacy. And it was comfortable being just another face in the crowd, another listing in the phone book. There was a kind of safety in it. And he wasn't sure if he was ready, or even wanted, to lose it. But at least he had his pseudonym to hide behind. On the other hand, if *Losing Time* beat all the odds and became a commerical success he'd have to come out of his cosy closet. And according to Laura the only way there was the slightest chance of that, was for him to stop hiding *now* and get out there among the crowds and do some shouting.

'Books don't sell themselves, you know,' she kept on saying. 'Just like dog food or office furniture or whatever it is that you waste your talents on hyping. We'll be lucky if *Losing Time* comes out as a sub-leader. It's a first novel and you're an unknown author.' She really knew how to boost a guy's confidence sometimes. 'Take Steve King when he was into his Bachman jig. When *Thinner* came out with Richard Bachman on the cover it sold twenty-eight thousand. And when somebody let the cat out of the bag and Stephen King's name went on the cover it sold two hundred and eighty thousand. Think about it.'

'Do I have to?' was his reaction. He pointed out that nobody would give a damn whether he wrote as Jeff Coolidge or C. J. Warren. 'What's the difference? Who's heard of either?'

'Exactly. So you've got to sell yourself.'

And Laura, as usual, was right. The book was out and in the stores. Some of the stores. Not the major chains. There were no special displays hailing bright new author, no dump-bins at the checkouts, just another book filling shelf space. A stillbirth.

So no more rainchecks. 'I've been working on a new angle,' she had said when they were arranging the meeting.

'What new angle?' Very suspicious.

'I'll explain over lunch.'

Jeff didn't think he was going to have much of an appetite.

He moved away from the window, turning himself from author to adman. He plugged in the new computer which had taken the place of his office typewriter and reached for the instruction books. There was one for the micro, two for the word-processing software that he was supposed to be planning the campaign for, one for the disk drive, one for the printer . . . At least the VDU was easy enough to understand – you just switched it on and waited for the picture.

Or did you? Suppose there was a power cut, what then? Answer me that. You can't, can you? He smirked at the blank screen in front of him, feeling decidedly superior to it. Give me a typewriter any day. Or even a pad and pencil. He picked up the two books that came with the software and felt almost offended by their combined thickness. Word processing. He shuddered at the term. Words shouldn't be 'processed', they should be gentled, nurtured, searched for and teased along until each one is carefully positioned in exactly the right place . . .

He sighed. That was exactly what he wanted to be doing right now – sitting back at home working on the new book and being there for Danny when he got back home from school instead of having the kid wait for him at some other kid's place. A parcel. Poste restante. He wished for about the millionth time since *Losing Time* had first been accepted for publication that he had the guts to quit Sherman Whitney and really go for it, be a full-time writer instead of a part-time dabbler with words. But he was finding the second novel slow going while the bills, unfortunately, were just the opposite. He wasn't too worried about bestsellers and fast bucks – here he paused a moment, allowing himself to thrill to the scary fantasy of writing The Big One, Monopoly money royalty cheques, Johnny Carson interviews – just so long as he could earn enough to keep the wolf from the door. If he'd had only himself to think about he'd have done it, no hesitation, just handed in his notice and revelled in his garret, but with a child to think about too . . . it wasn't on. Not yet awhile. But maybe a leave of absence, some kind of extended unpaid vacation, sabbatical? He could probably scrape enough together to keep them going for six months or so . . .

Dave Grantley's voice from the doorway jolted him back to the realities of the present. He quickly filed away the leave of absence idea for later consideration and turned his concentration on the Senior VP, who wanted to know how he was doing with the new software account. 'Any angle on it yet, Jeff? I know it's early days but they're screaming for layouts already and the art department needs something to go on.' He crossed over to Jeff's desk and casually examined a couple of the manuals. 'Some beast, huh? IBM mainframe in miniature. Personally, I'd rather have a stable of secretaries. They got better legs.'

Jeff gave a dutiful grin, promised to come up with something by yesterday at the latest and then glared at the door as Grantley left again. He dragged his mind back to the electronic puzzle in front of him and tried to force his attention on how to understand it, how to control it, how to *sell* it. It was only a tool, dammit. They were in homes and offices all over the world, even schoolkids used them these days, so how come he was regarding it like it had AIDS or something? How come *he* was the one who had to make it lovable, desirable, special, better than the competition? And how come he couldn't?

Because he was only half there, that's how come. When you try to hold down too many roles all at the same time, some of them are bound to fluff their lines. This job – all his jobs – needed a whole person. Or two. Or three. Then he smiled as a thought struck him. Look up the Yellow Pages, Coolidge, and call a shrink. 'Hey, doc, has anyone invented an injection yet to *induce* multiple schizophrenia? Preferably physical as well as psychological. No? Darned shame. Work on it, will you? Schizophrenia. Many hands make light work. Or instead of many hands, only one computer. Programmed with our client's software package . . .

Ideas began to come at last, slowly and then speeding up a little as, gingerly and then with a little more confidence, Jeff began to play around with the King Kong of executive toys on the desk in front of him. Maybe, just maybe, this thing was more than a gimmicky toy after all. And maybe, just maybe, he could even find a use for one of these himself! It could never replace that essentially creative act of ripping a sheet out of the typewriter and crumpling it into a snowball but suppose, once you'd dragged your hundred thousand words from brain to paper, you realised that your Ronald character was really a George or a Michael. All you had to do was . . . he looked at the instructions . . . type the command to change it, press the return key and Ronald was no more. Magic. Could even have its uses in the next Presidential Campaign.

He was downing his third coffee and enjoying himself thoroughly when the phone buzzed. 'There's a Mz Laura Babski calling, Jeff. Shall I put her on?'

He looked at his watch. Only an hour till he was supposed to be meeting her for lunch. Must be her turn to play the raincheck game, or so he hoped. He said he'd take the call.

'Jeff. Laura. Terrific news. Couldn't wait till lunch.' With those few words she managed to sound brisk, breathless and in a desperate hurry as she always did. 'Are you sitting down?'

'For God's sake, Laura. What? What is it? Tell me.' Jeff's heart was suddenly pounding. His agent's phone calls always had that effect on him. In person he could cope with her but on the phone she terrified the life out of him. She was formidable. But that's what made her one of the best.

'It's *Losing Time*. Maybe we should have called it *Marking Time*, honey. Have you seen New York?'

'What? I live . . . What are you going on about?'

'*New York!* The magazine. Today's issue.' Laura spoke slowly but impatiently, spelling it out with her voice and relishing each word. 'Rhoda. Koenig. Has. Reviewed. Your. Book.'

Silence.

'Jeff?'

'Shit. Go on, tell me the worst, how bad is it?'

His agent did something he'd never heard her do before. She laughed. 'Oh, ye of little faith. Honey, she loves it. It's terrific. Really good. Positively glowing.'

'Don't bullshit me.'

'Would I? But we've got to follow it through. Now. Next week there'll be another good review and it won't be your book, it'll be somebody else's. Now's the time. We've got to push it or it'll just roll over and die on us. I talked to Pam Mackenzie at Coliseum just now and she's right with us so bring your diary to lunch. See you later.' She rang off.

Jeff found himself in the classic pose of staring open-mouthed at the receiver in his hand wondering if he'd just heard right or if he'd imagined the whole conversation. This was it then. Pam Mackenzie was his publisher's senior Publicity Manager. He was aware of his heartbeat, his breathing. He made a determined effort to slow them both down. There was something else he had to do, too. Ah, that was it – put the phone down. Then he picked it up again and buzzed the receptionist. 'Have you got today's *New York* out there? You do? I need it. Guard it with your life, I'm on my way!'

And he was.

Chapter Three

She breezed back into the office well after three o'clock with a grin to overpower the cheesiest of Cheshire Cats. 'Hi! Do you want the good news or the bad news?'

Linda looked up from her typewriter. 'Kate O'Connell, I do believe you're tipsy.'

'I wouldn't say that.' She raised a hip and perched herself on the corner of Linda's desk. She slipped off. 'Well, maybe just the teeeensiest little bit. Call it drowning my sorrows.' She giggled.

Linda was beginning to look concerned. This wasn't the Kate she knew at all. 'What do you mean, good news or bad?' she asked with a suspicious glare. 'You'd better give me the bad.'

'Okay. The bad news is that I was right all along. *Kate In Company* is being axed.'

Linda looked at her boss aghast. The woman was mad. Not as in angry but as in loony – she was still smiling. 'What? They can't! Come on, Kate, stop kidding around.'

'No kidding. The. Chop.' She accompanied the words by slicing her finger across her throat. 'Scout's honour.'

'I can't believe it,' Linda said flatly. 'So what's the good news, then? If there could be any after that.'

'Oh, there could, there could. *Kate In Company* disappears from Wednesdays and Fridays. Totally. Never again to darken the hallowed schedules of TV7. As of the end of this run. That's . . .' She started to count on her fingers then dismissed the exercise with an airy wave saying, 'Oh, whenever. Maths was never my strong point. A few more weeks, anyway . . .'

'Kate,' Linda pleaded. 'Tell me. Please.'

'Ah. But.' She paused for dramatic effect. The pause was just a little too long.

'But *what*?' The poor girl was practically screaming.

'But. Try *The O'Connell Encounter* for size. The autumn schedules. Only one show a week, mind, but . . .' she smiled '. . . how does Saturday nights grab you? Leading up to the evening news?'

There was no immediate reply. Kate watched the changes of expression fly across Linda's face – disbelief, horror, exultation all in a split second. Eventually just one word fell out of her mouth: 'Gosh.'

Kate burst out laughing. Prime time. At last. And soon. 'And no more clashes between me and Julian, either,' she went on. 'Responsibility has been firmly delineated. He's to be producer in an administrative role only. Editorial responsibility is mine, all mine! Oh, the power. I love it, I *love* it!' she finished gleefully.

The idea behind *The O'Connell Encounter* had been Kate's own. She'd worked on it, prepared papers on it and put it up to the Programme Planning Board months ago, in the days when Ed was merely Head of News and Current Affairs. Since when – nothing. Just a memo from Ed Franklin acknowledging receipt and ending with a thank you but under the company's present economic constraints the Board decision was no thanks. He didn't need to go into details. Everybody who worked at TV7, from the scraggy cat in the cellar to the fat cats up on the seventh floor, knew that ratings were falling and advertising revenue was following suit. And unlike the BBC they didn't have taxpayers' licence money as their regular financing. So first there was talk of paring programme budgets, then it was mutterings of cutbacks in the support services (horrified miaowling noise from the cellars), followed by gloom-laden warnings of the ultimate sanction – 'personnel reduction'.

The fact that Management had had a change of mind was testimony to the high regard in which Kate was held. *The O'Connell Encounter* was going to be a high budget show. High risk, too, but hopefully a high flyer. A sort of Custer's Last Stand against the Dallasty soaps, quiz shows or current affairs heavies that were the alternative weekend viewing. If it worked it would be the best thing to hit British TV screens since . . . Kate couldn't immediately bring anything remotely similar to mind.

But 'if it worked' were the operative words. The problem was not in the anticipated viewing figures – everyone is a Peeping Tom at heart – nor in the logistics of actually getting the show on the air. The problem might well be in finding enough subjects willing to air their linen, be it dirty, clean or indifferent, to fill a twelve-week run. A studio interview, no matter how probing, is one thing. But taking in Kate O'Connell and a film crew as house guests for a few days beforehand is quite a different matter. And that was the basic idea. A sixty-minute slot comprising an informal studio talk show format but with a filmed biography of the subject fed into it – a sort of composite 'week in the life of', warts and all. The titillation of visual eavesdropping. Like *Kate In Company* the new show was to be recorded in front of an audience – they couldn't risk all that intercutting 'live' – but it would be one hell of a test for Kate's presentation skills, guiding the interview in and out of the film smoothly so the joins didn't show. With any luck – and a great deal of hard work – *The O'Connell Encounter* would be pure magic. Compulsive viewing.

She hoped. Oh, how she hoped. Because the end of the run just happened to coincide with the end of her current contract. A shadow flitted briefly across her face. It didn't bear thinking about. So she decided not to. Not yet awhile anyway. 'So, Linda, what do you think about the title?' she asked after she'd finished explaining the new format.

'Mm, not bad. Seeing as they're so keen on using alliteration it could've been worse. Ding dong, *O'Connell Calling!*'

She giggled. It was such a heady relief after the worries of the morning that silliness was the inevitable result. 'Oh God. *Colliding with Kate.*'

'*O'Connell's Quirky Quest for Skeletons in the Cupboard!*'

Kate hiccupped. 'No. Doesn't work. Wait, I think I've

got it!' Grandly she exclaimed, 'Ladies and Gentlemen, we proudly present . . . *Keyhole Kate!*'

'How about *Kate Up Queer Street?*' said Alex rather sourly as he stepped out of her shower that evening. 'Damn it, why are there never any clean towels in here, Kate?' he asked as he came through into the bedroom dripping and naked.

'Because I hate doing the laundry.' She shrugged. She was sitting up in the rumpled bed looking extremely pleased with herself and unashamedly appraising her lover's body as he walked towards her. He was slightly built – five foot eight or nine, only a few inches taller than Kate herself, and not particularly muscular – but she liked his body, it reminded her of a boy's. She had this fantasy sometimes, as she ran her hands over his smooth chest, that she was making love to a fifteen year old. And sometimes his performance matched up to it; he was so eager, hungry for her, desirous of and delighted by her that he'd come too soon, before she was ready. 'Oh Kate, Kate. Oh. Do you know what you do to me?' he'd whisper.

Stupid question.

Then she'd wait a little while and they'd do it again, her way. Like now.

'Come back to bed,' she demanded.

'*Wet?*'

She smiled and nodded, thinking: 'You said it!'

'Woman, you're insatiable!'

Not exactly. More like – not sated *yet*. She held out her hand, he took it and she drew him back into the bed, drying him with her body, playing with him, *playing* him, until he was moaning quietly and she cried out, 'Now! I want you inside me *now!*'

It was nearly ten o'clock before they made a second attempt at getting out of bed. This time they were more successful. Hunger is a very powerful motivator. Kate dressed quickly in old Levi's and a seen-better-days sweater. She was off duty and, as far as she was concerned, so was style, elegance and chic: all those things belonged in the work place. Home was the place for comfort and convenience. She wasn't quite a closet slob but sometimes she felt she came pretty close to it. The sweater, which had once been a glorious Kaffe Fassett original, had suffered rather badly during Mrs Pickles' leave of absence when Kate had made a one-off foray into domesticity. She'd hand-washed it (so far so good) then pegged it out on a line sopping wet. It now hung over her slender frame like a limp rainbow, drooping below her bottom and with cuffs turned back twice to give her hands a little breathing space.

Alex watched as she wiped off the remains of her eye make-up, pushed her shoulder length honey coloured hair back behind her ears and covered her head with a pure silk Hermès scarf *à la* Princess Anne. If it wasn't for the designer labels she could have been a refugee from a building site. And she was still the most desirable creature he'd ever known.

'Will I do?' she asked, turning to face him for inspection.

'Delectable.'

'That's not what I meant.'

'I know. And yes, you'll do. Nobody would know you from Eve. Or Adam, for that matter.'

'Thanks. Two quarter pounders with cheese, then. I won't be long.'

While Kate scavenged along Chiswick High Road looking for a McDonald's or a Burger King or a Wendy's, for she really fancied a burger and fries and would brook no objection, Alex showered again and attempted to make himself look as though he'd spent the evening sitting on the front benches of the House of Commons.

It was a debatable point which of them would be most inconvenienced by being recognised. Alex Pritchard had a pretty high political profile. Newly elevated to the Cabinet in the last government reshuffle, personable and articulate and therefore often pushed forward for the *Jimmy Young Show* or *Question Time*, at forty-eight he

36

was tipped by those in the know as a future party leader. With a solid reputation and (Kate tried not to think about them too often) a wife and two young daughters, he was understandably wary about venturing out into the streets of Chiswick when he was supposed to be in Westminster awaiting a late-night division.

He stood under the spray, carefully avoiding getting his hair wet. As a politician he could avoid giving a direct answer to pretty well any question but explaining newly-shampooed hair when he climbed into bed with Elizabeth later defeated even him. He closed his eyes as he gingerly soaped round his foreskin and still sensitive glans. Kate, ah, Kate! He was obsessed by her. Possessed by her. Often, he wished he'd never met her.

Kate, meanwhile, was standing in a typically slow queue for supposedly fast food, enjoying being incognito. It was a game she liked to play when she was in the mood and she had it down to a fine art. It was a facile little game, but a challenge nonetheless. She had a theory that anyone, even the Princess of Wales, could go about unrecognised if they wanted to – it was all to do with *thinking* invisible. If you act like ordinary Mrs Jones, people will assume that's who you are: just another body taking up air space.

It worked again. The boy behind the counter gave her a brief puzzled glance as if he'd seen her before some-where and couldn't quite think where, but they were fairly busy so she escaped without having to go through the 'don't I know you/no I don't think so' routine. She scored herself eight out of ten, not noticing the man standing directly behind her in the queue. And why should she? Even if she'd had eyes in the back of her head he was still pretty unmemorable, the sort of man the police would describe as 'average height, average build, clean-shaven, average length brown hair, aged between twenty and forty'.

But Mr Average had noticed Kate O'Connell. And her double order. On a whim, a hunch, whatever journalese you choose, the gossip column stringer for one of the less reputable tabloids abandoned his physical hunger in preference to satisfying that other, constant hunger – to break a juicy story. Unobtrusively he followed Kate down the road.

It wasn't until she and Alex were both settled in the kitchen chewing burgers, licking fingers and stealing each other's fries that Kate picked up on his earlier comment about her new show. 'What did you mean, Alex, when you called it *Kate Up Queer Street?*'

He stopped chewing, swallowed and looked across at her. A little frown, a little hesitation. 'Do you really want to know what I think? Honest, considered opinion?'

She nodded and mumbled 'Mm,' still enthusiastically occupied with eating. God, these burgers were a treat.

Alex dabbed at his mouth with the paper napkin and wiped his fingers before saying, 'Well . . .' in a very measured tone.

She almost expected him to rise to his feet and call her his honourable friend or something. 'Come on, Alex, you're not in Parliament now. No speeches, just give it to me straight. If that's possible for a politician.' She said it teasingly.

'Has anybody ever told you, Ms O'Connell, that your interview technique can occasionally verge on the irreverent?'

'I should hope so. Has anybody ever told you you're evading the issue? Come on, what don't you like about it?'

He sighed. 'Well, if you really want to know my opinion I can sum it up in just two words . . .' He paused. Alex was very good at pausing for effect. Almost as good as Kate. 'It stinks.'

It was so unexpected that she flinched. 'What do you mean? It'll be marvellous television.' She sounded affronted and hurt.

'Marvellous television,' he echoed scathingly. 'That's all you people ever think about, isn't it?' The memory of their first meeting – when she'd provided 'marvellous television' by making him look an idiot on *Kate In*

Company – still niggled at him. Not many people were able to get the better of him in an argument but she'd managed it. It was one of the reasons he'd decided to pursue her, but he brushed that aside now and shook his head, despairing of her, of himself, of the fascination she held for him.

Kate interpreted the gesture as one of disdain and her hackles began to rise. What did he know about it, cloistered away in the venerable halls of Westminster? 'Okay,' she challenged. 'Just how do you see it then, Mr Guardian of Public Viewing Habits?'

That hitched him even higher on to his high horse. 'I find the whole concept somewhat offensive. An unwarranted and rather squalid invasion of someone's privacy.'

'Oh, really?' It wasn't just hackles now, it was flexing claws as well. Pompous, pontificating little know-it-all. 'Well, I would have thought that rather depended on whether one had anything to hide. And nobody's forced to be on the show. They can always say no. But don't worry, darling, I wasn't considering asking *you* to be on it.' She gathered up the empty food cartons, shoved them into the takeaway bag and crammed the lot into the fliptop bin which would have been straining at its seams if it had any.

'Thanks a lot. I wouldn't dream of accepting if you did.'

'I wouldn't ask you in the first place.'

'I wouldn't accept.'

'You wouldn't get the chance.'

'Stop being silly.'

She was really into the swing of it now. How quickly casual banter can change into personal confrontation. 'Your life would hardly be interesting enough anyway. Apart from the fragment of it that *I* occupy,' she flung out cattishly.

'Don't flatter yourself, my dear.' He sounded so cold. She couldn't believe this was the same man whose breath had been hot on her nakedness only an hour ago.

'I don't,' she countered. '*You're* the one who should

39

be flattered. There are millions of men out there whom I've never even met who'd drool at the thought of changing places with you and solely on account that I occasionally allow you to share my bed. If they knew about you, that is. But of course, we have to be very careful that people *don't* know, don't we? Can't risk snooping little reporters or squalid TV people finding out that the oh-so-respectable Alex Pritchard, Cabinet Minister, has a woman on the side, now, can we?' She only stopped there because she'd run out of breath.

Alex looked at her stonily. He seemed to have decided that the best sort of reply would be a dignified silence. But he couldn't manage one. 'Well, I don't think I'll be sharing your bed for much longer, Kate. You and your inflated ego don't leave much room for a third occupant.'

(Ouch!)

He walked rather stiffly over to the door, picked up his umbrella and briefcase, then turned to look at her again. He didn't say goodbye or even goodnight. He just said, 'Well?'

If that was supposed to be some sort of ultimatum he could keep it. She forced her face into a cool smile. The Kate O'Connell smile. 'Well. I assume this means you won't be free on Sunday afternoon. I'm going to see an old friend of mine and I was going to ask you if you'd like to come along but forget it, it doesn't matter.' She said it as if she didn't give two hoots one way or the other. She did, though. She hadn't really intended to ask him – he wasn't the only one with a public and professional reputation to uphold – but a little part of her had secretly whispered that it would be nice. If only for an hour or two. How lovely it would be to actually be with her lover in public, in the company of other people, talking in a group, being seen as just another couple. She realised that, apart from in the very beginning when they were tentatively feeling their way into a relationship, she'd never actually been with him when other people were around. It was always in private, just the two of them. Prudent and discreet. Or furtive and secret, depending on the state of your guilt. And yet the fact that he was entrenched in a marriage had been one of his attractions. It made him safe. No risk of complications. No demands that she should give up one scrap of her independence to cater for his needs, because someone else already did all that for him. Right now she didn't appreciate the irony and she sighed. There was only one thing left to say so she said it. ''Bye, Alex.'

But he still didn't go. 'Kate . . .'

She looked at her watch. 'The House is sitting rather late tonight, isn't it? Interesting debate? Poor Alex, he works *so* hard. Never mind, I'm sure Elizabeth will be able to soothe his tired brow.'

'Goodnight, Kate,' he said quietly. 'I'll call you.'

She kept her eyes fixed firmly on the table, forcing back the tears that impudently threatened to blur her vision, constrict her throat. It was a small victory but she won it. 'No, Alex. I think it would be better if you didn't.' Then she looked round. There was no way of telling if he'd heard her words or not. He was already gone.

The man in the street waited patiently.

True to form, the people's elected representative took no notice of him. Alex kept to the shadows and walked quickly away from Kate's house, along the street, past lots of empty parking spaces, round the corner, along another treelined street until at the far end of it he unlocked the door of his very shiny maroon Rover. He climbed in and pulled the door closed again. It gave that satisfying quiet 'thunk' of quality engineering and design. He sat back in the seat for a moment, hands on the wheel, arms braced straight as if preparing himself to make the transition between one world and another. A moment's pause then his body slumped a little, he turned the ignition and the engine purred into life. He drove away.

The man stayed in the shadows until the car was out of sight then he took a little notebook out of his coat pocket and jotted down the Rover's registration number. Before putting the ballpoint pen away again he used it to scratch his nose – an unconscious gesture of salute to the organ which told him he was on to something.

If Alex did phone Kate over the next couple of days she wasn't aware of it. All hell broke loose. Dr Sullivan of diet-and-health books fame had a mild heart attack on Thursday afternoon and was rushed to hospital. On Thursday evening, just as she got home, Kate was summoned back to work again. A garbled telex had just come in from Lagos. There'd been another military coup, the airports had been closed and TV7's African Correspondent, who was going to start off his home leave by adding a little weight to counterbalance Friday's programme, was stuck in Nigeria for the duration. Kate and Julian spent the whole of Thursday evening in the office making frantic phone calls and calling in old favours. At one point Kate even gave serious consideration to asking Alex to be on the show. If you can call three seconds 'serious consideration'.

It was close on midnight before she got home again and she was back in the office by seven thirty Friday morning digesting hastily scribbled research notes along with soggy toast and powerfully black coffee from the canteen. There had been last-minute cancellations with the programme before of course, but not at such short notice – and never both of the guests at once. And in and amongst that little lot she'd been hassled on the phone by a rather pushy New York literary agent who even Linda hadn't been able to field off. 'She's been phoning since Monday. I've used up all the stock excuses.'

'Tell her I'm dead.'

'I tried that. She didn't believe me. Kate, please, get her off my back, will you? As a personal favour to me.'

'Not now, Linda. Say I'll call her back.'

Linda glared a threat across the office. Kate sighed. 'Oh, go on then, put the woman through.'

Kate's end of the conversation went something like this: 'Yes? What's it called? No, I'm afraid I haven't had the opportunity . . . Who did you say it's by? Never heard of him.'

Laura Babski countered it with, 'You will, Mz O'Connell, you will. And I'm giving you first refusal. Do you want to go down in history as the one who turned down C. J. Warren? Or do you want the kudos of being the one who spotted him first?'

That had a certain appeal. A flagless semaphore flapped between Kate and Linda during this exchange resulting in Linda rummaging amongst a sea of books on the floor under the windowsill and rising in triumph like an incongruous Aphrodite, waving the novel in question before her.

'Okay,' said Kate. 'Tell you what I'll do, I'll have a look at it over the weekend and get back to you.' Note, she hadn't said *which* weekend. She put the phone down and said to Linda, 'Find out everything you can about this whatsisname, can you? Just in case. Oh, and while you're at it, check with the grapevine and see if Wogan or Ross of any of that lot have been showing interest.' Then she dropped the book into her briefcase and hurried down to Make-up.

They made it. The closing credits began to roll, the studio lights dimmed, the monitor cut from Kate's face to the programme caption and the floor manager yelled, 'Okay, children, relax!' Kate grinned. Impossible command. She was high as a kite. Wonderful stuff, adrenalin. The hormonal equivalent of the life and soul of the party. Guaranteed to get you going but with a skin like a rhinoceros – never takes the hint when it's time to leave. The studio audience began to mumble their way through the exits and Kate ducked behind the set which was already being dismantled to make way for the next booking. She picked her way across the cables and wires on the painted concrete floor, her eyes not yet adjusted after the glare of the studio lights, and pulled rather weakly at the heavy soundproofed door. The back corridor was refreshingly cool and gloomy.

'Darling!' She turned to see Julian hurrying close

behind. 'Kate, my precious angel, you were wonderful. Hold on a minute so I can give you a kiss and make all the boys madly jealous.'

'Ah, but which one of us will they be jealous of?' She gave him a big hug and then held him away from her and studied him for a moment. It hadn't crossed her mind until now but . . . 'Julian? Are you doing anything on Sunday afternoon?'

So much for the mythical millions of virile men drooling at the idea of being Kate O'Connell's date, she thought, standing on Mo's doorstep with Julian waiting for someone to answer the bell. She loved Julian dearly and was used to his flamboyant style of dress but he really had gone over the top this time. He couldn't have advertised his leanings any more obviously if he'd been wearing a placard.

'When I'm at work I'm a little more discreet,' he'd whispered in her ear with a greeting kiss, 'but when it's playtime I'm allowed to be as camp as a row of tents if I'm in the mood!'

'I take it you're in the mood.'

He flipped a wrist and pouted. 'Mmm. Deliciously. Do you like it?' he asked, giving a little twirl to show off the peach silk Three Musketeers-type shirt.

'Gorgeous. Can I borrow it sometime?'

'Only if you tell me the name of that outrageously sexy scent you're wearing.'

'I'll buy you a bottle for Christmas.'

'Deal.'

She'd been a bit worried that they'd stick out like two fistfuls of sore thumbs at the Levys' afternoon gathering. She felt that the pair of them together positively screamed, 'Look at us – we're The Beautiful Media People!' Although it was supposed to be just a private little party with a few old friends, Kate hadn't been able to resist doing herself up to the nines. Discreetly, of course. But hell, when you're an expert with make-up and you earn the sort of salary that lets you buy your ready-to-wears in Bond Street and you're meeting people who used to know you in the days when you were dressed by Oxfam . . . She'd chosen the Halston pure silk jersey skirt and blouse in a soft oyster shade which flattered her hair and complexion and made her teeth seem very white. She wore the blouse outside the skirt and nipped it in at the waist with a broad belt of taupe suede leather which exactly matched the colour of her high heeled peep-toe shoes. Eighteen carat gold Paloma Picasso earrings and a bracelet which she'd chosen at Tiffany's yesterday morning to cheer herself up completed the outfit.

It was Mo who answered the door. She stood there for a second, grinning, eyeing Kate slowly and methodically from head to toe before saying, 'You *cow!* Just look at you. I hate you!'

It was the nicest compliment Kate had been paid for ages. 'You don't look so bad yourself for a thirty year old wife and mother of two. Happy birthday!' She brought out the package she'd been hiding behind her back. 'Can we come in now?'

Mo looked at Julian. 'Your friend can. Not sure about you, though. Wait there while I make sure Ben's chained up in the cupboard.' Laughing, she ushered them both into the kitchen where Ben, most definitely not chained up anywhere, did his duty as host by thrusting large glasses of pinkish liquid at them. Kate looked at hers with suspicion. 'It's punch,' Ben said a little defensively. 'Mixed it myself. Go carefully. It's a fairly explosive recipe.'

'Delicious,' said Julian, gulping down half of his in one go. 'Now then, just *who* is that divine creature standing over there by the window? He looks so *soul*ful.'

Ben laughed. 'Not soulful, just drunk. And I don't think he's – er – quite your type. But let me introduce you to . . .' He took Julian's arm and led him off. Kate and Mo grinned at each other and were just launching into, 'Well, how are you *really* . . .' when Kate was almost knocked off balance by a miniature bundle of concentrated energy known as Sammy, followed closely by another one, and then another. Children of all sizes seemed to be everywhere, scampering around, weaving in between grown-up legs, clambering over furniture. 'More chaotic than I was expecting, I'm afraid,' said Mo a little ruefully, 'but an afternoon "do" solves everybody's babysitting problems. They're all smashed out of their tiny minds. The kids, I mean. One of the little blighters discovered my secret hoard of brandy liqueur chocolates and . . . well, you can see for yourself. I don't *think* any of them's been sick yet,' she muttered as she wandered off to answer the door again, shaking her head.

Kate was soon reclaimed by Ben, who'd settled Julian in a corner happily chatting up a tall, rather butch-looking, bearded chap who was clad from top to toe in the softest of brown leather. 'Writes soap operas,' he said. 'Thought they might have a few things in common . . .'

'Just a few old friends'. The walls were almost bulging under the pressure and for the next hour she was too busy being circulated to have much chance of a real good natter with Mo. She deftly fielded the inevitable, 'TV7? Oh, I'm a staunch BBC addict myself,' and the, 'Hope you don't mind my saying but you look a lot older than you do on the box,' and the, 'You fell on your feet, didn't you, landing a jammy job like that, all that money for working a two-hour week,' and tactfully laughed off a couple of requests for her autograph. By the time she was rescued by Mo she was almost ready to climb on to a table and shout at the top of her voice, 'Hey, everybody, it's *me*, Katy O'Connell, remember? It's only a bloody job, for God's sake! I'm still *me!*'

'Fancy a break?' asked Mo, taking her by the elbow and leading her off. 'Becky's due for a feed. Half an hour's peace and quiet. Come on upstairs,' and moments later she was sitting on the marital bed, leaning against a pile of coats and watching Mo settle herself and the baby into a rocking chair.

'My God, Mo, your boobs are enormous!' she said as the blouse was unbuttoned and one huge breast unzipped from its casing.

Mo smirked. 'Aren't they just. Ben's in his element.'

'I'll bet. But what about you? Doesn't it hurt? I mean doesn't she bite or anything?'

'Does it hurt you when a lover's having his way with yours?' Mo countered. The same dear, blunt and to the point Mo. 'And she hasn't got any teeth yet, anyway.' She looked at Kate seriously for a moment. 'You ought to try it sometime. You know — marriage, motherhood, the whole bit. Anyone on the horizon? I take it that Julian isn't exactly in the running?'

Kate smiled. 'Correct. There was someone but it wouldn't have worked. We broke up this week as a matter of fact. At least I think we did.'

'Oh, lovey, I'm sorry. Was it serious? What happened? Or don't you want to talk about it?' As Kate didn't immediately reply she went on, 'I'll bet it was your career, wasn't it? Your fame and fortune getting in the way of his male ego or something? God, men are pathetic sometimes.' She sounded quite angry.

'No, it wasn't anything as old-fashioned as that. Not this time, anyway. It was quite simple. He's married.'

'Oh, Kate, Katy, what are we going to do with you?' Mo said, her voice full of affectionate concern. 'Look, if I weren't a bit hampered right now I'd give you a big hug. Consider yourself hugged, okay?'

'Okay. And consider yourself hugged back.' She stood up and wandered around the room, curious eyes constantly drawn back to the event that was taking place at Mo's breast. Fascinating, yet at the same time a little off-putting. 'So,' she said brightly, 'how about you? You're looking well on all this, I must say. Aren't you supposed to be harassed and downtrodden with bags under your eyes and only coming to life when somebody mentions bowel movements or something?'

'That was yesterday,' said Mo, inserting her little finger into Becky's mouth and easing the protesting face away from her nipple. 'Shush, my lovey, don't be so impatient, it's coming, it's coming,' she crooned while doing up one side and undoing the other. She hitched the infant into her other arm and looked down at her, smiling as the little mouth greedily latched on to her swollen nipple. 'Piglet!' she said fondly, then turned her attention back to Kate as if there'd been no interruption. 'Anyway, when you've just had a baby it's not your eyes you get bags under.' She was utterly serious. 'Everywhere else, yes. Stomach, boobs, thighs . . . Oh well. And I can be as enthralled by the consistency of baby crap as the next mother but you don't want to hear about all that, surely?'

Kate knelt on the floor by Mo's feet and tentatively stroked the silk-fine hair which downed the back of the baby's head. 'You're quite right. I don't,' she said, smiling up at her friend. 'But leaving out the finer points of infant plumbing, what's it like, Mo? I mean, with Ben and Sammy and the baby and all this . . . domesticity? Don't you miss teaching?'

'The cut and thrust of the weekly staff meeting, the nail-biting drama of the coach trip to Stratford?' Mo laughed. 'Can't say that I do.'

'But what about the intellectual stimulation, the challenges, your independence . . .'

'Not to mention the money,' Mo cut in.

'But seriously, you can't even say that your *body's* your own any more,' Kate protested with a final little pat at the baby's head before she resumed pacing the room. 'I mean you haven't even got a *nanny!*'

Mo burst out laughing. 'You don't have to sound so affronted! Some of us actually like this motherhood business.'

'Well yes, I can see the attraction in husbands and children.' She thought suddenly of Alex and the two young daughters he spoke of with such pride. She'd even wished, fleetingly, and a while ago now, that she'd been the one to bear them. 'Trouble is you have to have the babies before you get to the children.'

The baby unplugged herself and burped a milky curdled splodge down the front of her mother's blouse. Mo gave a resigned sigh. 'Don't I know it. But you can't leave it too long, Katy. Never send to know for whom the biological clock ticks; it ticks for thee. Or something. Here . . .' she said, standing up and holding out her daughter. 'Take her for a bit will you, while I get changed.'

'But I'll drop her!'

'No, you won't. Sit down.'

They swopped places and Becky snuggled into Kate's lap unconcerned about her surrogate's apprehension. Kate, despite her misgivings, found herself relaxing into the chair, rocking it slowly, gently stroking a chubby miniature arm and watching, a little awestruck, as the tiny fingers curled around one of her big ones. 'She's so very . . .' Words like 'fascinating, miraculous, exquisite' were floating around in her head but what she said was, '. . . little.' It sounded a bit lame.

'She's nearly twelve pounds,' Mo contradicted proudly. 'Just about what I need to lose, and before you start agreeing with me,' she went on quickly, 'I'm perfectly well aware that my bum looks like an elephant's and my belly's like a soggy cream puff with snail tracks all over it.' She grinned at Kate's look of incomprehension. 'Stretch marks, woman, stretch marks. But once I've got her weaned it'll be diet and exercise and Jane Fonda eat your heart out! Don't laugh. This time I mean it.'

'I'm not laughing.'

'Good.' She rummaged around in the wardrobe for a moment then emerged with a clean blouse on a hanger. 'God, I'll be glad when I can start wearing proper clothes again.' She said it almost hungrily. 'A knee-length dress that fastens down the back! Or when you go to bed to be able to take off the same clothes that you put on that morning. But not when you've got a burpy baby. Come on, give her to me and I'll put her in her cot. With any luck she might go to sleep for a while.'

That's when Kate had a mild mental aberration. 'You go on downstairs and enjoy your party. Forget about being a mother for a while. Take a break. Me and Becky are quite comfortable. Go on, piss off, woman, before I change my mind.'

Kate blinked and Mo wasn't there.

She gently shifted the baby's position and kissed her forehead as she stirred slightly. 'There, there,' she crooned, 'we're perfectly all right on our own, aren't we, my pet?' She looked down into the gazing slate blue eyes and wondered what it must feel like to be so . . . so new. And what it must feel like to be in charge of such innocence – the responsibility of it, all those basic things still waiting to be taught, all the dangers you had to look out for and everything you had to provide. Everything. Simple as that. If this baby were left on its own for any length of time it would die. Fact. Heavy. It made the forthcoming *O'Connell Encounter* with its film schedules and nice little stockpile of prerecorded programmes seem like a doddle.

The bedroom door opened and Mo was back.

'That was bloody quick,' said Kate. 'What's up? Don't you trust me?'

''Course I do,' lied Mo. 'It's just that someone's arrived who Ben is dying for you to meet. Well, actually you've already met but Ben has a warped sense of humour.'

'What are you talking about?'

'One of your ex-victims!' Mo's eyes were sparkling with anticipation. 'Blame my husband, not me. I didn't invite them, Ben did, but come on down, I want to watch the fireworks.'

'Oh, I see. This is supposed to be the cabaret, is it? All right, who is it?'

'I think it was about nine, no, ten months ago you took him to pieces on the telly, yes it was, because I remember I was still throwing up all over the place and . . .'

'Oh my God!'

'What on earth's the matter?'

'It . . . it's leaking!' It was almost a shriek. Kate leaped to her feet holding the bundle of baby at arm's length in front of her, an expression of sheer horror on her face. 'It's bloody peed on me!'

Mo calmly reclaimed her daughter and pooh-poohed

the tiny dark patch of dampness on Kate's skirt. 'Nothing that a quick blast of the hairdryer won't cure. And she's a she, not an it,' she said, quickly turning towards the cot in an effort to hide her grin. She laid the now grizzling baby down and got the hairdryer from the dressing table cupboard.

'But it's *pee!* It'll stain. And smell. Oh God, and this is silk!'

'It won't stain, honestly. Baby pee is just like water. Come here, sit down, it'll be all right.'

And it was. Five minutes later Mo expertly lodged the baby between hip and crooked elbow and hurried a slightly ruffled Kate towards the door. Kate was muttering, 'Call yourself a friend? Look, you do realise, don't you, that I get through at least four of these people a week? I might not even remember him or her. Or it. Tell me the name at least.'

'And spoil Ben's fun? No way. That's what introductions are for.'

Ben joined them and they formed a little procession of three-and-a-fragment through the downstairs rooms of the house while they searched out the new arrivals. He explained how he'd come to be on party invitation terms with one of Kate's TV guests whilst being tantalisingly careful not to give any incriminating hints as to identity. Being a barrister he was rather good at that kind of thing. The target was finally sighted out in the garden where quite a few of the guests were enjoying the warmth of an early summer's afternoon. 'Ah, there they are,' he said, just as Julian sidled up looking a little pink and shifty.

'Kate!' He clutched at her elbow and whispered, 'Petal, I must have a word.' He was quite agitated.

'Just a minute, lovey, I've got to . . .' She held up the wrist that was firmly enclosed in Ben's hand as their host said, 'Come on! You come too, Julian, this'll be fun.'

Julian protested, 'Yes, but . . .'

But it was too late. A second later Ben had tapped the shoulder of a man who was standing with his back to them, his arm resting lightly across the shoulders of a woman at his side. The couple turned, smiling.

Kate smiled, turning cold. And somewhere to the left of her Ben's voice made the introductions while the man smiled fixedly at her and the woman stood serenely, smugly, *pregnantly*, at his side. 'Elizabeth, I'd like you to meet Kate O'Connell. And Alex, well, I believe you two have already met once before?' He was thoroughly enjoying himself. 'Mr and Mrs Alex Pritchard, Kate O'Connell.'

Chapter Four

If you had to choose just one word with which to describe Laura Babski, Jeff thought, while she outlined her plans for pushing *Losing Time*, that word would have to be 'uncompromising'. She was tall, yet wore high-heeled shoes which took her to the six foot mark; chunkily built, yet wore square-cut jackets in vivid colours — yellows, fuschias, electric blues; she was short-sighted yet spurned contact lenses, using large, tortoiseshell-framed spectacles variously: on the end of her nose, waving about in her hand or pushed back high into the mass of wiry hair which was uncompromisingly pepper and salt. Her make-up did nothing either to disguise or accentuate her rather small eyes, rather large nose, or the cheek and jawbones directly cloned from a middle-aged Joan Crawford. When Laura walked into a room, you noticed her. She made sure of it.

It's not surprising that he couldn't seem to get across to her why he had this nagging sense of reluctance to get involved in anything to do with personal publicity. She didn't have to point out to him that it was odd, coming from an advertising exec. — he knew that himself — but Laura said it anyway. She would.

He tried to explain what it had been like for him when he was writing *Losing Time*, how he'd written it primarily for *himself*. Yes, he'd wanted it to be published, had fantasies about it being successful and him going on to write another book and another, but all that was never really thought through, it was just accepted as part of the writer's dream, not real, irrelevant. He was not, or hadn't been until now, aware of a public to be account-able to, a readership or whatever word you wanted to use, which in its final distillation meant total strangers reading his book and agreeing or disagreeing but essentially seeing right into his mind. It made him feel exposed and vulnerable. 'It's like,' he said ruminatively, eyes fixed on his beer, 'having a wart on your left testicle or something and suddenly the whole world is having a good look.'

'The whole world? We should be so lucky,' she said. 'Have you, by the way?' There was a hint of lechery in her eye. If she were ten years younger and didn't have a rule about not making out with clients she wouldn't have had to ask, she'd have known through personal experience. At least that's what she liked to think.

He looked up at her then with a frank grin and said, 'The wart or the balls? But you know what I mean, Laura. There's a lot of *me* in the book. The real me, the private me. So long as I'm just a name on the cover, that's okay, I can handle it. But all these interviews you're suggesting. A whole publicity tour?'

'So? What are you ashamed of? You're a nice guy. It comes across. Nothing wrong with that. Besides, if you're such a private person you should be writing thrillers or a gothic romance, not a first-person semi-autobiographical novel! Look, it's part of the package, Jeff, you can't be a *successful* writer without having the publicity. Not at this stage anyway. Besides,' she added with a touch of cynicism, 'all writers are closet exhibitionists. Admit it, part of you is drooling at the thought of being rich and famous.'

True. But he wasn't going to admit it. 'I always thought one of the few good things about being a grown-up,' he said, 'was that you don't have to do things you don't want to do. There's nobody standing over you with a whip any more making sure you eat all the greens. And I don't want to do this.'

Laura considered his point then said, 'But you're not a grown-up, Jeff, you're a writer. The two things are mutually exclusive.' She reached across the table which was still strewn with the débris of their meal, and patted the back of his hand. The gesture and the voice she used were meant to be soothing. 'Besides, honey, it's not you

54

we're trying to sell, it's the book. You'll be talking about the words, not the writer.' She watched him take the idea, toss it around a little, start to point out that they came to one and the same thing. Enough is enough. Soother switched to sadist. 'That whip you were talking about? We can still use it. No more arguments, Jeff, you've got to do it, it's in your contract.'

'It is?'

'Clause 24, sub-section b.'

'No get out, I suppose?'

Laura smiled and shook her head.

'Stupid question, huh?'

The shake turned to a nod with the smoothest of transitions.

'And you realise that putting me on show could be an unmitigated disaster, the kiss of death, an unholy . . .'

'Bullshit. You'll be terrific.' She sounded absolutely certain of it.

When he and Danny were going round the supermarket that evening Jeff began to think he might be the object of some conspiracy. Danny found the idea of his dad going on the radio or maybe even on the television one of the most exciting things since Al Dexter had knocked Coach Thomson out cold with a baseball last season. He couldn't wait to tell the guys at school, he'd be class hero for months on the strength of it. Up till now his dad's writing had been not much more than a mildly interesting nuisance to him but having a father on television, wow, that would be really something.

'Hold your horses, nobody said anything about TV! Not yet. Nothing definite.'

Danny was pushing the trolley and Jeff was walking alongside him throwing things into it from the shelves and adjusting the steering every so often. They'd had a serious discussion about spaghetti hoops or alphabets, opted for cornflakes over puffed wheat because the free gift was better and Danny had delivered a lecture on low-fat milk because dairy foods were bad for Jeff at his age and he ought to think of his heart. Then they wandered through the records and books shelves and Danny whooped with delight when he saw that they were stocking his dad's novel. Seeing it in the supermarket, that made it real. Anybody could write a book and get it sold in a bookstore, (oh yeah? thought Jeff), but to make the tiny hardcover section in the supermarket, that was something else! He insisted on putting a copy in with the shopping.

Jeff felt exactly the same way. It really was beginning to happen. That was when he had mentioned, casually, that he might have to do some interviews sometime soon and how would Danny feel about his old man making a fool of himself in public?

The response was so enthusiastic that Jeff wondered if Laura had been working on him in secret. At the checkout Danny picked up the book, waved it in the air and said loudly, 'My dad wrote this.'

Jeff blushed and quickly took it from him. The girl on the till looked up and said, 'Yeah?'

'Yeah!' Danny's tone dared her to disbelieve him. 'C. J. Warren. That's him, my dad. Want his autograph?'

Her eyes flickered over Jeff then rested on his face with a spark of interest. And it wasn't because the kid claimed he'd written a book. 'Sure,' she said. Little sideways smile, hint of challenge, a second's eye to eye contact. 'On this.' She slid the credit card slip over to him and Jeff quickly signed it with his real name, took the bags from the packer and made for the exit with his head down. He was embarrassed and he was proud and he was going to have to get used to reconciling the two emotions. He was also going to have to do some serious thinking about his life. Short term and long term.

Short term, Danny was going to stay with his Grandma and Grandpa, Jeff's parents, up at Gilberts Pond for the long vacation. That was coming up pretty soon. Then, sometime in the summer months, Jeff usually took time off from Sherman Whitney and drove up to the lake to stay with them. But now he was going to have to fit a publicity tour into his vacation time and miss out on summer with the family. Unless he went for it, jumped in with both feet and instead of taking two or three weeks off for the summer, took time off for good.

Late that night when he popped his head round the door to check on Danny on his way to bed he didn't just glance in and listen quietly for a second or two as usual. This time he went all the way in, walked softly across the carpet and sat down on the floor beside his son's bed, careful not to wake him. He could just make out the boy's features in the dim light of the glow-worm lamp that Danny still insisted on having but his eyes adjusted quickly as he sat and gazed at the sleeping child. He wanted to reach out and stroke the blond head but resisted for fear of disturbing him.

So there he sat in the near darkness with the silence stirred only by the sound of shallow, rhythmic breathing. The sound was soothing to his soul and he thought: Danny, do you know just how much I love you, how much a part of me you are? It frightened him, sometimes, the power of the love that he felt, the fact that he would kill for this child without a moment's hesitation. Yet it wasn't a possessive love. He didn't regard Danny as belonging to him, rather that he belonged to Danny. His love for the child was automatic, it was just there, as much a part of him as his heart, his lungs, his brain. But the love he got in return, that was different. It was pretty automatic now, while Danny was little, but not something to be taken for granted. As Danny grew up, so the love he had for his father would have to be earned, and Jeff knew that he had no rights over his child, only obligations to him. Those obligations were a part of his dilemma. Did he have the right, as Danny's parent, to jack in a good, steady income so's he could go chasing his own dream? On the strength of a good review and a proposed publicity tour? The answer had to be no. But he wanted it to be yes. In spite of what he'd said to Laura.

He sighed and looked around the room, the details of it now quite clear, the nightlight seeming almost too bright. There were silver stars and moons and rocketships on the blue ceiling that Jenny had insisted on painting when she was pregnant, certain that the baby would be a boy, with Jeff having palpitations every time she went up the stepladder and her laughing down at him over her beautiful big belly telling him she was perfectly fit. There was the big teddy bear cushion that she had sewn, and the drapes and the bedspread with the comic strip print that she had made after he was born 'for when he's older'. Had she known somehow, even then? It was as if she were already preparing, stocking up on the things her baby would need when she wouldn't be here to see to it. He stroked the bedspread, almost caressing it. What should I do, Jenny? he asked inside his mind. If you were here now, what would you say I should do?

But he knew damn well the sort of thing she would have said. Like the time when he'd just graduated from Harvard Business School and Jennifer still had her final year to do at Radcliffe. He'd been offered a position at a small agency in Boston which meant they could have got married straight away and lived there until she finished at college. Or he could take up the Sherman Whitney offer – a lowlier position but with much brighter long term prospects. But that meant he would have to live in New York and they'd only see each other weekends. She'd just hugged him tight and told him, 'Count me out of this. I'll be here for you whatever you decide but you have to decide for yourself, for your own sake. Trust yourself, follow your gut feelings. Listen to your instincts, my love, they always tell the truth. Hell, they were right about me, weren't they?' she said with a wide grin. 'Didn't you end up with the best and brightest and wonderfullest girl in the whole of America?'

'And so humble. But you're not being much use to me now, lady, I need some help here!'

Then she'd giggled and looked up at him and said, 'Do you know, I can see right up your nose?'

Then he'd grabbed a pillow and swatted her with it and she'd run away and he'd chased her round the room until she caught him and they'd collapsed in a tangled heap on the bed and made love for hours.

He smiled at the memory. But it didn't help any. Listen to your instincts. Thanks. Sure.

Which one?

By Friday he was still no clearer. He'd put out tentative feelers at the office about taking extended leave. Stamped on like a bug. But now the idea had taken hold of him it wasn't going to let go. He had to explore all the avenues, follow it through to the end. Probably a bitter one, he thought as he picked up the phone.

'Laura. Can you spare me half an hour or so? After work maybe, around six?'

'Jeff. You must be psychic. I was just going to call you. But shall we say seven? Make an evening of it?'

'I can't. Have to pick up Danny from football practice.'

'That's awkward.' A cogitative pause then, 'Okay. Come along at six. I'll do my best to be back by then.'

'Don't bust a gut.'

'For you, Jeff?' she said sweet as a lemon. 'As if I would. Got to go now, there's a call on the other line.'

There was a click and the phone went dead. Laura, as usual, never wasted her breath on inconsequential niceties like 'goodbye'.

True to her word, Laura did not bust a gut. He was shown into her empty office in Queens at six on the dot and asked to wait. 'I shouldn't think she'll be long. Coffee, or can I fix you a drink?' asked her assistant. Jeff declined and the girl shrugged. 'Well, sit down and make yourself comfortable.' She left him.

There was a choice between one half of a loved-looking couch (the other half was heaped with manuscripts) or a faded armchair which looked lumpy but comfortable. He chose the armchair, sank into it and wished he'd accepted the offer of a drink. He waited.

Laura's office was the antithesis of everything Sherman

Whitney's interior designer held dear. Jeff liked it. It was like a large den-cum-family room, very lived in. Her desk was in one corner stacked with a litter of paper, every available bit of wall space was covered with shelves crammed with books, and much of the floor was hidden under precarious columns of manuscripts, variously bound, boxed or hugged by rubber bands, each more than a ream thick and every page covered with typed words that had come from somebody's imagination. It was phenomenal to realise that every word in this room, in print or type, had most likely been read at some time or other by the woman who should have been sitting here with him. Now. He looked at his watch. Five after six. He studied the titles on the shelves. Most of them were new to him. And most of them, he assumed, were written by her clients. He searched the shelves and at last he spotted a couple of copies of *Losing Time* among them.

Another ten minutes before she arrived. Laura always did that — 'arrived'. You couldn't imagine her simply entering a room, just walking in. '. . . And make sure that gets in the mail tonight and could you just call Schiller to confirm Monday before you go, honey. Thanks, have a nice weekend. Jeff. You haven't been waiting long?' The phone rang before he could answer. 'Tell them I'm in a meeting, take the number and I'll call them back. Then go on home,' she said to her assistant then she closed the communicating door, turned back to Jeff and said, 'Drink.' It was more of an order than an invitation.

'Bourbon?'

She poured two. 'Hold these.' She gave him both glasses while the manuscripts on the couch were unceremoniously rehoused on the carpet and Laura took their place. She draped herself along the length of the two-seater with a satisfied little sigh then reclaimed her glass from Jeff and said, 'Cheers.' She took a long drink then looked at him like she knew something he didn't.

Ominous. He wasn't in the mood for playing games and besides he hadn't the time. 'Thanks for fitting me in,

Laura, I know you're busy and I can't stay long so I'll get straight to the point. Money. I want your honest opinion. Truth. Realities. You don't have to let me down gently. I need to know how much you reckon *Losing Time*'s going to earn. In hard cash.'

She raised an eyebrow, took off her glasses and started to polish them with the edge of a brilliant jade neckscarf as she said, again with that infuriating secret-knowledgeable expression, a half smile, a twinkle in the myopically naked eyes, 'Well now . . . that depends.'

'Come on, Laura, give. I need to know.' He was sitting forward on the edge of the chair. Edgy.

She replaced the spectacles on the bridge of her nose and decided to play with him a little longer. 'Could be you'll just about recover the advances. Could be it'll do better.'

'How much better? Figures, I need figures.'

'A couple of hundred, maybe more,' she said watching his reaction. He slumped a little. Wilted. Like a plant desperately in need of a good watering. That's when she turned on the sprinkler. 'Thousand, that is. Two or three hundred thousand. Dollars. Maybe more, maybe less, but now I've clinched the Hoffmans deal . . .'

He looked back at her in silence for a moment. When he found his words they were parrot-like with repetition. And squeaky. 'Deal? Hoffmans? You don't mean Hoffmans Paperbacks. Do you. Do you?'

Laura regarded this kind of thing as one of the perks of her job. It hadn't happened often yet but it would. Jeff Coolidge wasn't the only one whose career was on the upturn. 'I do.' Game playing over, she grinned at him, sharing his burgeoning delight. 'That's why I was a little late. I spent the last hour at Hoffmans sorting out the fine print. All you have to do, honey, is sign on the proverbial dotted. Coliseum comes in for a percentage of the paperback advance of course, and we mustn't forget *my* ten percent of your share but . . .'

She didn't get the chance to go into any more detail. Jeff leapt from his chair with a whoop that even Danny couldn't have bettered, crossed the space between them in one bound, dragged his agent to her feet and waltzed her, protesting, round the room. The bourbon and a pile of manuscripts went flying.

Eventually Laura managed to say, 'But it's up to you now, Jeff. First the publicity and second, we want a quick follow-up, so get those fingers on the typewriter and get moving. How's the new one coming? Finished the first half yet?'

Right now he hadn't a clue. 'Nearly,' he said.

'Because I think it might be helpful if Aaron had a look at it at this stage. Make sure it's on the right lines.'

'Yes, sure, as soon as . . .' He shook his head, no room in it for thoughts of Aaron his Coliseum editor just now. 'Hoffmans Paperbacks,' he said reverently. Then his shoulders squared. 'I'll do it, Laura. I won't let you – us, them, anybody – down. When do I start? The publicity. Papers, glossies, radio, TV, let me at 'em, when do I start?'

So much for her delicate little hothouse plant. My God, he was turning into a triffid before her eyes. 'Soon,' she said. 'Pam Mackenzie will be on to you next week with the details. In the meantime, honey, is your passport up to date?'

'Passport?' There he went again, part of him thought dispassionately. What am I, some sort of echo?

'England,' she said. 'London. There's a TV show over there that would be just perfect for you. Give you some practice before we get you on CBS or NBC. We thought *The Brad Marvin Show* . . . anyway, that's later. Want to see how you pan out first, don't want to risk you shitting on your own doorstep – not that you will, of course,' she added quickly. 'So I'm in touch with a woman called Kate O'Connell, she's the frontwoman for the British show. Nothing definite yet but I should know by next week . . .'

The rest of it went over his head. An incongruous little brass and glass carriage clock chimed the half hour delicately from Laura's desk. 'Laura, I can't take all this in yet. Give me a couple of days and I might be able to think straight. Passport. Yes. Look, I've got to go. Danny.' He gave her a smacking great kiss on the mouth and then left. This time he was the one who forgot to say goodbye.

He celebrated by treating Danny to as much Big Mac and chocolate shake as he could manage then they took in a movie and drove round Times Square and along Broadway to admire the lights of the adverts and the shows. 'Hey, Dad, do you think they'll make it into a film? Who'll you have for the leading man and who'll play the lady, will they get Brooke Shields?' Danny was in love with Brooke Shields. Last week it had been Tatum O'Neil. At seven he should have been hero-worshipping Mr T or the Incredible Hulk. Or Kermit.

'Who knows?' answered Jeff. 'I wouldn't think they'd make a movie, but who knows?' He'd been having fant-asies on the same lines himself so he could hardly squash Danny's.

When they got back to the apartment and Danny had been sick and he'd finally settled him down to sleep after a glass of milk and a cookie, Jeff wandered around the place for a while feeling a little at a loss. He wanted to share the good thing that was happening to him. With an adult. Sure, there were people he could call, friends he could turn to, but that wasn't what he needed. Even if Nancy had been around she wouldn't have filled the need – the need to share this with someone special, the soul-mate, the other half, call them what you will. He put a Vivaldi record on the hi-fi and turned the volume knob to low so's not to disturb Danny. It didn't quite suit his mood. Rachmaninov would have been better but you need to play that loud and he didn't feel like enclosing his mind in the headphones. That's fine when you want to turn in on yourself but he wanted to reach outwards, to fill the room with something other than his own thoughts. For the first time in a long while his self-sufficiency was breaking down. The feeling was called loneliness, something he'd been too busy to acknowledge during the last few years. There'd been lots of times when he was down or worried or weighted with responsibilities, and others when he was happy or coping or winning through – a myriad of states of mind that all added up to being just another man. But now, now that he had a positive *joy* to share, this was when loneliness bruised him.

He picked up the phone and called his folks. After going over the details for Danny's summer at Gilberts Pond and fixing up the delivery date he added, quite casually, considering, 'Oh, by the way, there's good news on the book.'

'They like the new one? Thank goodness for that. Now maybe you can take it a little easier for a while, you work too hard, Jeff, you'll wear yourself out. You looked a little peaky last time we saw you . . .'

He smiled as she prattled on. Ever since Danny's appearance in the world he'd had a whole lot more patience with his mother. He knew what she felt now. 'No, it's not that, Mom, and I'm fine, honest. Great. It's the first one, *Losing Time*, it's going to be in paperback!'

'Oh, that's nice.'

She had no idea. 'Nice. *Nice?*' He shook his head, still smiling. 'Yeah, Mom. It's very nice.'

But over the weekend the high began to wear off and the pressure began to take its place. There was real money riding on him now. Somebody had to come up with the goods. Correction, *he* had to come up with the goods. He fed another sheet of virgin paper into his typewriter and made a start. He tapped out the number 173 at the top of the page. He was aiming for around five hundred. Minimum. And Aaron was waiting to see the first half. And he'd told Laura he was nearly there. So he told himself: come on, Coolidge. You already know all the words. All you have to do is sort them into the right order and write them down. No problem. (He wished.)

'Dad? Can I go play ball? In the park. You come too.'

'Danny, I'm trying to work. Another time, huh?'

'But it's *Sunday*. Can't you do *that* another time? I want you to come play ball with me.'

'Sorry, Chief, but if I don't . . .'

'Aw shit.'

'Danny!'

'Just for half an hour? Huh? Pleeease? Dad?' The electric typewriter hummed between them and Danny glared at it and then at his father. The pleading turned to truculence. 'It's not fair. Why do you have to write on a Sunday?'

Under the circumstances it was a fair question. Jeff had always maintained that of all the things that money could buy the only one that mattered was time. Release from the life sentence of nine till five labour. Time to do the things you really want to do instead of the things you have to do. He switched off the typewriter with decision. 'You're absolutely right,' he said. 'It isn't fair. So we'll change it, huh?'

And he did – first thing next morning when Dave Grantley shouldered his way through the office door, arms cradling a weight of pamphlets, photographs, shiny brochures. 'The major new IBM account. The TV campaign. We're shooting for it, Jeff old buddy. Here, have yourself another baby.' He dropped the slithering infant on to Jeff's desk.

Time, space, out from under all this bullshit. Jeff looked across at the Senior VP and said, 'Better go find another daddy, then, because this one's leaving.'

'You can't be serious.' Even as he said it, one glance at Coolidge's face told him the man had never been more serious in his life. 'Okay. Come on. Give,' he said, eyes narrowing. 'Who are you going to? What have they offered? Who's been headhunting?' It never even occurred to him that Jeff's 'little hobby' might have anything to do with it.

Jeff enlightened him.

'You're quitting? On the strength of one book? Don't be a fool, Jeff. You haven't thought it through. There's long term security to consider, not to mention a little thing like loyalty. To Sherman Whitney.'

'Then *don't* mention it. Here, you may as well have your copy now.' Jeff handed him a photostat of the resignation letter he'd dashed off at home last night.

Grantley gave it a cursory glance and handed it right back. 'You can't do this, Jeff.'

Jeff smiled and said, 'Watch me.'

Chapter Five

Not for Kate O'Connell to wish for a hole in the ground to open up and swallow her – she wanted a bloody great crater. Now! However, as that kind of seismic disturbance is hardly the done thing in suburban Stamford Brook she had to fall back on her reputation for being the 'youngest old pro in the business'.

She proffered her hand. 'What a pleasant surprise to see you again,' she said smoothly. Alex's hand felt slightly clammy. She dropped it quickly, inordinately gratified that she wasn't the only one putting on a show.

'I didn't know you knew Levy,' said Alex, stupidly, Kate thought.

'Why on earth should you, darling?' smiled the other point on the triangle.

A good question. Very good. Too good. Artful. Cunning.

Nonsense. 'And Mrs Pritchard. A pleasure to meet you,' said Kate, lying. 'I didn't expect you to be so . . .' (she almost said 'pregnant') '. . . young.'

Elizabeth didn't seem to see anything odd in the statement, she merely dipped her head in acknowledgement of a compliment then with a charming touch of self-deprecation said, 'I only wish I felt it.' She rested both hands proudly on her stomach by way of explanation Kate could well have done without. 'Another twelve weeks to go,' she went on, though nobody had asked her. 'Alex is hoping for a boy this time . . .'

Kate nodded and smiled and made what she hoped were appropriate noises while she took in every detail of the pregnant woman who stood before her. She was indeed younger than Kate had expected. Probably thirty-one, thirty-twoish. She was tiny. Apart from the six-month proclamation of an active sex life. The face was pretty but looked a little tired. As did the floral print maternity dress in its pretty-pale pastels with three too many drooping frills round the neckline and the hem which undulated pregnantly upwards at the front. Elizabeth's hair was short and neat and dark. And dull, contrary to all the rumours about pregnancy bloom. Kate gave an unconscious little toss of her own luxuriantly gleaming mane while Elizabeth switched the conversation from introspective pregnancy to interest in Kate's career and how fascinating it must be and do tell me all about the new programme Ben mentioned you were working on and so on . . . And on and on.

Crater? Make that an abyss, please. Anything to escape from the emotional tumult that was raging inside. Guilt, there was a touch of that. And anger. No, an illogical fury at Alex for his two-timing deception. Dutifully screwing your wife is one thing. Getting her pregnant is quite another. And, most disturbing of all, Kate found herself shocked through with envy. Not because Elizabeth was Alex's wife but because of everything he and their marriage and their family represented. Everything Kate didn't have.

She tried to dismiss Elizabeth Pritchard as a boring, bovine lump. It didn't work. She tried categorising her as a pathetic housewifely parasite. That didn't work, either. Almost in desperation she fixed her as a scheming shrew who deserved an unfaithful husband. But it was patently obvious to Kate's innate honesty that Elizabeth was none of these things. What she was, which was worse than any of them, was *nice*.

Oh shit.

She hadn't given Alex's family a thought at first. Back in the hospitality suite after the show Alex's marital status had been irrelevant, he was just another interview over with, another guest to be plied with drinks as he waited for a car to come and pick him up and take him out of her life as quickly as he'd entered it. But it didn't work out that way with this one. He was different. The show might be over but he showed no intention of quietly slipping out of her life.

'Well,' he said, eyeing her up and down with a speculative and, yes, appreciative look in his eye. 'I think the least you could do is offer a return bout. You had your wicked way with me, only fair that I should get my turn?'

She eyed him back just as blatantly. She was used to being treated as the thinking man's sex-object but she could give as good as she got. And the man standing before her was . . . interesting, in spite of the grey pinstripe suit. The standard British mouse-coloured hair was wavy and just a little too long to sit neatly with the shirt collar. He was thin, a little too thin for Kate's tastes, but it suited the angular bones of his face and seemed to emphasise the lines which radiated from the corners of his eyes when he smiled – something he hadn't done too often in front of the cameras.

Intellectually, too, there was enough in Alex Pritchard, newest member of the Cabinet, to merit further exploration. He was obviously intelligent, dedicated to his ideals and just young enough to still have some, with a touch of pomposity that she found highly amusing. All this was tempered by an enthusiasm that was almost gauche.

'And just what sort of return bout did you have in mind, Mr Pritchard?' she asked coolly, giving no hint that her thoughts already had him stripped naked. Hairless chest, she decided, long, thin cock. She turned out to be only half-right. It was a game she often played but usually it was before or during an interview, to give herself a psychological edge. This time the motives were much more personal, purely for fun. Except maybe 'pure' wasn't quite the right word.

'How about lunch? Sunday? We could drive out to the country somewhere to a quiet little restaurant.'

She didn't think about it. She just said, 'Okay.'

And so it had begun, the first of the many ways in which he would surprise her. She'd expected some county-fied pub, all buffet and broad oak beams, but he'd driven into the heart of Buckinghamshire, off the main roads and into country lanes, from the country lanes into winding single-track roads sided by tall hedgerows, and eventually down a cart track into the middle of a beech forest where he'd stopped the car, taken a blanket and a bag from the back seat and walked off, beckoning for her to follow. She did. Five minutes later they were seated on the ground beneath a spreading green canopy through which the sunlight filtered, dappling the tartan blanket with splotches of brightness. He opened the bag and took out a cottage loaf, a cold roast chicken, a bottle of champagne and two tin mugs. 'This'll be a bit fizzy,' he said, easing out the cork. 'Mind your head.'

The cork shot out of the bottle, she squeaked, they laughed and he poured. It was almost undrinkably fizzy and it was warm to the tongue and it was the nicest champagne she'd ever tasted. They both fell on the food, ravenous and unmannered as children, tearing at the chicken with their fingers, dabbing the grease away with hunks of bread. August was at its peak and it was one of those glorious and all too rare afternoons where the sky is like an unexpected birthday present all wrapped in blue and tied up with wisps of high white cloud. Replete, drowsy and just a little tipsy, they laid back on the rug with their heads in the shade and gazed upwards at the bright green of the leaves, almost translucent, backlit by the sun. Kate hadn't felt so un-Kate-like for ages. She felt totally relaxed and rather young and silly, as though she was a little girl again who'd just found a new playmate. 'Listen,' she said softly.

He was quiet for a moment, listening. Then he smiled and asked, 'To what?'

'The silence.'

'Loud, isn't it?'

'Mm.'

It was late into the evening when he took her home and at the doorstep, declining her invitation for a coffee, he said, 'No, it's late, I'd better be getting back.' She didn't think anything of it at the time and he just stood there, looking at her in silence for a moment. 'It's been a lovely day. And you're a lovely lady. I'd like to do it again. May I call you sometime?'

'Okay.'

Then he brushed her cheek lightly with his finger. It was the first skin-to-skin physical contact since the polite handshakes at the studios and the echo of that tiny caress stayed on her face even as she watched him drive away.

He called her the next day – at seven-thirty in the morning – and then every day for the rest of the week at the office or at home in the evening or sometimes both. They met again on the Saturday. And on Sunday they became lovers.

At first it was fun. More than that. It was heady and exciting and he filled her thoughts every moment when she wasn't working and sometimes he'd intrude even then. That was when she admitted to herself that although she couldn't in all honesty say that she loved him, the term 'in love' might well be appropriate. And that's when the fact that he was married began to hurt.

He used to ask her sometimes, if she was happy. And she'd always say 'yes', because she was, right then, that minute – he was there. But she spent a lot of time hurting. Not a deep pain, more of a nagging ache. It was all to do with not knowing when she was going to see him again. It was always 'I'll call you', and 'maybe', because they both had other commitments. But there was a lot of waiting, and lots of times when she wanted him and he wasn't there and she couldn't pick up the phone and call him at home, just to remind herself that he was still in the world somewhere.

All they ever had was a few hours, snatched here and there, to squeeze the joy out of before they parted again. There was Alex, with his life; and Kate with hers; and the two of them meeting somewhere in the middle where all other considerations were put aside. At night, or in the afternoon, or whatever time of day it was that he left her bed to dress and go out into the world again, she'd think of him in other rooms, other buildings, with other people. They all had more of him than she did. Sometimes, (a little too often) because it would help make her strong and because in a funny sort of way it eased her burgeoning guilt, she used to remind herself how it wasn't her he turned to when things got bad. It wasn't Kate who held his head and stroked away his fears. And often, a little too often, she would push away the knowledge that it wasn't her he was being unfaithful to.

And now that it was all over, when all those times that she'd promised herself 'just one more time' had been used up, she was facing the woman she had variously resented, pitied, hated, envied, dismissed, and lately, sympathised with for being married to Alex.

'Mummy! Daddy!' Two little girls with classic golden curls. 'Sammy's got a pet bunny in a hatch at the bottom of the garden. Come see, it's got *pink* eyes and it's all fluffy, can we have one too?'

'Hutch, darling, not hatch,' said Alex, caressing one moppet head indulgently while Elizabeth squatted down to give the other one a proprietorial hug. Kate saw her glance up at Mo, a kind of shared knowledge, a smiling pride, a sisterhood of mothers. And Mo had the insensitivity to glow back at her.

It was too much. Sickeningly too much. Even for Kate. She looked at her watch. It was a hackneyed but effective escape. 'Goodness, is that the time? Do excuse me but I'm afraid I have to be going.'

'Oh, Kate, must you?' It was Mo speaking. 'But we've hardly had a chance to natter.'

'Yes, I'm sorry.' She turned to Alex. 'It was so nice to see you again. And to meet you,' this last to Elizabeth. Then, 'Julian, are you okay for a lift home?'

He was. 'See you tomorrow, petal, bright and early,' and he kissed her cheek.

Ben did likewise and said not to leave it too long before she came to see them and Mo said she'd come and help find her coat, dumping little Rebecca into her husband's arms and hurrying after Kate.

She caught up with her at the bedroom door. 'Hey, hold on, woman, where's the fire?'

Kate dragged her into the room, closed the door behind them and leaned her back against it. She'd have locked it, too, except there wasn't a lock. She let out a deep breath and then said, as if she were muttering her way through a shopping list, 'Shit. Piss. Bugger. Fuck.'

'Anything the matter?' asked Mo.

Kate gave a little snort. 'Oh, nothing, nothing. Just your bloody husband and his bloody surprises. You remember that married man I was telling you about? Well you've just met him. And his wife.'

'Oh. Oh dear.'

'Oh *dear*?' repeated Kate. 'Dear Mo, surely you can do better than that!'

Mo started to giggle. Quietly at first until Kate caught the infection and the two women were hugging each other and shaking with hysterics. 'I think,' Kate dragged out eventually, 'I could do with a drink. Any more of those chocolate liqueurs hidden in here?'

She drove away from Stamford Brook like a bat out of hell. Her parting shot to Mo was, 'No problem is so big or so complicated that it can't be run away from!' though it was not a philosophy to which she usually subscribed. And anyway, she told herself as she ran all the way home like the fifth little piggy, there was no problem. Alex was in the past tense. She just wished she'd had the satisfaction of the affair having had a definite end. Her quiet 'perhaps you'd better not call me' and Alex's acquiescence (how dare he not call her!) had a distinctly whimperish feel to it.

She let herself in through the back door and locked it again behind her. The kitchen looked amazingly clean and tidy considering Mrs Pickles hadn't been in since Friday. There had been a time – a few hours ago – when she'd have felt smug and self-sufficient and independent and private because there was no one but herself to mess

73

up her domain. Now it struck her as depressing. Sterile. Just a place. With things in it instead of people.

She filled the kettle, switched it on, reached for the teabags then changed direction and took down the tin of Twinings Lapsang Soochong instead. Loose leaves. Made in a china pot. With a Limoges cup and saucer. And chocolate digestives on a plate. And a tray covered by a lacy cloth would have been a nice touch. She felt in need of a little pampering and she was the only one around who was going to do it for her so she damnwell got on with it. Except she didn't possess a lacy tray-cloth and the small noises of pouring water, chink of teapot lid, teaspoon on saucer – they all sounded terribly loud against the silence of her empty house.

She switched on the radio and wondered if she should buy a cat. Or five.

An hour or so later she was in another world. The peed-on Halston had been replaced by a Marks and Spencer cotton velour jogging suit. The half-drunk cup of Lapsang had been replaced by an earthenware mug of dunked teabag home brew and Kate was curled up in the armchair by the window in the sitting room oblivious to the sunny evening that was busying itself around her garden. She was doing a rare and wonderful thing. She was reading a novel. For pleasure.

It hadn't started out that way. It had begun with Kate gazing aimlessly at the muddy Thames. The distant sea tide was coming in, making the river flow disconcertingly backwards. It was one of the little quirks of nature that rather appealed to her. It was about the only thing that did in the listless, vapid inertia that had settled on her. Nothing to do and nobody to do it with. Muddy. Like the river. However, unlike the river she was not going to allow her mind to drift backwards because in that direction lurked Elizabeth Pregnant Pritchard and Earth Mother Mo and all those other people with other people embraced about them. So Kate embraced her own two favourite maxims: 'sod 'em all' and 'throw yourself into your work'. She'd taken the book from her briefcase and thrown it and herself into the armchair.

Her intention was to scan it, absorb the gist of it and get it out of the way so that when the agent rang again she could dismiss her and her new boy wonder with a clear conscience. But the best laid plans of mice and Kate ... The book was good. A real CGR, as she and Mo used to say in the old days when they had time to indulge themselves in discussing the latest novel – a Cracking Good Read. Kate's 'scanning' turned to reading which changed to thorough absorption which was later dissected and resulted in her saying to Julian at TV7 the next morning, 'Have we got a suitable empty slot on *Kate In Company* for an American novelist?'

The book landed on Julian's desk with a flat thunk. He touched it with one finger, slid it round and read the author's name from the cover. 'Never heard of him.' His tone was even more dismissive than his words. 'Petal, I know your mind's on bigger and better things now with the *Encounter* but that's no reason to let *Kate In Company* fizzle out with the dregs from the dustbin.'

'What's up with you this morning?' she asked. Julian looked decidedly dreggish himself. He was one of those people for whom the Monday Morning Feeling was a chronic and debilitating (for the rest of his colleagues) affliction but today he looked as though it might have turned terminal.

'Nothing's up,' he said tartly. 'That, my love, is the whole problem. Or rather, it was last night. Bloody men,' he muttered.

So Kate wasn't the only one whose love life was in the doldrums. She grinned. 'I'll second that. But at least your lovers don't go round throwing pregnant wives in your face.'

'True.' The beginnings of a smile began to twitch at a corner of his mouth. 'I wish we'd had a mini crew there. Some *O'Connell Encounter*, eh? That'll teach you not to mix business with pleasure.'

'Speaking of business,' she said, tapping the book and

decisively changing the subject, 'C. J. Warren and *Losing Time. Kate In Company*. How about it? Word has it that he'll really take off. No harm in us being among the first to give him a bit of exposure.'

Julian considered and then shrugged. Then he said, 'Oh, what the hell, why not? The last two programmes are glaringly empty so far. Oh, roll on the *Encounter*, with all those delicious advance bookings,' he added as an aside. 'But yes, if we can couple him with somebody interesting . . .'

'I was thinking on the lines of American upstart kitchen table writer versus the Best of British – say Jackie Collins or Jeffrey Archer, somebody like that with a bit of bite to them.'

Julian's smile finally made it across the whole of his mouth. He nodded approvingly. 'I like it. Where's the contact number?'

Although Kate would have denied it vehemently there was a certain truth in Julian's earlier reference to the old show taking second place in competition with the rising eagerness to get on with planning the new one. The framework, the basic format of *The O'Connell Encounter* was fixed but the content wasn't. And Kate, with full editorial control in her own fair hands at last, was quite willing to discuss with Julian (frequently) and Ed Franklin (occasionally, if she was cornered) nebulous things like aims and style and tone even though she knew that you couldn't really formulate something like that beforehand no matter how succinctly erudite you were when you spoke to the Head of Programming, or how lyrical you waxed in the club bar with your producer, or how picky you were whenever you were picking over somebody else's brains. Ideally a new series evolves, finds its own way in its own time.

The fly in the ointment was that TV7 was by no stretch of the imagination an 'ideal' world these days. At the back of Kate's mind was always that sense of urgency, that gnawing feeling that she was only going to get one shot. The company's purse was puckering, strings tightening, and Kate had an employment contract with an expiry date on it. She had to hit bullseye first time. And she intended to.

Her days were pretty full. The evenings she found a little harder. She could see no reason why that should be so – the 'other woman' gets used to having lots of evenings to herself – but there'd been a subtle change to the tenor of her life and she couldn't quite put her finger on it. She tried to but it was like trying to imagine a triangle whose angles add up to more or less than 180 degrees. She couldn't do it. But there was something. A new restlessness, a new dissatisfaction, a need, a gap. Some new space had opened up inside her these last few days and it made her feel uncomfortable. Hungry. She thought the *Encounter* would fill it.

In the meantime, of course, good old *Kate In Company* continued to happen. Its guests were booked, researched, interviewed, recorded, transmitted – a well-oiled (sometimes in all senses of the phrase thanks to the hospitality suite) production line. But, oh, she was longing for the series to be over so she and the team could devote their full attention to the *Encounter*. She was impatient to get on with it, get her teeth into it. One phase of her career was over, nearly. A phase that had lasted nearly a decade and taken her from nervous inexperience to confident expertise. She was ready now for the next phase. But *Kate In Company* still had two weeks to run and she was champing at the start line and nobody was going to shout 'go' until the closing credits of the closing programme rolled up the screen and off into their great resting place in the sky. Only then would the *Encounter* officially come into existence and only then would she be free of the constraints of having to be in London in the studio at a fixed time twice a week every week. Once *Kate in Company* was off the air there'd be a few weeks' lull before they started on the rigours of filming for the new show. She was going to use that period to the full. Headhunting. Not just here but in the States.

She filled her evenings by finalising the details of the trip. She was actually owed six weeks' paid leave from TV7 and if she didn't take a break now there wasn't much hope of one in the foreseeable future so she opted for four weeks busman's holiday, headhunting to feed her new baby.

The first three weeks were all fixed up – courtesy of the United States Government and an official programme intended 'to give distinguished visitors from throughout the world the opportunity to observe aspects of American social, economic, political, cultural and educational institutions and practices, as well as to make useful professional contacts'. That was what the blurb said. And that part of the trip was to include Los Angeles and *The Brad Marvin Show* and an attempt to finalise Joan Collins while she was in Hollywood. Then there was Dallas and the Spellings and/or the Shapiros, there was a stopover in Florida to suss out the recording industry, but the biggest scalp as far as Kate was concerned, was Carmel and small-town politics with its Mayor, Clint Eastwood.

For the last week, she intended to freewheel it, maybe taking an odd day or so to throw herself into the anonymous sightseeing tourist role. There was New York, of course, she was going to 'do' New York first thing – two nights and a day to break the journey from London to LA – then after the 'official' part . . . she dug out her atlas and considered Niagara Falls, the Grand Canyon, the whole of the West Coast, the Great Lakes . . . A quick calculation ruled out at least half of the places she wanted to explore but it didn't matter because that wasn't the main point of the expedition. She combed through her contacts book – fat, dog-eared and indispensable – and drew up a Stateside network of media contacts, friends, relatives, relatives of friends and so on, as a backup list just in case she didn't get an unofficial invitation to spend the rest of her vacation as houseguest of a minor politician on the Pacific Coast.

'I'm madly jealous,' said Julian one Friday afternoon

with another *Kate In Company* in the can and only two more left to do. 'There's you, off on holiday while I'll be . . .'

'*Holiday*?' she cut in. 'Do you mind – this is a legitimate business trip and don't you forget it! I'll be working my socks off over there. Well – most of the time,' she conceded.

'Just make sure you bring us back a few megastars to fill up our wallboard,' said an unmollified Julian.

'I'll do my damndest.'

The wallboard in question was in the main production office – an open plan room which had Julian's and Kate's separate offices tacked to its edges a bit like private side wards in a hospital – and was the *Encounter's* master plan. It was white plastic laminate, about five feet wide by three feet high, ruled into columns and boxes waiting for names, location dates and places, editing channel bookings, studio dates and all the other information which needed to be seen-at-a-glance by anyone concerned with the programme. Wipe-off felt pens dangled by its side attached to the wall on long pieces of string – very high tech, very efficient. The colour coding system was equally complex and equally efficient – green for 'go', amber for 'maybe', anything else for 'anything else'. But at the moment, green was conspicuous by its absence. There was, however, an encouraging proliferation of amber, including Joan Collins, who was to carry the flag for the ordinary British girl made good, and Costas Stavros, the multi-millionaire Greek shipping magnate cum part-time playboy to represent the typical international businessman.

Kate was working on the idea of categories rather than just a hotch-potch of big names, though if the name was BIG then all the better. She wanted royalty, a sporting hero(ine), music, politics, stage and screen, a rising star, a fallen star, a living legend . . . and down the right-hand side of the wallboard was a list of prospective candidates written in, willy-nilly, some of whom she didn't reckon they had a cat in hell's chance of bagging but there was no harm in having a go. Gorbachev or Reagan, for instance, or the reclusive Garbo/Bardot/Coe threesome; when anybody came up with a name that caught her fancy she'd tell them, 'Well, don't just stand there, write it on the wall!'

She looked at the wallboard now. Somebody had certainly been doing some writing up.

'Just thought you might like a few suggestions, seeing as you're going to be over there anyway,' said Julian, looking as innocent as a choirboy caught with his skirts up.

Kate grinned as she read the list out loud. 'Abraham Lincoln. I see. He's politics, I suppose.' She squinted a little as she deciphered the rest of Julian's scrawl. 'Is that Howard Hughes? And Gloria Vanderbilt, Frank Sinatra, Henry Ford, Jimi Hendrix, Graham Bell . . . Erm, Julian, my love, I don't like to mention this but most of these people appear to be a little dead.'

'Never judge by appearances, my precious,' he said sagely. 'Besides, since when did you let a mere detail like that get in your way?' He grinned. 'Do your damndest, petal.'

She shook her head at him and said with great affection, 'You're sick, Julian, you know that?'

The latest audience research figures were looking pretty sick, too. Ed Franklin shook his head and pushed the sheets of paper to one side along with the memory of the 'little chat' he'd just had with the Chairman of the Board of Directors. It wasn't often that any of them put in an appearance outside the Directors' Meetings – most of them only bothered to turn up for the AGM which was how Ed and the TV7 management team preferred it – but since all the hoo-ha over the previous HP's departure and the accompanying division of opinion over who should succeed, Sir Arnold had been keeping a close eye on his protégé's progress. Ed didn't like feeling that he was in Bickerdyke's pocket but however much he told himself he'd won the appointment on his own merits and could prove he was more than worthy of it, the fact remained that he was sitting in the Head of Programming's office only because Sir Arnold Bickerdyke's casting vote had put him there. It was an uneasy feeling.

Jeff wasn't feeling too comfortable with himself, either. He checked his watch against the digital readout on the wall. Ten after ten. Twenty minutes and counting. He wished they hadn't arrived so early and could think of a million other things he'd rather be doing on a Saturday morning than sitting in the lobby of a radio station in Newburgh keeping Danny in check and swallowing vending machine coffee. What he could really do with was a stiff drink . . . He caught the thought in mid-air and threw it aside with shame. But it was his own fault – if they hadn't gotten here so early he wouldn't have had the time to get half so nervous. It would have been easy; just arrive, coat off, leash Danny to a doorpost somewhere and straight in to face the microphone and get it over with.

It seemed like only yesterday he was in his agent's office, flying. Saying something stupid like 'let me at 'em!' Except it wasn't yesterday, it was some weeks and a career ago. He'd worked out his notice, added on the leave due to him, shucked off a steady job and staked everything on making *Losing Time* a winning one. He'd actually been eager when he'd asked Laura, 'When do I start?'

Now.

And it felt more like 'them' being let at 'him' than the other way round.

'A little radio station, just to get you blooded,' Laura had said when she called him with the finalised arrangements the other day. Or had she said 'bloodied'? He wasn't too sure. 'Then off you go to London to practise your TV image on Kate O'Connell, then when you get back we'll have your tour-proper all lined up and . . . This is it, Jeff, honey. You're on your way. Any questions?'

Like a fool, he'd said, 'No.'

So here he was. With Danny. En route to Gilberts Pond with a brief stopover to get bloodied, then settle Danny in for the summer, just nipping over to England, Chief, won't be long, then off again to God knows where and, oh shit, why had he ever let himself in for all this?

Eighteen and a half minutes to go. And counting. The seconds flicked at him monotonously. Slowly. Inexorably.

'Dad. Dad, will I be able to come in with you? Please, Dad, can I?' His stage whisper left a lot to be desired and the receptionist smiled at Jeff but he couldn't tell whether it signalled, 'isn't he cute?' or, 'poor you'. Danny was bouncing up and down on the seat cushion. 'I promise I'll be quiet. I want to watch. Do you think they'll let me press a button or something? I want to be a disc jockey when I grow up.'

'Oh yeah, since when?' Last he'd heard it was US President. But there was no reason why he shouldn't combine the two. 'Danny, please,' his voice was tense, 'shut it.' He tempered the words with a pat on the top of Danny's head.

The silence lasted until ten-fifteen and thirty-seven seconds. 'Dad? You okay?' Danny tugged at his sleeve and Jeff made a determined effort to stop fiddling with the zipper on his jacket. He took his son's small hand in his two big ones and held it tight. For his own comfort, not Danny's. He forced his mouth into the shape of a confident smile and said, 'I'm fine.'

It was a barefaced lie. Unless being scared witless qualifies as fine. He felt such a moron. A grown man, talented advertising executive, skilled manipulator of ideas, confident at handling presentations, clients or Sherman Whitney directors – yet scared witless at being interviewed on some little radio station he'd never even heard of. Incapacitated by momentous problems like, should he leave his coat in reception, take it in with him or wear it? Will it rustle? Will it matter? He could feel his throat constricting and he knew with more certainty than he'd ever felt in his life that when the red light came on and he had to say something earth-shatteringly important like

82

'hello' into a live microphone he'd ... smile? Nod his head? Die? All in a strangulated silence.

'If you'd like to come this way, Mr Warren?'

Jeff didn't move. The name didn't register until Danny dug him in the ribs. 'That's you, Dad, come on.'

'Oh, uh.' He cleared his throat. 'Yes.'

'Would your little boy like to watch?' the woman asked as she gestured towards the double doors that led to the studio area.

Danny was on his feet and by her side in a flash pulling at Jeff's hand and saying, 'Terrific, can I, great, come on Dad!'

'No problem,' she confirmed. 'What's your name?'

'Danny.'

'Right then, Danny, you come with me and you can watch your father from the cubicle. Ever been in a radio station before ... ?' She and Danny were through the doors already and Jeff was still wondering what to do with his coat.

He followed them quickly, wishing for about the twentieth time already that morning that he'd chosen something simple and uncomplicated for his lifelong ambition. Truck driver, beach bum, brain surgeon, anything would do so long as it wasn't author-doing-first-publicity-interview. A red light bulb glared above a heavy door on his left. The moment it blinked out the receptionist pushed the door open, pushed Jeff through it, closed it again and disappeared, taking Danny his lifeline with her.

He blinked, trying to adjust his vision to the dim light inside the studio. There was only one window and that was to another room – the 'cubicle', he supposed, when his son's reassuring face suddenly appeared grinning behind the glass.

'Hi, I'm Deke Jackson,' said a dark brown voice which belonged to a plump, bearded gnome on the other side of an array of record players, tape machines and miscellaneous knobs and slider switches of unidentifiable purpose. 'Sit down, be with you in a sec.'

Jeff did as he was told and silently watched the man

plug large cassettes into slots, select a record, throw a switch, set the record with a deft spin of a digit, flick the switch back then dislodge his headphones so that one ear was covered and the other peeked out from under. 'Right,' said Deke, 'all set. Do you want to use cans or not?'

'Oh. I, uh . . . cans?'

'Forget it, just take your cue from me and I'll point at you when your mike's open. Just ignore all the hardware,' he swept his arm over the desk of equipment. 'Don't let it put you off, pretend it's just you and me having a rap – most likely is, anyway. Who listens this time of day, they're all out shopping or drinking coffee or . . .' The last word blended into a yawn as he glanced from the record that was playing to the pristine publicity copy of Jeff's book which was to one side of the record deck. 'Okay by you if we go a bit earlier than we arranged? In the next link, after this disc. So we've got about one minute thirty left if you'd just quickly tell me about your book because I haven't read it. Oh yeah, and what's the C. J. stand for, what do I call you?'

Until that moment Jeff hadn't given it a thought. It actually stood for Coolidge, Jeffrey, but he could hardly say that and he didn't suppose for one minute that 'Mr Warren' would be appropriate. 'Er, just C. J. I'm known as C. J.,' he said, 'and there's no way I can sum up the book before . . .' He could see the stylus rapidly approaching the hole in the middle of the record and his feeling of panic was spiralling just as quickly. His voice sounded a couple of pitches higher than Danny's. Jesus. Laura, why did I let you talk me into this? I wanna go home.

Another yawn. 'Don't you worry about a thing, C. J. I'll just go by the blurb. Oh-oh, shorter than I thought,' he said as the music began to fade away, 'here we go then.'

The studio speakers suddenly cut out as Deke slid a red-knobbed fader switch in front of him and his incongruous voice, so laid back he should have been speaking through a hole in the floorboards, intoned melodically, 'Twenty-five after ten on WKLM . . .' Jeff fought against an almost overwhelming physical compulsion to cough, sneeze and hiccup all at the same time. '. . . Deke Jackson here with this morning's guest, the author of,' his eyes flickered to the book jacket but there was no pause in the speech, '*Losing Time* which is hitting the bestseller lists with a bullet. C. J. Warren. Hi, C. J.' And just like in the old Uncle Sam Needs You billboard the stubby finger stabbed the air and pointed straight at him.

Contrary to all his expectations, Jeff didn't die. 'Hi,' he said. It wasn't too difficult.

'So, tell us about your book, C. J., for those who haven't read it yet. What's it about?'

Sneaky. 'You tell 'em, Deke.'

There was a glint in the deejay's eyes that said he wasn't going to be caught out that easily and he grinned. 'Don't want to give away the plot, do we? But it's . . .' Eyes shifting to the book, one hand sliding it silently in front of him, he turned it over and read the blurb off the back of the jacket. Jeff was impressed. There were just enough half-hesitations and ums and broken sentences to make it sound as if he was spouting it off the top of his head. Again without a rustle, he opened the book, glanced at a page and finished, 'You've written it in the first person, the main character is obviously very much yourself talking, so just how autobiographical is it?'

'Not very,' he lied.

'Oh, come on C. J., every first-novelist says that. Come clean.'

'Do they? Well, I'll just take it as a compliment to my writing that you think it's all true. Some of it is, of course, things have to be based on personal experience, but mainly it's fiction,' he lied again trying to close up the holes Deke Jackson was punching through his armour.

Twenty minutes, two records and three 'links' later it was all over and the funny thing was he could hardly remember a word of what he'd said. Even stranger, he came out of the studios feeling . . . high as a kite, almost looking round surprised that there were no autograph hunters clamouring for his signature, no groupies fighting for his body. Just him and Danny standing on the sidewalk blinking at the sunlight, startled to find it was still there, like when you come out of the movies on a midsummer's evening and it feels odd that the sky is still pale. 'Well, Chief, what did you think of your old man? Did I do okay? Did you enjoy it? Still want to be a disc jockey?'

'Sure, Dad. It was neat.' But he sounded a little offhand and gave no indication which question that was supposed to be the answer to.

Jeff looked up and down the unfamiliar street, sixty miles and a world away from Manhattan. 'So what now? The rest of the day is ours. What do you want to do with it, kiddo? Straight up to Gilberts Pond or we could find a pizza, go and explore the sights, take a picnic somewhere first?'

Danny sighed softly and looked down at his feet. 'I dunno. I'm not hungry. Can we just go?'

'Sure thing.' But he was puzzled at the lack of enthusiasm. He hunkered down to bring his eyes to Danny's level and rested his hands lightly on the child's shoulders. 'Hey. Come on, what's bugging you?'

'I'm okay.'

'You're not. This is me you're talking to, your Dad and I know you.' He was all parent now, gentle, concerned. Paperback rights and promotion tours, none of that hype mattered a damn. Danny did. 'Come on, Chief, tell.'

'Well, those things you were saying in there about your book and . . . and about Mom, my Mommy . . .' Danny was trying hard to be older than his years but he couldn't keep the tremor from round the edge of his voice. 'It's . . . Daddy, I can't remember her! Am I bad? Is that why she died? I know I loved her but I can't remember my own Mommy and I try to but I can't . . .' A fat tear welled up and spilled down his cheek. He wiped his eyes on his sleeve almost aggressively but the tears kept right on coming.

86

Jeff had been dreading something like this. There was no way he could publicise *Losing Time* without some reference to the past, to the personal tragedy that, although fictionalised, was at the book's core. The pen-name was some kind of protection but it wasn't enough. He should never have brought the child along with him. Shouldn't have done the interview, period.

'Oh, Danny.' Jeff pulled his little boy towards him and hugged him tight. Danny's head rested against his shoulder and Jeff screwed his eyes tight shut against the twofold grip of pain that suddenly closed around him – Danny's pain and his own. He stroked Danny's head with one hand while the other continued to hold the little body close against his own, giving, and maybe taking, all the comfort and security he could. 'Now you listen to me,' he said once Danny's sobbing began to ease off. 'You're *not* bad and don't you ever think it. It's a long time since Mommy died and you weren't even two yet. It's not bad that you don't remember her, it's natural. Mommy would have been proud that you're growing up so normal.'

He went on, finding the words from somewhere, not knowing if they were true or not, just hoping that somehow they'd be the right ones. 'She died because she got sick, that's all. She got very sick and nobody could make her better, but if anybody helped her at all, it was you, Danny. You helped your Mommy most of all by loving her. And you do remember that, you just said so. And Mommy loved you back. That's all that matters, Danny, that you loved her and she loved you. That's the only thing you have to remember . . .' Dear God, he prayed silently, let my words help this child, heal this child, let me not leave any more scars for him to deal with.

Danny sniffed loudly then raised his head from Jeff's shoulder and looked at him with big, tear-bright eyes. 'I love you, Daddy.'

Daddy. He hadn't heard that name in a long while. 'Yeah.' He managed a smile. 'And I love you back. But

87

will you still love me when I'm rich and famous?' He asked it jokingly, to shake them both out of the blues, but the answer mattered.

'Aw, wow, are we really gonna be rich and famous?' He gazed up at his father as though he were being offered a free trip round the moon and back.

Jeff ruffled his hair and grinned. The 'we' hadn't gone unnoticed. 'Well, maybe just a little bit. I'll see what I can do about it, huh?'

But Danny's surge of enthusiasm was brief. He subsided into a state more akin to someone who was faced with a new school semester after a long vacation of freedom, rather than someone whose actual circumstances were the other way round.

Up till now the annual decamp from city to lakeside, from over-diligent father to over-indulgent grandparents, had been an occasion for high spirits and bubbling excitement. Days of cowboys and indians with the Straker boys, hunting expeditions, fishing trips, hammering more nails into the treehouse, getting dirty, backpacking all the way round to the other side of the lake – and no math tests – days stretching to weeks stretching to an infinity of summer. Childhood. But this year it seemed Danny had done some growing up. He spent the rest of the drive via the scenic route up through the Catskills trying a little too hard not to feel that he was being dumped like a parcel.

He was still in an awkward mood the next morning – half of him skittish like a young pony given its head, here at the lake with the summer still spreading before him and a couple of caretakers he could twist round his little finger, or at least who let him think he could. Then the other part of him wanting to cling to the parental body like a baby monkey terrified of letting go. Daddy was going away tomorrow, leaving him behind. Daddy would be on his own in London and all those other places without Danny to keep an eye on him. The plane might crash. He might get run over. He might get to *like* being on his own. He might . . . Danny could think of a thousand things that might stop his father coming back again next month. Next month can be a long way away when you're only seven years old.

It came to a head Sunday evening. Jeff was going back to New York to spend the night at the apartment before taking an early flight from Kennedy Airport to Heathrow on Monday morning. Not just that, but when he was through there he wouldn't be coming straight back to Gilberts Pond. He was going off somewhere else, all over the place, everywhere, it seemed to Danny, except where *he* was.

Jeff was putting him to bed. 'Hey, come on, Chief, I'll be back before you know it. If you think about it it's no different to any other summer. I've always had to go back to New York.'

'It is, so. Then you had to go to work. And you were back at home. But you're not going to the agency, you don't have to go to work anywhere. You could stay here with us.'

'But what I'm doing *is* work, Danny. It's just a different kind.'

'But you're going to *London.*' He sounded really pissed about it. 'It isn't fair. Why can't I come *with* you? *London*, Dad!'

Jeff settled himself on the edge of the bed and tried to explain. First, he'd find it hard to describe Danny as an essential expense to the British publishers, Millenium, who were footing the bill, and second, there was no way he was going to pay for an extra air-ticket just so Danny could come on a three-day trip.

'But you just made all that money. Because of selling those rights. Thousands and thousands, you said. It sounded pretty rich to me.'

'Right. But I haven't *got* it yet. That's only promised money. About as useful as Monopoly money. You don't buy airplane tickets and hotel rooms on promises.' The finer points of the credit card society Jeff decided could keep for when Danny was a bit older. 'Besides,' he went on, 'I'm going to have enough to worry about looking after myself over there without having to keep an eye on you too.'

'I wouldn't be any trouble. I'd be good. I was good at WKLM, wasn't I?'

'This is different. It's a different country and television's a whole different ball game.'

Danny didn't see it. His face took on that about-to-crumple look. 'I wouldn't be in your way. I promise.'

'Danny.' Jeff's voice was soft and serious. 'Don't *ever* think you'd be in my way. Never, you hear? You come first.' But Danny was looking at the bedclothes, not at his father. Jeff reached out and tilted his chin up, making him look at him, see the truth in his eyes. 'You come first,' he repeated. 'Remember that.'

'Then take me with you.'

'I can't.'

'Why not?'

At last, he hit on a logic that even Danny couldn't refute. 'Because you don't have a passport.' He tried not to sound too triumphant. 'But I promise, when I get back we'll get it all fixed up. And as soon as I've finished the first draft of the new book, here's another promise. The money should be through by then so we'll go to Europe, just the two of us. London, Rome, Paris, wherever you want to go, Chief. How does that sound?'

Danny looked at him sort of sideways. 'Like a bribe,' he said.

Chapter Six

Millennium, the small London publishing house which had the British rights on his book, were really pulling out all the stops to make Jeff feel *Losing Time* was one of their 'leaders' and he, one of their prestige authors. They flew him tourist class. The limousine waiting for him at Heathrow airport was black, with an orange For Hire light on its roof and he had to stand in line till it was his turn to climb into one. And when he gave the driver his destination it was not the Dorchester or the Connaught nor even the Park Lane Hilton, but a three-star hotel near Marylebone Railway Station where he was booked in for two, not three, nights' bed and breakfast. He arrived Monday evening, local time. The show was being recorded Wednesday early afternoon. The return date on his flight ticket was Wednesday night. They were really pulling out all the stops.

He sat in the reception lobby at TV7 the next lunchtime, waiting. For a long time. This was to be the research meeting – background information, pre-show briefing, that kind of thing. It was just as well the programme wasn't being taped till tomorrow because right now he felt – as he'd overheard a fellow hotel guest put it rather picturesquely this morning – 'bleedin' knackered'. And depressed.

He hadn't managed much sleep. By the time his body was telling him it was tired his watch was telling him it was four in the morning, local time. But he'd forced himself out of bed again at eight-thirty – just in time to catch breakfast, buy himself an A-Z Street Atlas from the hotel foyer and check out TV7's location, which didn't seem to be too far away. He wasn't due to meet Ms O'Connell until one so he had plenty of time in hand to get his act and his metabolism together – to take a walk, see one or two sights maybe and, as he checked out page 60b again, keep a promise he'd made all those years ago. Ten years. Hard to believe.

He wandered along Marylebone Road, heading east. It was hardly the hub of tourist London. A residential block on his right, built with dirty red bricks, louring and sullen, rows of dark windows, old-fashioned with florid, twiddly bits decorating the upper brickwork and an estate agent's sign advertising refurbished luxury one and two-bedroom apartments. A gothic Victorian monstrosity that should have been swathed in a legendary London fog.

No fog. Just exhaust fumes. Even at this time of day – surely well past the morning peak period – the road was jammed with traffic. Tall red buses, black taxis, cars, trucks, suicidal pushbikes with little dayglo orange flags sticking out to one side signalling 'this is my road space, keep out'. The sign was ignored by those vehicles with the luxury of four walls and a roof.

A city is a city is a city, he thought as he walked on. Buildings, people, traffic. But he was used to all that. What he wasn't accustomed to was all the sky. In London you didn't have to look upwards in order to see it. It was much lower than in Manhattan. No towering scrapers to support it, just an expanse of pale grey sheeting, always in view.

He stopped at the intersection and looked for the street sign. He found it. Tacked to the wall of an employment agency, up above the shop front. This was it, then. Ten years on and he was here. While the other pedestrians had their eyes on the traffic or the traffic signals or the little illuminated red man which told them not to cross over the road yet, Jeff's remained fixed, fixated, on the street sign.

BAKER STREET. In black capital letters on a dirty white rectangular background. 'NW1' in red. A thin underlining and beneath it in smaller red letters CITY OF WESTMINSTER. A city within a city. Just like the past is within the present, he thought somewhat philosophically.

Narrowly escaping death (he didn't notice) he crossed to the opposite sidewalk and made his way down Baker Street itself, following the direction of the traffic. He was looking for a coffee shop or some place he could sit for a while so he could burrow back in time and wallow in the memories that this place, or rather its name, held for him. He dismissed the Sherlock Holmes Hotel. That wasn't Baker Street's claim to fame, not for Jeff. He walked on. A fruit stall. No, a shop with its front opened right up on to the sidewalk, bananas and apples and grapes and pineapples and peaches and a range of unidentifiable but identifiably exotic fruits displayed with draftsmanlike precision in wicker baskets with big hooped handles. He was tempted to buy an apple but didn't want to spoil the layout. He kept on walking.

Eventually he settled on a burger bar. Something else that was the same the world over. He bought a coffee, took it over to a table by the window. Sat. Sipped. Scalding hot. Played with the little plastic stirring stick. Snapped it into four pieces without realising. Gazed out the plate glass window not really seeing anything while the coffee turned from hot to warm to stone cold and memories of Jennifer flooded him.

1978. Gerry Rafferty shooting up the charts. Jenny going into orgasms over the saxophone intro.

Baker Street.

Her all-time favourite record. 'It'll still give me goosebumps when I'm eighty,' she declared. You say that kind of thing when you're young and certain that whatever 'it' is, 'it' will never happen to you. And half-joking, half-serious, but completely solemn, they'd made a pact that one day when they had the time and the money they'd drink a cup of coffee together somewhere in Baker Street, London, England.

And here he was. Except he hadn't drunk the coffee. And Baker Street turned out to be just another street. And Jenny hadn't kept her half of the bargain.

He could feel an anger rising inside. It was sudden and quite illogical and at first it was aimed specifically at

Jenny. Simply because she wasn't here. Like he'd been stood up. Like she'd done it on purpose. She should have been here to drink the coffee and to look at the street sign and to go with him to TV7 and say things like, 'my husband, the author.'

The anger was quick to rise, just as quick to fade. By the time he was outside again a different emotion had taken its place and it was turned against himself. He felt stupid. Pathetic. Making some kind of sick pilgrimage to keep a promise that Jenny, if she'd lived, probably wouldn't even have remembered. He strode back up Baker Street closing the shutters on pop songs and fairy-tale endings that don't happen. He pushed his private history firmly to the back of his mind. The past is past and the dead are dead and they have no business intruding into the present of C. J. Warren, rising author, on his way to a London television studio. No part of his private life, past or present, had anything to do with that. He was here as C. J. Warren, period . . .

He found TV7 housed in one of London's excuses for a tower block. Can't be more than fifteen storeys high, he thought with a touch of superiority and the native New Yorker's proprietorial pride. He pushed through the revolving doors, resisted the momentary impulse to make the full circle and go straight out again, and approached the long low desk area at centre back of the lobby. There were screened-off exits on either side of it, the screens covered in chocolate hessian with blow-up stills from the station's programmes tacked up for decoration and publicity. The invitation to go and look at them was offset by a pair of burly doormen, one to each screen, in maroon uniforms and peaked hats. The only people allowed past the screens were the ones who flashed ID cards at the guardians.

He approached the reception desk. There were three women behind it. He chose the one on the far right who looked uncannily like Margaret Thatcher, told her he had an appointment with Kate O'Connell for one o'clock and finished by saying needlessly, 'I'm a little early.'

'Please take a seat.' She gestured to an area over to her right, Jeff's left. 'I'll inform Miss O'Connell's office that you're here.' The words were perfectly civil but the tone left him with a feeling that he'd been reprimanded by a schoolteacher. Probably something to do with her hairstyle – the colour of butterscotch candy and just as stiff.

He sat. And he did all the things that people waiting for other people usually do. He crossed his legs, gazed around, inspected the décor, uncrossed his legs, wished he smoked so's he'd have something to do with his hands, folded them together, unfolded them and finally reached for a newspaper – *The Independent* – which he opened but did not read.

The reception lobby was large and square and high-tech modern, all done out in beiges and creams and chocolate browns. Half of it was a main thruway, the other half, where Jeff was, was the visitors' seating area. Its dozen or so easychairs, in shiny chrome and brown leather, were too low and too long in the seat to be called easy and were screened off on two sides by a latticework partition, a bit like an open-fronted cage. Sitting there offered no feeling of protection or privacy. Jeff knew now what it felt like to be inside a display cabinet.

The place was pretty busy, it being lunchtime, and all the people who passed by looked pretty busy, too. Nobody sauntered. He didn't know which direction Kate O'Connell would come from, nor what she looked like, so he started to play the guessing game from behind the shelter of his newspaper. It couldn't be her, she was too fat. It couldn't be this one, she was too ugly. It couldn't be that one – too old, and her face, though interesting, was a little too lived in. He knew he was being sexist in his dismissals but he also knew that that was how TV companies worked the world over. Male television presenters could be baggy-eyed, bald and fifty. Female ones were always younger and more beautiful. Or if they weren't they were worked on damned hard to make them look as if they were.

He watched the people and he watched the clock and

he soon got bored with doing both. Not just bored but irritated, too. He'd been early. He knew he'd have to wait. But the clock behind the reception desk informed him that he was no longer waiting on his own time, he was waiting on Kate O'Connell's time. It was ten after one. She was late. That illogical anger he'd felt against Jennifer back in Baker Street began to gnaw at him again but this time its target was Miss High and Mighty TV Star O'Connell. He might have felt differently if he'd been back home in New York, or anywhere in the States because to a certain extent even if the TV station itself was hostile territory he'd still have been on home ground. As it was he was thinking: I'm a stranger in a foreign land and I'm here on my own and I left my kid behind all upset and I travelled thousands of miles to get here just to meet this woman and I'm jet-lagged and tired and nervous as hell and the least, the very *least*, she could do is offer me the courtesy of being on time.

He refolded the newspaper with a sharp little jerk and skimmed it back on to the low table in front of him. At least, that was the intention. *The Independent*, true to its name, had other ideas. It skimmed the table all right. And went on skimming. Through the air, in a graceful low arc, to land on the floor right in front of a pair of hurrying feet. Female feet. Which had been hurrying in his direction.

'Whoops-ee!' said a singsong voice as its owner bent to retrieve the paper. The face was momentarily hidden by a tumble of ginger frizz then the girl straightened and grinned at him. 'Are you my American author?'

'Are you Kate O'Connell?'

The surprise in his voice made her grin even wider. 'You *are* my author,' she said. Then she held out her hand, took his unproffered one and shook it heartily. 'Linda Ross,' she said, 'PA, researcher and general dogs-body to *Kate In Company*. Sorry I'm late. Are you hungry? There's a super little wine bar just round the corner I thought we could go to. It gets quite busy but the food's worth it. They do a wonderful bean and alfalfa salad so I thought we'd find ourselves a corner in there and just generally get to know each other . . .'

She hadn't exactly pushed him out of the building, it was more of a gentle steer, but they were outside before there was a break in the flow big enough for him to interject, 'Will Miss O'Connell be meeting us there then, or what?'

'Kate? Oh, no, you don't get to meet her till tomorrow. Normal custom and practice. I do the research, or sometimes Julian, our producer, does if it's a big enough fish.' She realised the faux pas and covered it with a confidential, 'He's sweet but he can be a bit of a groupie sometimes. Anyway, we do the research then Kate takes the notes and turns them into a scintillating interview.'

Jeff said a little cynically, 'Same the world over. The workers do all the work and the stars get all the credit.'

'And take the public flack, don't forget. There are advantages to being safely behind the scenes.' Linda was totally sincere. She wouldn't have swopped places with Kate for all the herbal tea in China. Or wherever. She might have swapped faces or bodies or salaries, but the job itself, never.

'I know. I'm a backroom guy myself. Wish I'd stayed there,' Jeff muttered.

'Don't worry. No need to be nervous. Kate's a super lady. You'll be fine.'

He didn't look as though he believed a word of it. That was because he didn't.

Linda reassured him again. 'She's a pussycat. Really. So. Let's get down to business, shall we? A bit of personal background first . . . ?'

Linda returned to the office a couple of hours later to find her 'pussycat' in a decidedly unkittenish mood. Its tail was twitching and its paws had flexing claws. Which was a shame, because Linda had not had much joy from her afternoon of getting down to business.

Kate, however, didn't even ask about it. She waved a piece of paper in front of Linda's nose with the words,

'Can you believe this?' 'This' was a standard company memo addressed to all departments from the Catering Controller. Kate stopped flapping it about and read it out. '*Please note that as part of the management efficiency initiative the third floor tea bar will cease operations blah, blah, blah . . . Staff requiring refreshments outside Restaurant opening times will find vending machines for both drinks and snacks have been situated on alternate floors.* Efficiency initiative!' she repeated scathingly. 'How many more euphemisms will they think up? Cutbacks. That's what it is. More bloody cutbacks.'

'Vending machines?' said Linda with disgust. 'What about my fresh juice?'

'Sod your juice, what about *Joyce*? They've made her redundant, the bastards.'

'They can't sack her! Not Joyce. She's more important to the running of this place than all the Board of Management put together.'

'*We* know that. *They* probably know it. But it's not much consolation for Joycie, is it? We'll have to do something.'

'Poor Joyce . . .'

'A petition,' said Kate decisively. 'The bigger the better. Every single member of staff. Where's our Staff Directory? Ring all Heads of Departments' secretaries and get them to co-ordinate their own patches. We'll be the central collection office. What do you think?'

Linda took a deep breath. 'I think,' she said carefully, 'you should forget about Joyce for a minute and concentrate on our American author. We might just have a slight problem . . .'

TV7 sent a limo to the hotel to pick him up. His self-esteem rating went up five points. Linda was hovering in Reception waiting to greet him. Score another five. She led him past the maroon guards, down a flight of stairs and into a plushly-carpeted room containing furniture, a floral display (dried flowers and grasses in mixed shades of fawn), a large TV set and a side table draped by a white cloth on which were spread out plates of sandwiches, cold chicken pieces, tea and coffee pots and, much more interesting, an array of assorted bottles.

He supposed Linda was trying to chivvy him out of his nervousness when she asked, 'Can I get you anything? Tannin? Caffeine? A bit of dead hen?'

'Any bourbon?'

'Doubt it.' She studied the bottles. 'Will Scotch do?' She poured a scanty single measure for Jeff, squirted some soda water over a slice of lemon for herself and said, 'Go easy on that stuff. We'd rather have you sober.'

Jeff took a sip. He could have drunk the whole bottle and still stayed sober, he was so uptight.

'It's the worst part, the waiting,' said Linda with all the sympathy of one who was not about to be executed.

'Is it?' he replied, not convinced. He kept reminding himself that he'd survived – hell, conquered – the radio interview back in Newburgh. And this was going to be easier in a way because it was recorded, not live, so it wouldn't matter if he fluffed it, they could always edit it afterwards. And he was here to talk about his work. The book. C. J. Warren, not Jeff Coolidge. Laura had said so. He'd said so. To himself, over and over, and to Linda, over and over, yesterday at the briefing. He'd made it quite clear.

Then suddenly it was time and he was being led to the studio set without so much as a brief pre-show hello from the frontwoman.

Brilliant lights. The proverbial sea of faces watching him. Worse, Jeff could see the sea quite clearly. Hulking TV cameras sneaking about on the end of snakelike cables. Technicians with earphones, semaphoring out of camera shot. People wearing jeans and clipboards, lurking, moving on exaggerated tiptoe.

Jeff, acutely aware of it all, trying hard not to be distracted, concentrating on putting one foot in front of the other so's not to trip in front of the cameras.

Kate O'Connell, apparently oblivious to it all, moving across her territory with a confident grace, a welcoming smile.

She looked nothing like the lioness he'd been imagining. He'd built up a hard, won't-let-you-off-the-hook type image. Kind of Barbara Walters with extra sharpened claws. Imposing, full of presence – and definitely not to be stroked. But this woman was nothing like that. For a start she was little – petite and slim, no more than five foot three or four. There was a delicacy about her and a beauty that whispered rather than shouted at him. All peaches and cream and smooth as silk and honey-coloured hair tumbling free about her shoulders. Nothing too fearsome here, he thought.

She led him to a big squashy sofa and as he sat she settled herself next to him, her body angled towards him, her legs crossed, one arm draped along the backrest as easy as if she'd been in her own living room. She was so natural, so seemingly devoid of airs and graces during her opening conversation that Jeff found himself almost relaxing, almost ready to believe that this whole thing was going to be a pushover after all. He couldn't think what he'd been so uptight about.

Which was, of course, exactly what Kate intended him to feel. She began to inch her way into the heavier stuff. 'Why don't you write under your real name? Something to hide?' Asked with a pleasant smile.

'Nothing to hide. More something to hide behind.'

She gestured minimally at the set, the cameras, the audience. 'You Americans have strange tastes in hidey-holes.'

Cue audience laughter.

Laugh with them, Jeff. 'I didn't mean . . .'

Quick as a flash, 'What *did* you mean then? Changing your name can't change the facts. *Losing Time*'s a true story, right?'

'Wrong. It isn't.'

A delicately arched eyebrow. 'You mean you're telling us that the remarkable similarity between what's happened to you personally and what happens to the guy in your book is – how do they put it – purely coincidental?'

'Well no, of course not, all fiction must be based on fact somewhere along the line but . . .'

Gotcha. 'So given that the story's based on fact, is that why you used a pseudonym . . .' and straight in with the punchline right below the belt, '– shame at having blatantly commercialised the death of your wife?'

By the time Jeffrey Archer joined them on the set, Jeff Coolidge felt he'd been put through a mangle. Squeezed dry, thoroughly squashed and permanently creased.

Later, when he could bring himself to perform an autopsy, he acknowledged to himself that it had been useful. Certainly the book had been given a good plug. Certainly he'd picked up a tip or two on interview technique by watching the real professional author at work, although Archer had the inbuilt advantage of being an ex-politician: well practised at putting across everything that he wanted to put across and never mind what the questions were. And certainly Jeff was glad that his first trial by television had taken place outside the USA. All in all you could say it had been a useful learning experience. Certainly. But that didn't mean he had to like the teacher.

He saw her only briefly after the show. He wasn't sure what he expected – some kind of post-production party, get the drinks out, pats on the backs and let's all tell each other how wonderful we are darling – but Jeffrey Archer's limousine was already waiting to whisk him off to Broadcasting House for a spot on the BBC's *John Dunn Show*, O'Connell was deeply engrossed in a discussion with the producer about what and where they should cut because they'd overrun by 'nearly a whole bleeding minute', and Linda Ross was accosting every staff member she came across threatening destruction and death by chemical warfare if they didn't sign some petition she was thrusting in their faces.

'Sorry you have to hang around like this,' said Kate ever so pleasantly once she'd actually noticed he was still there. 'Your car shouldn't be long.' She was making a real effort to be friendly now. 'Was it your first time on television?'

So it was that obvious. He managed a sardonic little smile. 'The virgin deflowered.'

'Well, you know what they say – you'll enjoy it more the next time.' No 'well done' or 'it wasn't too bad' or any attempt to play nursemaid to Jeff's ego. 'So. What now? Where does your publicity tour take you next?'

'All the way back to the airport. Flying back tonight. Coast to coast tour starts in a couple of days. I'll be here, there and everywhere for weeks. *Brad Marvin Show*, *Good Morning America*, that kind of thing . . .' That was supposed to impress her.

If it did, she didn't let on. 'Best of luck.' Said in a tone of voice that implied he'd need it? Then she held out her hand, said it had been a pleasure meeting him, and with no further attempt at inconsequential pleasantries, she turned away.

'And fuck you too, lady,' he muttered, but nobody heard.

Chapter Seven

'Well. Five million, ninety-seven thousand, three hundred and sixty-four down, and one to go.'

'It's never that many?' Julian looked momentarily confused.

'No, dear, it isn't that many. It just feels like it.' Kate was perched on the arm of a chair in Julian's office. The contents of the hospitality cupboard were spread about the room along with the entire production team. It was pretty squashed and not very salubrious. Only the television set rose above it all, sitting on top of the stationery cupboard, switched on, warmed up and waiting for the final transmission of the last ever *Kate In Company*. It was an alcoholically nostalgic gathering.

'Remember the one when Kate's bra strap came unhinged halfway through . . .'

'But Kate didn't.'

'And that one where what's his name, you know, the pianist fella, tripped on the dais . . .'

'And we almost got sued . . .'

And so it went on. And when the broadcast was over and Kate realised she didn't have to wind herself up to record another show straight after it she felt exhilarated by the sheer freedom of it. She'd expected to be sad, even a little tearful, or at the very least be filled with a sense of anticlimax. But there was none of that. As the closing signature tune competed with the spontaneous smattering of applause from the other members of the team she just inclined her head in recognition of the compliment and then grinning, went over to the set and switched it off. The screen faded to dark grey silence and she clapped her hands together. 'Okay, children, mush mush! Don't just sit there. Drink up. We've got a new series to get underway!'

Drinks were drunk and rude comments were exchanged and the room gradually cleared with smiles and parting shots of 'Slave driver!' and 'it's all right for you, we're the ones who have to do all the hard work,' until only Kate and Julian were left.

Julian meticulously shared out the last inch of the scotch between their two glasses and put the empty bottle into the waste bin. It clinked against two others. 'Well, it's all over,' he said, settling back into his chair with a beatific smile.

Kate's response was a devilish grin. 'Uh-uh,' she corrected. 'It's only just beginning.'

Her statement was not entirely accurate. They'd made more than a beginning already. And she made sure it was thoroughly consolidated during the couple of weeks before her foray across the Atlantic. The wallboard was looking encouragingly healthy with two of the amber coloured 'maybe's' changed to brilliant, beautiful, all-systems-go emerald green – with names, filming dates, locations and studio sessions agreed, arranged – *confirmed*.

Kate was particularly pleased about getting Tamsin Coe. Known as 'The Face' in the sixties, she had been up there with 'The Shrimp' and Twiggy for eight glorious years of international cover shots and pots of money, until a car crash at the age of thirty-one had put an end to her modelling career and she retired to Barbados amidst unconfirmed rumours of horrific disfigurement. She had occasionally been spotted by the paparazzi, but always under big hats, filmy veils and dark glasses. Her quote, 'leave me be', had become almost as legendary a catch-phrase as Garbo's 'I vant to be alone'. Kate's own catch-phrase – 'no harm in trying' – had pulled off the coup. A long letter, three even longer telephone calls and a very large dollop of persuasive charm had resulted in a confirmed booking and the promise of a few days' filming in the Caribbean.

Linda wrote up the details on the wallboard. Barbados came beneath the Costas Stavros entry, where the film location read, *Stavros' private villa, Island of Hydra*. She was decidedly disgruntled. 'Don't ever try telling me it's tough at the top. First, swanning around the States on a freebie, then all expenses paid to the Greek Islands and Barbados. What I can't work out is, if I'm as indispensable as we all know I am, how come you don't need your PA when you go on location?'

'Precisely *because* you're indispensable. We need you here to run the shop while we're away. Besides,' said Kate, 'don't believe all they tell you about travel broadening the mind. It merely numbs the spirit. All you get is Spanish Tummy and jet lag.'

'I wouldn't mind having my spirit numbed by the likes of Costas Stavros, honest. Now that's what I call a real man. Rich, rugged and ruthless. Mmm.' Her eyes took on a faraway-in-paradise look as she went on, 'And to think, I'll actually get to meet him.' She faced her boss squarely. 'I *am* going to be needed in the studio for the interview recordings, aren't I?' It was a statement of intent, not a question.

'Oh, Linda, don't go all groupie on me. They're only people, you know, just as boring and mundane as the rest of us.'

'Try telling that to our beloved HP and see what happens.'

'But, lovey, we don't expect you to work overtime, to give up your evenings, maybe even weekends.' Kate was teasing now. The recording sessions could be any time, depending on the star's availability. 'After all the hard work you put in during the day, really, we couldn't ask you to make that sort of sacrifice. No, it's all right, we'll manage without you somehow.'

'No, you won't. I'm indispensable, remember? And for Costas Stavros I won't even put in an overtime claim.'

Linda's magnanimous dedication to duty was nothing compared to Kate's as she posed briefly for the airport stringer under the mini-barrage from his flashgun. It was the definitive signal that she was not yet off-duty. So long as a 'personality' is in public they belong to the public.

Fact of fame. It was a fact Kate heartily disliked but Heathrow airport is hardly the place to try the scruffy incognito game. She spared a smile and a brief sympathetic thought for the photographer, a slightly down-at-heel freelance, desperate enough to spend his days at an airport on the offchance of finding a few scraps to feed his hungry camera, plump out his pay cheque. Then she forgot all about him as she hurried off along the endless corridor towards the sanctuary of VIP first-class air travel.

Not very long afterwards she would have exchanged places with the earthbound photographer willingly. She was strapped into the chair, checking that the seatbelt was fastened securely. For the fifth time. Her insides clenched themselves into a tight little ball. With prickles on. As if she'd swallowed a hedgehog whole. Flying always did this to her. Well, not so much the flying part as the take-off part, those first few thrusting moments when you know it's too late to change your mind. A bit like losing your virginity. She longed for somebody's hand to squeeze. Preferably a friend's, but any old hand would do. She made a conscious effort to relax, to think alpha-waves. She made a conscious effort to be logical, to remind herself that statistically there's more likelihood of suffering a fatal accident in your own home than in a plane crash. Neither effort was successful. Please God, she silently prayed, make them hurry up with the drinks trolley.

As they didn't crash on take-off her prayer was soon answered. The weather looked good, the Captain on the intercom promised a smooth flight, so she decided to settle back and enjoy the next few hours while she could, before she had to worry about crashing during the descent.

Although she knew that according to her body clock it was nearly midnight, her wristwatch and the light skies told her it was still early evening, local time. She'd felt a little weary when the Boeing landed and she was disgorged into the confines of JFK International but by the time she'd gone through the officialese of immigration control and luggage reclamation and customs she was wide awake again. Jet lag stood no chance against the first-time thrill of standing on genuine American concrete.

She climbed into a rather battered yellow taxi cab and gave her destination. Then she tried to find a position of comfort on the badly sprung back seat. By the time they were driving through suburban Queens with its cemetery-clad hillsides she gave it up as a bad job but it didn't matter because the driver was providing adequate distraction. He could have been sent straight from TV7's Drama Casting Unit: the archetypal New York cabbie, sallow-skinned, stubbly-chinned and a Polish Irish American accent she had to concentrate on to understand.

He pointed out one or two places of interest to her during the half-hour drive into the city. 'You know something?' he asked, indicating a huge complex to their right. The building rose pale into the now-darkening evening and looked to Kate like a somewhat stale wedding cake. 'That's the Cornell Medical Center,' he said, without waiting to hear if she knew it or not. 'Second oldest hospital in the nation.'

'And how old would that be?'

'Well now, the building's more recent but the Center was founded over two hundred years ago under a royal charter from your own King George.' He spoke with the respect due to an ancient monument. Whether this was for the royalty or the hospital she wasn't sure but she rather liked having her own personal king.

'Really? How fascinating,' she replied with an unconscious exaggeration of her perfect Queen's English. Only a couple of hundred years ago, eh? Practically new.

The taxi disgorged her under the canopy of the hotel's main entrance where she stood with bones feeling stiff and bruised, surrounded by her luggage, two doormen and a gaggle of bellboys. She was soon checked in and alone in her room on the fifteenth floor looking out over a gothic church which crouched incongruously across the street. The view wasn't bad. The room was even better.

She explored it quickly, taking off her shoes to let her toes luxuriate in the thick pile carpet, then went into the bathroom. *Very* nice. She splashed her face and hands with cold water to freshen herself up and felt deliciously decadent for defiling the pristine arrangement of towels – four huge bath sheets and at least six hand towels, all fat and fluffy. So many of them. If you could afford something like two hundred quid a night for the hotel room, how come they expected you to be so dirty?

Back in the main room she switched on the television to keep her company while she unpacked and before long she was channel hopping with a slightly manic abandon. Every so often she'd stop in her tracks and gaze at the screen, head tilted to one side and forgetting to breathe. It wasn't just the plethora of channels that did it, nor the variety of the programmes and the insistence and frequency of the commercials. She already knew what to expect from American TV – it was very upfront, very . . . American. But knowing in your mind and actually watching the reality are two entirely different things.

She thought of the sedate Public Information Broadcasts back home which occasionally slip out as a late night afterthought, advising Londoners that pavements are for pensioners and young mums with pushchairs and not for parking cars on. She compared it with the jangling jingle from the New York State Health Department which sang brightly, 'VD gets ar-rou-ound!' Very health conscious, these New Yorkers. Maybe that's why there were so many towels. She stubbed out a cigarette to the catchy rhythm of the American Lung Association's 'Do the cigarette mash' and then lit up another one in defiance while she called room service. Settling for a steak and fries, she awarded herself a gold star for remembering to say fries not chips.

Two more tips later, hunger satisfied and mind still swirling with enjoyment of All Things American, she switched off the set, took a notebook and pen from her handbag and stretched out on the king-size bed enjoying the relative silence afforded by the double glazing. She settled herself back into the pillows – all six of them – and started to write.

She added a few more items to the list over a late breakfast in her room then edited it down to manageable proportions as she finished her coffee. The Circle Line boat trip was out, for a start. She didn't want to sit watching Manhattan glide past her, she wanted to be inside Manhattan, zipping about in the thick of it.

They say that when you visit New York for the first time you either love it or loathe it. Kate's only intimate contact with the city so far had been limited to the few steps taken across the sidewalk from the taxi to the hotel entrance yet already she'd got the bug, was infected by the get up and go, the energy, the effervescent atmosphere that seemed to come from simply being there, in New York. She went into action. And, as in everything else she did, she played her tourist role to the full. By the end of the first day she felt hot, dishevelled, breathless and hungry. She also felt small. Physically little, still not accustomed to buildings so high that you actually notice laws of perspective in action. The sheer physical impact of New York was indescribable. She was like a kid in a toyshop just before Christmas with a tame millionaire uncle in tow – she didn't know where to begin, just wanted to grab hold of passing elbows and say, 'Hey, wow, look at that, isn't it fantastic, where next, more please!'

She gawped at the twin towers of the World Trade Center, edged around the steam emanating from manholes like lids on an eerie underworld, window shopped (which took monumental strength of will) along Fifth Avenue, and by lunchtime was ready for the Empire State Building. Wisely she didn't eat anything until afterwards, still reeling from the turbo-charged elevator which whizzed her up through eighty floors in less than a minute, and then up again, still another twenty-two storeys before the top. She thought she might take in some art and culture in the afternoon, visit the Guggenheim perhaps, then again she could go really over the top and take a horse-drawn carriage ride around Central Park . . .

There was a moment when Kate O'Connell, sensible, efficient career woman, reared her head and she considered going back to the hotel and phoning the office in London for a progress report. The moment was brief. The Katy part of her was so caught up in the delights of the Big Apple that she decided a postcard would suffice and she wandered off along Broadway instead, thinking gaily, 'Just call me Eve!' In retrospect it was probably not the wisest of decisions.

But the thing she was loving most of all about her stopover in New York was the feeling of being totally, wonderfully, anonymous. Here she wasn't Kate O'Connell the woman on the telly, she was just another face in the crowd, another tourist with a slightly quirky accent who hadn't really got to grips with the vocabulary yet. The only time anyone gave her more than a passing glance was when she asked a policeman (my God, his hand rested lightly on a gun butt) where the nearest pillar box was.

This renewed sense of being just Katy rather than *the* Kate O'Connell didn't last long. After a good night's sleep and a lazy bath, she packed away the jeans and T-shirt, put on the new Donna Karan and went off to La Guardia airport for the four and a half hour flight to Los Angeles and three weeks of being a distinguished visitor under the hospitable auspices of the United States Government. First stop, Joan Collins, to finalise the details and change her from provisional to definite, then Mel Hurley and an insider's view of producing the talk show, American style.

Jeff took a plane from Detroit to LA, tacked an extra three hours on to his body clock, notched up another hundred or so points on the stress scale and scored something like ten thousand on the personal self-esteem rating – which had been scoring pretty high, pretty well all the time, in the weeks since he'd skulked away from Kate O'Connell at TV7.

This was it. The end of the tour. And keeping to all the rules they'd saved the best till last. *The Brad Marvin Show*. The Big One.

He was used to hard work. At least he'd thought so until the publicity tour had gotten underway. It could have been weeks, months, or simply a lifetime, he didn't know any more. The days and nights had merged into a blur of hotel rooms, radio and TV studios, interviews before breakfast, mid-afternoon, late at night. Planes and trains and taxis and courtesy cars, bookstore signing sessions, photographers from the local press. He was an old hand at it all now. A real pro. He'd learned his lessons well and it was paying off. You didn't have to search the shelves any more to find a solitary copy of his book. There were stacks of them. In dumpbins at store entrances. Even displayed in storefront windows. The stops had been well and truly pulled out, printers and distributors working overtime. Coliseum and Pam Mackenzie had hyped him to the top – with a little help from Jeff himself. He'd done it all and seen it all from London to New York, Washington DC to Chicago, Memphis to Denver to Seattle and not necessarily in that order.

And then Hollywood hit him. The City of Angels. And Beverly Hills.

The Brad Marvin Show sent a car out to the airport to pick him up. Some car. A bronze Mercedes, long and sleek, with seating for a baseball team in the back. And its own bar. The driver took his much travelled zip-up suitcase and set it carefully in the trunk as if it contained the treasures of Fort Knox. The bag sat like a solitary pebble on the floor of a vast cavern.

They drew up at the entrance to the hotel, a low curving façade of peach-washed arches and tinted glass. A uniformed doorman and three porters materialised to ensure smooth transition from car to lobby. In a mad rush of extravagance he handed a ten-dollar bill to the man who opened the car door. Then had a not-so-mad rush of certainty that ten dollars was nowhere near what the man was expecting.

The porter stood guard by Jeff's bag at the reception desk. The clerk looked up smiling and said, 'Mr Warren?' as Jeff approached. And Jeff wasn't wearing a label. A key was handed to the porter. 'This way, sir.'

Jeff followed him along a peach-coloured, marble-floored corridor past franchise boutiques displaying chinchilla slippers and ruby-studded cigarette cases and out of the hotel into the protected precincts of the gardens, where winding paths bordered by mini-jungles of exotic blooms ensured the individual privacy of the guest bungalows.

His had a sitting room, a bedroom with two double beds in it and a bathroom with a tub you could swim in. He chose a telephone – there was one in each room, naturally – and asked, 'Could I have room service, please?'

He could.

'Could I have some iced tea, please?'

'Certainly, Mr Warren.'

He hadn't given his name or number but you expect nothing less in Wonderland. Then the big kid inside who'd been straining to get to the surface ever since the arrival of the Mercedes suddenly broke free of his leash and added, 'With a side order of strawberry sandwiches. In white bread. Sprinkled with raw cane sugar.' Go for it, Jeff baby.

He put the phone down, sank into an armchair and shook his head, grinning at his surroundings. OTT! Way over. Unreal. Disneyland for grownups. That couldn't have been Victoria Principal he'd glimpsed diving into the pool, he told himself firmly. Could it? And that gleaming piece of poetry in metal that purred up behind them at the entrance wasn't really driven by Mick Jagger. Was it? And if the long, blonde woman with the matching long, bronzed legs was Jerry Hall, then my name isn't Jeff Coolidge.

'Mr Warren?' said the voice which accompanied the knock on his door.

He choked back a disbelieving groan and answered it.

There was a bellboy presenting him with a bottle of bourbon. His favourite brand. Of course. 'Compliments of *The Brad Marvin Show*' said the ticket strangling its neck and Jeff's memory instantly zeroed in on his first taste of television hospitality. 'Up yours, TV7,' he thought. 'In America, we do it *right*.'

Originally he'd been scheduled to have a meeting with Mel Hurley, the show's producer, that afternoon but it turned out the guy was going to be tied up with some visiting VIP and Jeff was getting his assistant instead. His ego wasn't so fragile these days. He didn't take it as a personal affront. And when he saw Veronica he decided he'd got the best of the bargain.

Veronica Straus looked like a California press agent's dream. She was one foxy lady – with her smooth limbs, smooth tan and the sunglasses pushed into smooth sun-streaked hair, she could have been Farrah Fawcett's sister. She was wearing what appeared to be a fairly standard uniform – cool cotton and denim with Gucci accessories.

They were sitting on the shaded terrace of the Flamingo Lounge and she was just coming to the end of her probings and preparations. 'Don't worry about a thing,' she said. 'Brad is one of the best. You'll feel like you're just sitting around in your own home having a conversation with an old buddy. Really.'

Jeff smiled at that one. He'd collected a lot of 'old buddies' recently. Standard chat line. What happened next wasn't standard. Veronica reached across and stroked the back of his hand. Twice. Kind of languorously. Reassurance or come-on, he didn't know. But the afternoon was hot, the breeze was hot, *he* was hot. And not just because of the climate. He turned his hand over so there was a long stroke of palms then next thing he knew his was stranded belly up on the table while hers was waving at a big, (that's big like a bear) bearded guy who was hovering over by the doorway mouthing things at her and pointing at his wristwatch.

Jeff didn't like the look of the competition. He put his hand round a drink which more by luck than navigation was his own glass, and covered his retreat with a joking, 'Make my day. Tell me that's just your brother.'

Veronica gave a little smile acknowledging the frisson. 'Sorry,' she said. '*Not* my brother.' Then she nearly floored him with, 'He's my secretary. He'll wait.'

Jeff smiled again.

'But I do have to go,' she went on. 'We'll send a car for you at six.'

'But the show doesn't start until seven-thirty, does it? An hour and a half's a long time to hang around at the studios with nothing to do but get nervous.' In keeping with the surroundings, subtlety abandoned him and he went on, 'I might need my hand held. Or something.'

She stood up, big blue eyes narrowing, giving him the once-over. Just when Jeff thought his overtures had fallen on very stony ground she leaned towards him, sheeny curve of cleavage showing tantalisingly from V of buttoned blouse, and said, just low enough so's he wasn't sure he heard right, 'Easy. No problem. What say I pick you up at five instead?'

She didn't wait for an answer. A quick smile then she turned, collected Bear-man and was gone.

Jeff stayed on the terrace savouring the remains of his drink, picking out odd words from their conversation and playing around with them. Writer's habit.

Easy.

Pick you up at five.

Pick up.

Easy pick up.

One thing was for sure – if anybody around here was an easy pick up it had been him, not Veronica. All hail to the emancipated woman, he thought as he headed for the pool to cool off.

He felt like a prince. Make that a king. Or perhaps like a schoolkid suddenly showered with candy. He looked around and really would have pinched himself to test if he was dreaming except he thought somebody might see him do it. Here he was, sitting on the edge of a turquoise pool dangling his feet in the same water that the ex-Pammy Ewing had just been swimming in and over there, under a big umbrella, he couldn't believe it but it was true, the diminutive Michael J. Fox was lounging on a lounger deeply engrossed in a book. A big, chunky hardcover. With *Losing Time* in glinting silver letters on the jacket. And as if that wasn't enough, there was the imminent arrival of a beautiful blonde who was going to come to his bungalow to . . . pick him up.

He left the poolside and padded through the tropical gardens, rubber flip flop sandals making little flapping noises on the neatly manicured pathways. He was much more apprehensive about the imminent confrontation with Veronica than all the Brad Marvin or Kate O'Connell shows put together. Okay, so over the last two or three weeks he'd noticed that women were showing an unaccustomed interest in his person. Bookstore groupies, radio station hangers-on, hotel maids who looked at him like he was Somebody. It made him feel good. It made him feel, for the first time in years, that he was worth looking at in his own right – as something other than, 'Danny's dad', or 'Sherman Whitney's hack', or 'Nancy's convenient stopover'. Put simply, his self-image had shifted, and not too subtly. But feeling good about your own appeal and actually putting it to the test are two different ball games . . . And Jeff hadn't been laid in a long time. He was assuming (hoping, longing, *willing*,) that that circumstance was about to take a turn for the better.

He could have read the Flamingo Lounge scenario all wrong, of course. Most likely had, he told himself as he put the key in the door to his bungalow. Veronica could be calling round early merely to give a little pre-show coaching on TV interviewee technique. Could be. If she even turned up.

He opened the door and the cool, conditioned air

115

inside wrapped around him bringing on the shivers and another little problem – clothes. Which to wear? How many? Any? He had no idea of the etiquette of this type of assignation. He decided to think it over while he took a shower – just in case his luck was in, he didn't want to be tasting of sweat and chlorine. As it happened, that decision took away the need to make any sartorial ones.

Veronica was early. He'd left the door unlocked. She let herself in, called out her presence and found him in the bedroom wearing just – and only just – a towel.

'Hi,' she said.

And he said, rather pointlessly, 'You're early.'

Her reply was a cat-with-the-cream smile and she began deftly to unfasten the little pearl buttons on her blouse, eyes never leaving him, hungrily taking in his naked torso, the curve of hard muscle under damp skin. The lady didn't mess about. Her blouse dropped to the floor, she stepped out of high-heeled sandals, wriggled free of the tight designer jeans and that was it. Before Jeff could say, 'Nice to see you, can I get you a drink?' his hard-on was nudging aside the towel and her hand was inside it, helping.

Neither Jeff nor Veronica made any pretence at polite conversation. They didn't even kiss much. Not mouth-to-mouth, anyway. They fell on to the nearest of the two beds and explored each other avidly with fingers, palms, lips, tongues. Veronica ran her hands over her own body as well as his, pushing her pert breasts up towards him, teasing her nipples, daring him to resist them. He couldn't. Then she trailed a forefinger downwards, over his flat belly, spiralling it round his cock then grasping, squeezing, like she was milking him while with her other hand she caressed herself between the legs then brought the fingers back up to touch his lips saying, 'See how wet I am for you. Taste me.'

He took her glistening fingers into his mouth and sucked their silky wetness while Veronica made little moaning sounds as he put his arms around her and rolled their bodies round so he was on his back and she was bestride him, ready to sink herself on to his aching, ramrod-like cock. If he didn't get into her quick he was going to burst.

'No, not yet,' she murmured. 'Let me put it on for you.' Then she was leaning across him, her breasts flattened against his chest, nipples like hard little beads, while she reached for the bedside drawer and started fumbling inside it. Her voice was urgent, impatient. 'Where are they? Where do you keep them?'

'What? Come back here, woman.'

'What do you mean – what? Condoms. Durex. Fucksake, CJ, where *are* they?'

'You're not on the pill?'

'What's the pill got to do with anything?' she said, sitting up again, squatting on his thighs, hands on his hipbones like she was poised to vault off him. Which she was. 'You mean you don't carry any? You think I'm going to make out with you without *wearing* anything? And you from *New York*? Hey, baby, I might be hot for you but I'm not crazy. Haven't you heard of AIDS?'

'Sure but . . . You don't think *I* . . . ?' He could feel it ebbing away. See it. Leaning over, limp, deflating even quicker than his ego. 'Jesus, Veronica. Look, I wasn't expecting this.' He put his hands on her hips and eased her off him. He was getting pins and needles in his legs.

'Obviously,' she said, reaching for a sheet.

He grabbed a piece of it for himself. 'I don't have any. I wasn't planning on getting laid. And I don't carry them around with me because I don't *screw* around. Simple and boring as that. Sorry.' He shrugged. He felt really dumb.

'Ha!' It was a sharp, short, derisive sound. 'You'll be telling me next that nice boys don't.'

'I wouldn't know. I'm not into boys.'

She began to soften. A little laugh. 'Well, thank God for that.'

'Besides,' he said, 'if you're so careful, how come you didn't bring your own?'

'Because I don't screw around either. Do you think

this is all part of *The Brad Marvin Show* regular service or something?'

He didn't know whether it was or not and frankly, at that moment he didn't give a damn one way or the other, but the look in Veronica's eyes told him not to labour the point. 'I hoped it wasn't.'

'*Isn't*,' she corrected as she edged back across the bed and started caressing him again under the sheet.

'Hey, I thought you didn't want to make out with a naked New Yorker?'

Her lips and tongue were teasing their way towards his groin and her words were muffled against his tensed belly as she said, 'So? There are ways and means, baby. Haven't you heard of safe sex?'

He felt, rather than saw her smile, before her mouth closed over him, a warm wet sheath for his stiffened cock.

The limousine had been waiting nearly half an hour before Jeff and Veronica, both looking squeaky clean and very smiley, bent their damp heads to climb into the back of it. They didn't speak much on the way to the studios and when they did no eavesdropper would ever have guessed what these two people had just spent the last half hour doing to each other in the shower.

Once inside the car Veronica became very much the working girl again. She briefed him on make-up: 'Don't want shiny noses causing flare, do we?' She briefed him on hospitality: 'It'll be flowing like water so watch yourself. Save the heavy stuff for after the show.' And she briefed him on her husband . . .

'Your *what*?'

'Carl. My husband. He'll be along later, so be cool, huh?'

'Oh, shit.'

Brad Marvin, as Veronica had said earlier that afternoon, was either one of the best or *the* best. Jeff sailed through the programme, catching the ball when it was in his court, holding on to it for just long enough, tossing it back to Brad who caught it, adjusted the angle to give a bit more shine, angled it back to Jeff's best side. At least, that's what Jeff felt, but he was half smashed already thanks to Veronica's little bombshell, so his opinion didn't count.

Up in the gallery in front of the bank of screens, while the director and the technicians got on with the business end of the production, the producer's opinion was soberly favourable. He nodded, leaned over to his companion and said, 'It's going well. What do you think, Kate? Is it much like at TV7?'

Kate O'Connell didn't take her eyes off the main monitor for a second. 'I think,' she said slowly, voice not hiding her surprise, 'the man must have had a personality transplant. Jeff. C. J. Warren. I can't believe the change in him – in just these few weeks. My God, I wish he'd been like this when I had my go at him.'

Mel agreed. 'Must say you had me a little worried back there when you told me how uptight he was on your show. But just look at him now. A natural.' He grinned. 'It's the California air that does it, you know.'

'Really? "Come to California! Instant sun, sea, sex and stardom".' Then she paused, like the penny had just dropped. 'That's it. That was the missing ingredient. Charisma. To be basic, sex. Look at him.' She went on, not taking her eyes off the monitor, 'Look how he's making up to old whatsername, Floella, he's got the old bag eating out of his hand. And there's not much doubt which part of him that Mary Magdalen girl wants to eat. My God, he's come out of his shell, I bet he's just gone and sold his book to about half the female population of America.'

Mel looked doubtfully from Kate to the screen and back again. Sure, the guy was relaxed, charming, nice smile, but . . . 'Come on, Kate. Burt Reynolds he ain't.'

'True. But neither is . . .' she tried to think of an example and quickly found one, '. . . Jeff Bridges, for instance. That's who he reminds me of. Totally different of course but same *type*. First impression, nice looking

119

but nothing to write home about – till he looks at the camera, or a woman. Then he can be so damned sexy you just want to . . .' she broke off with a smile and a shrug.

Mel looked at her quizzically. 'Which Jeff? Warren or Bridges?'

'Either. Both. This is a purely professional, objective opinion, you understand?' she said, intentionally contradicting the words with a mucky little half-smile. 'You, er, wouldn't happen to be having Jeff Bridges on the show later, would you?'

The producer shook his head regretfully. 'But you never know your luck. Everybody who's anybody in this town is going to be at the party tonight.'

They were in the hospitality room after the show – the everybodies, the anybodies and the newly-elevated 'somebodies', which included Jeff and the other guests on the programme: a middle-aged lady sex therapist called Floella Glickman whose outspoken tongue had made her into an overnight sensation; Mary Magdalen, a raunchy leather-clad soul singer and Thomas Allen, the rising young British actor who'd just taken over the reincarnation of a character in *Dominion*, the latest ratings winner from the Spelling stable.

The atmosphere was totally different from that which had filled the room only an hour or so before. Then it had been electric with nerves, as if you might get a shock of static if you accidentally brushed up against someone and all Jeff had wanted to do then was get it over with, get the hell out before Veronica's other half turned up, and tomorrow, maybe even tonight, get on a plane and head off for Gilberts Pond, Danny, writing, rest and sanctuary. He was more relaxed now, but it was an exhilarated sort of relaxation, broad smiles and mutual compliments and it wasn't just the drinks that made everybody so high. He could understand how a person could get hooked on this kind of thing. He wasn't so eager to get away now. A little sad the publicity tour was at an end. Maybe he should stay on in Hollywood for a couple of days? Mentally he shook his head. It swam a little.

'Hey, C.J.?' There was a tug at his arm. 'C.J., you're miles away. Penny for them.'

The brunette in black leather. Mary. 'Sorry,' he said. 'Anyway, don't waste your money, they weren't worth that much.' He supposed he should get the singer's autograph for Danny. Later maybe.

Her arm slid inside his. 'Come on. Party time. The cars are here. Play your cards right and I'll dump my bodyguards and give you the job.'

He grinned at her. 'Play your cards right and I might just take it. What party?'

Thomas Allen joined them. A man to man thump on the shoulders, a lascivious wink and, 'Come on, C.J. Charlene Prince waits for no man. So are we all going to her party or are we all going to her party?'

Jeff gave a nonchalant little shrug. 'Guess we're going to the party,' he said, and followed the departing celebrities along down the yellow brick road.

Chapter Eight

Even when your name's Kate O'Connell it's not every day you get to share a guest list with Elizabeth Taylor, Shakira and Michael Caine, Tom Selleck, Richard Gere, Joanna Woodward and Paul Newman, Jane Fonda, Ryan O'Neal and Farrah ... every time she thought she'd exhausted the supply of those oh so familiar strangers' faces from big and little screen, hey presto, another one popped out of the woodwork, or in this case, the pink-tinted mirrored walls of the Prince mansion ballroom.

The house wasn't so much somebody's home as a film set from Hollywood in its heyday. You were left in no doubt of it from the moment you arrived: a huddle of paparazzi outside the twelve-foot high security gates, the whirr of cameras operating on the motordrive principle – shoot everybody and you're bound to get Somebody. Uniformed guards checking names off lists as the slow train of Rolls-Royces, stretched-out Cadillacs, Ferraris and Mercedes glided past with the occasional gesture to the fashion for ecology-conscious small cars in the shape of the Porsche sports model.

The freshly-raked gravel driveway, through which only the most rashly suicidal of weeds would dare to show its growing tip, cut a geometrically perfect ellipse through the expansive lawns which fronted the Princes' Bel Air mansion. A team of Beautiful Youths in tight yellow trousers and uniform T-shirts stood ready to take the keys and the cars while the famous and not quite so famous and I'm-*with*-somebody-famous made their way up the Italian Palladian style stairways which swept a graceful double curve to the front doors. The Princes seemed to have everything in the plural – in and out driveways, Siamese twin doorsteps, double carved mahogany front doors and, Kate had little doubt, two swimming pools out back? She discovered later that she was almost right if you count an Italian-tiled, orgy-sized jacuzzi as a pool. She thought it was taking the His and Hers syndrome just a little too far.

Kate stood in the ballroom next to Mel Hurley and his wife Angela, part but not part of the conversation that was ping-ponging between them and a State Senator and the Spielbergs. It was probably very interesting but Kate was still half-expecting Astaire and Rogers to come gallivanting across the marble floor any minute, complete with top hat, white tie and tails, and ostrich feathers getting up everyone's noses. Except that nobody had started dancing yet.

The party was still in its cocktail phase with silent waiters carrying drinks on silver trays and olive-skinned maids in black dresses and frilly white pinnies offering platters of hors d'oeuvres to all and sundry as the luminaries drifted from cluster to cluster and God forbid there should be a black hole anywhere. The men were expensively casual, the women were smoothed, painted, coiffured, massaged, exercised and pin-tucked to perfection in their Lagerfelds and Lacroix.

Kate, on the inside feeling more and more the big-eyed little girl from small time, small screen, small country, did not however look out of place on the outside. She discreetly flew the flag for Britain in a tried and tested and conveniently packable Bruce Oldfield creation which she'd bought for last year's Royal Variety Performance at the London Palladium. She reckoned that if it was good enough to wear when meeting Her Majesty the Queen it should certainly be good enough for Hollywood's 'royal' family. And it was. An effusive welcome from Ms Prince herself with a, 'What a ravishing little dress,' and a none-too subtle leer from the man who had long been resigned to being known as 'Mr Charlene Prince', confirmed it. The dress was one of Kate's favourites and she'd packed it more in hope than in certainty. Midnight blue slubbed silk, a simple wraparound shift draped from one shoulder and fastened there by a silver filigree butterfly pin. It was as light as a feather, comfortable as nakedness, looked as though one tweak at the pin would leave its wearer exactly that (a totally false impression), and was virtually uncreasable.

'Ah, the workers have arrived,' said Mel Hurley, looking towards the gilt-covered double archway, which reminded Kate of McDonalds, to where *The Brad Marvin Show* entourage were making their entrance into the ballroom. Kate was amused to see the erstwhile reticent and uptight Mr Coolidge/Warren appearing cool and nonchalant with an ebony beauty clinging to one arm and an ivory beauty glued to the other and looking as though he wished he had an extra limb or three to accommodate more such drapery.

The difference a few short weeks can make. The power of the media. That first heady thrill of fame. Kate remembered the feeling. And she'd remembered, back in the days when it first started happening for her, to keep her head on her shoulders and her feet on the ground even if she could now afford to clad them in Guccis. She watched Jeff with interest – the new star, base metal turned instantly to Golden Boy through the fickle alchemy of public taste. He had two choices: he would either handle it or he'd succumb to it and start believing in his own myth. She wondered which it would be. And she decided that either way he might well make a fascinating subject for a close encounter of the O'Connell kind.

She smoothly excused herself from present company, lifted a glass of champagne from a passing tray and made her way across the quickly-filling room, spotting the Hoffmans and Warren Beatty on the way. She saw Jeff before he saw her. His cool exterior seemed to have slipped a little, maybe because Jackie Collins had just greeted him like an old friend before going over to have a brief word with her sister. He looked slightly glazed, slightly fazed, and was still clothed in women.

Kate's opening line was simple if hardly original. 'Hello, Jeff. Or is it strictly C. J. these days?'

His surprise at seeing her outweighed any consideration of manners. 'How in hell did *you* get here?'

She smiled. 'The same as you, I imagine. By limo. Here, have a drink.' She offered him the champagne glass, which he took. 'Actually, I'm combining a business trip with a short holiday,' she went on pleasantly.

'Which is this – business or pleasure?'

She gave a little grimace at the surroundings. 'Would you believe, purely business? I had a long meeting this morning then was closeted with Mel, your producer, all afternoon picking up a few more tricks of the trade. I watched the show. You were very good. You've obviously been getting plenty of experience since London.'

So this was the visiting VIP, Jeff thought. Might have known. And still, ever so subtly, coming out with the acid. He briefly introduced his companions and muttered some inanity about it being a small world, which was supposed to end their conversation.

'Save the clichés, Jeff. Can we talk business?'

'Do we have any to talk about?'

'We may have. If you can tear yourself away from your charming companions for a moment.'

It was said with sincerity but Jeff only heard sarcasm. 'Don't go away, ladies,' he said, loosening himself from the black leathered singer and the sun-streaked blonde. 'I doubt if this'll take long.' He followed Kate as she made a winding path through the groups of people towards the massive French windows which opened on to the pool area.

Mary Magdalen shrugged. She'd intended to get CJ away from this overblown secretary type but this wasn't how she'd planned the extraction. Still, business is, after all, what Hollywood parties are for and it was time she got down to some. She smoothed her supple miniskirt to show off her equally supple frame and set off to cruise the room in search of a movie producer or studio head, she wasn't fussy. Madonna wasn't the only one who could do it.

Veronica, suddenly left on her own, put on her Farrah

smile and practised being 'cool'. Which was just as well because moments later a big familiar hand rested on her shoulder and a big familiar voice said, 'There you are, hon. I was beginning to think I'd lost you. I was hoping you might have managed to get away for an hour or so, earlier. Guess you had a hard day, huh?'

Veronica leaned her cheek against Carl's hand and muttered softly, 'Yes. 'Fraid I got a little tied up.'

Jeff and Kate stood on the terrace which overlooked the floodlit swimming pool. Jeff thought: fantasy land. Kate thought: nice place to visit but I wouldn't want to live here.

Timothy Dalton, looking as suave as his portrayals of 007, spotted Kate and gave a wave of greeting in her direction. Both Kate and Jeff waved back.

'You know Tim?' Kate asked.

'Our publicity tours crossed paths in Chicago. Or maybe Memphis. Somewhere.' Very blasé.

She smiled to herself. She still thought of Dalton primarily as a classical stage actor. 'Going back to what you said about it being a small world,' she said conversationally, 'I have this pet theory . . .'

'Thought you didn't approve of clichés.'

'I don't,' she said. 'You see, my theory is that it's not the world that's small, but its population. I reckon, and I think tonight proves it, that there are actually only about three hundred real people on the whole planet and wherever you go you keep on bumping into them or into somebody else who knows them.'

'That so? And where do the other ninety billion come in?'

'Cardboard cutouts,' she said sagely. 'Look, there's a prime example, over there.'

Jeff looked. He wasn't altogether sure what she was getting at but decided to play along. 'That's not a cardboard cutout,' he said. 'It's a Barbie doll.'

She laughed. 'Same difference.'

The lady in question turned, as if she knew she was being discussed. She fixed her eyes on Jeff, seemed to flicker a recognition, then gave him a blatant come-on smile.

'You collect dolls then?' Kate asked, amused.

Jeff raised his glass slightly in Barbie's direction. 'Not yet,' he said appreciatively. 'But I think I soon will.' He turned back to Kate, voice suddenly brisk, eyes scanning her face like she was the small print on a contract. 'So what was this business you want to talk about?'

Whatever it was about him, the look, the smile, that indefinable 'something' that she'd nevertheless attempted to define to Mel Hurley back at the studios — it was missing when Jeff Coolidge looked at Kate O'Connell. You really know how to make a woman feel like a businessman, she thought. But what the hell. She was looking for an *O'Connell Encounter*, not a *Brief Encounter*. She explained about the new programme, its format, the transmission schedule, finishing with, 'So that's basically why I'm over here. Looking for prospective subjects. Headhunting.'

'Another "lifestyles of the rich and famous", huh? Well, you've come to the right place. Look around, take your pick.'

'I already did and she said yes. But you've missed the point, this isn't what I'm after. A movie star is a movie star is a movie star and I've got Joan Collins lined up. And Clint Eastwood, fingers crossed.' An incongruously girlish little grin accompanied the physical gesture then suddenly she was all high-power talk again. 'Just a few final details to thrash out when I see him in Carmel tomorrow. But that's the kind of thing I mean, you see — not just a movie star. Not just fame or money. Something more than that. Or *less* than that, depending on your perspective.'

He took her point. She had some nerve. 'And that's where you think I come in, I suppose. Thanks.'

She was totally nonplussed by the reaction. 'For goodness' sake, man, put your prickles away. Why do you take everything I say as a personal putdown? I've never met anybody so much on the defensive!'

'And there's another personal attack.'

'Don't be silly.' She was running out of patience. 'All I was saying is that I'm looking for people who have something more to offer than mere glamour . . .'

'I believe the word you used was "less".'

'But what I meant was . . .' And now who was on the defensive? 'Oh, stop quibbling over semantics,' she said testily.

'Semantics is my business, or had you forgotten?'

The way he was acting she did indeed find it hard to remember that this was the same man who'd written *Losing Time* so sensitively. But she wasn't going to be put off. Slowly and deliberately she ignored the whole interruption and went right back to her original point. 'I'm looking for more – or less,' she emphasised stubbornly, 'than fame and glamour. I want to show . . . well, "real people", if you like. The ordinary human being beneath the trappings. There are plenty enough talk shows around for the cardboard cutouts. And the Barbie dolls,' she added as Jeff's attention had once more been diverted by the balloon-breasted nymphet, now minimally attired in strappy little swimsuit that had more cutaway than cloth. She was poised – or rather, posed – on the end of the springboard about to make a no-doubt graceful dive into the deep end while various of the male guests ogled their desire to make a dive into *her* deep end. Kate resisted the urge to sidle up behind her and give the girl a hefty, *un*graceful shove. After due pause for admiration the dive was executed, a little splashily, and the would-be starlet climbed out of the water, long wet hair sleeked over the glistening, golden brown shoulders.

'Look at that . . . tan. Nice,' murmured Jeff.

Kate tried hard to keep the irritation out of her voice. 'Now, maybe. Another few years and she'll be riddled with wrinkles and skin cancer. Silly girl.'

There was a twinkle in Jeff's eyes as he looked back at Kate. 'Careful,' he said. 'Your claws are showing.'

'Typical,' she said witheringly. 'I state a medical fact

and you reduce it to petty bitchiness. You really are unbelievable, Mr Coolidge. And, I might add, insulting.'

'So how come you want to fit me into these plans of yours?'

She attempted to look down her nose at him, which was difficult as her target was some eight or nine inches taller than her as she said, and now she *was* being bitchy, 'To be honest I'm no longer altogether sure. I had this spur of the moment idea that you might make an interesting person for the *Encounter*. But as you seem to be getting more and more two-dimensional by the minute, I'll have to give it some more thought.'

Jeff reckoned he carried it off rather well. A slight couldn't care less shrug, very casual. Then he handed back his empty champagne glass. 'Well, thanks anyway. For the drink. You let me know when you've sorted your ideas out. You can call my agent.' An apt departure line, he thought.

Silly bugger, thought Kate, and went over to have a chat with Joan Collins who at their meeting that morning had, contrary to popular image, turned out to be utterly charming with a wicked sense of humour that turned Kate into an instant fan for life. *The O'Connell Encounter* with the British girl made good was now well past the agreement in principle stage. Kate only hoped that Clint Eastwood would be half so accommodating. God, what a line up this show was going to have . . .

Jeff flung himself back into the mainstream party. He spotted Veronica dancing with a thick-necked, bullet-headed, broad-shouldered guy who looked as though he'd be more at home in knee pads and helmet than the tailored cream jacket that squeezed itself around his muscles. Athletics major. Football hero. Cheerleaders' wetdream. Carl? He decided it wouldn't be wise to make close enquiries and carried on cruising. He could search out Mary, maybe. Or follow up on the Barbie doll. But the interest he'd shown in that direction had been a put-on, some juvenile attempt to get under the O'Connell woman's skin. And it had worked. So much for making the contacts, playing the game.

He quietly watched the glitterati glittering around him. When he'd arrived he'd felt part of it all, one of them, a star in his own right, albeit a new and smallish one. All the magic of tinsel town. But as the evening wore on the shine began to wear off. He thought about Kate O'Connell and cringed over his petulant behaviour towards her. Couldn't believe his off-hand rejection of a programme that would have given him equal time and billing with the likes of Clint Eastwood. Realised she'd been singling him out as one of the 'real people' in her weird cardboard cutout theory. Couldn't for the life of him work out why.

Decided not to bother.

The Hurleys and their houseguest were back home in Angelo Drive by midnight. Kate was driving up to Carmel in the morning and wanted a reasonable night's sleep. Mel and Angie, who'd been to countless Charlene Prince parties, were quite happy to concur, especially as Angie had an early session with her tennis coach (she had not yet decided if she should have an affair with him) and Mel was a veteran of the Hollywood business breakfast.

In retrospect Kate regarded the Los Angeles visit as an unmitigated success, the best possible start to her tour of duty. Apart from the coup with Collins she'd made a pretty useful contact in Mel Hurley. He'd even hinted that next time Brad Marvin took a vacation it might not be a bad idea to have Kate do the stand-in if her home commitments allowed . . . And the more she played around with it, the more she was attracted to the idea of doing an *Encounter* on Coolidge, even if she didn't much like the man beneath the pretty packaging. She wasn't inclined to do him any favours but the camera would love him and he did fit the 'rising star' category to a 'T'. And she always did like a challenge. His obvious lack of enthusiasm for her programme – and her person – only fired her determination to get him.

She could see it now. Her eyes narrowed a little

maliciously as she ran through it. She wouldn't have to work too hard to make a good programme out of the Coolidge/Warren dichotomy. With a little judicious fiddling she could practically put it together with scissors and tape. Stick together some clips from her own interview with him on *Kate In Company*, the bits where he'd come across as touchy, diffident, *human*. Juxtapose them with a few (carefully edited) sections begged, borrowed or bought from *The Brad Marvin Show*. Shoot location film of the man strutting about his own haunts in New York, add a nice, needling live interview and hey presto, Jekyll and Hyde updated!

She smiled at his pathetic attempt at a put-down. Call his agent, indeed. Well watch out, Coolidge, because before she got back to New York, she intended to do just that. And when they next met she'd get past that touchy exterior of his and charm the pants off him till she had him just where she wanted him — ripe for assassination.

Sunday morning in the Levy household and somewhere beneath the débris a kitchen lies hidden.

Ben, in overnight stubble, snagged terry towel robe and jogging suit trousers, yawned behind the sports pages. Sammy, still in his Spiderman pyjamas, was hypnotised by Garfield while the baby on the floor in the bouncing lie-back cradle gurgled (intelligently, of course) at an elasticated string of pink plastic bunny rabbits. Mo, in quilted housecoat with fresh Milupa stain down the front, was barely able to remember the long and lazy lie-ins of yore when she and Ben-her-lover hadn't realised what luxury it was to read the Sunday papers in bed. She glanced up from the colour supplement to Ben-her-husband and decided the Photocall pages were the prettier option.

There they were, the Beautiful People, caught unawares in not-so-beautiful poses. Except for one. Kate, being different as usual, had looked very beautiful indeed in designer clothes with designer hand luggage when she took off last week to take the States by storm. Mo felt a stab of envy, for even best friends are subject to human frailty. Then she read the caption and the envy disappeared.

The delectable Ms O'Connell minus her constant companion. Maybe he's tied up at Number Ten. Or maybe that's the story he saves for his pregnant wife.

'Oh shit,' muttered Mo, forgetting present company.

'Dad-dee!' Danny hurtled towards him, crashed into his hips, bulletted his head into his father's stomach and squeezed with every ounce of his small, proud strength.

Jeff picked him up and swung him round in the air, laughing. 'Hi there, Chief. Didya miss me?' He put the boy back on the ground again.

'That much,' said Danny, holding his hands about a foot apart.

'*How* much?'

'*That* much!' And the arms were stretched wide, fingers straining outwards.

'That's more like it. And I've missed you, too.'

'How much?'

'*This* much!' and he wrapped his arms all the way round the small boy and hugged and hugged.

Bedtime was a little late that night. Danny had to check that his father ate enough supper. Then he had to make sure that the bags were all unpacked properly and put away out of sight. Then he crept outside and removed the ignition keys from the car and snuck them upstairs and under his own pillow just to be on the safe side. And then he had to show off his burgeoning postcard collection.

'He's been up to his elbows in flour paste all afternoon so's his scrapbook would be ready in time,' said William, Jeff's father.

'Leaving me to clear up the mess,' added Jeff's mother Emily, fondly.

So Jeff dutifully sat at the table next to his son, slowly turning the thick, waving pages and looking again at the pictures he'd selected in this city and that, sometimes with care, sometimes in haste, to send home to his son. It had been a way of sharing the tour with him, a way of showing that he wasn't forgotten even if, at times, he most certainly had been. Danny had turned the postcards into a complete record of the publicity tour, set out with painstaking care in date order. Complete except for the last page – the Hollywood card hadn't arrived yet.

'But we'll walk over to the General Store in the morning and pick up the mail. Maybe it'll be there tomorrow.'

'And maybe Mrs Straker will ask for your autograph. Do you think she will, Dad?'

'Ma Straker has known me since I was knee high to a grasshopper, even smaller than you. Now what would she be wanting with my autograph?' said Jeff fondly. And secretly thinking it would be a real kick if she did.

If admiring the scrapbook was a slow process – which it was as Danny demanded a blow by blow account of where he went, what the hotel was like, who he met, who said what, for each city, with Emily and William taking just as much interest in the answers as their grandson – filling in *The Brad Marvin Show* and the Charlene Prince party took even longer. And then they had to watch the video twice more. Of course Emily Coolidge had taped it. If they hadn't had a video recorder she'd have crawled a hundred miles on hands and knees to get one. Not that she would have admitted it to Jeff. Danny fired excited comments all the way through it like, 'Wow, did you see that, Mary Magdalen actually touched you!'

Jeff smiled enigmatically. Emily's eyes flickered between her son on screen and her son in the flesh with a quiet glow of pride lighting her face, while William made the occasional 'hrrmph' noise, particularly through the Floella Glickman highlights. Jeff, embraced by and embracing the comfortable familiarity of the rambling old house at Gilberts Pond, looked at the images on the screen and cringed with embarrassment as if that were some stranger with an uncanny physical resemblance but it had nothing to do with *him*, with here and now.

'Okay, that's it, the sideshow's over,' he said suddenly, and not just referring to *The Brad Marvin Show*. He switched off the set before Danny could flip it into rewind for another take. 'Come on, Chief. Move. Time you were in bed. Way past time.'

Danny's protests were tired but insistent. So was Jeff. Jeff won.

Ed Franklin liked to be at his desk at TV7 early on Monday mornings so he could quietly gather his thoughts and make the transition between weekend and work a gentle process. He idly leafed through the pile of news-papers which had been delivered to his office over the weekend. Unfortunately, he, like Mo Levy, was a Photo-call fan.

Julian barely had time to take off his coat and send one of the girls for a coffee before he was summoned to the Head of Programming's office. The offending photo-graph and caption was thrust unceremoniously under his nose and Ed growled, 'What the fuck is all this about?'

Julian had no need to feign innocent confusion. He didn't believe in wasting good money on Sunday news-papers because there was never any news in them, so he hadn't seen the item Ed was poking a nicotine-stained forefinger at. He looked at the photo and thought Kate looked very pretty. Then he read the byline, tried not to visibly blanch and declared, 'I haven't the slightest idea.'

Ed ignored him. 'Who is it? Who's she been fucking? Is it true? Or can we sue?'

'It's just harmless gossip, Ed. Nothing to get het-up about. Besides, you can't be serious. Sue? Think of the publicity.' He wished he'd kept his mouth shut.

Ed did calm down. Very quickly. He thought for a moment then said, 'Now *there's* a point. Good idea, Julian.'

'What idea? I never have ideas! I just said, didn't I?'

Ed ignored him again. 'Hmm. We'll give it a little

while, see if anybody picks up on it. Wouldn't do the ratings any harm to have a bit of scandal around transmission date, would it? And if it all dies a quiet death, well . . . we'll just have to see.'

Weeks later, when Julian tried to recall the interview, he could never be sure whether Ed had said; 'We'll just have to see' or 'We'll just have to see to it.' But for the moment he went back to his office and filed it away as yet another little thing he had to worry about. The little things, he could cope with. It was the big things that were getting to him. And the biggest thing right now was not having heard from Kate apart from one postcard from New York.

He stood in his office doorway and shouted for Linda.

Linda, who regarded Kate, not Julian, as her boss, stayed in her own office space and shouted back, 'It's all right, come in, I'm not too busy.'

The fine point of one-upmanship escaped him completely. He went to Linda with a passing glare at Kate's big, empty desk. 'What the hell's she up to, the silly cow,' he said. 'Have you got a copy of her itinerary? Why hasn't she called us? Where's she supposed to be today? Have we got a contact number? How are we supposed to get any real work done around here if she doesn't let us know what she's fixing up at her end? We'll just have to go ahead and if we clash with what she's fixed up, tough. On her. She might be the Editor but I'm still the Producer around here and I'm bloody well going to produce!'

'G'morning, Julian,' said Linda. 'Had a nice weekend?' and she calmly turned to look at a sheet of A4 tacked on the wall beside her. 'She's in Dallas by now. Staying at the Hyatt Regency. Soaps and the Spellings, I believe.'

'Ring her.'

Linda shook her head. 'It's God o'clock in the morning over there. *You* do it.'

'Is it? Oh. Well, maybe later. Catch her about breakfast time. You work it out, I never was much good at sums, specially on Monday mornings.' He pulled up a chair and sat down heavily. He immediately got up again to close the office door. Resuming his seat he said in confidential tones, 'Linda, what do you know about Kate's, er, social life?'

'Ah. You saw it too?'

He shook his head. 'Not till just now. When Ed Franklin showed it to me.'

'Oh.' It was a long drawn out sound, full of bad omen. Then there was a brief but brightening pause. 'Still, what's a little gossip? Who cares in this day and age?'

'Tell that to John Profumo.'

'Who?'

'Okay, try Cecil Parkinson.'

'Oh come on, this is hardly the same league. Just ignore it. I'm sure it'll go away.'

'So tell that to Ed Franklin.'

'I would, with pleasure, except we're not speaking. The petition was ignored. The vending machines won. And because I'm a lady I won't say where I'd like to shove them.'

Neither Linda nor Julian phoned Kate in the end because she beat them to it. High as a kite, she was. 'Linda, how's things, is Julian there? Get him to come and listen in on my extension, will you, lovey?'

Julian didn't wait for a formal invitation. He'd leapt to his feet every time Linda's phone had rung.

'You're not going to believe this, but believe it anyway,' said Kate. 'First, you can write up our Joanie in green. All fixed.' She gave the dates. 'So can you get the bookings out, fix the crew, editing, the lot?'

Linda scribbled down the details while Julian nodded eagerly, earlier testiness at his star forgotten. So was the fact that you can't hear a nod on a telephone line.

Kate took silence to mean consent and gleefully pulled her rabbit out of the hat. 'And as for our "living legend" category, how about if I said . . .' for a woman she didn't do a bad impersonation of Dirty Harry '. . . I'm going to make your day!' She paused to let it sink in.

Linda was quickest off the mark. She squealed. Then

she pulled her professionalism together and said, 'You don't mean . . . Kate, you didn't really get . . .'

Yes, she did, She'd driven in a hire car from Los Angeles through Santa Barbara and then along the coast road, every bump and hairpin bend of which had increased the collywobbles. It wasn't the road that did it, nor the breathsnatching vistas of ocean, forest and hills that accosted her from every new bend. It was the thought of the forthcoming meeting. Clint Eastwood. In person. Why should Kate O'Connell be immune? No reason, no reason at all.

She arrived at Los Ondas on San Antonio Street a good half hour early. Took in the high fence surrounding his house, the side windows clouded by salt blown in from the Pacific. Being early was almost as bad form as being late so she drove on, cruised around the immaculately tree-lined little town with its antique shops and Spanish-style adobe houses and ever so discreet olde worlde atmosphere. It was much more than a world(e) away from Beverly Hills. And Clint Eastwood, when he greeted her, was a world away from the cheroot-chewing name-less cowboy or the steel-glinting streetwise cop or any other role you care to conjure. Greying hair, lined and craggy face, loose skin around the neck. Clothed in unre-markable but good quality navy blue blazer and charcoal grey slacks. He looked older than she'd expected, which is to say he almost looked his age. Her first impression was that if you passed him in the street you probably wouldn't give him a second glance.

Then he held out his hand and smiled a greeting. It flashed through her mind that she'd read somewhere that he liked his women short and blonde. For once in her life Kate O'Connell was glad she was only five foot three.

'The upshot was,' she went on, 'it's a yes, so long as we can come to an agreement on the dates because he's planning another movie and much as he keeps denying ambitions to run for Governor of California . . . anyway, that's details, mere details. Because we will agree on the dates,' she said with confidence. 'If we have to rearrange transmission schedules or do him as a one-off special, we'll agree on the dates! So,' you could hear the grin in her voice as she went on, 'am I brilliant, or am I brilliant?'

'And so modest,' said Linda, also grinning. 'Anything else?'

'I'll never tell.'

'She means about work, petal,' said Julian.

'Oh, that. Yes, plenty. I can't believe this place. The Spellings are looking hopeful. Forget the Ewings and the Carringtons and the whatever all those other soap characters are, I'm working on the creator himself. The way these people live! Makes the Ewings look like scrubby little dirt farmers. Anyway, I'm lunching with Aaron today, then sitting in on a script conference this afternoon and, hell, you don't want to hear my engagements book, I've hardly a minute to call my own. So wish me luck then it's next stop Miami.'

'What's in Miami? Apart from a beach,' said Julian getting another word in, even if it was edgeways.

'Criteria Studios. And at the moment, Barbra Streisand recording her little heart out. Guess who's been invited to sit in on a session? Anyway, that's about it from my end. How've you been doing?'

They hadn't been doing too badly. The current Formula One Motor Racing World Champion (Nigel Mansell had done it at last) said he'd be delighted. Pity they'd already missed out on the British or the Monaco Grand Prix but the Austrian was hopeful, and Nigel's Isle of Man home would make a good enough location.

'Splendid, splendid,' said Kate.

And Kate wasn't the only one who could perform tricks with rabbits. 'Now you'd better start practising your ma'ams and your curtsies, my petal,' went on Julian with justifiable pride, 'because so long as we angle it on her charity work, the Princess Royal has indicated possible consent.'

Linda and Julian grinned smugly at each other when the very expensive reverse charge transatlantic phone connection was finally broken. They went through to the main office and ostentatiously took it in turns to update the wallboard. Then they and the small audience of researchers stood back to admire the handiwork.

Stavros, Collins, Eastwood, Mansell, Coe, Spelling, Streisand and the Princess Royal. More than half of them confirmed or as good as, the rest of them provisional and only four more slots to fill.

'Go for Thatcher,' Kate had said just before she hung up. 'And by the way, Linda, how's that book doing — you remember, C.J. Warren, our quiet American? Is it selling back home?'

'Must be. People are reading it on the tube. And W. H. Smith have got window displays. Why?'

'Great. I'll get to work on our rising star, then. In fact I've already started.'

Chapter Nine

Jeff had taken over the guest bedroom as his study/workroom for the duration, although since he'd been back at Gilberts Pond he hadn't achieved much of either. The typewriter was on the table which stood under the window which had a magnificent view across the water to the far side of the lake. On a sunny, blue-skied day like today it was damn near impossible to concentrate his brain on working when that organ seemed hell bent on directing his eyes out over the satiny water instead of on to the sheets of paper in front of him. So he sat, chin on hands instead of hands on keys, watching his father and his son, their fishing rods making a V-shaped antenna from the wooden rowboat.

The place ought to be a perfect hideaway for an author. Ought to be as easy to sail through the writing of a novel as the little boat found it to sail across the calm waters of Gilberts Pond. But Jeff Coolidge, much as he complained about it when he was there, was a city man – accustomed to city noises and a desk which had an unrestricted view of a blank wall. He was also used to permanence and to his own space. The spare room was fine enough except for the knowledge that all it would take was one phone call from his sister, Helen, and he and his typewriter, notes, reference books and rough draft copy would be thrown out on their ass. And it was a certainty that at some point before the summer was through Helen and her family would decide to pay a visit. As was only right and proper. They had as much right to the place and the parents as he and Danny did.

Jeff could see it all. The house would become a writer's hellhole, with a total population of five adults, three children and one dog. And only four bedrooms. There would be nowhere for him to work, short of clearing out the old woodshed and moving himself in there complete with stereo and headphones to block out the adult chatter, the juvenile play-shrieks and the canine doing its damndest to out-noisy them all. The woodshed idea struck him as pretty good, whether Helen came to stay or not. He might mention it to his parents later. Danny could help him clear the place out, fix it up a little – he might enjoy that and it would give them a chance to do something special together, get back some of that special closeness that they had in New York and which seemed to have faded a little since Jeff's protracted absence on tour.

He worried over the change in Danny. It was as if the child didn't see Jeff as the same man any more. Not just 'my dad' but 'my dad the famous writer, the TV star'. Pride and resentment were all mixed up together in the child's head. There were the clingy moods. There were the off-hand moods. There were the interested in or bored by his work moods. And sometimes there were the down-right cussed moods when whatever Jeff said or suggested, Danny took umbrage. Kids. One day you think you know them through and through, the next you find yourself trying to relate to somebody you've never met before. Jeff, conscious that over the last couple of months he'd hardly been the ideal parent, made excuses for his less than ideal offspring. He reminded himself that it was all part of growing up. Just another developmental stage. Something. Nothing.

Tomorrow or the next day, as soon as he got to the end of this chapter, he'd take a day off and take Danny off somewhere, just the two of them.

But gazing out over the lake thinking about Danny, Helen and the woodshed were hardly the best route to get Jeff to the end of the chapter. He pulled himself back to the task in hand and re-read the day's output so far. Only three pages in to Chapter Nine and more x's than clean lines. He fed another sheet into his typewriter and had just about got the flow of inspiration to the rate of a brackish trickle when the ringing of the telephone caulked it up again. His father and Danny were out on the lake. Emily was over in Gilberts Hollow. So who had to provide the answering service? With a curse he clomped downstairs.

'Hi there, stranger. Just checking you out. How's things going?' Laura's rasping New York voice sounded incongruous in the lakeside house.

'Okay. Slowly. I'm finding it kind of hard to get into all this peace and quiet but it's coming along.'

She laughed. 'Not two weeks away from the limelight and he's missing it already. And to think I once had you marked down for a closet hermit! What you need, honey, is a quick, bracing shot of sweltering city stink and humidity. Correction. What you're going to get.'

'What? Expand.'

'Two things. First, *Lifetime* want to do a spread on you, photos, in-depth piece, the lot. It's great timing. *The Brad Marvin Show* is yesterday's news, the tour's cold . . .'

'Already? After I slogged my guts out?'

'The way of the world, Jeff. This'll be the perfect shot in the arm. So that's settled, you'll do it?'

'Sure. Great. What's the second thing?'

'Kate O'Connell.'

The name hit Jeff like a slug from a sniper. 'What does *she* want?' he asked suspiciously.

'You, honey, what else?' Laura explained about the phone call she'd had from the lady herself from Washington. She was going to be in New York for a couple of days and as she and Jeff had already talked about this new programme she was setting up she wondered if he'd given it any more thought and could Laura fix up a meeting?

'If *I'd* given it any more thought?'

'That's what she said.' Laura congratulated him. 'You certainly came up with the goods, didn't you? I said you could do it. Anyway, when you have your meeting, just make sure you consolidate your hold . . .' Jeff didn't have the heart to disillusion her. 'This *Encounter* programme

142

would just about clinch you in Britain, so meet with her, be nice to her, give her a good time. Just get yourself on that show. She's already got Eastwood and Streisand and Joan Collins . . .'

Jeff could recall practically every word of their previous conversation and the memory made him curl up. 'Yes. I know. She just happened to drop a few names into the conversation herself. I guess she thought I'd be good contrast material.'

'Oh God,' groaned the agent. 'You and your fragile ego.' Her voice was impatient. 'What's with you, Jeff honey, a permanent slow puncture? Don't answer that. I'll set it up and call you back. Just be there and don't screw up. Screw *her* if you have to, but get yourself on *The O'Connell Encounter*, okay?'

He sighed. 'Okay. Give me the time and the place and I'll do my best. But Laura?'

'What?'

'No casting couch. I'd rather make out with an ice-bucket.'

Laura chuckled. 'That can be quite nice,' she said enigmatically, and hung up.

He went outside for a breath of normality. William and Danny were on their way back to the landing stage, Danny waving at him, looking like today was going to be an 'I love my daddy' day. Jeff braced himself to give the news that he was about to desert him again, even if it was only going to be for a couple of days or so. Then he thought: why the hell should I?

He ambled down to the end of the landing stage and without waiting for the boat to come alongside he shouted out, 'Hey, Chief! Wanna come back to New York with me for a couple of days?'

'No way,' said Jeff. He was standing awkwardly, trying to look as if it was the sort of thing he did every day – leaning against a tree in Central Park reading his own novel and holding it at an awkwardly ostentatious angle to give the lens an unobstructed view of the cover. His

143

shoulders ached. His face ached. The smile had gone through the 'fixed' stage and straight on to the one where the cheek muscles go into involuntary spasm. And Danny was sitting over there on a bench, watching. Frowning. Little shakes of the head now and then. Doing more directing than the photographer. But at least he didn't look bored.

'Okay, relax,' said the photographer, trying with little success to hide his rising despair. He couldn't understand what was wrong with the man. He'd seen him on TV talk shows and he'd been okay then. He straightened, gazed round in a frantic search for inspiration then fiddled with the screws on the tripod and unfastened the Hassleblad. He came over to Jeff saying, 'Right, I got an idea. Come on. Just relax. Enjoy.' He put his arm round Jeff's shoulders and hugged him briefly. It was like hugging the tree. 'Hey, man, loosen up. I'm a photographer, not a dentist. This is only a camera.'

Jeff tried on a little humour. 'Yeah, sure. But to level with you, I think I'd prefer the dentist's drill.'

The photographer didn't get the joke. 'Don't worry about it,' he said, though *he* was beginning to. 'Let's go for an action shot. How about this, you're happy. No . . . ecstatic. This is your first book, not only did you get it published but you ended up with a bestseller on your hands. You've fulfilled a lifelong ambition. So you feel like jumping for joy, right?'

'Right,' said Jeff flatly.

'So *do* it. Hang loose, man. Start over there by your kid then run towards me, fling your arms out and leap in the air. Simple.'

'You've got to be kidding. No way.'

'No?'

Jeff shook his head firmly. 'How about if I just sit on the grass and look self-conscious?'

'Compromise. Go for soulful.'

Jeff managed a half-smile. The camera took its opportunity and clicked.

'That's my boy,' said the photographer. Then, glancing

across to Danny he said, 'Hey, how about a couple of shots with you and your boy? Just to finish off the roll?'

Danny leapt to his feet and said, 'Great!' at the same moment that Jeff shook his head and gave a not-to-be-argued-with, 'No. Are you crazy? He stays out of it.'

'Aw, Dad.'

'Come on, man, why not?'

'Because I'm not having my son's picture splashed across the pages of a national magazine. What do you want – an open invitation to kidnappers, child molesters or any other lunatic out there who might want to make an easy buck? No way.'

It was a fair argument. But it took the shine from Danny's eyes, took a little of the shine off their day.

Later, when the photographer had packed up his equipment and gone back to his darkroom and Jeff and Danny were watching an impromptu game of baseball being played out with a grey and balding tennis ball and a piece of Parks Property tree, Jeff draped his arm over Danny's shoulders and said, 'Enjoying yourself, Chief?'

'Yes. Great. You?'

'Yes. Great.' The white lie sounded distinctly dingy, even to its perpetrator. Jeff's problem was twofold. First, being C. J. Warren in front of the TV cameras and an unseen audience of millions is a pushover compared with doing it in front of a live audience of one, that 'one' being your own child, the one person in the world you want to shine for, the one person in the world who can see through your every false smile. And second, having Danny tag along for a photo session was just about acceptable in terms of professional etiquette but taking him to a business dinner in the evening . . . ? Yet the only alternative was to cancel because he hadn't been able to get a sitter. Even the next door neighbours were away. He had a pretty good idea how Kate O'Connell was going to react when he turned up complete with entourage in miniature. Maybe he *should* cancel. It wasn't exactly going to be the thrill meeting of the century.

As soon as they got back to the apartment he tried to

145

extricate himself. At least, he called Laura and asked if there was any chance the meeting could be postponed. Until next year? Next century?

'Jeff,' she said with a firmness she usually reserved for publishers' accountants, 'Get off the phone. Go take a shower. Get yourself over to that hotel. Go.'

So he braced himself and called the hotel and the O'Connell woman wasn't there. 'Okay, take a message, will you? And please make sure she gets it as soon as she returns.' The message was brief and to the point and it made no apologies. Danny was a fact of life and she was just going to have to accept that. But he finished with a flash of the humour that Kate had not yet seen, 'Oh, and will you put, "By the way, don't worry, he's house-trained"? Thanks.'

Turning to Danny he warned, not altogether joking, 'And you'd better be!'

Kate got back to the hotel feeling hot, dishevelled and breathless. She'd spent the afternoon on the Circle Line boat trip and the vessel had chosen today, of all days in the last fifteen years, to break down, coughing and spluttering, somewhere in the vicinity of Triboro Bridge – right round the other side of Manhattan Island. Profuse apologies, of course. And they'd resuscitated it eventually. But it was now a little after seven o'clock and by her standards, ingrained through years of watching the second-hands on clock faces rather than the leisurely minute hands, that was late. Very. Horribly. Impossibly, if she was going to make herself look anything like decent before Coolidge arrived.

She hurried to the desk to claim her room key and the clerk handed her a note along with it. She read it on her way to the elevators, narrowly missing a bellboy who did a neat sidestep to avoid her. Its contents did not please. So, not just Coolidge now, but Coolidge and Son. No doubt some precocious little brat as jumped up as his father. Terrific.

She shoved the note into her shoulder bag and waited,

tapping her toes impatiently as she stood at the bank of elevators watching people sauntering (all of them leisurely and immaculately) across the plushy carpeted lobby. She knew she looked distinctly out of place. The women she saw were all smartly elegant – the type who would have immaculate toenail varnish – and none of them looked as though they knew how to sweat. Kate herself felt sticky and freezing cold and very much aware of the fact that her nipples were noticeably erect. Damn and blast the air conditioning.

When she reached her room the first thing she did was place a call to Jeff's home number. No reply. Another damn and blast. She hated high speed changes. She turned on the shower, peeled off her clothes, pinned up her hair and stepped under the spray, avoiding getting her face wet. A three-minute rinse off, one-minute rub down, press damp flannel over make-up, cotton bud round the mascara, touch up eyes, cheekbones and lips, brush through hair leaving it a little shaggy-looking but extremely flattering, a quick spray from the new bottle of *Giorgio* she'd picked up in Beverly Hills, then into the casual elegance of a wool crêpe dress in clean, clear lemon. At twenty-eight minutes past seven she was in the elevator looking, if not exactly feeling, as if she could hold her own with anyone from the pages – or the offices – of *Vogue*.

And woe betide the Coolidges if, after all this, they dared to turn up even one minute late. Because although her intention was to charm, it was by now balanced on a knife-edge and we wouldn't want to get anybody's bloodstains on the restaurant carpet, now, would we?

In the event the cleaning service had an easy night. Jeff had decided that the best way to handle the meeting was to try and forget all previous impressions, both his of her and those he assumed she had of him, and make a fresh start. Laura had said it: do whatever you have to do but get yourself on that show. He intended to, within the bounds of personal morality.

The maitre d' showed him and Danny to a suitably

prominent table with a gratifying, 'Mr Warren, isn't it? May I say I enjoyed reading your book. Miss O'Connell will be down shortly, sir.' Jeff wasn't sure whether he scored, or lost, points by being seated first but he reckoned five minutes early was a safer bet than five minutes late.

Danny was too excited to have any concern for timing. He was going to have dinner with a TV star. Not one like his Dad, but a *real* one, even if she wasn't an American one. With every entrance to the room he nudged and whispered eagerly, 'Is that her?' The objects of his anticipation ranged from jail-bait to a blue-haired matron who had to be seventy if she was a day.

'No. And don't point. Stop staring. Don't slouch, sit up straight. Stop fidgeting . . .' Jeff heard himself. Shrugged and touched Danny's hand. 'Sorry, Chief. You're doing okay. I'm just a bit edgy I guess.'

'Don't worry, Dad. I'll be as good as gold. I won't let you down.'

Jeff smiled. He leaned forward confidentially, and stage-whispered, 'To be honest, Chief, it wasn't you I was worried about.'

At seven-thirty precisely she stood by their table. Jeff leaped to his feet and offered his hand as the maitre d' beat him to it in holding out a chair for her. A look from Jeff then Danny, too, was on his feet. 'This is my son, Danny. Danny, this is Miss O'Connell.'

'Pleased to meet you, ma'am,' said Danny in a small voice, suddenly an overawed little boy.

Kate smiled at him as she sat down. A good-looking child. Nice manners. So far. She despatched the still hovering maitre d' with a statement that they'd like to order drinks now, then as the man dutifully hurried away to summon the appropriate waiter Kate turned to Jeff and remarked pleasantly, 'Your agent tells me you're living somewhere out in the country for the summer – I do hope you didn't drag yourself back to the city just on my account?'

As if she thought he would. 'I didn't,' he said, then

remembered he was supposed to be nice to her and added, 'there were a couple of other business things to attend to so it all worked in quite conveniently.'

'Well, I'm glad you could make it, Jeff. Or do you prefer C. J. these days?'

There was a slight self-deprecating shrug. 'Jeff, I think. I couldn't quite get comfortable with that C. J. guy.'

There was a sparkle in her eye as she said, 'What a lot we have in common.' It was a sort of test. To see if his prickles came out.

They didn't. He just looked at her with an answering spark and said, 'Well, it's a beginning.'

But it was a slow one. The business of menus and ordering kept the social intercourse going for a few more minutes but soon the prandial exchanges seemed to trickle away into a little pool of silence which was rippled only by the 'plop' of a stray word from neighbouring conversations. Kate switched her attention to the boy who looked spruce and scrubbed and was presenting a perfect example of the 'children should be seen and not heard' dictum. She had very little experience of dealing directly with children so she didn't bother trying, she simply talked to Danny the same way she'd talk to any adult. And accorded an equal amount of interest in and respect for his utterances – which shortly began to exceed the 'yes, ma'am' and 'no, ma'am' limits.

'Are you really a big TV star back in England? I mean, do people come up to you in places like this and ask for your autograph? Ma'am?'

She smiled. 'Yes, sometimes. Why? Don't I live up to your expectations?'

'Oh, I didn't mean, I mean yes, I mean . . .'

'Come to think of it,' she said, narrowing her eyes and giving him the sort of once-over she might have reserved for a chat-up, 'You don't look much like a schoolboy to me.'

'I don't?'

She shook her head and said seriously, 'Far too debonair.'

Puzzled look.

'It's okay, Danny, that's a compliment,' Jeff put in.

A slight preening and a pleased grin. 'Thank you, ma'am.'

'The name is Kate,' she said, touching his chin with a light fist.

'Kate,' the boy repeated. 'I'll try, ma'am.'

She laughed and wanted to hug him.

Danny was in heaven. The early tentative sideways glances at Kate when he thought she wasn't looking had turned to open gazes even when she was. Danny Coolidge was having dinner, just like a grown up, with a real, live TV star. And she was so-o-o-o pretty. And she was talking to him like he was a grown up too. And she thought he was debonair. He was going to look it up in the dictionary just as soon as they got home, and just wait till the Straker boys heard all about this! It made Mary Magdalen touching his Dad on *The Brad Marvin Show* pale into insignificance.

You could say that Danny was star-struck. Except it wouldn't fully express what he was feeling. Kate shone like a sun queen, sitting there right next to him in her yellow dress. He wished somebody would take a photo of them, so's he could prove it was really happening. Better still, he wished he could wrap her up and take her back to Gilberts Pond with them. See what the Straker boys would say about that!

While Danny fell in love and occasionally remembered to eat a fork-sized package of ravioli, Jeff made inroads on a lasagne and Kate twiddled at her spaghetti and got down to the business end of the meeting.

'With your *Encounter*,' she said, choosing her words carefully, which is to say she lied through her teeth, 'we'll be aiming for subtlety, a delicacy of touch that just isn't possible within the confines of an ordinary talk show . . .'

'I noticed.'

She smiled. 'Yes. *Kate In Company* was a bit of a baptism by fire, wasn't it? Sorry about that. But it made good television. And I dare say it pushed up your sales figures by a measurable degree. Anyway, that's history and you're an old hand at the game now. Pity, in a way. It would have been nice to do the *Encounter* before you became so adept at handling the media. Your Brad Marvin was excellent, even if the show itself is a little shallow. Now that's where the *Encounter* comes into its own. You see, the angle isn't *what* you've accomplished, but how and why and the effect it's all had on you as a person, an ordinary man, a father . . . it'll be an in-depth study, if you like, a potted biography, a lot to do with Jeff Coolidge and not much to do with C. J. Warren.'

She expected him to back off there, slam the shutters down, so she went on quickly, 'and that's why we'd handle your *Encounter* particularly delicately. It would be easy for the intrusive nature of television to destroy that essential ordinariness, if you'll excuse the expression, that we particularly want to get across. If we were to show you as just another bestselling author it would defeat the object.'

'Which is? Tell me again?'

'Look. You're the personification of Joe Public's dream come true. How many people say, "I could write a book" or "If only I'd thought of that I could have made a fortune?" You know the syndrome. My point being that you didn't just think about it, you *did* it. You took the dream and you made it happen. But you're still – well, almost, because you haven't made a habit of it yet, – you're still more akin to Joe Public than Harold Robbins. At least, that's how I want to show you. Which is where the delicate touch comes in.' She took another forkful of her now cool spaghetti and said in closing, 'Well, what do you think?'

It was all accomplished disconcertingly quickly, considering the way he'd reacted to the *Encounter* suggestion on the night of the Hollywood All-Stars. She'd been determined he'd capitulate eventually, even if it took the rest of her stay in America to persuade him, but she hadn't expected him to be so wantonly easy. You couldn't really say he capitulated because he didn't even take a token stance to capitulate from. He said 'okay'. Just like that. And they hadn't even started on the main course yet.

'Wonderful,' she said. 'That's settled then.' The waiter took away the empty spaghetti dish and Kate wondered what they were going to do for the rest of the evening – just *eat*? Perhaps throw in some drinking and being merry for good measure?

As if reading her mind Jeff picked up the bottle of claret and refilled her glass, then his own, then poured a drop for Danny which he watered down to the palest pink, continental style. 'A toast,' he said.

Kate raised her glass. 'To a successful programme?'

He shook his head. 'Uh-uh. To pussycats.'

'What . . . ?'

'Pussycats.' He drank the toast then offered merely, 'Ask your assistant,' by way of illumination.

It was close enough to what she had in mind. She drank, mentally toasting, 'Cat and mouse.' Then in the best Tom and Jerry tradition she dedicated the rest of the evening to pawing out his weak spots. Sorry, furthering her objective research. She found it increasingly difficult, however, to support the strutting upstart/jumped-up little pillock theme she'd set her sights on. Three times they'd met and three different people she'd met. And this latest one was rather fanciable. Maybe she should be doing a game show, in which the host proclaims, 'Will the real Jeff Coolidge please step forward?'

She continued a gentle probing under the guise of easy conversation. 'Tell me more about, what's it called, Gilberts Pond? I envy you having somewhere like that to escape to. Must be fantastic for you, Danny, being able to live there every summer.'

Danny agreed with enthusiasm. 'Will you be filming there too?' He could see it now. Tom and Robbie Straker sick with jealousy while he, Danny, was filmed for TV. 'I'll let you film my treehouse if you like.' Jeff nearly choked in surprise. The treehouse was strictly off-limits for grown ups. Invitation only. Except no one over thirteen years old had ever *had* an invite. Until now. 'I mean, you couldn't make a film about my Dad without me there too, could you?' continued Danny with all the certainty of one who still lived in a world where Santa Claus rides through the sky with sacks of toys for all good boys and girls.

'I'd like . . .'

'No.'

Kate looked at Jeff with almost as much shock as Danny did.

'Not Gilberts Pond. And definitely not Danny. Sorry, not for public consumption. Not even with a delicate touch.'

'Aw, Dad!'

Kate nearly joined in with, 'Aw, Jeff!' She looked from one to the other – adamant father, nakedly disappointed child struggling between stoicism, defiance and the humiliation of threatening tears. She felt for him. 'Sorry,' she said diplomatically. 'I just assumed . . . but it's your decision of course, Jeff. Anyway, we don't have to bother with the finer details right now. Plenty of time to discuss locations later.'

'No discussion,' said Jeff. 'Danny stays out of it.'

'But Dad.'

'Enough. Two choices. You stay out of the film or we both stay out of the film. There are plenty of other authors around and Miss O'Connell wouldn't have any trouble finding a replacement. I'm still not sure why she fixed on me anyway. So that's it, subject closed. Now, what do you want for dessert?'

Danny subsided into a quiet defiance behind the menu while the grown ups opted for cheese, coffee and manufactured as opposed to spontaneous conversation. Jeff's contribution was, 'I'm still curious. Without going over old battlegrounds, there are other writers who've hit the jackpot first time around. So what made you decide on this one?'

'Honest answer?'

He grimaced but said yes.

153

'You're photogenic. You won't crack the camera. You're nice to look at.'

He wasn't too sure but he asked anyway, 'Are you being sexist?'

'Blatantly,' she said in a very matter-of-fact manner. 'Fifty-two per cent of the population – and you can therefore assume, of the audience – are women. I have to be scrupulously fair in dealing out the sex objects.'

He looked at her not sure if she was putting him on or deadly serious. And not sure which he would have preferred. 'Thanks,' he said. Then added, 'I think.'

Danny, who'd been soaking up their every word like blotting paper and understanding far more than the adults gave him credit for, as is the way with kids, looked from Kate to his father and then back to Kate again, declaring with a tinge of vindictiveness, 'He's far too old to be a sex object.'

Jeff laughed.

Kate refrained. 'Hmm.' She looked as though she were giving the matter solemn consideration. 'You might have a point there, Danny. Just how old is he?'

'He's way over *thirty*.'

'That *is* pretty old,' she replied. 'But,' (sigh) 'I have a job to do. Beggars can't be choosers.'

Jeff pushed away his plate and with good grace said, 'Well, if you two whippersnappers will excuse me for a moment, I have to take my creaking old bones to the men's room. I won't be long.'

'Take your time,' said Kate smiling. 'I have a thing about younger men anyway,' and she took hold of Danny's hand and squeezed it, which went some way towards making up for his earlier disappointment.

The only other hitch in the evening's proceedings came in the form of a wrangle over who was going to pick up the bill. Jeff wanted to pay, especially as he'd brought Danny along uninvited. Kate was even more insistent. In the game she was playing, she/he who picks up the bill pulls the strings. She signed for them all on her hotel bill

154

then walked her guests to the lobby. 'My people will be in touch with you then, to talk about dates,' she said.

Danny tugged at her arm. 'Kate, would you do me a favour?'

'If I can, Danny. What sort of favour?'

He looked sideways at his father. 'It's kind of confidential.'

'Would you excuse us for a moment, Jeff?' They stepped to one side and carried on a brief but muted conversation while Jeff watched — Kate looking serious, nodding her head. Danny holding out his hand, Kate shaking it. They returned.

'What was all that about?'

'Confidential,' said the woman and the boy in concert.

The next morning a boxed single yellow rose arrived along with her breakfast. The accompanying card read: *'Thank you for a lovely evening. Love from Danny. P.S. In repayment of your hospitality, can my dad take you out tonight?'*

She rang the apartment. 'Did you send the rose or was it that gorgeous child of yours?'

'I cannot tell a lie.' He sighed. 'It was me. Disappointed?'

'Of course.'

'Now *I'm* disappointed. But how about it anyway? I just happen to have a couple of tickets for Radio City and seeing as Danny's got himself a date with his sitter . . .'

'What?' A shock-horror voice. 'He's being unfaithful to me already?'

''Fraid so. These younger guys are so fickle. I know I'm only second best but will I do instead?'

'Well, I suppose it would be a shame to waste those tickets.' Or the opportunity to talk him round on Danny and Gilberts Pond.

Or to waste all the hard work Jeff had put into fixing it when they'd got home last night. I love you, Mrs Raskovitch, he thought and wondered why he hadn't thought of her yesterday.

As for tonight's little plan, nothing devious, just that

he didn't like feeling beholden. And as she'd mentioned she was staying in New York for a couple more days there was no harm in consolidation. He was a bit worried that without his home life thrown in she just *might* come up with a substitute and if she dropped him, at best Laura would kill him. Besides, he felt like a night on the town. And a night on the town with a beautiful woman on his arm was even better. Even if she *was* Kate O'Connell.

He picked her up at seven and they took a cab along Sixth Avenue to the corner of the Rockerfeller Center. The Rockettes were in top form, all legs and sequins and precision high kicks and Jeff pointed out the architectural highlights. Of the building. An art déco palace of chandeliers, mirrors and glitz that nearly got demolished in the progressive seventies. 'But it was saved by a public outcry. Along with the Wurlitzer,' he pointed out. 'The world's biggest.'

'You don't say,' she teased.

'And before we go, you must visit the Ladies' Room.'

'How do you know I must?'

'No, I mean you must see it. It's magnificent. So I'm told.'

So she did and it was. Circular mirrors and smooth rounded corners and a garden of a mural which grew out of the carpet edges and blended into a cloudy ceiling sky. 'It's a bit over the top for me,' she said when she met him again in the foyer. 'No matter how well you've painted your face, the decorator did a better job on the walls.' It was the perfect opening for a compliment and Jeff didn't take it. He just looked at her and smiled and his eyes said it all. She liked what she didn't hear.

After the show he took her for drinks in the Rainbow Room sixty-five floors up in the RCA Building then maintaining a tit-for-tat attitude she took him back to the Skylight Lounge at her hotel for a nightcap. They found a table by the vast expanse of window wall which looked out over the nightlit city. Jeff pointed out one or three more landmarks for her and she said that when he came to London she'd return the favour if the visit wasn't as brief as his last one. 'The aerial view isn't as good but on the ground I think we win hands down. More breathing space. And our policemen don't wear guns.'

He looked at her hard for a moment. 'How come you're always trying to score points?'

It surprised her. 'Am I? I didn't know there was a competition going on.' Then she smiled at him. 'Out of interest, did I win?'

'Out of interest, would it matter?' he countered, not allowing that sparkling smile to get to him.

She sipped her brandy and shrugged. Jeff read it as a 'yes'.

'Tell me more about your country hidey-hole,' she said, 'seeing as I'm not going to be allowed to see it for myself.'

Jeff complied, waxed lyrical even, now he felt its sanctuary was safe from public exposure. Funny how, once he was away from it, the place seemed idyllic. A bit like when you have kids.

'Sounds really beautiful,' she said in a moment of genuine wistfulness.

'It is.' Maybe it was the brandy or maybe he was just trying to make up to Danny a little for banning TV crews from the lake but he said, 'Actually, I was, Danny was wondering if you'd like to see it anyway? He's desperate to show you off to his friends.'

She smiled at that. 'But you're the star over here, not me.'

'Yeah. But I'm just his old dad. So what do you think? Now your duty tour's over you could come stay for a few days' vacation if your plans aren't too fixed.' It was said in full confidence that her plans would be nailed, screwed and glued but at least he could go home to Danny with a clear conscience that he'd made the gesture.

'I'd love to,' she said.

There was a moment's panic which he covered by smiling, but he was nothing if not adaptable. He quickly added up all the pros of the situation and they cancelled out the cons easily. 'Great,' he said at the same moment that the smile reached his eyes, 'I'll call my folks then.'

'Isn't it a bit late?'

But he was already making for the telephone.

'Jeff? What's the matter, what's happened, why are you calling at this time of night?'

'You weren't in bed, were you?'

'No, but . . .'

Jeff, who kept an eye on Kate across the room not quite believing what he was letting himself in for, explained. Would they mind an extra person for a few days? Business. He'd move his gear out of the spare room. They hadn't heard from Helen, had they?

Helen was not expected. No, they wouldn't mind. In fact, they'd be delighted. The English television lady. Interesting. 'Is she nice? Is she married?' asked his mother.

'I don't know,' he answered to both questions.

So it was settled. Jeff and Danny would pick her up in the morning and Kate was to get a taste of the real American way of life, home cooking, simple hospitality, a respite from hotels and restaurants and tourist traps. She somehow doubted that Gilberts Hollow would have a Neiman Marcus, but at least AmEx would be pleased. (Or maybe not.) By the time she had packed her bags and settled her bill the next morning she still hadn't worked out whether it was herself, Jeff or even Danny who'd done all the manipulating. Not that it mattered.

And by the time Jeff had closed up the apartment the next morning and got Danny and their things loaded into the car all ready to go and collect the lady, all he wondered was – who in hell had spiked his brandy?

Chapter Ten

They drove up the Hudson Valley on the Interstate 87 with Danny, at Kate's insistence and who was he to quarrel with anything she said, in the front seat and Kate herself settled comfortably in the back of Jeff's beat up BMW. She'd decided, now that she'd secured her infiltration into the enemy camp, that there was no reason she shouldn't relax and enjoy herself while she was at it. With the *Encounter* practically sewn up the best thing she could do now, for herself and the programme, was enjoy the break so when she got back she could attack the assembly of the final product fully refreshed and energised.

'If you look at the map,' said Danny, determined to be a perfect host, 'you see this bumpy bit between the Catskills and the Adirondacks, look, straight up to Albany then head left for about fifty miles . . .' His finger jolted about on the map as he tried to show her their destination. ''Cept we turn off way before Albany, about here . . .' He twisted his body round still further so he was half stuck between his and the driver's seat.

'Danny. Sit down. Sit still. I'm sure Kate's quite capable of reading a map.' Jeff was a little hungover and a little wary and the words came out with a sharp edge which he regretted.

Danny shot him an aggrieved glance. A bouncing puppy slapped down.

'It's amazing,' said Kate as if she'd noticed nothing, 'do you realise we're going to pass by Leeds? I was born near there, you know. A town called Halifax. Have you heard of it?'

'Halifax, Nova Scotia?' asked Danny, surprised.

'No, you dumbo! Halifax, Yorkshire, England. The original one.' She ruffled his hair affectionately then turned back to the map. 'Oh, and look, we'll be going through Durham! And there's Stockport. And Selkirk.' Her enthusiasm was infectious. 'And Cambridge and Kingston and . . . Troy, Amsterdam, Rome. Don't you people have anything original?'

'Sure we do, don't we, Danny?' said Jeff by way of a peace offering. 'There's, uh . . . come on, Chief, think of something quick, there's national pride at stake here.' An arch glance at his passenger in the rear view mirror, 'Not to mention a few points to score!'

'I got it, I got it. Betcha don't have a Peekamoose Mountain!'

'Peekamoose. No, you've got me there,' she conceded. 'But we've got a Snake Pass. Don't think it has any snakes, though.'

'That's silly,' said the boy. 'Why's it called Snake Pass, then?'

'Because it wiggles like a snake, wiseguy.' And she wriggled her fingers into the nape of his neck making his shoulders hunch up with giggles.

They arrived at the little township of Gilberts Hollow early afternoon and Kate felt like she was driving into another film set. This one was a ramshackle and abandoned film set. There was a general store, all shutters and clapboard; a garage and petrol station with just two pumps, one with a faded *Out of Order* placard hanging round its neck on a loop of knotted twine. They passed maybe a dozen or so other buildings then came to a little wooden church sitting pretty in perpetual Sunday best of smart white paint with green doors and trimmings. That's where the main street and the hardtop ended, forking into a couple of dirt tracks which ran along either side of the neatly kept cemetery. They took the left turn which wound through a forest of tall trees allowing an occasional tantalising glimpse of shiny water from the lake's edge. A few hundred yards more and the track became a small clearing into which was snuggled a house, again covered in clapboard, with a veranda running along the front and a rocking chair and a little table and a broom leaning up against the doorframe. It was an *Anne of Green Gables* sort of house except the paintwork was the wrong colour.

'I don't believe this,' said Kate. 'Don't tell me – your mother's known locally as Old Ma Coolidge and she's got grey hair in a bun and she sits out here with your father, smoking a pipe!'

Jeff laughed. 'She doesn't smoke the pipe. But my father does.' He brought the car to a halt, pulled on the handbrake and gave a quick blast on the horn.

Danny flung open the door and tumbled out, running up to the veranda shouting, 'Grandma! Grandpa, we're here! Come on, come and meet Kate!'

And out came a smiling woman with grey hair. And that was where any resemblance to Kate's imagined image gave out. Mrs Coolidge was the epitome of genteel elegance, comfortable graciousness. The clothes – slacks and a toning cotton blouse – were casual but expensive-looking, the smile was warm and welcoming. She embraced Danny, put her arm round Jeff's waist and hugged him as he kissed her, and all the while her bright eyes were on Kate, taking her in, summing her up. She must have liked what she saw because she quickly disentangled herself from her menfolk, took Kate's hand and led her into the house saying, 'Welcome to Gilberts Pond, my dear. I'm so pleased to meet you, you must be tired after the journey. Come and I'll show you where you can freshen up while those two unload the trunk.'

'Thank you,' said Kate. 'And thank you so much for inviting me, Mrs Coolidge, it's very . . .'

'You must call me Emily, my dear, and I shall call you Kate.' She led her guest upstairs and showed her to a pretty, light-filled bedroom, all plain pine furniture and crisp cotton prints.

'Oh, how lovely,' Kate said, meaning it. A spontaneous appreciation.

'I'm glad you like it, my dear. I hope you'll be comfortable.' Emily indicated the paper-strewn table underneath the window with an apology. 'Jeff's work. I didn't dare touch it. He'll soon clear it out of the way for you.'

Kate protested she didn't want to cause any disruption but Emily brushed the protest aside with a brisk, 'Nonsense. Now, the bathroom's just along there, come on down as soon as you're ready, we eat in the kitchen and I've baked a ham and there's fresh bread and salads ready when you are.'

'Thanks. We didn't stop off for lunch and we're all ravenous.'

Emily smiled. 'I thought you might be. *Knew* Danny would be. He always is. Now I'd best see if I can find that wayward husband of mine. He went off fishing straight after breakfast but . . . oh,' she said, pointing out of the window, 'there he is now.' Emily Coolidge opened the casement, waved vigorously then cupped her hands round her mouth and shouted, 'They're here, Will!'

It wasn't a very loud shout but her voice must have carried well over the water because a tiny figure in a tiny rowing boat out on the middle of the glimmering lake waved back and began to make its way slowly towards the ramshackle landing stage.

'Now, where are my boys with your things?' She bustled over to the door. Jeff appeared on cue carrying Kate's suitcases and overnight bag. 'About time,' she said. 'I'll leave you to it then. Don't be long, you two. Danny?' she called as she left, 'where are you? Come on down to the landing with me and help Grandpa.' Her voice receded.

Jeff put the bags on the floor. Kate was standing by the window, her hand resting lightly on his worktable, eyes glancing at the loose pages spread all over it. Here in this room, this familiar, personal environment, to Jeff she suddenly seemed predatory, the cool O'Connell woman again, ready to search out all his intimacies for future exposure. He wished he'd never asked her here, wished she hadn't accepted. Wondered why on earth she had. Suspected he knew the answer. He said, 'I'll get all

162

that stuff out of your way.' He moved, as if he were going to do it right now, that minute. Which he was.

'No, please, it isn't necessary. I'll make myself scarce when you want to work, I wouldn't dream of . . .'

'It's no trouble.' A little brusque and not to be denied. He was already shuffling papers into neat piles.

Their hands brushed fleetingly and his jerked away as if stung. Kate moved to sit on the bed and watch him. Even though his back was turned to her his body language said: tension. As if he were about to grab and run.

'Jeff.'

He stilled, but didn't turn.

'Honestly, I wish you wouldn't do this on my account,' she insisted quietly. 'Leave it. I don't need the table.' The more she was fussed over, the more uncomfortable she felt.

He turned. He was hugging the manuscript to his chest. She smiled. 'I'm not going to steal it, you know.'

'I never thought . . .'

She stood and took a step towards him. You don't interview people on camera for as long as Kate had been doing without picking up some hints in lay psychology. 'And,' she said tentatively, 'just in case you thought I accepted your invitation so's I could snoop around, dig up your murky past for the *Encounter* or something . . . forget it. I told you. This is a holiday. I'm off duty now. Okay? Scout's honour?' She made an approximation of a scout salute.

You could see him beginning to relax. There was a brief light of appreciation in his eyes as he said, 'I find it hard to imagine you as a girl scout.' Understatement of the year.

She never had been. Not even a Brownie. An enigmatic smile sufficed for her reply. So much for scout's honour.

'I'll see you downstairs then,' he said. A casual exit. But he was still clutching his precious pieces of paper . . .

William Coolidge was a large, robust man in his late sixties with thick grey hair and a well-trimmed wiry beard. The eyes which sparkled behind the rimless spectacles were a pale grey-blue, alert, missing nothing. Young eyes in an old but still handsome face. He fixed them on Kate. 'So, you're the young woman with designs on our son, eh, going to turn him into an international celebrity?'

'Did he say that?' Kate tossed a speculative glance towards Jeff.

'Dad!' said Jeff.

'Well, you are, aren't you?' piped up Danny.

'Danny!' said Jeff.

'Come and eat,' said Emily calmly.

And how they ate. Kate sailed through a second helping of pink and succulent ham, had no difficulty removing her allotted portion of rice and coleslaw, and flinched only slightly at the sight of a golden crusted apple pie.

'How come you're so skinny when you eat so much?' asked Danny.

'Danny. Manners.' That was Emily.

Kate finished her last mouthful then pushed the dish away with a small sigh of satisfaction before saying, 'Actually, Danny, I'm not skinny at all. The real me is a fat little piglet constantly struggling to get out.'

Danny giggled.

'And if your grandmother keeps on serving meals like this,' she went on, 'the piglet will win hands down.' She turned to Emily with a smile. 'That was delicious. Thank you. Let me help clear the dishes.'

'I wouldn't dream of it. You just relax and enjoy yourself.'

'Jeff, why don't you and Kate go for a walk, show her round the place?' suggested William.

'Great!' said Danny. 'We could go up along the lakeside, I'll show you where the creek comes in. There's minnows and the best place for swimming. Can you swim, Kate? I'll teach you if you can't.' The boy was already pulling at her arm, secure in his possession of her.

Jeff was about to take the easy way out and let Danny play host when Emily cut in, 'Not you, Danny. I have a couple of chores for you.'

'Tomorrow morning, Danny, first thing,' said Kate. 'You can show me the minnows then. Just you and me, okay? Is it a date?'

'Just you and me?' face brightening.

Kate nodded.

'It's a date!' said Danny.

Emily's motherly hospitality, William's bluff friendliness, Danny's all too transparent delight in her presence, had done much to augment Kate's declared predisposition to be 'off duty'. Jeff, the actual host, was still guarded, a little quiet. So was Kate – quietly schizoid. 'Katy' was coming to the fore, much as 'Kate O'Connell' kept trying to butt in. Katy thought Jeff was rather nice. Kate struggled valiantly to find traces of the upstart C. J. Warren.

Katy was winning.

It was a perfect afternoon. Hot but not too hot. A faint breeze, lukewarm and refreshing. The clean, empty smell of fresh water. Quiet lapping of little waves against the stony shoreline. Trees whispering, green leaves dappling their shade upon the man and the woman who walked beneath them.

They talked of the place itself and how Jeff came to be connected with it. How the house at Gilberts Pond had been their summer home for as long as he could remember, the annual escape from New York where he was brought up in a mixture of faded gentility and corporate management. 'My mother provided the "old blood" from Providence, Rhode Island; my father provided the "new money" from moulding plastics in Brooklyn. Not a fortune. Middle management. But enough for this. So when he retired they sold up and moved here permanently. Caught my first fish here, cut myself when I gutted it. Learned to swim. Had a tangle with some poison ivy once. Climbed trees. Fell out and cut my leg. Want to see the battle scars?'

She declined the offer, wishing she had a tape recorder hidden about her person. 'So you had a normal, happy childhood. How refreshingly boring! I'll let you into a secret. So did I. We never had enough money for a spare house, though. People don't do that kind of thing in Halifax, not the part that we lived in, anyway. But we had a big garden. Not all ours — we lived on a Victorian terrace and all the gardens were joined together, no fences, and this communal driveway along the front, so there was this huge space to play in, me and the other kids. We liked it down the Bottom best . . .'

'The where?'

'Down the Bottom, that's what we called it.' She warmed to the theme, unused to the luxury of talking about herself. Enjoying it. 'Apparently when the developers built the terrace — 1861, it was — they were going to build another one facing it and they got as far as excavating the foundations then ran out of money. So that became the bottom garden, like a small valley with trees all up the edges.' Her eyes and voice softened with the distance of memory. 'A magic garden. And in the winter — it always snowed of course — we had a fantastic sledging track through the trees. And we were cowboys and indians, pirates and princesses . . .'

'Which were you?'

She smiled. 'The pirate. Or the sheriff. I was a bit of a bully.'

He let it pass. 'Do you ever go back?'

Her face clouded. 'I did, once. About five years ago. We moved from there when I was fifteen, you see. But I went back, just to have a look. I wish I hadn't.'

'Progress?' he asked sympathetically.

She pulled a face. 'Hardly. Dereliction, more like. It was so sad. A rundown slum. The big gates that kept us safe, just rotted wood hanging off the hinges and nobody'd repaired them or cared. And right there in the middle of the gardens, in front of the terrace right on the drive, somebody'd built a bungalow. Just sitting there, with a chickenwire fence round it, a horrid little pebble-dash box slap bang in the middle of where I learned to ride my first two-wheeler!'

Jeff shook his head. 'Some people have a nerve.'

'And at the far end – we were forbidden to crawl through the fence, though we did, of course – there used to be a bowling green. The groundsman was an ogre.' She smiled. 'Poor old chap. He was probably very sweet to his grandchildren. Anyway, that's a block of council flats now. Our houses have probably gone too by now. Pulled them down, I expect. I don't know. And I don't think I'll go back to find out. They were such splendid houses. Mosaic tiles on the floor, and carved oak panels and big brass door handles and bells from when they used to have servants. Our bells still worked. And attics, and cellars . . .' Her voice trailed off and she came back to the present, halted beside a gnarled and knobbly tree. She patted its bark in affectionate remembrance and turned to Jeff. He was standing close, and she had this uncomfortable feeling that he was looking into her rather than at her. 'So,' she said quickly, 'you're not the only one round here who can climb trees, Jeff Coolidge.'

'Oh yeah?'

'Yeah,' she parried.

'Prove it,' he challenged.

'Certainly not.' She leaned back against the tree trunk and gazed around, still a little entangled by her childhood. TV7, *The O'Connell Encounter*, the media woman and her quarry – they all seemed to have gone away. Buried in an abeyance file to be dealt with some other time. Not now. 'Now' was just a wooded shore, a shiny lake, warm skin, warm feelings . . . 'This is so lovely,' she said, not particularly to Jeff.

'So are you.' It slipped out without thought, naked and honest.

There was a brief moment, a moment when she looked up at him in silence, when only their eyes spoke, when she wanted to, could have, reached out, brushed back the hair that fell over his forehead . . .

She brushed away the moment. Abruptly she pushed

herself away from the tree and walked down to the water's edge.

Jeff stayed where he was, watching her as she picked up little pebbles and skimmed them across the surface. She was very skilful. A beautiful picture. 'You're very good,' he called out.

She turned to him, smiling, putting her arm up to shield the sun from her eyes. 'Thank you.'

'Tell me, Miss O'Connell,' he said as he came to her side, 'are you this good at everything you do?'

She considered. 'That depends. If I put my heart into it. I try my best.'

'Formidable. And apart from your career and climbing trees and skimming stones, what other things do you put your heart into, Kate?'

She looked as though she were giving the question serious thought until the frown turned into a grin and she said, 'Eating! And it must be teatime!'

He looked at his watch. 'You're right,' he said. 'Come on, we'd best be getting back, they'll be wondering what's happened to us.'

And so am I, she thought. So am I.

It was just a stray thought, not caught in the passing.

They returned to more food and easy chairs, lazy conversation in front of an unlit log fire, Danny and his grandfather playing checkers (William making no allowances for youth and winning every game) and Emily asking Kate about her home, her work, her background. Jeff watched and listened while she answered what she chose. The evening darkened and Danny, allowed first-night privileges of staying up late, fell asleep sitting on the floor propped up against Jeff's legs with his head on his arms and his arms on his daddy's knees. Jeff lightly stroked the boy's hair, Emily tiptoed out to make coffee, William quietly folded the checkerboard and put the counters into a battered tin box.

Kate sat curled up in a corner of the couch, her bare toes snuggled underneath a patchwork cushion, and watched the family scene, almost feeling a part of it. It was a good feeling. Wishing she *were* a part of it, or of something like it, something of her *own* like it. That wasn't quite such a good feeling. And then she took to wondering about the other woman who used to sit here, belonging to it. William and Emily's daughter-in-law. Danny's mother. Jeff's wife. That was an uncomfortable feeling.

Jeff eased himself out from under Danny's weight and with practised skill he picked the boy up and positioned him comfortably in his arms so that his head was resting on Jeff's shoulder. The boy woke just enough to say mumbled goodnights to everyone. William kissed him and he squirmed sleepily. 'Beard tickles,' he said. Emily put down the coffee tray and smoothed the hair back out of his eyes with a gentle touch. 'Goodnight darling,' she said to him. 'Sweet dreams.' Danny smiled and closed his heavy eyelids. 'G'night, Grandma.'

'Goodnight, Danny,' said Kate, wanting to get up and kiss him too but feeling it was not her place. She blew him a kiss instead. 'Don't forget about tomorrow.'

'Minnows,' he murmured, eyes still closed. He nestled deeper into his father's arms as Jeff carried him up the stairs.

William crossed to the hearth and took pipe and tobacco pouch from the mantelpiece. He sat down in the big easy chair by the fireplace and began the business of lighting up: filling, tamping, lighting, sucking, tamping again. 'One of life's exquisite pleasures,' he said to no one in particular. 'A pipe before bedtime.' Emily poured the coffee into giant-sized mugs, sugared one and took it to him. She set it down on a little table by his side and he smiled up at her, took her hand as she perched on the arm of his chair. 'And a beautiful woman to tell me I smoke too much,' he added.

'Did I say a word, one word?'

He drew on the pipe again and said, 'It's all in the eyes, Kate. Married as long as we've been, you don't need to talk much any more. She just nags me with her eyes.'

Emily cuffed him lightly on the shoulder. It was almost a caress. 'Don't you listen to him, my dear,' she said. 'His mind wanders. Old fool.'

He patted the liver-spotted hand which had stayed in place resting on his shoulder. 'Must be an old fool – to have put up with you for all these years.'

They smiled at each other, years of shared memories showing in the look. Kate suddenly felt terribly out of place alone on her couch in a house full of friendly strangers.

Jeff came back down. 'Out like a light,' he said. He picked up a couple of coffees and joined Kate on the couch. She drew in her legs a little.

William gave a hefty yawn and tapped his pipe into the hearth. 'Well, guess I'll be turning in, too.' There was a brief pause. 'Eh, Em?'

'Oh. Yes.' She drained her cup. 'Well, goodnight you two. Don't be too late, now.'

And then it was just Kate and Jeff in an empty room whose walls reverberated with the echoes of other nights like this, only not like this – there'd been a slightly younger William and Emily, a smaller version of Danny upstairs in his bed, and Jeff down here, on this same couch maybe, with someone else, not Kate. Or so it seemed to her. She shivered slightly, told herself she was being stupid and, besides, it was nothing to do with her. These were their memories, not hers. She had no right to them.

'Cold?' he asked.

'No.'

He studied her for a moment. 'What's the matter?'

'Nothing. I was just thinking,' she said vaguely.

'Well stop it. You're on vacation. You're not supposed to think.'

'Tell me about Jennifer.' There, it was out. With all the tact of a steamroller. 'You must have had so many happy times here.' Her tongue ran on regardless, no stopping it now. 'But you still come back. Year after year. Doesn't it hurt?'

170

He didn't flinch. She'd almost expected him to. 'Not any more,' he said.

She probed on. A career-long habit difficult to break. She wanted to *know*. And not just for the programme's sake. She wanted to lay the ghost. 'What was she like? What happened? Why are there no photographs?' It had been bothering her, the fact that there were no framed photographs around the room.

'I hid them all away,' he said, straightfaced. 'Didn't want to risk my personal bric à brac having an *O'Connell Encounter*.'

And she would have believed it, too, except that then he grinned.

'We're just not a photos in frames sort of family,' he said. 'There are plenty of photographs. Want to see them? I warn you, it could take all night,' and he went to the crammed bookshelf at the side of the fireplace and dragged down three heavy albums. 'How far back do you want to go? Mom and Dad's wedding? Me in diapers down by the lake? My graduation day? My wedding day? Danny in diapers down by the lake?'

The voice was lighthearted enough but she got the message. 'Look, forget it,' she said. 'I don't want to pry.'

He put the books down. 'Hey. Look at me.'

She was.

He knelt before her and took both her hands in his. The touch sent an involuntary shiver through her. 'That was a cheap dig just then and I'm sorry. But this *Encounter* business, it kind of gets in the way sometimes you know?'

She nodded. 'I know.'

He didn't get up and he didn't let go of her hands. 'Can we get something straight?' He hadn't been rehearsing this, hadn't even acknowledged that it was coming. But it was here. And Jeff, being an innately honest man, had to find the words for it. Lay it on the line and *say* the words. 'I do want you to know me, Kate. I want *you* to know me. Everything there is. And I want to know you. I want you to . . . I want you . . .' He

171

shrugged, let go her hands, looked straight into her eyes not smiling. 'I just want you.'

Kate didn't answer straight away. She had to concentrate on breathing. When she did speak her voice was soft, almost a whisper. 'And I want you, Jeff.'

The admission hung in the air between them, waiting to be taken up.

Or not.

She reached a fingertip to touch his hair. Soft. Her hand dropped to her lap again and she looked away, anywhere except into the eyes which were watching her, trying to read her signals. She shifted position to break the impasse. Unfolded her legs, sat up straight. Reclaimed herself. 'But it wouldn't be very professional of us, would it?' she said.

He stood. Made a business of it, turned it into a parody of an old man with creaking bones. A little humour saves many a face. 'You're right, it would hardly be sensible,' he said. Then he smiled. 'Damn it to hell.'

She smiled too. 'So come on, Coolidge. Don't just stand there, get the albums.' Then she added, 'And you can skip the ancient history. Start with the baby snaps, the ones where you're lying naked on a rug.'

And there they all were. Frozen moments in black and white, later in colour. Jeff as a boy, Jeff as a teenager, Jeff with Jennifer. So that was Jennifer. A perfect Beach Boys' California Girl. Sun-streaked hair, cut-off jeans, Seventies child personified. There was even a picture where she had flowers in her hair. Then there was Jennifer pregnant and serene, Jennifer smiling at the new baby, Jeff and Jennifer with Danny. Then just Jeff and Danny.

All those memories, little pieces of stiff paper stuck down into a book.

He closed it.

She touched his hand. 'I'm sorry,' she said quietly. 'You don't look at these very often, do you? It's hurt you.'

'No.' He smiled at her. 'I mean, no, I don't look at

them very often, and no, it doesn't hurt any more. Why should it? I had it *all* for a while. Some people never even get close.'

Don't I know it, thought Kate.

He talked in muted undertones; she listened. In a way it was much more intimate than lovemaking would have been. She felt honoured that he should lay it all before her. It all came out, how he and Jennifer had met, fallen in love, married, had a baby. Straight out of a storybook except for the part that should have said, 'and they lived happily ever after'.

'She was twenty-eight years old,' he said.

Kate shuddered inside. Thought of herself a year younger, thought of herself being told, 'It's cancer of the liver. You have weeks, maybe months.' Dear God.

'We were thinking of trying to have another child,' he said flatly. 'So she went for a check up. And nine weeks later she was . . . dead.' He sounded still puzzled by it.

'Don't, Jeff. Please, you don't have to tell me any more.'

He was suddenly vehement, almost shouting at her. 'I want to. Listen, damn you, I want you to listen!' Then he took a steadying breath. 'I'm sorry. But, please, I *want* to talk about it, about her. That's the hardest part, especially at first – people, friends, family even, not *letting* you talk about it, changing the subject, avoiding the issue, avoiding *you*. Me. Danny. The ones who are left. It's such a . . .' he struggled to find the word. 'Such a damned *insult*! Don't you see? It negates a whole *life*. God, it used to make me so angry.' He smiled then, a little sheepishly. 'I guess it still does. Sorry, Kate, it's not you, it's just that dying is such a taboo subject. But we all do it. Jenny just did it before she was supposed to. She broke the rules. That makes people very uncomfortable.'

It was the first year that had been the hardest, he went on. Those twelve months dotted with merciless and unavoidable reminders. Thanksgiving, Christmas, New Year, Jenny's birthday, his birthday, Danny's birthday, their anniversary, the endless list of recurring events when it was impossible to do anything but think, 'This time last year . . .' Then there were the one-off occasions to face: a cousin's wedding, the first solo invitation to a place where you used to be a couple. And after that the business of starting over, trying to remember how to ask a girl for a date, getting to know someone, going through all the business of what books/films/music/food/politics you have in common. And eventually, touching, kissing, making love, to someone who was not Jennifer. And trying not to feel guilty about it, reminding himself that he was not being unfaithful. He allowed himself a little smile as he said, 'I got over that hurdle eventually.'

And Kate thought: this is the other side of loving someone, the dark side of the moon. It scared the hell out of her.

But he hadn't finished. In a way the difficulties in the sheer logistics of running his life had helped. Danny was the biggest problem – what does a working man do when he has a two year old to look after as well? But the child was also his lifeline, a solace, a joy. And a source of strength. Or at least, a reason to be strong, to get on with it.

'What *did* you do about caring for Danny?' she asked.

'Exactly what millions of working *women* do about pre-school childcare. I advertised for help.' At the time he'd have been hard pushed to afford it, he explained, but short of going back to live with Emily and William there seemed little alternative. He knew his folks would have welcomed them both with open arms but he couldn't do that. It would have been a cop-out, a role change. 'Like saying, I don't want to be a father, I want to go back to being your son.' So he made his plans and composed the ad and hurt inside at the thought of leaving Danny with a stranger all day and tore himself apart with imagining his baby being neglected or abused while he was out at work. He did all that and forgot to reckon with his mother.

Kate smiled. 'Don't tell me. I can imagine.'

'She sure put her foot down!' How could he even

think of allowing *her grandchild* to be looked after by a stranger, she'd demanded? Someone who might forget that he didn't like eggs or that strawberries brought him out in a rash, someone who might *not wash their hands* after emptying his potty? How dare he think of advertising without asking her first? And so it was settled. Jeff withdrew the ad and they stayed where they were, and until Danny was old enough to start school Mrs Coolidge would arrive after breakfast and enjoy herself thoroughly with her grandson all day until his daddy came home from work and prised her out of the door. Danny flourished, Emily grew ten years younger and life for Jeff gradually began to take on, if not exactly a sparkle, then at least a muted patina. He had his son, he had his home, he had the occasional girlfriend, he had his work and he had his book. 'And now,' he said, 'all I need is another one. Oh, Kate, they've got to like the new one.'

'Is it any good?'

He considered for a moment. 'To be quite honest, I haven't a clue. I think it is, I hope it is – what there is of it. But I'm too close to it to judge. It could be a heap of garbage for all I know.'

She dismissed the statement with a laugh. 'Just believe in yourself, Coolidge. You'll get there.'

'Wherever "there" happens to be. And what about you, Kate? Where are you going, where do you want to be?'

She hid a yawn behind her hand. 'Right now, as of this minute, I'm sorry to admit it but I think I want to be tucked up in my bed.'

He had to say it. 'Alone?'

Definitely. Business/pleasure taboos to one side, Jeff might have succeeded in accepting the girl in the photos as part of the past but Kate had had to assimilate the re-run in one concentrated sitting. She needed a little space. 'I'm very tired,' she said, uncurling herself from the couch and stretching. 'And I have an early date in the morning, remember?'

175

'Ah yes. My rival taking you down to the creek. Heavy competititon.'

'No contest,' she said.

'Yeah, but for who?'

Instead of answering she gave herself up to the pleasures of an uninhibited yawn which, its energy spent, finally extinguished itself in a little shudder and a sleepy smile. 'Goodnight, Jeff. See you in the morning.' And she went up to bed where she did not lay awake for hours reviewing the day's highlights. She fell asleep almost as soon as her head touched the pillow.

Jeff was the one who lay awake. He was beyond tiredness now, well into his third wind, and he stretched himself out naked on top of the sheets allowing a warm breeze drifting through the open window to soothe his skin. Every little bit of him felt alive, tingling, and he thought of Kate lying in a different bed, so close to his own, just a wall away. Would she come to him in the night?

No way.

Should he go to her?

Same answer.

Eventually, he slept.

Chapter Eleven

'The question is, gentlemen, can we afford to go ahead with it?'

The weekly sub-committee meeting was taking place in the HP's office. Only three members of the Board of Management were present: Ed Franklin, who led the meeting; Hallam Mariot, the Advertising and Revenue Controller, a tall, dishevelled man who went about constantly wrapped in a fog of his own making, and who was known amongst the humbler members of TV7's staff as 'the Great Pipe in the Sky'; and Iain Donaldson, Finance and Administration Controller known, much to his consternation but a job title is a job title and the initials were the cross he had to bear, as 'Controller of Fuck All'. It was Donaldson who had posed the question.

Three pairs of eyes scanned again their copies of Julian's glowing, not to mention crowing, Producer's Progress Report. Two pairs fixed on the figures halfway down the second page – Julian's ineffectual attempt to hide 'the bottom line'. His estimated final budget was frighteningly high, even for television.

Ed Franklin was looking at the first page. And the names and locations thereon. Tamsin Coe, Barbados. She'd been his ivory towered princess, his image of female perfection. Many was the night, years ago, when he'd retired to the bathroom with a stolen copy of *Vogue* while his wife was asleep in face cream and rollers. Then there was the Princess Royal, the real princess, the thinking man's favourite member of 'the family firm'. Stavros, Eastwood, Mansell, Collins . . . Impressed wasn't the word. Somehow Kate – and here he gave himself a pat on the back for allowing her full editorial control – had managed to find someone for everyone's fantasy, admiration or just plain, malicious curiosity. But the locations! Greece to Barbados to Austria to the States, to England, to the States again . . . He shook his head. He put the report on the table and sat back in his chair, about to make his pronouncement.

'No.' The voice was firm. 'The question *is*, can we afford not to? Hallam? What's your view on this?'

The discussion continued.

The children were pink and shining and ready for bed. Bathtime was over and they were downstairs again with clean teeth (in Becky's case, clean gums), clean pyjamas and clean fingernails. It was one of Mo's favourite times of day and it was a Tuesday so there was *Eastenders* on the telly which for some reason both children, even the baby, adored. It kept them quiet while she and Ben went through their nightly ritual of having a sherry to the accompaniment of did you have a good day at the office, dear, and how's your day been with the children?

'Interesting.' Ben's answer, not Mo's. 'Had a phone call today from Elizabeth Pritchard. Remember – pretty little thing, pregnant, Alex Pritchard's wife, the party?'

'Oh, her. What did she want?'

'Can't say, really. I mean I could, but I can't, if you know what I mean. Just a chat.'

'You and your professional confidences,' said Mo with a disgruntled click of the tongue. 'What did you mention it for, then?'

'Well . . . now this is a purely hypothetical question, of course . . .'

'Of course,' said Mo, mollified. 'Go on. Hypothetical what?'

'What would you do if you were pregnant and you found out I'd been having an affair, a serious one it seems – hypothetically?'

She came close to him and whispered right into his ear, 'I'd cut off your balls and put them in a pickle jar on the mantelpiece.'

'No, come on, seriously.'

'Who's joking?' she said very seriously. 'Anyway, what

are you saying? What's Elizabeth Pritchard ringing you for? You're company law, not marital. She's not after a divorce, is she? Hypothetical question, of course.'

'No. Asking about injunctions, actually. Litigation. Sueing. She was pretty upset, clutching at straws, pathetic really. Rang me because she knew me. I calmed her down, explained she hadn't a hope in hell – seems she read something in some gossip rag at the hairdressers. It didn't actually name names but it gave enough heavy-handed hints to identify the Minister in question. To his wife, at least.' He took a sip of his sherry and went on, musing. 'I must say I feel sorry for her. Poor woman. What sort of bitch is it that tries to take a husband away from a pregnant mother?'

'Now hold on a minute, what about Ka . . .' Maureen Levy, bite your tongue off. She'd been about to say, 'What about Kate's side of it?' She threw out a desperate 'Cake! What about a piece of cake, anybody?'

Ben looked at his wife curiously. 'You all right, love?'

'Yes, please!' said Sammy.

Mo, committed, went to the cupboard, took out the cake tin, cut a small wedge for Sammy and a smaller one for herself; forced herself to take a bite as though it were perfectly natural to be eating chocolate fudge cake with dry sherry before dinner. She smiled brightly at her son. 'Special treat. All the more delicious because it feels naughty.' She swallowed with difficulty. It was a wonderful performance. Kate would have been proud of her. And so she should, she thought. God, the things we do for our female friends. But a promise is a promise, a confidence is a confidence. Even from Ben. She could keep one, if he couldn't.

'Mo, are you sure you're all right? *You're* not, er . . .' He glanced towards her belly, then to Rebecca, then back to her belly again. Silently he mouthed the word, 'pregnant'.

'God forbid!' she said, sitting again, reaching for her Tio Pepe and finishing it in one gulp. Equilibrium restored she went on as if nothing untoward had occurred. 'Anyway, I should have thought it was the husband who was the villain of the piece, if anybody. Strikes me your honourable friend isn't quite so honourable as he makes out to be.'

Ben shook his head. 'Stupid bugg . . . chap. If he had to do it he should have been more discreet about it.' Casually he picked up the bottle and offered Mo a refill. She shook her head. He refreshed his own glass and smirked a little. 'Hypothetically, I wonder what the bit on the side's like, where he picked her up?'

That's right, she thought. You keep *on* wondering. 'Don't ask me,' she said disdainfully. 'Have a game of squash with him and ask him in the locker room.'

'Bit on the side of what?' said Sammy.

'Eat your cake,' ordered Mo.

Jeff woke up vaguely disappointed to realise that he'd slept the night through undisturbed. He stretched. Gradually registered that the sun was shining into his room at too high an angle. Looked at his watch. Gone eleven already!

He sprang off the bed, dressed quickly in only swim-trunks and jeans, and went through to the bathroom. He cleaned his teeth, studied his face in the mirror and ran a hand over his jaw. What the hell, an overnight stubble was supposed to be quite trendy so he merely raked his fingers through his hair and dashed off downstairs hoping that he looked unkempt and sexy rather than merely bedraggled.

The house was deserted but there was coffee on the stove. He poured a cup and went outside with it into the warm shade of the porch where sounds of laughter and splashing water came to him from down by the landing stage. He drank the coffee, took the empty cup back inside, took the stairs three at a time, took a towel from his room, took off the jeans and took himself back outside again. Once he was round the side of the house he switched to a nonchalant pace and ambled down to the lakeside where Danny was watching him from the water like a sleek and shiny seal pup and Kate was sitting on the bleached wooden boards watching Danny.

Her hair was hanging loose and damp and glinting in the sunshine, she was wearing a backless one-piece swimsuit in a brilliant emerald which fitted her like a second skin and when Danny waved and called out, 'Hi, Dad,' she turned and waved too. He slipped the towel from off his shoulder and held it casually, wishing he'd kept his jeans on.

'Good morning, slugabed,' she said.

'Come on in,' said Danny.

He dropped the towel and dived off the end of the staging before he had time to reconsider. He came up spluttering from the shock of the icy water. But that was one embarrassment cured, anyway. He took a few strong strokes out into the lake, turned, swam back. He sensed Kate watching him and he felt stupidly self-conscious, wanting to get out of the water because it was freezing his balls off, wanting to stay in it because it was a shield.

She stood up, a graceful movement, then picked up a towel and said, 'Danny, it's time you got dry, you've been in there long enough, you'll turn blue.' She held out her hand so the boy could clamber up on to the landing. She wrapped the little body in the towel, rubbed him down, tickling him, hugging him as he wriggled.

Watching them together made Jeff's eyes smart.

He swam towards them and hauled himself on to the planks resting on his arms so he was half in, half out of the water. 'Where's Mom and Dad?' he asked as a neutral substitute for all the things he really wanted to say.

'They took a walk into Gilberts Hollow to pick up the mail,' she said instead of reaching out and running her hands over his hard-muscled shoulders. Sunshine and warm skin always made her feel randy. And Alex was a long time ago. And Jeff was here.

'I'm hungry,' said Danny, still too young to think of hiding his baser instincts.

'Run on up to the house and get dressed then,' said

181

Jeff as he pulled himself properly out of the water, 'and we'll be along in a little while.'

Kate put on the terry-towelling robe Emily had provided her with earlier, then sat hugging her legs and resting her chin on her knees. Jeff rubbed himself down briskly. Kate watched.

She wished he had a paunch. Or plump, soft thighs. Or a bald and spotty chest. Or a fat bum. Anything to turn her off. He didn't. Squinting at him in the glaring sun she had to admit, quite objectively if hardly dispassionately, that he had a beautiful body. The kind of body a Greek god would have had if *she'd* had a hand in designing it.

'Penny for them,' he said, watching her watching him.

He was dry now, towelled hair spiky, looking clean and rough at the same time. God, she thought, now there's food for fantasy. She reached up to his hand and pulled herself to her feet. 'Buyer beware,' she said.

'Ah, but you owe me.'

'Do I?'

'You do.' He turned her to face him, resting his hand lightly on that vulnerable curve where neck and shoulder join, could feel the steady throbbing of her pulse beneath his thumb. Contrasts of rough and smooth, the towelling collar, the silky skin. He spoke quietly. 'I told you last night, I want to know you, Kate. Who you are, where you've come from, where you're going to. But you ran out on me.'

'I never run away,' she said. 'I just have good timing.' His hand was still and its slightly damp coolness burned into her hot skin. Soon, she thought, just a second or two more, then I'll move away.

'We're back!' Someone else with 'timing'. It was William and he was making his way towards them. 'Em says lunch in half an hour.'

That afternoon they went out, Jeff, Danny and Kate. Took a drive out to Cobleskill to have a look at the Howe Caverns. Jeff couldn't work today. Half the day was gone already and what kind of host sleeps through most of the morning then leaves his guest to her own devices the rest of the day? Not this one. Besides, it was good to see Danny so lit up.

'Don't forget your coats,' said Emily, eyeing Kate's bare arms as they were about to leave. 'It gets very chilly down in those caves.'

Kate sat in the front of the car this time, gazing through the windscreen at the passing scenery. Very pretty. Almost English, but not quite. There was something about the quality of the light, the subtle difference in the colours, shades of green a fraction of a tone away from the greens that she was used to. Then there were the more obvious things: the architecture; driving on the wrong side of the road; the accent of the man who was speaking to her. 'Need to stop for some gas soon.' Even his vocabulary. It all reminded her that she was a stranger in a foreign land, just a woman on holiday, on her own. A few days and she'd be gone. This was borrowed time. Even the man and the boy, borrowed people, *with* her but not *hers*. Story of her life.

Wistful. Fey. A funny kind of mood clothed her. She was never sure when or where on that journey she took the decision, nor even if there was a decision involved. But somewhere between Gilberts Pond and Cobleskill, at some point in time that was outside of time, it came to her that she *could* make it all her own. For a little while at least. Take them, take it, take all of it. Wrap them around her and pretend they were hers. Literally, 'borrow them'. Just to see what it felt like. Just for an afternoon.

It was possibly not the wisest thing she ever did. But it was quite interesting.

She allowed Jeff to pay for the entrance fees while she stood by with Danny. Just like she imagined Mo might do with Ben and the children. Inside the caverns Danny was between them, holding her hand, holding Jeff's hand. People would look at them, she thought, and assume they were a family: father, mother, son. It became a game to her. One she kept secret from the other participants, of course – that way she wouldn't have to pay any forfeits.

There was a refreshment area nearby with a playpark for children – slides, swings, a monstrous 'old woman who lived in the shoe' house, made of yellow and brown plastic. So Danny played and Kate and Jeff drank coffee sitting at a wooden slatted bench-table, watching him, while the afternoon turned sultry, glaring sun replaced by an expanse of low, yellow-grey cloud. The air was heavy.

'There'll be a storm later, I bet,' Jeff said as they drove back to the house at Gilberts Pond. It was just something to say. Kate seemed to have been very quiet that afternoon. Contented enough, but gone private, wrapped inside herself. He'd seen quite a few Kate O'Connells now, and here was yet another one.

Dusk fell, oppressive and sticky. The storm had yet to break. Danny, irritable now from tiredness and the heat, climbed the stairs heavily, complaining about having to go to bed.

'Tell you what,' said Kate, finished with her game and offering just because she wanted to, 'you give me a shout when you're all washed and tucked up and I'll come and tell you a story. Would you like that?'

'Can you tell stories out of your head or do you have to read them from a book?'

'I am a woman of amazing talent,' she said. 'Which would you like?'

'Will you make one up specially for me?'

Shit, she thought. 'I will,' she said. 'Now go on. Up those stairs.'

Jeff, who'd been quite willing to let Kate step in – it saved him from having to come the heavy father – said, 'You're very good with him. He doesn't often take to strangers like he's taken to you.'

Kate was disproportionately pleased. She made light of it. 'He's a nice kid. I rather like him, too. In fact I have this secret plan to kidnap him and take him home with me.'

He threw her a curious look. 'What about you? Do you plan to have kids of your own one day?'

She shrugged. 'I haven't really thought about it,' (oh, really?). 'Maybe. There's time.'

Yes, he thought. We all assume that. We have to.

'Anyway,' she said, 'there are one or two other things I want to do first.'

'Like find the right man?'

She laughed. 'I didn't realise you were so conventional. But to answer the question – not necessarily. All you need are the right genes. That's with a g not a j. Actually, I was thinking more on the lines of establishing my career, a solid home base, financial security, top rung of the ladder – you know, little things like that.'

'A thoroughly modern woman,' he said.

'No.' She was serious now. 'Just a person, Jeff. Male or female has nothing to do with it. Why shouldn't I want those things for myself? Want to get them for myself? Nobody'd even think to question it if I had a penis.'

He put his hands up in defence and backed off. 'Who's questioning? Hey, you're looking at a liberated man, here!' He laughed. 'Sexual equality, yes please. I tell you, the times I've wished I had a husband around the place to help out!'

She laughed with him. 'And the times I've wanted a wife!' Then Danny called out that he was ready. She looked at Jeff and grimaced. 'Like now?'

He shook his head. 'Uh-uh. You offered. You're on your own, lady.' Then, just as she reached the top of the stairs, he relented. A little. 'Kate?'

She turned.

'He's into dragons.'

He gave it five minutes before he went upstairs. The door to Danny's room was ajar and he stood outside for a moment, listening. The woman's voice was warm and low and he couldn't quite make out all the words. Something about Prince Daniel and his laser sword . . . the bionic dragon . . . the greatest victory in intergalactic battle . . . ? He pushed on the door and went in quietly as Kate drew her story to its close.

'And so Daniel was proclaimed King and he ruled over

185

his people wisely and never again did any of the dragon people dare to fly their ships anywhere near the Planet Gilbertus.' She kissed her fingertips and touched them to the child's forehead. 'And so they all lived happily ever after,' she said. 'Except for the dragons.'

'That was some story,' said Jeff. 'But I missed the beginning. If I get the popcorn can I stay for the second showing?'

'Sorry,' she said, patting Danny's hand on top of the bedcover, 'that was for ticket holders only. Danny had the only ticket.'

When she left them Jeff sat on the edge of the bed looking at his boy. 'Well, Chief. Has it been a good day? You don't mind having a houseguest with us?'

Danny yawned. 'She's great. And she's ever so clever. When you were still in bed this morning I took her down to the creek and she showed me how to tickle minnows. Bet even Grandpa can't do that.' Another yawn. Heavy eyelids.

'Did she indeed?' he said, impressed. But it didn't really surprise him. Was there anything she couldn't do if she set her mind to it? Walk on water? Fly to the moon? Bring it back again? (And share it?)

He settled Danny to sleep and tiptoed out leaving the door ajar so the upstairs light filtered into the room.

The weather seemed to have made everyone restless. William was prowling about the veranda like a caged lion, Emily in the rocking chair was fanning herself – little fluttery movements with a southern belle concertina fan straight out of *Gone With the Wind*. 'William. *Do* something,' she ordered. 'Go out and do a raindance, anything!'

He gave her an arch look. 'You know darn well the mumbo-jumbo sticks are over at Joe's place being serviced. We got any beer in the refrigerator? Kate? Jeff?'

Kate demurred. She was leaning on the rail gazing dreamily out into the darkness. She hadn't felt so — away from it all, free of it all, whatever 'it all' was, not for a very long time. The sky above was black velvet. Neither moon nor stars pierced its stifling blanket. 'Actually I was wondering if you have such a thing as a storm lantern,' she said turning to them. 'Would it be foolhardy of me if I were to go for a swim? I've always wanted to do it. Go swimming, at night, outdoors. Could I, do you think?'

'Ah, memories of youth, eh, Em?' But William said yes, they did have a lantern and she'd be perfectly safe.

'But stay close by the landing stage, won't you, dear?' said Emily.

Jeff, overcome by chivalry, forsook the offer of a cold beer and said, 'It's okay, Mom, I'll go with her, make sure she's all right.'

'Good idea,' Emily agreed. 'As for me, I think a cold shower would be a little more sedate.'

They hooked the lantern on to one of the posts which supported the landing stage. Behind and above them, the windows of the house made squares of yellow light in a dark shape, the land between invisible in the night making the house seem like a boat, floating. Kate and Jeff cocooned inside their own little sphere of yellow light from the lantern.

She took off her robe and lost no warmth, only its weight and texture. The air was blood heat so if you stood quite still you couldn't tell where your skin ended, where the air began. You couldn't feel its touch. Warm. Womblike. And the lake was like a black mirror with only void at the limits of the lantern light. It was at once inviting and threatening, not quite so tempting in fact as in theory.

'This is a bit spooky,' she said with an uneasy little laugh. 'Perhaps I'll settle for a shower after all.'

'Coward,' he said and dived straight in, leaving her there alone in the light on the wooden boards.

She walked to the edge, looking for him to surface. The light failed to penetrate the water, just reflected back at her so she couldn't see the moving shape of his body below the ripples which circled outwards from his dive.

'Jeff?' she said tentatively. Seconds passed. A little firmer, 'Coolidge, where are you, don't muck around. Jeff?'

A splashing noise. A voice behind her. 'You called?' A teasing, mischievous face at the other side of the staging. 'You bastard,' she said, feeling ridiculously relieved. Then she, too, took a breath and dived straight into the black water before she could change her mind. She almost expected the surface of it to crack, splinter into shards as she broke it. Then she was below, weightless, turning and drifting in the cool water. Not as cold as it had been that morning. It wasn't all that deep – six, maybe eight feet. Her toes found the bed, pushed against the silt, yielding then firm. A couple of strokes and she surfaced, eyes closed and face up into the night. 'Oh!' she gasped. 'Oh, this is glorious!' She trod water, feeling exultant, vibrant, every square inch of her invigorated by the silky water on her bare skin.

'It's quite something, isn't it?' he asked, swimming to her side. 'It's even better if you're skinny-dipping. Ever done that?'

'No.'

'Want to try it?'

She smiled, reached out and put her hand on his head as if to ruffle the wet hair. 'You're incorrigible!' Then, with a quick and wicked thrust, she dunked him. And swam for her life.

He came up spluttering. 'Right. So the lady wants to play dirty, huh? You've asked for it.'

She was a strong swimmer. So was he. She felt young, free, playful – so she let him chase her then she let him catch her.

Physical contact, naked skin on naked skin, is allowable, unavoidable, when you're playing games in the water. So it was okay for them to touch, to clasp, for limbs to tangle.

They were treading water again, at the dim edges of the light, facing each other, hands on shoulders, timing it, tense and waiting for who was going to make the next move, wondering what the move would be. Apart from the bright yellow spot of the lantern away to the side of them, the world was in monochrome, shades of grey upon grey, and the eyes which challenged were wide with night vision, pupils black and fully dilated.

Vulnerable.

There was something – an imperceptible softening, a question or maybe an acknowledgment. Something changed in the eyes.

Suddenly she let go of him, turned and swam for the landing stage, round the other side, shielded from the house. She stayed in the water, holding on to one of the posts, not watching him, just waiting.

Then his hand touched her neck. She turned her face to him. Then she let go of the post and wrapped her arms around him instead. She kissed him. Softly but with growing hunger. Took his mouth for her own, licking his teeth, tasting his tongue, Jeff and the lakewater mingling in her mouth while her fingers moved in his wet hair, holding his head, not letting go, and her legs clasped around his hips so she could feel his sex pressing against her.

'Oh Kate, Katy, do you know what you're doing to me?' His voice was both harsh and soft as his lips moved across her face – her cheeks, eyelids, forehead, everywhere, a million wet little kisses reading her face in braille. 'You want me as much as I want you. I know you do. Don't think about it, Kate. Just let it *be*.'

She eased her face back from him, looking at him long and slow. She wasn't playing any games, not this time. 'Who's thinking?' she said softly.

She released him then and swam round to the ladder, climbed up out of the water. She waited for him, holding out her hand to him. The air warmed her and the wet swimsuit clung to her, revealing every smooth curve of her body – the indentation of her navel, the hard nipples pushing against the taut, shiny cloth. She waited for him, wanting him and knowing she would have him.

He picked up her robe, took her hand and they left

a trail of wet footprints behind them on the wooden boards.

'Under the trees,' she said quietly. 'I want to make love to you under the trees.'

'Put your shoes on, you'll hurt your feet.'

They weren't quite children of nature. It was not quite the Garden of Eden.

But as the darkness of the woodland enfolded them, the still-heavy air wrapping them up in the scent of green leaves, brown earth and night flowering blossom, they came pretty close to it.

He spread the robe on a smooth slope of grass, moss, last year's leaves. She didn't speak, just removed the shoes, knelt, reached her arms up and behind her neck to release the halter tie of the swimsuit. Jeff knelt in front of her, reached around her, found her fingers and stilled them. 'Let me,' he said. 'Let me do it.'

So she dropped her arms to her side, acquiescent, while he gently – indeed, almost hesitantly – peeled the swimsuit to her waist leaving her naked to the still, sultry air. Then he sat back on his haunches, looking at her full breasts, the nipples softer now, their areolae making dark circles against the paleness of her flesh. He shook his head slowly from side to side exhaling through his teeth. 'Kate. You're so beautiful.' He reached for her, placing his hands on her shoulders then skimming over their curves, stroking down her arms, back up again and across her throat with a delicacy of touch, a sureness of touch that made her whole body ache for him, his fingertips, his tongue, his maleness. Her head fell back, eyes closed, mouth slightly open, concentrating all her senses into that of touch – of being touched. He was moving the flat of his palms downwards to take her breasts, cupping them gently from underneath then enclosing them and finally, just as she felt she couldn't wait any longer, he drew his fingertips towards the nipples, taking them, rolling them gently between the pads of thumb and fore-finger making them grow and stiffen.

She made a little moan of pleasure as that poignant,

fierce singing of nerves shot a direct connection from her nipples to the centre of her sex. She felt the surge of warmth, the pulsing, the moistness between her lips, her thighs.

He was kissing her now, taking one hard bud between his lips, sucking on it, licking it, teasing around it with his tongue while his hands smoothed down over her waist to the tantalising swell of hip still clothed in the cool damp material of her swimsuit.

She eased him away from her then and deftly hooked her fingers into the swimsuit to slip it down over her hips. She stood and stepped out of it achieving nakedness with an unstudied grace of movement which almost took his breath away. She seemed to him like a pale and perfect sculpture with her smooth curve of thigh, the neat patch of hair shielding that secret part of her, a darker shade against the delicate swell of her abdomen.

He rose on to his knees and leaned forward. His hands were on the soft roundness of her buttocks, pulling her hips towards him so he could bury his face in the triangle of hair, feel its damp, springy texture against his lips. He breathed in the scent of her moistness and his tongue slid inside her soft and secret flesh to taste the very essence of her.

She shuddered at the feel of him, the heat of his breath, the soft wet caresses within her labia, around and across the tumescent bud at the gateway to her sex. Such wanting, such aching — to be opened, to be filled. She trembled at the edges of orgasm until she could stand it no longer, had just enough will to touch her palms to his forehead and tilt his face back from her. 'Please. No more,' she murmered. 'Stop. It's my turn.'

Jeff didn't argue.

There was no hesitancy in her touch. It was slow and sure, and took its time to savour these first explorations of his body. She ran her hands down his chest feeling the hard muscles flex involuntarily at her touch. She paused for an experimental moment to flirt with his nipples, to tease and suck at them. To her delight they responded,

191

hardening to little beads, showing her one of the ways to excite him. She loved the feel of him, the underlying hardness of the man's body. His skin was smooth, like running her hands over hot silk, sheened slightly with perspiration in the thick and humid air.

Lightly she brushed her fingers over the bulge of his erection, his penis hard and insistent, straining beneath the cloth. She stroked once, twice, featherlight. He made a little moan of pleasure, pain. The sound pleased her, increasing her own arousal. She could feel the throbbing in her engorged clitoris, wanted him to touch her there again, wanted to feel his shaft deep, deep inside of her, filling her.

She slipped her thumbs into the waist of his swim-trunks and pushed downwards, easing them over his penis, setting him free. She dipped her head to the glistening tip of it and licked, just once, with the flat of her tongue, tasting the slightly salt fluid. Straightening, she reached her hands to bring his mouth to hers. Her tongue found his, giving him the taste of himself.

They lay down then, nakedness pressed against nakedness, his penis, hard, pressing against her pubis; her breasts, soft, pressing against his chest, while his knee came between hers, easing her legs apart.

She turned her face aside and brought her hand to her mouth, licking it, sucking at her fingers, covering her palm in silky wetness, then she reached down to take him in her hand. Her fingers slid around him, easing the stretched foreskin further back from the sensitive tip, circling it with her slippery palm then placing the wet pad of her thumb on the very tip, so she could feel the little hole there. She opened her legs further and guided his penis so that it parted the lips of her sex. She moved her hips so the smooth head of his shaft slid across and around her swollen clitoris again and again and still again.

He tried to enter her but she would not let him. An urgently whispered, 'No. Not yet.'

An equally urgent, 'Kate. Oh Katy.' He deserted her

mouth and fell on her nipples, sucking and lapping at one, fondling the other, while his free hand moved down over her hip-bone, raising her from the ground a little so he could explore the crease of her buttocks, insinuating between her thighs from behind then spreading her soft folds apart, entering her with his fingers.

A little cry, and he felt her vagina contracting around his fingers as though she were trying to suck them into her and then she moaned, 'Now! I want you inside me now. Oh please, oh . . .' and she thrust her hips upward, her hand around his penis pushing him into her.

One, two, three thrusts, her hands on his clenched buttocks pulling him ever harder and deeper inside so she could feel him against the very depths of her, pounding against the entrance to her womb while the surge of heat rushed through her, stopping her breath, constricting her throat, blotting out all senses in the one engulfing ecstasy.

He thrust deeper and faster as she clasped him into her, her legs and arms wrapping round his body, her sex throbbing round his cock until he cried out, spilling into her, spurting his juices to mingle with hers inside the soft, warm, pulsating centre of her womanhood.

He tried to hide his face, bury it in her hair, but she would have none of it. She took his head in her hands and held his face before her so she could see, watch the agony and ecstasy on his face as he came, *see* the power she had. She felt him shudder, felt the warm weight of him when it was over. He dropped his head, eyes closed, shoulders hunched for a moment, then he eased himself up slightly to take back his weight.

She was still watching him. This was the telling moment, *after* the passion, when they had to become Kate and Jeff again, not merely woman and man. She waited. Sated and lethargic, she wanted no responsibility. She left it to Jeff to set the course of their changed relationship. She watched his face and she waited, silent and interested.

He smiled. Then he opened his eyes slowly, heavily,

and looked down at her. 'Kate,' he whispered. 'Oh, Katy.' The smile broadened. 'I guess you *do* know what you do to me.' And then, just like in the hackneyed old song, he kissed her. Very tenderly. For a long time.

They were lying side by side, facing each other, kissing and looking and stroking, taking the time, now that passion had been temporarily slaked, to discover the finer delights of their nakedness.

'Do you know, I've never done it in a wood before.'

'Me neither.'

Kisses. Caresses.

But Kate had begun to think about tomorrow. 'Jeff. There's something I want to say.'

'Uh-uh. I don't like the sound of that.'

A smile. 'I haven't said it yet.'

'Then don't.'

Silenced with a kiss. She decided it could wait. Tomorrow. In the daylight. With clothes on.

She lay on her back and stretched her arms up behind her head, closing her eyes and enjoying simply *being*.

And then it began. Quite suddenly and with no warning, not even a distant rumble. Rain. Warm rain. Rain such as Kate had never felt, and certainly never felt on naked stomach, breasts, thighs. Heavy, fat droplets of warm rain falling sporadically on her skin like drumming fingertips.

She didn't leap up and grab for clothing – not that there was much to grab for anyway – she just murmured contentedly, 'Oh, fuck.'

He laughed. 'What, again already?'

But she took his joke and turned it back on him. She reached for him, ran her hand across the hard flatness of his belly and down to his groin. Lightly she cupped his balls in her hand feeling the slack skin, the soft weight of them, then she ran a finger up to the thick base of his penis, feeling it leap for her, watching it stiffen at her touch. She smiled. 'Why not? I've never done it in the rain before.'

*

194

Emily was waiting up for them. She was in the kitchen, coffee steaming on the stove, a pile of fluffy towels ready on the table, when the screen door opened and in they came, dripping.

'I was just beginning to wonder if I should send out a search party,' she said lightly, worried to death. 'Did you have a good swim?'

'Wonderful. Then we went for a walk. It rained.' Jeff took one of the towels and wrapped it around Kate's shoulders, lifting her wet hair from underneath so it rested on top of the towel. Emily did not miss the little gesture.

Kate said, 'We were wet from swimming anyway so it didn't matter. It was so warm we just kept on walking. Sat for a while watching the rain on the lake. It's so beautiful here, Emily, it must be wonderful to have this all for your own. I'm sorry about your robe, it's a bit . . .' She was burbling, felt like she'd drunk glasses of heady wine. And the robe was more than a little wet. Bits of grass clung to it and there were muddy patches. Kate bundled it hastily and headed for the door. 'I'll just go up and get dry, I'll rinse this out for you . . .'

Jeff and his mother stood in the warm, bright kitchen with the rain dripping down the windows while Jeff towelled himself and dripped little puddles on to the floor. Emily poured coffee into two mugs then took a cloth from the drainer. She tossed it on to the table. 'Wipe up when you've finished,' she said. 'The floor's like an ice rink when it's wet.'

He indicated the two mugs. 'You not having one?'

She shook her head. 'Bed.' At the door she turned and looked at her son, standing there. 'Jeff?'

'Mm?' Very casual, still towelling.

'Be careful.'

'Go to bed, Mom.'

When Kate came back downstairs she had a towel wrapped around her head like a turban and she wore corduroy jeans with a loose cheesecloth shirt, buttoned up. Underneath it she wore a bra.

Jeff, also dry now, had donned a pair of faded denims and a soft cotton shirt which he wore unbuttoned, open like a jacket.

They sat at the table on hard wooden chairs, hands cupped around the steaming mugs, taking little sips and not saying anything. The rain had eased slightly. The storm, if storm there was, had passed over them before it truly broke, leaving them now with a soft pitter patter on the veranda roof outside the screen door. The night was still warm but it had lost its heaviness, washed away by the rain.

'Kate?'

Answered by a look from over the rim of the mug as she continued to drink.

'I want to sleep with you. Wake up in the morning with you next to me.'

She studied him as she considered the option. She considered it for quite a while before answering quietly, 'You're a nice man, Jeff. So understand when I say I'd like a little space now. Besides,' she shook her head and smiled at her own words, 'I wouldn't feel right. Not with your parents in the next room, and Danny. I know . . .' she held up a hand to stop his protest. 'We're adults and I don't suppose anybody would mind, but.' She shrugged. 'I just wouldn't feel right about it, okay?'

He didn't press her. She liked him for it. 'So. What are you going to do tomorrow? Back to the typewriter? Work on the masterpiece?'

He leaned back in the chair tilting it on two legs, stretching himself. 'I don't know. I sort of doubt it.'

She put her mug down. There was a decisiveness to it. 'Well, I must,' she said. 'I'd like to phone the office. I'll reverse the charges of course, TV7 will pay for it, but I'd better find out what's happening, see how they're doing with the dates and the film crews and all that. That be okay? I could always go into town and call from there.'

'And this is a lady who's on vacation? Off duty? Anybody ever told you you're a workaholic?'

She grinned. 'Anybody ever pointed out to you that you're obviously not?'

'Once or twice,' he agreed. 'But I think the words were "lazy, workshy, good for nothing bum".'

'Really. And who called you that?'

'Me, mostly. On the days when I can think of a million things I'd rather do than try to fill up a blank sheet of paper. Like today. Tomorrow, the day after, all the days while you're here.'

'Oh, no you don't,' she warned. 'Don't you go shifting your responsibility on to my shoulders, Coolidge, or I'll be away from here like a shot! Just go and write your book. I'll find plenty to keep me occupied. I might even get your mother to show me how to make an apple pie.'

He looked at her in mock horror changing to wonderment. 'And now – in the first of a new series – the megatalented Kate O'Connell – encounters – the baking apple!'

She pushed back her chair and stood – on her dignity. 'And if I wanted to,' she said, 'I could turn even that into a prime-time hit.' She joked, but there was a grain of belief beneath it.

He studied her. 'You know, Kate, one of the things I really like about you – it's that air of meek humility, that just perceptible lack of self-confidence . . .'

She sighed. 'It's a cross I have to bear.'

She lay awake, listening to the rain, listening to the noises of the house, the occasional quiet creaking as if the building were stretching itself, relaxing, falling asleep again. Kate was far from sleep, lying there, thinking of the man, replaying the evening, projecting herself and Jeff into tomorrow and directing the action, making final edits to the script she intended to use.

She was tempted to go back to her game – the one she'd played this afternoon. To allow herself this time, away from her own world, tasting a different one. Tempted therefore to leave her bed, tiptoe along the landing and slip into his bed, to lie with him, two warm bodies relaxed together in the trust of sleep. It was something she'd experienced rarely. Once or twice before Alex, once or twice with Alex. And now it was hers for the taking. Albeit temporarily.

Besides, she was not and never had been, a one-night stand lady.

Jeff had said earlier, 'Just let it *be*.'

And she could. If she wanted to. Let it.

For just a little while.

So long as he understood that's all it would be. So long as they both understood the rules – that this was temporary.

Chapter Twelve

She knew she'd seen it somewhere. Some reference, something – the tiniest twanging at the cords of memory.

She knelt on the pale peach, velvet-pile, pure wool carpet ignoring the pins and needles pricking through her calves, ignoring the dull ache at the small of her back and the burning sensation in her chest, just beneath the breastbone. Heartburn. She almost laughed. How appropriate.

Old newspapers, colour supplements, women's magazines, spilled across the floor in a random litter. And she, usually so houseproud. It was her daily personal challenge to make sure everything was spick and span and neat and pretty despite the ravages inflicted by her two young girls and their enthusiastic but somewhat untidy nanny. Normally Elizabeth wore her showpiece home like a badge of honour – no sticky fingerprints on her flower-print kitchen wallpaper; no line of grey fluff along the edges of her pale pastel carpets; no tricycle-inflicted wounds on her skirting boards. And here she was, in the centre of an unholy mess, even though she'd sent the girls off to her mother's for the weekend.

She continued the task. Pick up, search through, discard. One, then another and another. She flipped the pages quickly, sometimes violently, so they made sharp rustling noises and some of them even tore. The more she searched, the more her anger grew. Anger at herself for being so blind, not even *suspecting* something was going on. Anger at not being able to put her finger on those elusive lines of print she *knew* she'd seen somewhere – not the gossip rag, something else, connected to some woman, *the* woman. And of course anger – no, a hot, shaking fury – at Alex for causing it all. For his weakness, for his deceit, for his betrayal, and for his *carelessness* in getting found out. And thus making her look a fool. A pregnant, adoring, blind, humiliated fool.

She never thought she could sink to this. She'd already done the bedroom – flinging his suits out of the wardrobe, assiduously going through them, pocket by pocket, in search of something, anything to support the rumour, identify the mistress. She shuddered at the distasteful word. She'd ransacked his drawers, searched through the neat piles of underwear even though they'd been neatly piled by herself. The bathroom cabinet, his shaving case, the desk in the study. Everywhere she could think of where he might have left something – a packet of (another shudder) condoms, a hotel bill made out to a Mr and Mrs Smith – as if he'd be so stupid. She could even *see* herself being totally ridiculous. A hulking, lumbering, ludicrous figure. But she couldn't stop herself.

She picked up another magazine, glad for once that he liked to keep these things 'on file'. At the end of February, January's would be put out for the binmen. At the end of March, February's would follow. And so on, an orderly procession, through the year. And so she had nearly eight weeks' worth of print and paper to go at.

She went at it with a compulsive, almost manic, meticulousness.

The black Ministry car turned smoothly into the driveway and as it purred to a halt outside the front door the Cabinet Minister closed the lid of the scuffed red box and snapped the catches shut. Carrying it, two similar ones and a briefcase, he bade good evening to the driver, instructed him to pick him up again at seven-thirty sharp on Monday morning, then he stood on the doorstep waiting for the door to open. He did not usually have to bother fumbling around with latch keys. The door always opened for him when he returned to his constituency home for the weekend. Depending on the time of his arrival either his daughters or Elizabeth would be there looking out for him, waiting for him with smiles and hugs and kisses.

Today was no exception. The door opened and there stood his wife, serene and smiling as always and offering her pink cheek to be kissed.

'Where are the girls?' he asked as he dumped the Ministry boxes in the study, loosened his old school tie and carefully hung the suit jacket, a grey, pin-stripe, bespoke Savile Row job, over the back of a Hepplewhite chair.

Elizabeth had settled herself on the chintz-covered sofa when he entered the drawing room. She arranged her face into an innocent expression as she looked up with the words, 'They're staying at Mummy's this weekend. It's Tracey's weekend off. Don't you remember, I told you?' She hadn't.

'Oh yes, of course. Slipped my mind.' He was at the drinks cabinet with his back to her. He poured a gin and tonic for himself then turned and asked, 'Can I get you anything, darling? Soda? Orange?'

She just looked at him without replying. Her husband. Relaxing at home. He hadn't even unbuttoned his waistcoat. He unbuttoned more than that for *her*, the other one. 'What?'

'I asked you if you'd like a drink.' He frowned. 'Are you all right, pusskins? You look a bit flushed. You feeling okay, the baby . . . ?'

I've got backache and acid heartburn and varicose veins and piles and I weigh three stones more than I'm used to and I'm tired of carrying this parasite punching at my ribs and playing football with my bladder and . . . 'I'm fine,' she said and picked up her knitting needles.

He had the nerve to take her word for it.

He flopped into 'his' armchair – also in blossoming chintz – and looked around the room in satisfied contentment. Bright as a new pin. As always. But comfortable at the same time, with little touches around showing evidence of life – a couple of magazines on the coffee table, fresh flowers in the vases, the knitting bag by the sofa. It was his favourite room, the drawing room. Spacious for a new house these days, and light, with the wall of French window looking out over the garden at the back with its protected oak tree and panoramic views beyond the low fence – undulating fields, clumps of beech trees, right the way over to Marlow. You don't get views like *that* in the city, oh no.

He gave a contented little grunt as he settled deeper into the chair. 'What's for dinner?'

You. Grilled, roasted or skewered, take your pick. 'Fish and chips.'

'Oh.' Not so contented. 'Oh, well. Tell you what, darling, seeing as the girls aren't here, how about if I take you out tonight? Could pop down to the Shire Oak, if you like, they do things in baskets, don't they? Can't be too late though, my boxes are pretty full. Well? How about it?'

Scampi and chips in a plastic basket. You really know how to make a woman feel like a wife. 'I don't think so, if you don't mind, Alex. I'm not really feeling up to it. Actually I was rather looking forward to a quiet evening at home, just you and me . . .' She put down the knitting needles (which was just as well, considering) and picked up a slim magazine instead. Nonchalantly, she flipped through it.

'Oh. Righto. Whatever you want.' He finished the G and T, put the glass on the coaster on the little leather-topped table at the side of the chair, stood, stretched and said, 'Well, in that case I'll go and make a start on the boxes. Give me a shout when you're hungry and I'll go and get the fish and chips.'

Big of you. 'Sit down, Alex.'

'What?'

She fixed him with an unsmiling gaze. 'I – said – sit – down.' Her voice was controlled but the magazine she held in her hand was trembling. She put it down again, quickly. It was open at the Photocall pages. She swirled it round on the table so it was right side up to him. Picked up the other one, a copy of the gossipy trash she'd seen at the hairdresser's, the new copy she'd bought to bring home with her. Opened that one. Turned it, too, in his direction.

He didn't seem to see any significance in what she was doing with the magazines, just flopped back into his chair again with a heavy sigh. 'Okay. Go on. What have I done this time?' The voice was that of the long-suffering and infinitely patient. She was after all, pregnant. Very. He had to make allowances.

Elizabeth was going to make *none*. She could feel it coming. That stew of emotion that she'd managed to keep to a contained simmer all afternoon – since she'd found the reference to the constant companion, the pregnant wife, the picture of that woman so sure, so slick, so smiley, so *slim* – she could feel it all seething upwards, about to boil over, to spill and splash and scald all over their marriage. And she didn't feel the least bit like stopping it.

Suddenly she slammed her fist down on the table, a blow aimed straight at Kate O'Connell's head. Elizabeth's jaw muscles twitched and through clenched teeth she spat out, 'How could you? And if *I* can put two and two together, how many more people will be doing exactly that? You bastard. You . . . you . . .' She scooped up the magazines and flung them at him as hard as she could. They fluttered, crackled through the air.

He ducked to the side, even though he knew they'd never reach him. 'What on earth . . . what are you talking abou . . . have you gone mad, woman? What's the *matter* with you?'

She was on her feet, fists clenched, body trembling with fury, hatred, jealousy, while tears and carefully applied mascara both stung at her eyes. 'I'll tell you what's the *matter*, you . . . you *fucking* bastard!' she screamed.

He was still reeling from the shock of Elizabeth even knowing such language, let alone using it, when she followed with the body blow. Right below the belt.

'What's the *matter* is *fucking Kate O'Connell!*' She gave a short, bitter exclamation. 'Ha! Literally. What a laugh.' And the tears rolled down her face.

The days – just as tradition demands they should – flew by. It was the shortest week, yet in other ways it was the longest week, the week she took and set aside somewhere outside the world of Kate O'Connell.

The morning after the night of the rain, early, before anyone else had risen, Kate, who'd set the travel alarm just to be sure, crept along to Jeff's room, cautiously opened the door and entered.

The room was dim, thin curtains filtering out the harshness of a summer's day already broken. He was still asleep, his face turned towards the door, to where Kate stood. His hair was tousled against the white of the pillow and she could make out a faint shadow of stubble softening the firm line of his jaw. His mouth was open very slightly, his breathing quiet. She smiled at that. He didn't snore, then. Was there no end to the man's attraction? His shoulders were bare above the sheet and one arm was flung outwards as if he'd reached for something, in a dream perhaps, and found only an empty pillow. The sight touched her, there seemed a poignancy about the still figure and she felt she should perhaps tiptoe away again, that she had no right to witness the defenceless revelations of sleep.

But she did not go. She took a silent step closer, breathing very softly so's not to disturb him, although ultimately she must. She gave herself a moment longer to watch (watch over) his sleeping face and as she paused there she thought: remember this. Keep it. Savour it. So when the time comes, in just a few more days, you can say goodbye to it.

Another step and she was at the bedside. She sat, reached out and rested her hand on his shoulder, firmly but not enough to startle. 'Jeff.' The name was spoken quietly, somewhere between voice and whisper. 'Jeff, wake up. It's Kate. Katy.'

His eyes opened, closed, opened again and focused. 'Hello.' A sleepy murmur. 'How long have you been there?'

'Hours.'

'And you didn't wake me? Spoilsport.' He stretched and turned over on his back. 'Did I say outrageous things to you in my sleep?'

She scanned the length of him, outlined clearly beneath the single sheet. 'Shocking. Absolutely outrageous.'

'Bad as that, huh?' A yawn.

She stood. Turned her eyes away from his body and back to her purpose. 'Actually, I'm the one who's got some talking to do . . .'

'Oh God,' he groaned. 'A woman who talks before breakfast. Save me.'

'No, I'm serious, Jeff . . .'

'You think I wasn't?'

'Look. I'll go and make a pot of tea, will that help?'

'You can make *tea*? Katy, you're getting more domesticated by the minute.'

She wasn't used to being teased. Especially first thing in the morning. She rather liked it. 'I'll meet you in the kitchen.'

He winked and held a finger to the side of his nose. Stagewhispered, 'I'll be the one in the bathrobe. With a white rose in the lapel.'

She glanced heavenwards for help and left, shaking her head.

A few minutes later, with tea brewing in the pot and two cups out ready to receive it, Jeff wandered into the kitchen. A green toothbrush was pinned to his bathrobe collar.

'Fraud,' she said. 'Where's my white rose?'

'Nobody said it was going to be *your* rose, lady. Now sit down and deliver the goods. Start with my tea.'

She studied him, then sat down and poured out one cup, smiling. She drank. Replaced the cup delicately in its saucer. Looked at him innocently. 'Nobody said it was going to be *your* tea.'

'Okay.' He poured for himself and they sipped in silence for a moment or two. 'So. What is it? Don't tell me you dragged me out of bed at this hour of the day just to drink tea with me. What's on your mind, Katy? Come on, tell Uncle Jeff.'

She glanced at him then fixed her eyes on the tabletop as though she'd just discovered something inordinately interesting there. 'Seems a bit silly in the cold light of day. Like I'm making a big thing out of nothing at all.'

'I wouldn't know. I haven't heard it yet.'

She took a preparatory breath. Let it out again. Looked at him, eye to eye. 'Okay. Speech time. There are some things I want to get clear.' She stopped.

He waited.

'I've been thinking . . .'

'Good,' he said encouragingly.

'I'm serious.'

'Good,' he said again.

She ignored him and launched in. 'One, I don't make love with people lightly . . .'

'Good.'

'And if you say that one more time I'll thump you – I mean it.'

He clamped his lips together and folded his arms across his chest assuming an 'I'm listening intently' expression.

'And the other thing I don't do, to use a hackneyed phrase, is mix business with pleasure. So, if we're having an affair – which, all things considered, I suppose we are . . .'

Obediently silent, he made do with a nod.

'Then I want to make it clear from the start that it's got nothing to do with me as Kate O'Connell, if you see what I mean. When I come back with my film crew, when we put the *Encounter* together, none of this is going to make the slightest bit of difference. It'll be like it never happened, or like it happened to two different people. Do you understand what I'm saying?'

He didn't answer straight away. When he did it was, 'Sure I do. In a few days, goodbye Katy. In a few more weeks, hello Ms O'Connell, ma'am. That it?'

'More or less. Yes. Or putting it another way, goodbye Jeff, hello Mr Warren. So. How do you feel about that?'

Another slight pause then, 'Schizoid.'

'We're both adults. We can handle it.'

'And just suppose I don't want to, what happens then?'

She shrugged. 'Not a lot. I find somebody else for *The O'Connell Encounter*.'

'Are you blackmailing me?'

'Er . . . yes.'

He considered again. Then he shook his head, looked at her through narrowed eyes. There was no teasing light in them any more. 'You've got some nerve,' he said. Then he stood. Began to pace the room, stalking round the table, pausing every now and then to point at her, bend closer to her. 'You've also got one high-blown opinion of yourself, don't you? You think you can play around with people, move them around like pieces on a chessboard then put them to one side when they've served their purpose?'

'No, I didn't mea . . .'

He went on without listening. 'So what's this particular game called. I've got news for you, Katy. I'm not sure I like the rules.'

'It's not a game, I just . . .' She wasn't used to being on the defensive and she didn't like it. She focused on the green toothbrush stuck to his collar — it sort of gave her a superior edge. 'All I'm doing is taking the rules from your own book, Jeff. Or hadn't you noticed?'

He stopped. 'Expound.'

'With pleasure. But for goodness' sake sit down and finish your tea before it gets cold.'

He didn't, but she went on anyway. '*Losing Time*. It strikes at the core of current American philosophy, doesn't it? The first law of the Yuppie? Which is why it suddenly took off like it did. Go for it? If you want it go for it *now*? Life is short and time might me shorter than you think, so live it.' She looked at him. 'Isn't that right? Isn't that what it says? Have your cake *and* eat it?'

'That's an oversimplification.' He sat.

'That's beside the point.' Her voice softened. She reached out to touch him, place her hand on his arm.

'Jeff. Understand. All this . . . you, Danny, this place, the warmth that surrounds you . . . you have so much. And it's like I can share in it for a little while. Now. I didn't plan it, I wasn't expecting it, but it's like being given a taste of something I've always wanted and never quite managed to get. And now, for these few days, you, Danny, you've all made me feel like I'm part of it. And I like it.' She paused, looked at him frankly, somehow made herself strong by admitting the need. 'And *you*. I want you, to have you. For the little time that I can.'

'Who's arguing? You've got me.'

'But,' she said. 'I can't stay. And I can hardly take it all back with me, can I? It doesn't quite fit into the scheme of things.' A wry little smile. 'I live in England.'

'I noticed.'

'My life is in England. Yours is here. And God knows where your writing is going to take you but one thing's for sure, you're not going to stand still. Neither am I. But for a few days, we *can*. That's all I'm saying.'

'So what are we arguing about? Where's the problem?'

'It's not here, it's later. I'm just trying to make that part of it easier when it comes. Just want us both to know where we stand. Or where we *will* stand. That's all.'

'I see. Just one observation . . .'

'Fire away.'

'You talk too much.'

The days slipped through her fingers like soft, dry sand.

A sunny morning . . . Jeff working at a little table out on the veranda, head bent, scribbling furiously with a pencil and a yellow legal pad. Kate sitting in the rocking chair reading (great honour) the manuscript so far. Jeff suddenly looking up, saying, 'Excuse me, can I have a kiss please?' She complying, then saying, 'This is good, you know. Bloody good.'

'Which? The kiss or the manuscript?'

'Both.'

Then quietly continuing their occupations as if there'd been no interruption.

An overcast evening . . . but warm enough and dry. A barbeque in the yard out back of the Strakers' General Store. Kate on show – Danny showing her off. Kate indulging him, joining in the cowboys and indians with him and the other youngsters from Gilberts Hollow. Kate being shot and dying magnificently against the picket fence. Catching a look from Jeff as he helped out on cooks' detail, prodding manfully at a sizzling piece of beef.

Indoors . . . after lunch. Kate and Jeff and Danny clearing, washing, drying the dishes, packing Emily and William off for the afternoon with a promise of evening meal prepared for when they got back. Jeff and Danny doing most of the work while Kate directed operations then stunned them all (and took all the glory) by producing golden, crisp and light as air Yorkshire puddings. Being from Yorkshire, that was one thing she did know how to cook.

Danny in bed . . . Emily and William watching the television. Kate and Jeff going out for a drive to no place in particular, just to give the car a workout. Kate resting her hand lightly on Jeff's thigh, thinking what a shame it was that the BMW was the standard left-hand drive, fully automatic, American version. No hard male muscle flexing under her fingers as the driver depressed the clutch, shifted the gear lever. She smiled to herself.

He caught it. 'What are you thinking?'

Her smile broadened. 'Do you know, I've never done it in a car before?'

A screech of brakes.

Out on the lake . . . in the rowing boat in a soft drizzle. William and Danny and Kate in raincoats and an assortment of hats. Danny delving into a tin of squirming worms and maggots, offering to bait the hook for her. Kate accepting. William showing her how to cast the line. Sitting, musing, holding the rod, feeling the tug, squealing, 'I've done it! I've caught something!' Nearly upsetting the boat in her excitement. Reeling it in. Throwing the tiny, slippery, flapping thing back again.

Pulling a face at Jeff when they returned to find him waiting at the door with his hands on hips, scowling and growling, 'What, no supper?'

And her bedroom curtains, not quite closed, allowing a shaft of early morning light to cut across the still air and paint a soft grey crack on the wall opposite. Jeff next to her, asleep. Kate, who hadn't wanted to squander the night by sleeping, waking up disappointed to find that she had. Wishing the light would go away. Wishing the night, which was the last night, would come back and start all over again. Looking at her watch, tempted to turn back the hands. Knowing it wouldn't change anything.

She touched him. She brought him out of sleep by making love to him. Silently. Slowly. Lingeringly. Making it last. The last time.

Danny insisted on being up and around to say goodbye, even though they were leaving so early. He helped out with Kate's luggage, dragging a soft, heavy suitcase down the stairs behind him, thud, thud, thud.

Kate was down a few minutes later and after all the 'thank yous' and 'take cares' and 'safe journeys' there was nothing left to do but get in the car and go.

Emily came outside with them holding a brown paper bag which she tucked into the boot next to the luggage. 'Just a few things for you, dear,' she said to Jeff as she hugged him. 'Milk, bread, some cold ham and a little casserole you can heat up for your dinner tonight. And don't forget to bring back the dish.' A food parcel for the needy. The universal symbol of maternal love. He was only staying over in New York for the one night.

They stood on the porch and watched them go, William with his arm around Emily's shoulders, Emily with her arm around Danny's, all three figures waving. Kate waving back while Danny tore at her heart with his tear-bright eyes above a not very, but trying awfully hard to be, brave smile.

Once they were through Gilberts Hollow and on to the main roads Jeff and Kate didn't say much. They *talked* a lot – 'it's been a lovely week', 'we've enjoyed having you here', 'are you sure driving me back to New York isn't too much trouble?', 'none at all' – but they didn't *say* much.

New York. Jeff offered a coffee at the apartment, Kate accepted a straight drive to the airport. 'But there's nearly two hours before your plane goes,' he protested.

'Check-in time. And I happen to like mooching around airports on my own.'

'Whatever turns you on. You're the boss.'

'And don't you forget it.'

'No, ma'am.' He gave a quick salute, negating it with a friendly one-fingered gesture.

He pulled up the car right by the main entrance and turned off the engine. Then, resting his head sideways on his arms on the steering wheel, he looked at Kate as if he were imprinting her face on his memory. He had too much to say so he waited for her to say something first.

'Well, thanks for the lift, Jeff.'

(That wasn't it.)

'And for my week. It's been . . . really special.'

(That's more like it. Getting warmer.)

'Well. I guess it's goodbye time.'

(Uh-uh. Getting cold again.) 'Katy.'

Her turn to just look. And that's all that happened. She looked at him and he looked at her and they didn't say a word, didn't move, caught up in each other's eyes unsmiling, unblinking, while the world outside the car shrank, contracted. The sound of other cars pulling up, drawing away, the scream of aircraft taking off, landing, all the sounds in the world faded away to be replaced only by the sound of their own quiet breathing. She was held by his eyes, giving back gaze for gaze, seeing there all that she wanted to hear but didn't want to acknowledge. Timeless. And still no words were spoken.

Tap, tap. More insistent. Rap, rap, rap. A uniform. A voice. 'Come on, buddy, move it. You can't stop here.' An airport cop. A bucketful of cold water.

Kate wound her window down, a sort of reflex action. 'Oh, I'm awfully sorry, officer,' she said sounding awfully, awfully English. 'It's my fault. I'm just going,' and in one smooth movement she opened the door, swung her legs out and was standing in the world again. She closed the door and leaned through the open window, reaching across to Jeff, touching his arm.

'Goodbye, Jeff,' she said. 'Thanks for everything. Kiss Danny for me. And I'll see you . . .' she shrugged, changed it to, 'I'll be in touch. Take care.' She withdrew her hand, kissed the fingertips at him and turned to go.

'Katy?'

She stopped. If you tell me not to go, she thought, I won't go. Yes I will. But tell me anyway. She turned.

He was getting out of the car now and grinning. 'I think you forgot something.'

She looked blank and the uniform looked very impatient.

Jeff was unlocking the trunk. 'Your bags?'

The officer shook his head and threw a sympathetic look across to Jeff. Jeff caught it and tossed one back which said, 'Women!'

The cop smiled. 'Two minutes. Then I'll be back and you'll be gone, right? Have a nice flight, ma'am.' He nodded at Kate and walked away leaving Kate and Jeff stranded again, a little island on the kerb, Kate and Jeff and her luggage. She stood guard while he fetched a cart for her. They loaded it. She touched the handles.

Then she smiled up at him a little sheepishly. 'This is what they call a re-take,' she said. 'Get it right this time, O'Connell. G'bye, Jeff. Safe journey back home.'

'You too,' he said. 'And Katy?'

'Yes?'

'Just make sure you come back, huh?'

She smiled. 'Of course. I have to make you into an international celebrity, don't I?'

'Yeah,' he said. 'That too.' He bent down and kissed her forehead quickly. She turned, and he watched her walk away, pushing the cart with her back straight, head high. The invisible electronic beam broke for her, opened the doors for her, and she walked on through. She didn't look back. The doors closed behind her.

The traffic cop was bearing down on his car with a gimlet-eyed determination. Jeff leaped for it. There was a squeal of wheels as he drove off.

He considered driving straight into the parking lot, leaving it, chasing after her, buying a ticket, boarding the plane, 'Hi, fancy meeting you here . . .' Except he didn't have his passport with him. He went through all sorts of different scenarios while the car took him into the city on automatic pilot.

Jeff, back at the musty apartment, thinking of Kate and listening for planes flying overhead.

Kate, checked in and bags gone, mooching about the air terminal, thinking of Jeff and listening for her flight number over the speakers.

And soon, she was flying. Caught between the blue sky-ceiling and the white cloud-carpet. The hostess came along with the trolley asking if she wanted anything.

I want it *all*, she thought, but the girl was only offering drinks. Kate waved her away and determinedly waved thoughts of Jeff away, too. She closed her eyes. Rested her head back. Wished she could press a magic button and be transported instantaneously to her own little sitting room where Mo, unencumbered by either husband or offspring (if you're talking magic you may as well go the whole hog), would be ensconced in one armchair and she'd be in another and the only thing to come between them would be a bottle of wine.

How she longed for the release of a good long confession session! With the frankness and ease that only seems possible between long-standing female friends. If there was anybody in the world she could be absolutely honest with, absolutely *herself* with, it was Mo. No matter the long gaps between seeing each other, the even

213

greater gaps between their present lifestyles, when you've shared your deepest confidences about everything from *Paradise Lost* to virginity lost, you stay close.

But she couldn't have Mo either. At least, not yet.

Kate reached down to the bottom of her handbag and took out the packet of cigarettes that she miraculously hadn't touched for a whole week. She lit one. Drew the smoke deep into her lungs. Coughed. Drew in again. Felt dizzy. She looked at the burning tip of it, watched the steel-coloured smoke perform its sinuous slowdance in front of the plexiglass window. She leaned her head back again and gazed unseeing at the vast, bright emptiness outside until her eyes began to sting.

She told herself it was just the glare and the cigarette smoke.

Chapter Thirteen

The tarmac was black and shiny when they landed – black with the night, shiny with the rain, Heathrow at two in the morning. But being Kate O'Connell had its advantages. A uniformed chauffeur took her bags, guided her quickly to one of the TV7 fleet cars, settled her in the back seat before putting her cases in the boot, then got in behind the wheel and started up the engine.

'Straight home is it, Miss O'Connell?' said his chirpy Cockney voice.

'Please.'

'Chiswick then. Quite handy. I'm off to Richmond after I drop you off. Pick up Marina Welsh for the breakfast show. Didn't you have her on your programme once, Miss O'Connell? Yes, I'm sure you did, it was . . .'

She was back. Her own familiar world spread itself about her and closed her in as she sped down the M4 in the protective custody of a limousine and driver sent by the management to ensure the safe return of their rising star. Yes, the familiar world had its compensations. That other world, the one she'd left behind on the far side of the Atlantic, already seemed to be in another dimension as if she'd only dreamed it. This was home.

And as she unlocked the front door and switched on the lights she found it was a bright and sparkling home with fresh flowers on the dining table and a note from Mrs Pickles who'd left them there. She'd also left fresh milk in the fridge, fresh bread in the breadbin and a freshly baked steak and kidney pie in the freezer. Emily's food parcel. An echo from Gilberts Pond. Kate flopped down into her favourite squashy armchair with a little grunt of satisfaction.

Oh, the emotional comfort of familiar possessions! She looked around the room surveying her territory, checking her nest, smiling at the miscellany of inanimate objects which surrounded her. Books – hundreds of books, paperback fiction, heavyweight tomes from college days, even the tattered Angela Brazil and Enid Blyton stories from her childhood – Kate rarely had time to open them but she could never throw away a book. There was her collection of little chunks of rock, carefully dusted although there was nothing special about them. They weren't rare or precious or even beautiful, but they were precious to Kate – like the smog-stained lump of grey sandstone with the carving on it. It was a piece of All Soul's Church where her parents had been married and she herself was christened, which she'd retrieved from the rubble on the shocked day she paid a nostalgic visit and found they'd knocked it down.

She smiled as her eyes wandered about the room, reaffirming spiritual contact with all the little objects which were more than possessions. They were her familiars, linking past to present, a proof of passage, a confirmation of her existence. Yes, it was good to be home again.

She closed her eyes, took a deep breath and relaxed her body heavily into the cushions as she exhaled – a trick she'd been taught by her dentist who did a thriving sideline in hypnotherapy. She was tired but too hyped up from the journey, the culture clash of homecoming, the out of synch body-clock, to be sleepy. She was also feeling decidedly shop-soiled so, at God-o'clock on whatever morning it was now, the post and the ansaphone could wait.

She took her bags upstairs, heaved them on to the bed and scowled at them. She told herself it was only a chore, a simple mechanical action, just empty them and heap the lot into the laundry bin and forget it. She unfastened the clasps of the biggest case and the lid sprang open from the pressure of the squashed and crumpled contents. She began to sort through them.

And there she was, transported to that other world again. Kate, delving through her dirty washing and thinking: memories are made of this. Grains of California sand. Grass stains from the Straker barbecue. The swim-suit she'd worn at Gilberts Pond. She lingered over it briefly before squashing it resolutely into the linen basket; came to a full stop as she unearthed a florist's card which said: *P. S. Can my Dad take you out tonight?*

The memories came crashing through.

'Go away!' she said to them aloud, alone in her bedroom while the London rain spattered against her windowpanes.

Five more minutes of bustling activity succeeded in imposing a fair semblance of devastation on the precision order left by Mrs Pickles. Kate turned her back on it and headed for the bathroom.

She turned on the shower, contemplated having a brief and sterile fling with the shower head, but the idea had little appeal. It wasn't quick release she wanted so much as slo-o-ow release. Kisses and strokes and gentling embraces. Specifically, Jeff Coolidge's. She undressed, kicked the discarded clothing into a pile by the door, stepped into the bath, drew the curtain and allowed the spiky hot water to have its way with her, streaming over her shoulders, down her back to trickle around her toes then gurgle down the plughole taking some of her tension along with it. Warmth and steam and water noises. A welcome cocoon.

She slipped into a cotton kaftan, went back downstairs again and microwaved Mrs Pickles' pie while a pot of tea brewed. Then she demolished the pie in one go, opened the mail and spooled back the ansaphone tape.

Bleep. 'This is Mr Charter's secretary at the NatWest. He wondered if you could call in and see him sometime to discuss your current account. Perhaps you could ring us when you return to arrange a mutually convenient appointment? Thank you.'

No thanks.

Bleep. Click. Silence.

Bleep. 'You know, I really hate these things. That was me just now. I rang off so's I could arrange my speech but I still don't know how to put it, so I'll get straight

217

to the point.' There was a long pause, then, 'Something's happened. We've got to talk. But not on the phone, I have to see you. I'll ring again.'

Bleep. 'Bloody machines. It's Mo. Give us a ring when you get back. As *soon* as you get back, do you hear? I think we should have a confidential natter. It's important. But machines have ears, and so do cleaning ladies, so it'll have to keep. I hope. See you.'

How intriguing. First thing tomorrow, then. Or rather, she thought as she glanced at the clock, first thing later today.

Bleep. 'Damn and blast, where are you, Kate? I'm going to keep on calling until I get you. It's important. We have to talk.'

'Alex, you're a one-man epidemic!' she said to the machine in irritation. 'No way.'

Bleep. 'Hi, Petal. Julian here. I want to see you *before* you come in to the office. Make sure you phone me at home the minute you get back. So long as it's after eleven, of course. I sleep late, weekends.'

Doubly intriguing. How wonderful to be so in demand. She shrugged.

Bleep. Click. Silence.

Bleep. 'Hi. It's Jeff.'

Stop heart. Stop tape. Start them both up again. 'Jeff Coolidge. In the States. There I was, hoping I wouldn't wake you, and I end up talking to a machine. Just my luck, huh? Listen, I just called to say . . . Oh, Christ. Look, just . . . take care of yourself, huh? Goodnight, Kate's machine.'

The rest of the tape was blank. She looked at the little grey box, grinning at it like an idiot. She spooled the tape back for a second or two and played it through again. 'It's Jeff. Jeff Coolidge. In the States . . .'

How many Jeff Coolidges do you think I know, you sweet, sweet fool?

She poured herself another cup of tea. Lit a cigarette. 'Jeff bloody Coolidge!' she said at the phone, her smile turning upside down. 'Bloody men! And bloody

218

hormones! Oh, bloody hell!' She reached out and touched the telephone. Picked it up. Put it down again. What was the point?

She went upstairs to bed.

The clock on her bedside table was showing 14.55 when the insistent ringing of the telephone pushed its way into a dream then pushed the dream out of the way and finally woke her up. She cursed herself for not reconnecting the answering machine.

'Welcome home, petal.'

'Wha . . . ? Who . . . ? Julian? What time is it? What day is it?'

'Oh God, she's jet-lagged. It's Saturday, darling. Three o'clock on a typical summer's afternoon – the angels are having a pissing contest and all's wrong with the world. Now then, have you had an absolutely marvellous time, did you bring me back a gorgeous hunky baseball player, and why don't you let your producer take you out for drinkies tonight and fill you in on what's been happening back at the cat-house?'

'Terrific! *Has* much been happening? Did you miss me?'

'The answer is "madly" to both questions. You won't *believe* what's been going on.' A pause. 'Or maybe you will. And I warn you,' his voice dropped to a serious note, 'it's not all good.'

'Then tell me now, Julian.'

'It's not for the telephone. See you later then?'

'Come *on*, Julian.'

'All in good time, petal. And we'll go in my car, okay? I've no intention of entrusting my delicate and extremely precious body to someone who's spent the last four weeks driving around on the wrong side of the road. Pick you up about nine, then. See you later.'

She was thoroughly awake now, thoroughly back in her own world – and thoroughly disturbed by it. Without moving from the bed she made a quick call to her parents to let them know she was back unmugged, unraped and unmurdered; tried to get hold of Mo but there was no reply; was tempted to throw caution to the winds and give Alex a ring on his home number (serve him right) but thought better of it; and spent the afternoon giving her face and body a much needed five-thousand mile service – face-pack, leg wax, the full treatment – while worrying over Julian's ominous hints.

'Come here, you ravishing creature!' said Julian, standing on her doorstep with his arms flung wide demanding that Kate fall into them. She did, and received a bear hug that practically squeezed the breath out of her lungs, but as it was still raining she was quickly released and they made a dash for the shelter of the car.

Soon they were settled into a discreet alcove in the corner of a pub down by the Thames: the sort of pub that was dark and cosy and full of nooks and crannies and where the beams, once upon a time, had actually grown on trees and the horse-brasses had been part of the wardrobe of some long-ago Dobbin.

There was only one thing Julian loved more than spouting gossip and sometimes even *that* took second place, but tonight his résumé of who was sleeping with whom or wasn't any more or might be but nobody's quite sure yet, was delivered in thirty seconds flat ending with, 'And so, my darling, we come to the main event. Ready? Go on, have a slurp first, I think you're going to need it.'

'Just tell me, Julian,' she said tersely, not touching the drink.

He sighed. 'Well, there are two things really . . .' He stopped, wondering how best to put it.

'Go *on*.'

'Look, petal, it's not as bad as it sounds . . .'

'Julian . . .' she warned, not lightly.

'We'll come through it okay, really. In fact, when you think about it it's probably all for the best.'

The dwindling supply of her patience ran out and she kicked him under the table. None too gently. 'Tell me!'

He looked pained. 'The Seventh Floor's been rationalising our budget.'

She knew what that meant. 'How much? How bad is it?'

He spread his hands.

Kate was about as close to committing murder as she'd ever been. But she controlled the urge. 'Julian, how *bad*?'

His face assumed the expression of a Saint Bernard feeling terribly apologetic about it but his little brandy barrel was empty. 'They slashed at the jugular. Fifty percent.' Then he went on quickly, a little too brightly, 'But I did what I could. They were even talking about dropping the whole series at one stage but I managed to persuade Ed' (he'd done nothing of the sort) 'that would be cutting off their nose to spite their faces. So we still have an *Encounter*. Most of it. Well, two-thirds of it. They've cut the run from twelve to nine.'

'They can't do that!' She was horrified. Furious. 'And that's three-quarters, not two-thirds. But they can't do it. I won't let them.'

Faces turned.

'Sssh. They can. They have. Kate, you can't stop them. Don't try or they really will cut the whole bleeding lot and we'll be out on our arses. Calm down. There's nothing we can do about it. It's a *fait accompli*.'

She steadied herself. 'The bastards,' she muttered. 'And Ed Franklin's the biggest bastard of the lot. I thought he was on *our* side.'

'He *is*, petal. Believe me. He's the one who persuaded them to cut rather than cancel,' he said, forgetting he'd just claimed that glory for himself.

Kate noticed but let it pass. She took a steadying breath. 'You said a fifty percent cutback. One quarter of the series doesn't equal a half of the budget. What about the rest?'

He flapped his hand as if brushing away a maraudimg swarm of midges. 'Oh, we can fiddle that. A little creative accounting here and there. Leave it to me. As for the other thing, well, I'm sure it'll all blow over, probably has already but . . .'

'What other thing?'

He didn't risk beating about the bush. With Kate in this mood the risk of being beaten about the head was greater. 'The gossip columns have got hold of you and Pritchard. You haven't actually been named yet but the hints have been, shall we say, a little less than veiled? And Ed Franklin laps up the gossip columns.'

'Oh, great.'

'Well, it's your own fault, petal. Haven't I always said you should never mix business with pleasure? Anyway, my advice to you now is simply to deny it all. *If* anybody asks, which I'm sure they won't. I mean, it's hardly the scandal of the century, is it? And in the meantime, live like a nun. And make sure you're *seen* to live like a nun. As I said, it's probably something and nothing. Not even a storm in a teacup. More of a damp fart.'

She considered the latest piece of information. More to herself than to Julian she said, 'So *that* explains it. There's my answering machine working overtime and there was me thinking it was my irresistible charm that caused it.' Her wine glass was still practically full. She picked it up and studiously drank it dry. Then she placed it back on the table, centring it carefully on the beer mat. She looked up at Julian, gave a short, sharp sigh, pulled back her shoulders and said, 'Oh, well. *C'est la vie.* Look on the bright side. If it does turn into a scandal it'll do wonders for the ratings.' But the words didn't sound quite as brightly philosophical as she'd intended them to.

That's when a perfect stranger with imperfect timing tapped on her shoulder. 'Excuse me, but you're Kate O'Connell, aren't you? I wonder if you'd mind signing this beer mat for me?'

'Oh Katy,' said Mo with a mixture of sympathy and despair. 'Why don't you just get married, have kids, and settle down in anonymous suburbia? It has its charms, you know.'

Kate gave a grudging sigh. 'I must admit, at times the idea does have a certain appeal.'

'On the other hand . . .' Mo glanced round the room and appraised the wine glass she held with the appreciation of a Sotheby's connoisseur.

Only an hour before she'd been up to her elbows in the washing up bowl while her son was sitting on the floor staring goggle-eyed at the television set, oblivious to his sister who was propped up by a pile of cushions, busily teething and yelling in a most unladylike manner. Ben was in the little study, door firmly closed. A great way to spend a Sunday afternoon.

Then the phone rang. And rang and rang. 'Somebody get that, will you?' Mo had called out. 'Oh, damn and blast, do I have to do everything around here?' she muttered, answering it herself with soapy hands.

'Hi. It's me. I'm back. And I think I know what you wanted to talk to me about. Are you busy? Can me and my unopened bottle of dry white tempt you away from domestic bliss for an hour or so?'

'Hold on, Katy,' she said into the phone then called out, 'Ben? Would you mind, could you manage if . . .' Then she took a leaf out of what she imagined was Kate's book and changed it to a firm, 'Ben, I'm going out for an hour or so. I'll be at Kate's. You and Sammy can get your own tea for once. Give Becky the jar of strained chicken and vegetable. And the Bonjela's in the cupboard, I think you'll need it.'

And that's how Mo came to be sitting in an every-labour-saving-device-you-can-think-of kitchen which had a fridge with wine and Perrier water in its insides and no garish paintings stuck to its outsides. There was not a Mr Man nor a stray Lego brick to be seen. And she and Kate were drinking from extremely breakable, long-stemmed, Waterford crystal glasses.

Mo filled in all the details about the Pritchard business that she'd gleaned from Ben – which weren't many. 'But he talked sense into her. There's nothing she can do.

Anyway, I should have thought if anybody was going to sue for libel it would be you. Or Alex.'

'Except for the small detail that it's all true, of course.'

'What's that got to do with anything?' said Mo. 'Anyway, it's all over now.'

Kate shook her head. 'I'm not so sure. He's been pestering me. Well, pestering my answering machine. Wants to talk.'

'Well, for God's sake, don't! You keep well out of it, my girl. Keep your head down. His phone's probably bugged.'

'Oh, Mo!' Kate smiled. 'That's ludicrous. This is England.' A moment later, almost to herself, she said, 'How could I have been so *stupid*? It's not as if I even loved the man, not really.'

'Hmm. Well, that's what you get for screwing around. You'll learn.'

'Oh, will I?' said Kate flatly. 'That's the other thing I wanted to talk to you about . . .'

And Mo's 'out for an hour or so' turned into three or four or more.

'Are you actually telling me you've finally gone and fallen in love?' asked Mo incredulously when Kate had finished a blow by blow account of her month in the States.

'Certainly not,' she said a little too certainly. And added, uncertainly, 'Well, maybe a little bit. But only with a *concept*. The idea of a home, family, you know . . .' She went on firmly, 'Anyway, he's an American. Hardly convenient.'

'Convenient!' Mo repeated the word with a kind of horror. 'God, woman, you're callous.'

'Oh, come on! A widower with a child and all sorts of shackles and a whole life going for him on the other side of the Atlantic - the whole scene cries out for a Betty Crocker Instant Wife Mix. Hardly my style, lovey. Besides, *my* life is here, my work is here. And that's another thing. I've learned my lesson as far as mixing work and my personal life is concerned, thank you.'

Mo sighed. There was a faraway look in her eyes. 'So it's *Brief Encounter* strikes again, eh?'

Kate laughed. 'You're an incurable romantic, Mo Levy. I'll stick with the O'Connell-type encounter, thank you very much. And let's face it,' she added with a touch of smugness, 'I'm not doing too badly out of it.'

'Ah, but there's more to life than money and careers and boardroom blood lettings and public scandal,' said Mo-the-sage.

'Sure there is,' replied Kate-the-realist. 'Like cleaning house and cooking meals and wiping shitty bottoms? I mean, take you for example. You're so busy being Ben's wife and Sammy's mother and Becky's . . . hell, the baby's whole life-support machine. I mean, when did you last stop and look at the label that says "Maureen Levy, Private Person"?'

'Okay, okay, so whatever way you choose there's bound to be pros and cons. And quite frankly the way things are at the moment I think I prefer my pros and cons to yours. Besides, you can't have everything.'

'Why the hell not?' cried Kate vehemently. 'I'll tell you something, Mo. I'm going to have a darned good shot at it – "Life, the Universe and Everything", as the *Hitch-Hiker's Guide* once said. And to hell with Jeff bloody Coolidge and Alex bloody Pritchard and Ed bloody Franklin and anybody else who thinks they're going to get in my way. I can outface the lot of them!'

'Atta girl!' said Mo.

It didn't occur to Kate to include Elizabeth Pritchard's name on the list of people she was willing to send across the river Styx.

Perhaps it should have done.

Chapter Fourteen

The city was an alien place. The air seemed heavier, the sky smaller. It got like this every year round about this time. Perspectives changed and instead of seeing the Big Apple all he could see was the maggots in it. The annual escape to Gilberts Pond used to be enough to unclog the energy channels and have him raring to get back in the thick of it but in recent summers the vacation had seemed never quite long enough, and the thick of it, when he returned, seemed just a little thicker each year. He was glad he was free of it, just visiting.

He walked along Fifth Avenue – a glitzy, rich heaven to some, a grimy canyon to Jeff – then turned into the building that housed Coliseum publishers. He sat in the reception area for ten minutes waiting for his new editor to come and get him. Or get to him. Depends which way you look at it. Everything and everyone else in this city was getting to him, no reason why this new guy should break the mould.

He'd got back to the apartment on Friday after leaving Kate at the airport and mooched around for a while wondering what to do with himself. He'd decided to call Laura. He had a feeling it might be a mistake. It was, sort of. Because he then had to call Danny and explain why he wouldn't be staying over in New York just for the one night like planned, it was going to be two or three. Maybe four.

'I'm sorry, Chief.'

'Aw, Dad.' The disappointment was naked, poignant.

The world revolves around little children, thought Jeff, or at least, the children believe that it does. Duty, loyalty, responsibility, those words apply to the parent, not the child. But this particular parent also had duties, responsibilities, to himself and his work – which ultimately were for Danny's benefit as well as his own. And Jeff's Coliseum editor had moved on to bigger and better publishers, said Laura. So Jeff had to break in a new one. Whom he'd never met. Whom he was going to meet, over lunch, on Monday. 'I'm real sorry, Danny, but it's very important. You know I'd rather be up there with you but . . .'

The silence on the end of the line stabbed him louder than any manipulative whining might have. Then, when the silence was broken by a subdued, 'Okay. I understand, Dad,' it was just about all he could take. Talk about guilt.

After that he called up his answering service. He wasn't expecting there to be anything much because all the people who mattered had the Gilberts Pond number. But he called anyway.

And they'd all crawled out of the woodwork.

Everybody he knew since grade school and some he didn't know he knew, had been calling to say it's been a long time and why don't we get together sometime old buddy. Dave Grantley from Sherman Whitney's. Even Nancy.

He wrote down the list of numbers to call back. If he felt like it. Later.

Then he took a walk.

'Hey, didn't I see you on the TV a coupla three weeks back?' said the barman as Jeff perched at the counter and ordered himself a long, cool beer. 'Aren't you C. J. . . . what was it, Allen, the actor on *The Brad Marvin Show*, when was it?'

'No,' replied Jeff tersely. 'I was the other guy, the sex therapist.' Bad joke. Bad mistake. Bad sex between the barman and his wife and Jeff heard all about it all the way down to the bottom of his glass.

'Do you have a telephone?'

'Sure.' The barman pointed to the wall booth.

Jeff escaped.

'Mr Coolidge! Well hello! This is Dave Grantley's

secretary. Remember? Rhoda? Gee . . . er . . . I'll put you through then.'

Mister Coolidge. A little while back she used to call him Jeffbaby.

'Jeff? Hi there. Good of you to call back. Just thought I'd give you a buzz to see how you are. Saw the show. And the spread in *Lifetime*. So how've you been keeping? *Where*'ve you been keeping? And aren't you the dark horse, writing bestsellers and never letting on that it was you. Telling us all that you were just a spare time scribbler. Jesus. No wonder you went and quit on us like that. Wouldn't I love the chance.'

'Liar. That agency's your blood and guts and you know it.'

A laugh. 'Yeah. True, I guess. Anyway, why I was phoning, Jeff – or should I call you C. J. these days?'

'Oh, don't worry about it, "sir" will do.'

'Bastard. Listen, how about a drink after work with somebody who used to know you before you were rich and famous?'

'Not rich yet. Still waiting for the cheques. And only famous till next week's headliner. And what's the matter, Dave, Arlene gone back to her mother again?'

'No such luck. You should see who we got sitting in your chair now. Some VP Creative Director! Boy, could I be creative with her. Things are looking up around here.'

'You mean you didn't call to beg me to come back?'

'Uh-uh.'

'In that case I'd love to have a drink with you. How about if I meet you at the agency? Be nice to drop in on the old place again. Seems like a lifetime since I lived there.'

It was a weird feeling entering the Matteson Building again. He felt like a displaced person. An outsider who used to be on the inside. Same elevators, same receptionists, same décor, same slick place. But it looked different. Funny, the strange look of familiar places once you've severed your links with them.

The people he used to work with didn't look any different. But they acted different. All broad smiles and enthusiastic greetings. Respect and envy in about equal parts and just a pinch of wariness in there – after all, a guy who has the temerity to ditch the rat race, and our glamorous, exciting, addictive, advertising rat race at that, can't really be, could never really have been, one of *us*. Like maybe it was Jeff who was the rat. But they were still eager to shake his paw.

And Dave Grantley was eager to share his credit. 'Didn't I always say he had talent? Good old Jeff. Scribbling away in secret. But I knew he'd make it.'

Jeff was introduced to Doran Wade, the woman who'd taken over his old position. He wished her good luck.

She smiled, thanked him, wished him the same and something about her attitude told him Dave was the one who was going to need the luck. Eighteen months, Jeff thought, two years at the most, she'll have that corner office for sure.

She was a tall woman, her height emphasised by uncompromising high-heeled shoes and dark, slim fitting, straight-skirted business suit. The epitome of the executive woman. Her dark hair was swept back severely from an angular face, the eyes, also dark – brown, almost black – looked at him forthrightly. The look seemed to say, 'I know exactly where I'm headed and I'm already well on my way'. She reminded him of Kate O'Connell.

Another twenty minutes of over-familiarity and badly-disguised envy and assurances that 'I could write a book, too, if only I had the time' (from everyone but Ms Wade) and he couldn't wait to be away from the place.

Then another half hour in Dave's company and he couldn't wait to be away from him, either. Fame, success, whatever word you want to use to define what had happened to Jeff, changes people a lot. Not the people it happens to but the people around them. Like Grantley. The only flashes of the Executive VP he was familiar with came as lustful innuendos about Charlene Prince's house party (Jeff wished he'd never mentioned it) and enquiries as to whether the groupies had latched on to him yet.

Jeff was sickened by it. As soon as he reasonably could, which was quite soon, he used the one excuse that he knew Grantley would find acceptable: 'Been great seeing you again, Dave, but I've got to go, got a date with a luscious blonde in exactly . . .' he looked at his watch for authenticity's sake, '. . . twenty-six minutes. Keep in touch, huh? See you,' and he was out of the bar and flagging a taxi as if he really *did* have to be in bed in under half an hour.

'Where to?'

That's a good question, thought Jeff, as his voice gave the apartment address.

Norman, the usually taciturn night doorman left the fortress of his desk and accompanied him chattily all the way to the elevator. All of five yards. During the journey he elicited a promise of a signed copy of *Losing Time*. And forgot to mention who was going to buy the copy to be signed.

Jeff closed the door thankfully behind him. Switched on lights though it was not yet dark, switched on the TV though he didn't intend watching, then turned on the shower which he did intend to use – he was feeling decidedly tacky.

A little while later he'd dug himself into a cosy bivouac at his desk. A pot of coffee, a carry-out pizza, the light from a single lamp. The quiet hum of an idling typewriter gradually metamorphosed into a spasmodic then increasingly steady clatter as his characters took over the action and all he had to do was listen, watch and write it down. The real world was the one that was taking place inside his head. The other one, the one he'd escaped from, with its products and campaigns and artwork and layouts and primary selling points and hooky little catch-phrases and people so upfront that they stab you in the chest not the back . . . that world didn't exist right now.

He read through the newborn paragraphs. Meeting new editor on Monday. 'Is it any good?' Kate had asked him once. He couldn't answer her then and he couldn't answer now as he re-read it. Her eventual declaration that it was 'bloody good' meant little. By that time it was hardly an objective verdict. Kate. Katy O'Connell from London, England. The typewriter hummed quietly. He reached for the phone. He knew it was breaking the rules – all that goodbye Katy, hello Ms O'Connell nonsense – but they were her rules, not his. He didn't recall ever actually agreeing to them.

In the event it didn't matter any which way because he got her answering machine . . .

The lunch meeting went off okay except for an underlying cross-current. Des Lakerman, Jeff's new editor, wanted to talk straight plot, character, plot, progress to date – and plot. Jeff just wanted to get to know the guy so he wouldn't be handing over his new baby to a total stranger.

They both gave a little and took a little. But it was hardly an instant meeting of like minds.

'Jeff, you've got to see my problem. All I have to work on is your synopsis and first three chapters. If I'm going to help you shape your novel into the follow up that *Losing Time* needs – deserves,' he added with a smile, 'then I've got to know where it's at now. So send me what you've done so far, let me read it and we can take it from there.'

'Fair enough. I take your point. But what are you saying – I sit around and twiddle my thumbs waiting for permission to carry on with the rest? What about the deadline?'

'We can be flexible on that if we have to. But keep on writing.' Another smile. 'Anyhow, writing's like sex. The more you do it the better it gets. And you're a good writer. But.' A pause which was meant to be significant.

Jeff sat right through it.

'That's not necessarily enough. The second book is always the problem one. You have a readership now, people are going to buy it because it's got your name on

231

the cover. So we don't want to leave them waiting too long. And if the new one doesn't come up to their expectations they won't bother to buy the one after that. Now that's where I come in. I'm paid to know what those expectations are. And help you meet them. So we have to work closely together on it. So you'll send me what you've done already? What is it, fifty, a hundred thousand words?'

'It'll be a few weeks,' said Jeff, not committing himself to length. 'I'll have to get it typed up properly, it's still only in draft.'

'Don't you worry about that, just send me a photostat of the draft. I'll be able to knock it into shape.'

Jeff left the meeting a little uneasy about the way Des' vocabulary had made a smooth transition from 'you' through 'we' to 'I'.

Whose book is it, anyway? he thought as he turned north on to the Interstate 87.

The question was answered when he got back to Gilberts Pond and opened the mail. He stared at the cheque. The advance had come through. And about time. A cool fifty thousand dollars.

It might be his baby, but it was Coliseum's property.

Kate kept the 'atta girl' philosophy to the forefront and carried it into TV7 with her on Monday morning. Early Monday morning. She wanted the office to herself for a while.

She sipped at the scalding hot, brown-tasting liquid from the vending machine and spared a fleeting moment to long for the old régime of but a few weeks ago. Joyce at the trolley, PPB planning programmes not cuts, and all's right with the world – even if it had been a somewhat narrower world than she now found herself in.

She studied the master plan wallboard and plunged back into positive thinking. One good thing about having three of the programmes sliced away – it meant the board was now full. Overflowing, in fact, like a veritable cornucopia. A nine-week run and ten names on the board.

Someone would have to go. There you are, Ed – instant expenditure cut and don't say I never do anything for you.

By the time Julian arrived she had a plan of action written out in longhand and waiting on his desk. 'It's just a rough draft,' she told him. 'I'll leave it to you to word it suitably for the Board or Franklin or whoever.'

He read it through, nodding mandarin-like. 'It makes sense.'

She threw him one of those looks which said: of course it does – *I* wrote it.

'Postpone Spelling,' he read aloud. He looked up at her. She was standing next to him, leaning over him, a guardian or an avenging angel, he hadn't worked out which yet. 'I like that. "Postpone". Still, I suppose it's more tactful.'

'Tact my foot. Forward with confidence. Infect the management with it. Of *course* there's going to be another series. Positive thinking, Julian.'

'If you say so, petal. But why Spelling?'

She explained, as if to a three year old, 'Because it's a one-off location. With a little juggling and a fair amount of cooperation from the gods we could combine the others. Eastwood and Collins are both West Coast. Ditto Coe, Streisand and Warren East Coast, even if Barbados is a bit southerly. The others are Europe or Britain so not much hassle there. And the other thing is that Spelling's the only one without a face – you know, big name but would *you* recognise him if he sat next to you in the canteen?'

'Makes sense. On the other hand it might be simpler just to junk the Warren. Last in, first out, principle.'

'No.'

The instant veto surprised him. But it was too early in the day to argue. He merely shrugged and said, 'You're the editor.'

It was a hectic time. Production team in full swing, meshing together like cogs in a well-oiled machine –

sometimes very well-oiled, especially after lunchtime in the club bar.

Contracts were sorted, film crews booked, travel plans finalised and hour upon hour passed when all that could be seen of Kate O'Connell was the top of her head as she read and re-read research notes, with elbows on desk, hands shading eyes, a literal tunnel vision.

Then there were the follow-up letters to her American Visitor Program hosts, with a very carefully composed one to Mel Hurley proffering a return invitation. A very useful contact. After all, Brad Marvin couldn't go on forever. A postcard of Tower Bridge addressed to Master D. W. Coolidge care of Gilberts Hollow was slipped into the out-tray. It was to become a habit, just a harmless habit.

And there were the usual summertime chores to be sorted out and fitted in or tactfully refused – the run-of-the-mill fête openings, the charity galas, the invitations to the all-star openings of London's next 'in' nightclubs. Would she be one of the judges in this year's Miss Southern Counties contest? No. Would she be the guest speaker at the next Women In Media Annual Conference? Yes. Would she care to attend a Royal Première in Leicester Square in the presence of Their Royal Highnesses, The Duke and Duchess of York? Most definitely. And . . .

They got the show on the road.

Kate: 'Come on, let's have some action around here. Now are we sure that Spelling's postponed and all the other bookings are confirmed?'

'You updated the wallboard . . .'

'Never mind that, what about the PPR? Julian, you're the producer, have you sent it?'

'Hey, hold it, hold it, who's the boss around here, you or me?'

'Quite frankly, lovey, I don't give a fart, so long as we get the ratings. So let's get going. Linda, who've we got for cameraman and sound recordist in Athens? Are they absolutely clear about what we're going to do? Happy with it? And where are those old cuttings from *Vogue*? If we start the Tamsin Coe with a full screen front page cover shot from the Sixties and just melt it into a still of the face as it is now, and then animate and into the film . . . What do you think, Julian?'

'My God, she's asking my opinion!'

'Don't worry,' said Linda soothingly, 'she always gets like this when the stress factor peaks. Over compensating. It'll go away in a couple of hours or so.'

Linda and Julian were looking at her like she was a specimen in a culture dish. 'Very funny,' said Kate. 'Meanwhile has anybody thought to collect our tickets for Athens? For tomorrow?'

'Hmm.' Julian stroked his beardless chin. 'My prognosis would be more like a couple of days than a couple of hours. Should we ignore it or pander to it? Your opinion please, Doctor Ross?'

Linda, with a perfectly straight face, said, 'Oh, pander to it, I think. Definitely pander, Doctor Howard.'

'Will you two be serious for one *minute*? The tickets?'

'Kate. Petal.' Julian flipped a glance to the plastic travel agency wallet sitting on the centre of her desktop.

'And of course the PPR's done. Last week. And this,' Linda tapped a fat blue folder on her desk, 'is the summary of the Stavros research. And you've got Pete on sound and Lorne on camera, same as you'll have for all the States locations.'

'Oh goody,' said Julian. 'Lorne's a nice boy.'

Linda calmly finished off her list and said, 'Anything else?'

Kate paused and looked at the other two looking at her. Julian was trying very hard not to smile but not quite succeeding. Linda had her arms folded across her chest making her appear defensive and aggressive at the same time. 'Yes,' said Kate, 'there *is* something else.' Suddenly she grinned. 'I'm sorry. And thanks.' She put her arms around them both and gave them a quick hug.

'Oh, did anybody remember to check on the ferry from Athens to Hydra?'

Linda slapped the flat of her hand against her forehead and glanced skyward. 'Damn it, you mean you're not going to *swim?*'

Kate laughed. 'All right, all right, you've made your point, both of you. But did anybody think to book us a car to Heathrow in the morning?' she added slyly.

'Yes!' Julian and Linda shouted back at her in unison.

Kate shrugged, took the blue folder from Linda's desk, sat at her own. 'I was only asking,' she muttered as she opened the folder and buried herself in its contents.

The phone rang. Linda answered it. '. . . Straight away? Yes, sir. I'll tell her.' Kate and Julian looked at her expectantly. 'Er, that was Mr Franklin. He wants to see Kate. In his office.'

'When?'

'Now.'

'I wonder what that could be about?' said Kate as if she didn't know. 'Oh well, best get going. Bye bye then, children.' She picked up her cup of tea and took it with her. 'See you later,' she said brightly.

Julian looked at Linda ominously. 'I hope,' he said.

Ed was sitting behind his desk, the regulation six inches bigger all round desk that denoted his senior management status. There were lots of little touches like that around the upper floors of TV7. Julian, as a producer, had carpet in his office but he could only have grey, green or brown (he'd chosen the green) and it didn't cover the whole floor. Ed's carpet was burgundy and it was wall to wall, and there was a too large for cosiness casual seating area covering half the room where he could entertain other executives and people to be impressed in the elegant comfort of low couches round a real teak veneer coffee table.

But Ed was sitting behind the desk pointedly pulling rank. 'Ah, Kate, my dear. Come in, sit down.'

She ignored the secretary's chair he indicated and settled herself into a sofa.

Ed wasn't going to relinquish the first point that easily. He remained desk-bound. For the indictment. 'I'll come straight to the point. This.' He stabbed a nicotine-stained finger at a photostated sheet of paper on his desk.

Its format was familiar. She had plenty of them herself. Handy compilations of press cuttings, compliments of TV7's library clippings service. She gave it a disdainful glance, not prepared to cross the room to take a closer look at it.

'You and Alex Pritchard.' Ed's voice was cold as he summarised the contents. 'It seems the gossip columns are trying to build up to another sex and politics scandal. Cabinet minister and, I quote, "a beautiful television personality".'

She nodded her head as if in graceful acceptance of a compliment. 'How sweet.' Then she said, 'I wonder who they can be referring to.'

'Look, Kate, between these walls, what you get up to in your own time is your own affair, excuse the pun, but when it impeaches your integrity as a front-line presenter for this company then it impeaches, *per se*, the integrity of TV7 itself . . .'

Pompous ass, she thought.

'Your position demands that you be politically unbiased, morally and personally and publicly irreproachable, and you must be seen to be so. In all respects. If you have a private life . . . well, frankly, it's best that you don't.'

Bloody nerve.

'This was folly, Kate, gross folly, even to think of getting involved in the first place. A senior politican, whom you met in the course of your work, in your position as a representative of TV7, and not only that but a married man, a family man, a pregnant wife . . . Oh Kate.' He shook his head and sighed deeply.

She almost expected him to follow it with, 'How could you *do* this to me?' rising to his feet like all the best thundering Victorians with finger thrusting doorwards ordering her never to darken that part of the architecture again. She was almost disappointed when all he did was relinquish the desk, throw himself heavily into the opposite sofa and light a cigarette. He didn't offer her one.

'Finished?' she asked.

He dragged on his cigarette and looked across at her and, oh Jesus, that was sympathy she saw in his eyes. 'Unfortunately, no,' he said, following the words with an ominously long silence which she filled up with all her secret horrors.

'You mean I'm fired?' voicing what she couldn't even let herself think about.

'Not quite. Not exactly,' he said.

'What the hell does that mean?' she burst out. 'Not quite fired. It's like saying not quite . . . not quite *dead*. You're either dead or you're not. So which is it, which am I?'

'Look, Kate, believe me I did my best with the Board of Management. Let's just say your life-support machine hasn't been unplugged yet. But it was a close call. Situation in constant review. Your contract comes up for renewal soon, don't forget.'

'Or termination.'

'Quite. And my hands are tied when it comes to a majority decision. So I advise you to keep a low profile. Very. You've got to come out of this smelling of roses.'

Some challenge. She thought about it then tossed him a half-smile. 'Oh well,' she said. 'All the best roses grow out of a pile of horse shit. Didn't you know that?'

Chapter Fifteen

They were using a non-intrusive filming technique: fly on the wall stuff with Kate keeping her on-camera profile about as high as a cellar, saving most of it for a voice-over commentary to be dubbed on later.

The technique had the practical advantage that it hardly disturbed the subject's routine. Whatever they happened to have planned, be it business, work, mayoral meeting, mucking out a stable, they just got on with it while Lorne, Pete, Kate and Julian as director, made themselves as unobtrusive as possible. As for the artistic considerations, well, it gave a (spurious) feeling of integrity and respect to what was actually much more revealing than the pushy, 'Hey, we're here with a film crew to ogle your every movement,' approach.

There were no 'set-ups' and no retakes. Actuality was the name of the footage. It had its hassles, of course – there were headaches and there were highs – but it was working.

Filming Costas Stavros at his Greek island hideaway scored mainly as a high – professionally and generally speaking. In particular, though, even sun-plumped olives, feta cheese, hot pitta bread and bottomless bottles of retsina and/or champagne couldn't help to disguise the slightly sour aftertaste which caught at the back of Kate's throat every time she remembered what might be brewing for her back home.

It was almost the end of the shoot. One more morning to film the aftermath of the villa-warming party would wrap up the social profile on Stavros then hop back to London, bone up on the Thatcher research, make a side-step to Chequers, then back to base for a quick burst of Joan Collins and manfriend on holiday in London, then was it a Mansell Grand Prix next, or Riding for the

Disabled with the Princess Royal? Take a deep breath, get your bearings and off we go again . . .

They were sitting at a table underneath an arbour of gnarled and twisting ancient vines and plucking spasmodically at the lush clusters of darkly purple grapes. Pete and Lorne were around somewhere putting their equipment to bed after a hard day and evening's work while Kate and Julian had snatched the opportunity to sneak off to a quiet hidey-hole like a couple of schoolchildren playing truant. Dusk had fallen into the arms of a balmy night, the air still and heavy and scented with the wild marjoram which grew on the hillside beyond the high white walls of the Stavros villa gardens. Julian swatted lazily at a marauding band of mosquitos and murmured, 'Ah, this is the life. What a way to earn a living, eh, petal?'

'You're just a sybaritic parasite at heart, aren't you, you old faker?' she said to him affectionately. She bit into another grape. Its juice was sweet. The expression which flitted briefly across her face was not.

'What's the matter, my angel? Come on, tell Uncle Jules.'

She sighed. 'You know perfectly well. The more I try not to think about it, the more I can't *help* thinking about it. And each time I run it through it gets more and more sordid.'

'What happened to all your positive thinking?'

A feeble joke: 'I'm not sure.'

'Petal, what you do in your own time is your own business, right?'

'Wrong,' she said. 'Not according to Ed Franklin.' She gave a little exclamation of disgust. 'Who'd have thought TV7 would get sucked into all this Victorian moral values crap? And if they have to, why can't they take on board some of the Victorian hypocrisy that used to go with it, that's what I want to know? It's not as if I'm still involved with him even! The affair's history, for God's sake. It's not fair!'

'Kate O'Connell, now just you listen to me.' This was

240

Julian's about-to-deliver-a-lecture voice. 'What's done is done. No use just sitting around on your pretty little backside and moaning about it.'

'What do you suggest I do? Throw myself into my work?' This, from someone who'd spent the last weeks doing nothing but, and doing it brilliantly.

'As if I could stop you,' he grinned. 'No. I was thinking perhaps it's time you entered the arena yourself. Come clean, go public, sell your story to the Sundays or something!'

'Really? A good, clean, mud-slinging contest? How sordid. And there was me having this quiet little fantasy of digging myself a nest in a very far away suburbia and turning into an anonymous housewife.'

'*Really?*' he imitated her inflection.

There was a long pause. Then Kate said, 'No. *Not* really.' She bit into another grape almost viciously.

Julian wondered whose head she was imagining it to be.

'Alex, I don't . . .' She stopped to concentrate on the breathing exercises. Light breaths, using only the top part of her lungs. Her chest rose and fell, rose and fell, and Alex kept on driving.

He kept to the speed limit, stopped at the red lights, wished he'd called an ambulance, wished, fleetingly, that the baby had chosen *Question Time*, any time, but not the bloody parliamentary summer recess, for its all too imminent maiden speech.

She relaxed into the seat again. Finished her sentence. 'I don't want you there. Oh, Christ . . .' The breathing was quicker. 'Another one . . .' she gasped.

Alex shot her a panicked glance. He wondered if they were going to have any choice in the matter.

They didn't.

Elizabeth felt a warm gush of fluid between her legs and the pale yellow wetness flooded her clothes, ran down her legs, dripping over the maroon leather upholstery, soaking into the carpet. She said, 'I'm sorry,' and kept on panting.

She was well into the second stage of labour by the time they reached Maternity. She was whisked away from him, straight into the delivery room, and he was still struggling with mask and gown when he heard the scream. Just one. A cry which seared down his spine with spikes of ice. Surely not human. Not Elizabeth?

Then there was silence.

Broken by that unmistakable, rasping bleating of the newborn.

An eternity passed.

A plump, squat, green-clad figure bustled through the swing doors. Brown eyes and glistening brown forehead visible above the mask. 'Are you the father?'

He took a step forward, pushed on the door.

'You can't go in yet.' The hand on his chest was firm. 'It's all right. They're both fine. It's a boy. But I'm afraid your wife tore quite badly, it was so quick. The doctor's seeing to her now. The waiting room's just along there.'

He followed her directions as if she were his Permanent Under Secretary. And he waited.

And waited some more.

Nobody came.

He walked apprehensively back along the corridor. Nobody stopped him. He came to the room, checked through the window in the door. Elizabeth.

Elizabeth suckling their baby. His son. He pushed on the door and entered.

She was gazing down at the tiny bundled creature nuzzling and rooting at her swollen breast. Her face was flushed, hair damp, the gentlest smile lifting the corners of her mouth.

Alex watched, motionless. He felt a rush of love for her, for them, wanted to hold her in his arms, beg her forgiveness, promise . . . anything. Anything. His wife, the mother of his children. He took a step forward.

Elizabeth caught the movement. Looked up at him.

And her face changed, the eyes deadened. Wearily, flatly, she said, 'Go away, Alex.'

The story had well and truly broken. No lone stringer at the airport this time, but a whole bank of flashguns, a jostle of eager reporters.

'When did you last see Alex Pritchard?'

'Did you know his wife's just had a baby boy?'

'Is it true that you're the other woman in the Pritchard Affair?'

'Now that the Pritchards have separated do you and the Minister intend to marry?'

It was target practice down at the asylum except the inmates were all trained marksmen.

Julian, looking somewhat pale, was dragging at her elbow and muttering, 'Just duck and keep on moving, petal.'

But Kate had no intention of ducking. She held her shoulders straight and her head proud. She did, however, keep on moving. It was also one of the rare occasions in her life when she opted for predictability as the best course – but she didn't actually say, 'No comment', she simply made none.

The TV7 limousine provided a sanctuary of sorts but it was a brief one. They turned into the quiet road along by the river and there they were, a stolid thicket outside her high garden wall. 'It's no good,' Kate said when the driver suggested they try round the back, 'they'll be there as well.'

'What now?' asked Julian. 'Feel like running the gauntlet?'

'No,' she said, trying on a brave smile. It wilted before it reached maturity. 'Just running.'

'You can come back to my place if you like.'

'Thanks, Julian, but . . . driver? Do you know Stamford Brook? And do you think you could get us there without being followed?'

Ten minutes later and a little travel-sick they drew up outside the Levy residence without having been stopped for speeding. Miracle number one. The street looked blissfully, beautifully, boringly deserted – suburbia on a weekday evening. Miracle number two.

Julian, assuming the mantle of the knight protecting the lady's honour, insisted Kate remain in the back seat until he checked out the premises. 'I'm not leaving you until I know you'll be all right,' he said. He rang the doorbell.

Mo answered it. 'Julian?' Very surprised.

'Hello. I have a fugitive in the car looking for sanctuary. Kate's place is swarming with the press. Can we come in?'

The children were in bed. Kate, Julian, Mo and Ben were sprawled about the sitting room carpet, although you couldn't see much of the carpet because it was covered in a week's worth of *Guardians*. 'For once in her life she's not complaining that I forget to put the rubbish out,' said Ben.

'Pity you don't get *The Sun*,' said Julian.

But the upshot was, as Ben and Mo had been almost certain, that no one had actually been named as the third party in the Pritchard affair. Kate's involvement was rumour, vile rumour and speculation.

'But is it true?' asked Ben, looking Kate straight in the face.

She held his gaze and gave back a firm, 'No comment.'

Ben grinned. 'Good girl. Just stick with that for as long as you can.'

Mo began to shuffle the papers together. She was quite vicious about it. 'So what now? Do you want to stay the night here or are you going to try and go home?'

'Got to face it sometime. Might as well get it over with.'

Mo left the papers in an untidy heap and stood up. 'Come on then. I'll give you a lift.'

'Time I was getting home too,' said Julian. Mo looked a question at him and he said, 'It's okay. Thanks, but I'll ring for a taxi.'

They turned off Chiswick High Road and wiggled

round into Sutton Court Road heading for the Strand on the Green by one of Mo's famous 'devious routes'. Her history of navigating by instinct had given her a knowledge of W4, 5 and 6 that would have been envied by many a cabbie. As she crossed the A4 and switched right into a warren of expensive back streets she said, 'Are you sure you want to do this? You can stay at our place for as long as you like, you know.'

'I know. And thanks. But I have a suitcase full of grubby clothes, a million and one things to do and . . .' She turned to Mo and smiled '. . . and you know damn well that I'm lying. I just want to be home, Mo. *My* home. Know what I mean?'

'Course I do.' They were in Riverview Grove now. Nearly there. 'Listen, Katy, do you want me to stay the night with you? I can if you like. Ben could cope.'

'Oh Mo. What would I do without you? But no, really, I'll be okay. You go on back home. I'll survive, honest.'

Mo grinned. 'I don't doubt it. It was the reporters I was worried about.'

She needn't have been. There were only two left and they were sitting on the fence across the road throwing chips at a couple of desultory ducks, making them swim for their supper. 'You know,' said Mo, 'if we called a bobby we could probably get them for loitering with intent.'

'Who? The ducks or the reporters?'

'The ducks, of course. Are you ready?'

'As I'll ever be.'

'Shall I create a diversion so you can nip in without them seeing you?'

'Like what? Run over the ducks?'

'Uh-uh. My car can't swim. I could run over the reporters, though?' Mo stopped the car. She quickly looked around then threw it into reverse and did a three-point turn.

'What *are* you doing?'

'You'll see.' Then, engine protesting, she backed along the street at high speed, jolting to a halt directly beside

Kate's gate so there was only the footpath between the passenger door and the passenger's private property. 'Now go on. Scoot. Try and call me tomorrow.'

Kate wasted no time in thankyous and goodnights. She was out of the car, keys at the ready, and unlocking the door into her garden before the reporters had recovered their frightened wits.

The gate slammed shut. The lock clicked. The newsmen banged their fists against the sturdy wood then dashed round the front of the car and scrabbled at Mo's window. 'Who are you? Was that Kate O'Connell?'

'No comment!' Mo shouted back at them as she slammed the car back into first gear and drove off laughing. She hadn't enjoyed herself so much in ages.

It was easier in the morning. It's wonderful what a few hours' sleep, a face of fresh make-up and a little Jean Muir tailoring can do for your perspective. Last night Kate had felt the weight of muggy stormclouds closing in on her. This morning she was going to breeze over the top of a storm in a teacup.

She left by the front door.

'Miss O'Connell, would you confirm that you are in fact the other woman involved in the Pritchard business?' Weary but persistent.

'No comment.'

'Are you denying it then?'

'No comment.'

TV7. Show the ID card. 'Morning, Miss O'Connell,' said the security man.

She almost said, 'No comment.'

'Morning, Kate,' sang Linda as her boss walked into the office. 'You got here then.'

Kate smiled. 'You could say that. So, how's things? Everything been running smoothly while we were away?'

'Like sandpaper.'

'Nothing changes.'

Kate was wrong on that score. Public opinion had changed.

The crank mail, the hate mail, started coming in handfuls. One or two a week used to be the norm. Now it was three or four a day.

'Oh, my God,' said Linda, sickened, as she gingerly pushed a crumpled piece of lined notepaper to the edge of her desk. The handwriting was hardly legible, the paper was smeared with a pale reddish-brown stain. It wasn't ink.

'*I've got something special for whores like you,*' read another one. The enclosed semen-filled handkerchief was a sampler.

'*Here's a lock of my hair,*' said another which scattered a shower of short, dark, wiry hairs over the office floor.

'*I'd like to cut your tits off,*' screamed another one, written in green felt tip and enclosing a naked and gleaming razor blade.

After that, anything addressed to Kate O'Connell was diverted via Security for vetting before she or her assistant saw it.

And Kate kept a low profile.

She spent her evenings, when they didn't involve any filming, working quietly at home in a sitting room furnished with cardboard boxes full of press cuttings. It never failed to surprise Kate just how many printed references there were to people who had a 'name'. Two-line snippets here, three-page colour spreads there. She reckoned she could probably have come up with a photocopy of Tamsin Coe's pet chihuahua's vaccination certificate somewhere – if such a creature ever existed.

When her head began to ache and facts began to blur into an impossible jigsaw puzzle before her eyes, she knew it was time to call it a day. She switched on the television set but watching it was too close to work for comfort so she switched it off again. She considered reading – a novel, a magazine, the phone directory. Even got as far as running a finger along the bookshelf but the thought of all that small print put her off. She toyed with the idea of taking a shower or making a phone call.

Mixing a face-pack, fixing a drink. Hitting McDonald's, knitting a sweater, writing a letter.

She settled for the drink and the telephone.

'Hi, Ben. Is Mo around?'

'Ah, the scarlet woman of W4.'

'Don't you start.' A moment later, 'Mo, how d'you fancy a night on the town?'

'Terrific. When?'

'Now.'

'My darling girl, it's gone eleven!' To hear her, you'd think Kate had suggested a trip to Pluto and back. 'Ben and I were just on our way to bed.'

Lucky for some. 'Oh. Yes of course. Silly idea anyway. Hope I didn't wake the kids.'

'So do I.'

'Look, how about if we go out for lunch?' suggested Kate feeling more and more incarcerated.

'Inflict Becky on a restaurant, you must be off your head. No. Tell you what, you come round here. Sunday lunch?'

'Lovely. Great. Thanks. See you then. 'Night, lovey.' Kate put down the phone and went to bed with a clipboard, a pencil and a fat blue folder for companionship.

'Darling,' said Lady Bickerdyke anxiously as she sat on the edge of Elizabeth's bed, 'I hate to see you like this. Are you sure you're doing the right thing? Daddy and I . . .'

'Don't fuss, Mummy. I'm perfectly all right. And I know exactly what I'm doing.' She glanced into the cradle at the side of the bed where Edward Alexander Arnold Pritchard slept the sleep of the soundly drunk. It was an antique cradle, hand-carved oak, a family heirloom (Bickerdyke side, not Pritchard) festooned in brand new pale blue frills. Elizabeth set it gently rocking. She smiled as she looked up at her mother. 'I'm just making sure Alex sweats a little. He'll come running. When I'm ready. You don't think he'd risk losing this, do you? His long-awaited son and heir?'

Lady Bickerdyke sighed. Looked from grandson to daughter. 'But *is* he? Sweating, as you put it? And *where* is he?'

'At home.'

'Maybe today. But what about tomorrow? Have you thought that while you're up here playing your touch-me-not games he's free and available and up for grabs by, I've got to say it, that O'Connell woman?'

A fleeting doubt crossed Elizabeth's brow. Then she said, with a stoicism that surprised her mother, 'I know. And that's the way I want it. Alex is the one who has to make the choice, Mummy. And I wouldn't want him back unless he'd made that choice. Was sure of it. I won't be second best.'

There was a dignity and a pride in the words that wrung at Lady Bickerdyke's heart. Her daughter, her little girl. Second best. Never.

'You're playing a dangerous game, Elizabeth. The woman has such a high profile. I mean, it's not as if she were some little floozy from Woolworths . . .' (As if Alex had ever set foot in Woolworths.) '. . . I mean, well, she'll be there, won't she, at the press of a button, in your own *drawing room*. Even if you're right and he's not, well, tempted any more, think of the humiliation. There she'll be, a constant reminder, flaunting herself from your own television set.' Lady Bickerdyke gave a little shudder. 'It doesn't bear thinking about.'

'That's where you're wrong, Mummy. I've thought about it a lot. And I was wondering . . .' Elizabeth's voice took on a slightly wheedling note. 'After all, TV7's one of Daddy's directorships, isn't it?'

'Well yes, but . . .' Lady Bickerdyke smiled then and patted Elizabeth's finely-boned hand. 'Well, well. Don't bother yourself about it any more, darling, just leave your father to me.'

That evening, when the two girls had said goodnight to their beautiful new baby brother and Elizabeth was taking a nap before dinner, Lady Bickerdyke had one of her 'quiet words' with her husband.

'You see my point, Arnold, surely? I won't have it, it's an impossible situation for Elizabeth to be in. Can't we do something, anything? Get the woman out of the way?' She gave a little shudder of distaste. 'Get her hanged, drawn and quartered, for all I care. She deserves it.' She poured two glasses of sherry and gave one to her husband. 'Surely you could tweak a few strings here and there, Arnold? After all, what's the point of having influence if you never *use* it?'

He considered. For so long that Lady Bickerdyke thought he might have forgotten what he was supposed to be considering. Then he said, 'Damn it, old girl, you're right!' He knocked back the sherry in one mouthful. Strode determinedly to the telephone, flipped open the leather-bound address book, ran his finger down the F's and dialled.

'Ah, Franklin, old chap, glad I caught you. Bickerdyke here.'

'Sir Arnold!'

'I was wondering if you fancied a round of golf on Sunday. Little matter I want to discuss with you . . .'

'You wouldn't believe the sick people out there,' Kate said to Mo that Sunday sandwiched between Stringfellow's and Gatcombe Park after she'd helped the Levys dismantle a roast chicken. Kate was washing up, Ben was drying and Mo was stacking the dishes on shelves. 'God knows what those poor guys in Security have been opening up during these last few days. It's sick. Really sick.'

'Frightening, I call it,' said Mo with a little clatter of crockery. 'If that's the price of fame, you can keep it.'

'Must I?' said Kate.

'But you've got to face it,' threw in Ben pragmatically, 'it's your own fault, Kate. You're the one who went digging your nose into beds that didn't belong to you.'

'Thanks a lot. And for the record, Levy,' she flicked a fistful of soap bubbles at him, 'I didn't. It was always on

250

my *own* bed.' She grinned. 'Well, not always on the bed, actually, but we won't go into the minor details.'

'Look Kate, I don't want to come down heavy on you, but speaking as a barrister I ought to warn you that you might just have to. In court.' It was most unlikely, because from what Ben had heard so far he doubted the Pritchards would get as far as the divorce courts, but it was his way of getting his own back for the way he'd been kept in the dark right up to the moment he'd put two and two together for himself and come up with his wife's best friend.

Mo groaned. 'You're not serious?' She looked even more horrified at the thought than Kate did.

'It depends,' he said, playing it out to the full. You could almost see his dusty wig. If he'd been wearing braces his thumbs would have been hooked into them just like if he'd been wearing his courtroom gown. As he didn't wear braces he made do with pacing up and down the kitchen flapping the teatowel around for emphasis. 'How vindictive is Elizabeth feeling, would Alex put up any kind of defence, would he counter-sue? Though I can't imagine he'd have any grounds against a sweet little thing like Elizabeth.'

The glance which passed between Mo and Kate practically groaned aloud. 'Don't say another word,' said Kate firmly. 'I don't want to hear.'

Later, they all went for a walk round the perimeter of the fenced-in green opposite the house. Mo pushed Rebecca in the lie-back buggy, Ben and Sammy were sporadically ahead of them or behind them depending on which one had kicked the football. Kate was part of it all and apart from it all, walking along thoughtfully and in silence.

Mo nudged her and grinned. 'Look at us. One big, happy cliché, eh?'

'So what's wrong with being a living cliché?' said Kate dolefully.

'Hey, come on, Katy, snap out of it. Just because you've got a slight touch of Kate O'Connell versus the rest of the world, so what's new? When did you ever like things easy? You used to thrive on this sort of thing.'

'Maybe it's old age. The big three-oh.'

'Bollocks.'

There was a slight pause, then Kate said, 'Or maybe I'm just jealous. Of you.'

'Well, I can understand that. Good-looking, intelligent husband. Beautiful, intelligent children . . .' She said it lightly but they both knew she believed every adjective. 'You know what your real problem is?'

'Which particular one are you referring to?'

'What you need, my girl, is a good man and a baby or two.' It was Mo-the-sage again. 'That'd put you to rights. That's what *real* life is all about.'

'Jesus.' Kate couldn't believe what she was hearing. 'You can take clichés a bit too far sometimes. Come off it, Mo, you can't be serious? Can you?' Kate wasn't too sure. And sometimes, she wasn't too sure that Mo was wrong.

Mo ignored her friend's disgust and went on blithely, 'But you're frightened. Shit-scared of really getting involved. You think you're going to lose your precious independence, or God forbid, somebody might come along who actually means more to you than your career. So you aim your emotions at safe targets. They're either gay like Julian, or they're married, or you're so damned choosy that a nice, ordinary, attractive, respectable, *available* man doesn't even get a look in.'

'You mean somebody like Ben, I suppose?'

'Hands off. I said "available". Actually, I was thinking more along the lines of your American friend.'

'Oh, not that again.'

'Why not? You'll be seeing him again soon, won't you? Just open your mind, not to mention your legs,' she added lowering her voice in deference to Sammy's proximity, 'and give it a go. And while you're at it you could always leave your birth pills at home.'

'You're off your head.'

252

'Lots of women do it these days. Opt for single mother-hood. And why not?'

'I'm not arguing. Don't think I haven't thought about it.'

'Well then?'

'Well what?'

'You and your randy writer.'

'Don't be ridiculous. It's going to be a straightforward professional engagement with C. J. Warren the author. Nothing more. Clear?'

'Methinks the lady doth protest too much,' sang Mo.

'Look, just leave it, will you? I wish I'd never told you. Forget it – *I* have. Just a holiday dalliance. I don't know what got into me.'

Mo smirked. 'Better delete what I just said about you being choosy then!'

'Cow.'

Ed had always regarded his Sunday afternoon round of golf as a gentlemanly recreation, a civilised way of getting physical exercise and mental therapy.

Sir Arnold Bickerdyke was about to change all that, like he'd changed the tenor of Ed's working life. First the power play at TV7 – and Ed wasn't grumbling. And now it intruded on to the golf course – Ed still wasn't grumbling – not to Sir Arnold's face, anyway.

'Ah, Ed old chap, glad you could make it,' had been the oh so civilised greeting. 'Wanted to have a quiet word . . .'

Quiet it had been. Like the first imperceptible rumblings that barely register on the Richter Scale and then wham, bang, the ground opens up and swallows you. To be more precise, Ed *wished* that it would.

'Do you have children, grandchildren, Ed?' He left no space for an answer. 'I have. A daughter. Only child. Oh, they're a worry, children. Even when they're grown up, well, she's still my little girl, you understand what I mean?'

Ed did, but he didn't understand what the Chairman of the Board of Directors was leading up to.

'My little Elizabeth. She's home with us now, just produced another grandchild, boy this time, splendid little fellow. But the point is, she's home with *us*. That husband of hers . . .' The pause was illustrated by a shake of the head and then a whacking great sweep at the ball which took it, much to Ed's consternation, on to the very edge of the green. He stood back while Ed took his turn to tee up. 'She married fairly well. Could have done much better for herself of course but at the time Alex seemed to be a decent sort of chap, good prospects.'

Elizabeth. Alex. The swathes of solid green golf course didn't seem quite so solid under his feet suddenly. Ed swung his club back.

'Good political prospects. Pritchard, you know. Alex Pritchard, that's my son-in-law.'

Terrific timing. Ed's driver swiped at the ball for a clear miss.

'Oh, bad luck, old chap. Try again.'

The trouble with people in high places doing you little favours like casting the vote that turns you into the Head of Programming is that they seem to think you owe them a little favour or two in return.

'My daughter means the world to me, Ed. Her happiness. And if there's anything I can do in my own little way to keep her happy, then by God I'll do it. Understand?'

By the time they were on the ninth hole Ed understood only too well. Play his cards right and who knows what further promotion might drop his way. Trouble was, he was lumbered with a sneaky little echo in the place recently vacated by his conscience, a little echo that kept insisting that it didn't particularly like the cards.

Chapter Sixteen

Danny had two scrapbooks now. The first, of his father's publicity tour, had given him the postcard collecting bug. The second, which he grandiosely called his 'British and European Collection', showed that the passing infection had developed into a full-blown, chronic syndrome.

Every day he took it upon himself to walk into Gilberts Hollow to see if there was any mail. Sometimes he'd go alone, sometimes with one or both of his grandparents, sometimes it was just Danny and his father, though that didn't happen too often because Jeff had become almost fanatical about putting in a regular day's writing with regular hours.

Danny wasn't sure what to make of it. Sometimes he thought his dad had really flipped the way he'd disappear upstairs with the words, 'I'm off to work now, see you later, have a good day,' just like he had a real job in a real office somewhere. He was convinced that if they had a subway from the kitchen to the spare bedroom Jeff would have taken it. The only saving grace was that he didn't put on a suit and tie in the mornings. Yet.

While Jeff worked, Danny did all the things that small boys do in the long days of summer out of school. He scraped his knees, got dirty, swam a lot, did secret things in the treehouse – and showed off a lot of picture postcards to anybody who'd look. And it wasn't just Tom and Robbie Straker who admired them: his dad showed an inordinate amount of interest in them, too.

The brief messages were bright, funny. Like the one of the Acropolis in Athens:

Roses are red, violets are smelly,
Ancient Greek history turns me to jelly.
(I believe that's 'Jello' to you colonials.)
love, Kate.

Jeff tried very hard to read between the lines but if there was anything there for him the ink was invisible. He was brought up short every time by the unchanging and all-encompassing postscript: '*Give my regards to your family.*'

An imposing stately mansion in the heart of the English countryside: '*The Prime Minister's country cottage*,' said the message.

A selection of tourist views of London – Big Ben, Buckingham Palace, the Crown Jewels, The Tower.

A card with an Austrian stamp, a picture of a Williams Formula One racing car: '*Kate tells me you're the real champ*,' signed by Nigel Mansell.

With every new one Jeff would shrug and say, 'What – she didn't send one for *me*?' It became a standing joke.

Except Jeff didn't find it all that funny. Not a card, not a letter, not a phone call. Nothing except documents from TV7 signed by people he didn't know confirming arrangements for *The O'Connell Encounter* with C. J. Warren.

The fact prodded at a whole hornets' nest of thoughts, feelings, tenaciously sticky memories that he'd been working hard at sealing over. Working hard but not too effectively. Ever since he'd left Kennedy Airport that crazy, seems-like-forever-ago day, it had been like he was two people.

One of them was like a little kid with a birthday coming up, or a hopeful adolescent on Valentine's Day carrying on a desperate love/hate relationship with the US mail, the telephone company. Every day he hoped, and every day he was disappointed. His phone calls were never transatlantic and his mail contained either junk, or window envelopes, or nothing.

The other Jeff was a sensible, logical, adult person who could say to himself, 'Okay, Coolidge, you picked up a little sting here so apply the standard remedies.'

He tried them all.

Dabbing at it with a cotton ball soaked in witch-hazel – homespun comfort at Gilberts Pond with his mother spouting her subtle philosophies like, 'I wish you could find yourself a nice girl, Jeff, the kind of girl who was brought up to be a wife and mother. I worry about you and Danny, living on your own in that apartment when he goes back to school. It's not . . . normal.'

He tried bathing the wound in warm water – took Dorothy Bemis out on a couple of evenings, nice meal, a movie over in Cooperstown, could have ended up in bed together. But it wouldn't have been 'making love', just 'making it'. The idea left him cold.

Latterly, it was applying a squirt of instant high-tech Freezeazy. He'd gone out and spent some of his cheque on a personal computer, disc drive, word processor, software, monitor and printer, which put paid, once and for all, to the idea of moving into the woodshed. But at least he didn't clatter any more. He clicked and beeped instead.

The last cure was working well – or at least, Jeff was. Averaging two thousand words a day of new stuff and that was after hacking all the old lot into his new toy first. Even better, as he read it through he'd enjoyed it, been quite impressed with some of it. Keep this up and he reckoned he'd have the first draft completed by Thanksgiving, no problem. Mind, he was pushing himself pretty hard, starting early, forgetting to take meal breaks, finishing late. And even when the first draft was done there'd be the re-writes to tackle. Still, he reminded himself, he had Des to guide him through that so it shouldn't prove too difficult.

He leaned back in the chair and stretched. He'd done enough for today. And he had to get Des' printout down to the post office before Beth Straker shut up the store. So, with a little pat of thanks, he switched off the hardware, picked up the satisfyingly heavy brown envelope and went in search of company.

William was out on the lake determined to fish for their supper. Emily had walked into Gilberts Hollow with a shopping bag to make sure they'd *get* supper. Danny was around somewhere being far too quiet to be up to

anything but mischief. Or so Jeff thought. 'Danny? Dan-
nee! Anybody home? Fancy a drive?'

No answer.

Jeff found Danny in his little bedroom at the back of
the house, window shut tight, and when Jeff entered, face
shut as tight as the window. 'Hey. What gives, Chief?'

Danny shrugged and turned a page of the book he
obviously wasn't reading.

'I've packed it in for the day. Wanna come for a drive?
I have to drop this in at the post office so maybe we'll
catch up with Grandma, give her a ride home again.
What do you say?'

No answer, not even a shrug this time.

'Okay, no problem, this can wait till tomorrow. How
about if we go out and play ball? My shoulders are stiff,
I could do with the exercise . . .'

Another page turned. Noisily.

Jeff had one more shot. 'Take a walk then . . . maybe
stroll out to Grandpa's boat?'

'That's silly.'

At last. 'I know it. But it got you talking to me. What's
the matter? I get the distinct feeling that suddenly my
face doesn't fit around here.'

'Go away, will you, Dad?'

Jeff did just the opposite. He sat on the bed, took the
book out of Danny's hands and felt his forehead to check
if he had a raised temperature.

The boy squirmed away. 'Leave me alone. I'm all right.
Just want to be on my own, okay?' he said irritably.

'No, it isn't okay,' said Jeff. 'On your own is okay but
being rude about it is not. A friendly request for company
should be met with a friendly answer. If it's no, that's
fine, but you watch your manners.' He paused to give
Danny a chance to apologise.

He did, grudgingly.

'That's better. Now if you really want to stay cooped
up in here all day, on a lovely afternoon like this, then
that's up to you and I'll leave you to it even though I
think you're off your head. But I'll leave you to it *after*

we've had a talk. So what's wrong? If it's something I've done then tell me. Maybe I ought to apologise but if I should it's only fair that you tell me why. Why the sulks?'

'I'm not sulking. What's it to you anyway? You're never around to notice.'

'Ah. Look, Chief, even though I'm here I still have to work, you know,' he pointed out reasonably. But since when can you reason with a kid who's upset?

'It's not real work,' Danny muttered. 'I liked it better when you had a proper job. At least then I knew. When you went to work you went to work and when you came home you came home. But now you're here all the time but you're still working. All the time. I liked it better before,' he repeated stolidly. 'The Pond is our vacation. Supposed to be.'

It was quite a speech for a boy of seven and it had a seven year old's impeccable logic: black is black, white is white, and don't bother me with shades of grey because I'm not interested.

'Uh-uh,' said Jeff, 'the lake is *your* vacation. Grown-ups don't always get one.' Danny still wasn't looking at him. Jeff wasn't even sure if he was listening or not. He went on anyway. Sort of casual, conversational. 'Things have been changing pretty fast recently, haven't they? We'd got ourselves a nice, comfortable routine going, year in, year out, you and me. We knew where we were going and we made a good team. But it's only the routine that's shifted, isn't it? The team's still the same.' He tucked a finger under Danny's chin and tilted his face round. 'Oh, Danny. I still need you. I need you on my side more than ever now.'

Danny didn't look as though he believed a word of it.

'Okay,' Jeff conceded. 'Maybe I have been working a little too hard recently. But if we stick at it, we'll get into another routine, one that suits us both. Except I can't do it all by myself, Chief. You're part of the picture.' He put his arm round Danny's shoulder and gave him a quick, firm hug. 'A very necessary part. Very important.'

Still no answer.

'Hey, come on, things aren't so bad. And it'll be worth it in the long run. But *now* is pretty crucial, you know. This second book has got to be good.'

'Why?'

'*Why?*'

'Yes. Why? You've done one already. Why do you have to go and do another one, why can't you just leave it there?'

Jeff couldn't help smiling. 'One word,' he said. 'Money.'

'But you've made lots,' Danny protested.

'Is that what you think? Time we had an economics lesson here. How's about if we do it outside, take that drive, and I'll try to explain things as we go along?'

Danny considered. Then he said, 'Okay.' They walked to the door, Jeff first, Danny following. Then Danny stopped. 'Dad?'

Jeff turned.

'Did you mean it?' A small voice, a face so full of insecurity that it churned at Jeff's guts. '*Do* you really need me?'

He could have cried, that the question needed to be asked. He smiled instead and held his arms stretched out wide. 'You betcha!' he said brightly. 'About *this* much. Times a million or so.'

Danny came to him and hugged him round the waist. Then he mumbled into his father's stomach, 'So why can't I come to New York with you when you go to do Kate's film? I'm the one she writes to. And if I'm part of the team, I want to be in the film as well.'

At last, the root of the problem. And it would have been real easy to fall back on 'You can't because I say so'. But Jeff was determined never to be that kind of father.

So they drove into Gilberts Hollow and on the way he tried to explain, in simple terms, all about the professional life/private life dichotomy. He applied it to Kate as well as himself, pointing out how difficult it would be for her to concentrate on making a good TV programme if Danny were around to remind her of all the fun things she'd rather be doing instead. He also explained, yet again, his reluctance to have either Danny, or Emily and William, or even Gilberts Pond itself, for that matter, exposed to public scrutiny.

He thought he made rather a good job of it.

'I think you're just being mean,' said Danny.

Maybe 'because I say so' would have been okay after all.

One morning, after about a week of trying out a new teamwork routine which involved Jeff taking an hour every day for lunch and coming downstairs again at five pm sharp, Danny and his grandparents took a stroll into Gilberts Hollow to pick up some provisions and see if there was any mail. Emily and William passed the time of day in the store with Mrs Straker while Danny went into the yard out back to brandish his new postcard at her sons.

'Jeff's ladyfriend certainly gets around, doesn't she?' said Beth Straker, storekeeper, postmistress, official repository of township gossip and reader of all open mail. 'Taken herself off to Barbados now, I see.'

'Yes. Nice girl,' and 'She's not his ladyfriend,' said William and Emily respectively and in unison.

Jeff didn't get to see the mail until he emerged for lunch, by which time Danny had been hard at work on the scrapbook. Jeff dutifully admired the silver sands and frondy palms of Discovery Bay and wished his son hadn't been quite so efficient with the cowgum. 'So what did she say on the back of it?'

'Oh, the usual.'

Jeff smiled. 'And she didn't send one for *me*?'

Danny shook his head and began flipping through his collection again. He muttered, as if it were the dullest thing in the universe, 'No. You only got a letter.'

Looking at the single page you'd never guess that Kate had been weeks composing it.

The first draft, which had begun, '*Darling*', had been

scribbled under the influence of Jeff's Ansaphone message and the bottle of wine she'd shared with Mo that first Sunday afternoon back from the States; the day she'd expansively declared she was going to have it all and to hell with everybody. She slept on it, tore it up and went to the office to work on the *Encounter* schedules instead.

The next attempt came shortly after she'd had her lecture from the Head of Programming. That one had started, '*Dear C. J.*', and after one or two alterations had finally been torn into little pieces and scattered from the deck of the Athens to Hydra ferry.

There was a straightforward, '*Dear Jeff*', version which started around the Austrian Formula One Grand Prix, grew more iron-fisted during the Margaret Thatcher profile, and was finally abandoned as altogether too inhibited and stuffy after Kate had spent a wonderful evening at Stringfellows sharing the social life of a vacationing Joan Collins & Co.

After that one came a, '*My dear Jeff*', prompted by Mo's 'open your mind and legs and give it a go' heart to heart. That one really belonged on perfumed pink notepaper with crimply-cut edges and had landed in the kitchen rubbish bin pretty damned sharpish.

The final version, again a plain, '*Dear Jeff*', had followed Kate's *Encounter* with the Princess Royal. It was businesslike but friendly, it got on with the job but showed a sense of humour, whilst at the same time drawing a line of protocol that was not to be crossed.

Never let it be said that Kate O'Connell was impressionable.

This last had been slept on, glossed up, cleaned and sanitised until, its author finally satisfied, it was dropped into a post office in Marhill Street, Bridgetown, Barbados, along with the habitual postcard to Coolidge Jnr, after Kate had done a quick recce of Cave Shepherd & Co, the island's leading department store.

Barbados had hit her like a wall. She'd walked directly from the Caribbean Airways DC–10 down the steps and on to the tacmac at Grantley Adams Airport and after

262

the controlled air conditioning of the flight it really was like walking into a wall of hot treacle. A rain shower had left the ground steaming and within moments Kate and her team were damp, sticky and perspiring from every pore.

Night had already fallen so they didn't see much of the island during the taxi ride from Christchurch up into St James. Kate was merely left with an impression – bumpy roads, wooden shacks, weatherworn paintwork and more bumpy, narrow roads.

They were staying at a small, family-run apartment hotel on the southern curve of Paynes Bay where the beach dwindled to hardly more than a pale ribbon between the hotel gardens and the sea. The two-storey buildings of the hotel complex formed a horseshoe shape with the open end towards the Caribbean and the central area filled by exotic blooms, tall uplit palm trees and a turquoise swimming pool glistening like a flat-cut jewel.

They checked in, checked out their rooms (each with bed-sitting room, balcony, bathroom and kitchenette area) then met up in the restaurant which was open along its long side to the gardens and the warm night air. The evening slid past them and in a little while Kate left the boys to reconnoitre the bar while she set off on an exploration of her own. She was ostensibly heading for her room and bed and a good night's sleep before their early start out to St John in the morning, but the surroundings enticed her into taking the scenic route.

The night was very like the island people themselves – warm, black and garrulous – and as she strolled through the gardens and on to the beach it was as if every one of her senses was alert, sharpened, tingling with a clean intensity of reception.

She ambled along the shoreline until the spillage from the garden lights no longer touched her. Then she sat on the sand to enjoy a few moments of doing nothing but simply existing, being there, becoming part of it all. It was what she called her 'refuelling time', when she could set aside the activities and demands of the day and concentrate on thinking about nothing at all. It wasn't always easy. Like it wasn't tonight. Her surroundings were too intrusive and though she could have tried to block them out she didn't really want to – they were giving her too much pleasure.

Communing with Nature – one tends to think of it in terms of peace, silence, tranquillity, but Kate didn't find it so. The noise! First there was the busy, high-pitched chirruping coming from the palm trees behind her – 'whistling tree frogs', the waiter called them when she had asked earlier, and by the sound of it they were whistling in their millions though she couldn't actually see any of them. Then, providing a sort of arhythmic harmony, there was the froth of foam which made an incongruous break in the placid sea surface where a coral reef to her left just peeped its nose out of the water. And hovering underneath it all there was the constant, soothing whisper of flat sea inching forwards and backwards over flat sand.

She stretched out her legs and watched as the lacy edges of the Caribbean performed a sort of courtship ritual with her toes. Inviting her, teasing her, caressing her, retreating again. Her fingers played with the gritty silkiness of fine-ground coral sand, bleached pale by centuries of sun and where it was dry it was still faintly warm to the touch. And the sky! She looked upwards and sighed with pleasure. It was a perfect travel brochure cliché – big and brilliant stars closer than she'd ever seen them, shining out of blueblack velvet.

She breathed slowly and deeply, smelling the air, tasting it, intoxicated by it, and she found herself engulfed in one of those rare and precious interludes when time steps outside itself and a minute could be an hour, an hour could be a microsecond, and all that matters is that you're there, a part of it, acute, aware, *alive*. The world seemed so intense with beauty that it almost hurt to give herself up to it. Correction. It did hurt. For a moment, one tiny, fleeting moment, she was pierced with loneliness, to be surrounded by such beauty and have no one there to share it with. Then, just as quickly, the feeling was pushed aside. Kate didn't *want* to share her world. At least, not until she'd made sure that she was thoroughly mistress of it.

She wandered, still barefoot, back along the beach and through the hotel gardens, infused with a confidence, a *certainty*, that everything was going her way. She thoroughly intended to keep it like that.

Unfortunately the world itself seemed to be in complete disagreement with the philosophy. It put its plans into action first thing in the morning. In this cosmic conspiracy, the conversation went: 'You want us to play ball with you, Kate? Okay, *you're* the ball.'

And it started very early. Kate was quietly minding her own business in the bathroom preparing for a shower when she stepped naked into the bathtub and on to a giant cockroach. It crunched and squelched under her bare heel. She squirmed all over, froze in a moment of sheer horror while her mind cried out: to hell with independence! Liberation sucks! I want a man on call to come and *deal* with this! She was left with neither time nor appetite for breakfast.

The bumpy drive up into the Parish of St John – on the rugged Atlantic side of the island, on road surfaces frequently washed away in past Barbadian downpours and in a hired mini-moke with shot suspension – didn't improve things.

Julian seemed to be balanced precariously on the passenger seat next to her, his silence broken only by an occasional quiet whimper, his face a picture of pink and pale in all the wrong places – eyes like squashed strawberries in last week's cheesecake. One look at him and she knew the morning's work was not going to be easy. Julian was the type of person whose hangovers don't *wear* off, they *rub* themselves off abrasively – on other people.

'Ouch!' That was Julian. 'Must you drive as if you're on safari?'

'Don't blame me, blame the public works department. And don't snap. You're not the only one who's had a bad start to the day.'

'It's not today that did it. Mind that . . . Aaargh! . . . pothole. It was those Happy Hour rum punches.'

'Happy Hour' had been somewhat elongated last night – all drinks at half-price to the new arrivals. Special offer, one night only, try our house special sir, you like it? Here, have another.

Locally produced high-proof rum, freshly plucked and squeezed limes, garnished with grated nutmeg grown in the hotel's own garden. Of course Julian had another.

And another.

And another.

Which didn't do much for his map-reading this morning. They went to Clifton Hall (wrong), the Villa Nova (also wrong), and all the way along the top of Hackleton's Cliff before Julian admitted defeat and thrust the map at Kate with the grace and patience of a two year old on a bad day.

She did an emergency stop. Pete and Lorne who were following drew to a more sedate halt beside her. They didn't want to send their equipment flying off the back seat. The new restraints at TV7 stated that they'd have to pay if they broke it.

Kate studied the map briefly to get her bearings then she turned it over to check on the *Places of Interest* blurb on the back. Glancing sideways at Julian she said innocently, 'Gosh, just look at this view. It's practically a sheer drop, and we're right on the edge, a thousand feet above sea-level.'

Julian clutched at the seat frame, arms rigid, eyes screwed shut. 'Can we go now, please?' he said, very calmly, through clamped teeth.

It took Kate only ten minutes to find Garrod Hall, the elegant Plantation House which had been rebuilt by one Mr Edmund Garrod after the devastating hurricane of 1831. The Great House and its thousand acres of sugar plantation had been sold separately at the turn of the century so the house in which Tamsin Coe now lived stood in five and a half acres of total privacy, a hillside oasis of frangipani, bougainvillaea, mahogany and Casuarina trees with the ubiquitous sprinkling of slender palms.

'Some retirement home,' muttered Kate as they drew to a halt, tyres scrunching on the crushed-shell driveway.

They were greeted by a plump Bajan woman in a green shirtwaister dress of protesting cotton and straining buttons. Her arms were folded over her ample bosom (no welcoming handshake) and she proclaimed, the very soul of hospitality, 'Yo's late. Mizz Tammy waited morning tea for you. Now I 'spect I'll have to make some more.' She stomped back into the shade of a doorway leaving the TV7 team to follow or not as they wished.

Julian's heroic attempt at a greeting smile flopped upside down as soon as the housekeeper's back was turned.

Kate, sharing his grimace, whispered, 'I'll bet she's a real pussycat underneath. You wait and see.'

She was wrong. It was the Barbados weather that turned out to be the pussycat – complete with flexing claws, flattened ears and twitching tail. The skies were in one of those, 'I'm so bored I don't know what to do with myself' moods – so the clouds played tag with the sun and chased around doing a bit of this, a bit of that and then trying out a bit of the other because it looked like it might be terrific fun.

Brilliant sunshine: Lorne complaining that the contrasts were too harsh and what the hell had somebody done with his gauze filter?

Looming grey cloud: not *enough* light now, where can he plug in his arcs and will somebody please help him with his fold-up reflector?

Sudden spears of drenching rain: cut! Cover the equipment, save the hardware not your hairdos and dash for the shelter of the trellis-work balustrade.

White-hot sun again: steaming gardens. And steaming tempers.

A plague of tantrums. Very infectious. And the reclusive Tamsin Coe had built up little resistance during the years in her self-imposed cloister.

They were in the gardens again, setting up after the downpour. Wild orchids with sodden heads bowed. Pete being dripped on by the huge plantain bunches high up in the trees and muttering about 'bloody bananas'. Julian actually stalking around peering at things through a frame made out of thumbs and fingers – and inadvertently stalking right through one of Tamsin's prized flowerbeds.

She blew. 'You *clumsy* little man, you *idiot*!' Then she turned to Kate in accusation. 'You *said* I'd hardly notice you were here! If I'd known it was going to be like this I'd never have agreed, *never*!' An agitated flutter of hands, a tremble of pretty pretty flower-print voile over rise and fall of scrawny bosom.

Kate paused, gave time for a little silence to establish after the outburst. Then she said, using a gentle, concerned, almost bedside tone, 'Why *did* you agree, Tamsin, after all these years of begging to be left alone?'

'Because I thought . . . I thought . . .' A face of naked appeal, suddenly very young-looking and vulnerable, 'If I got it over with, showed my face to the world once and for all, they, the media, you, would finally *let me be*.' Abruptly, she turned and hurried into the house.

Kate watched her go. Then she turned to Julian. 'You pillock,' she said. 'But we can take it from my question. It'll be magic. Did you get it all?'

Julian's turn to be the *prima donna*. 'No! Why the *hell* did you have to ask her just *then*? Couldn't you *see* we were still lining *up*? Am I the *only* pro*fess*ional around here?'

'You mean *none* of that went on film, not a word?'

Julian's chin went up in defiance, Lorne shrugged, Pete suddenly found his fingernails very interesting.

Kate withered them all with a glance and hurried off to pour oil on Miss Coe's troubled waters.

Just another one-of-those days . . .

The house was cool and shady inside. Cool and shady and quiet, almost museum-like. Period antiques, a lot of local mahogany furniture, nice pieces, all of them. The place almost sang with quiet elegance: it was gracious, tasteful, exquisite – and empty. It had no soul, just things. If you didn't already know the owner there wasn't a clue as to the type of person who lived there – apart from the penchant for antiques. It was the veritable gilded cage. But where was the lonely bird?

Kate knocked and pushed on interior doors, peeped her head around, not being able to help the feeling of intrusion. Eventually she tried the kitchen quarters at the back of the house and hesitantly called out the house-keeper's name. 'Milda? Milda, are you there?' She went in.

Milda looked up. Her face was as yielding as a brown-stone wall. She was preparing lunch and there wasn't a break in movement, just the stony glare. Spode platters adorned the chunky kitchen worktable and Milda was busily filling them with jumbo shrimps, lobster, some sort of stuffed grilled fish, rice and peas, a mix of fruit – melon, plantains, mangoes . . . slice, chop, mix, arrange, and all the while she grumbled, 'What you go upsettin' Miss Tammy for, tramplin' on her flowers, them flowers is her pride and joy, looks after them like they was babies . . .' Mutter, mutter.

Kate saved her apologies for the owner not the house-keeper. 'Do you know where she is?'

Milda's eyes rolled ceilingwards showing a crescent of muddy whites below the ebony irises. 'In her little sittin' room, I 'spect. 'S where she always goes – when she's of a mind to hide. Upstairs. Right above here.'

Kate turned to leave.

The chopping noises ceased. 'Mizz O'Connell?'

'Yes, Milda?'

Milda pointed a gleaming knife blade towards a teatray. Her voice unexpectedly softened, sounded a little sly. 'Why don't you take Mizz Tammy's tea with you, seein' as you're goin'? I'm too old to be runnin' up and down, up and down those stairs all mornin' like I had nothin' better to do with my time.'

Kate smiled. 'Peace offering?' She wasn't entirely sure whether it was Miss Coe or the housekeeper she'd be making it to.

Milda placed a second cup and saucer on the tray and with no further comment set about a christophine salad.

The door to the private sitting room was closed. Kate rapped lightly then waited. She was just about to knock again when a voice from within said, 'That you, Milda?'

'No, it's Kate O'Connell. I've brought you some more tea.' She opened the door without waiting for permission to enter.

The woman was seated in a high-backed wing chair which faced away from the window. The harsh, late morning light spilled around her rather than on her, making a backlit halo in the fair, fine curls which maturity had chosen in preference to the famous urchin-cut of yesteryear.

She was still beautiful – you can't have bone structure like that and not be – but it was a slightly papery, sharp-edged kind of beauty, which could have done with a little extra weight to pad out the ageing process, soften the angular features. The eyes which fixed on Kate were still large, still a startling Dresden blue, but there were fine lines around them now, cobweb etchings that suggested more than just the passage of time. But there was no mistaking 'The Face', the woman who with 'The Shrimp' and Twiggy, had formed the triumvirate epitomising the ideal of beauty twenty years before.

She sat straight in the chair, head at a regal tilt, spine unbending. Like a queen who'd decided not to hold audience today, there was a barrier around her. You couldn't see it, but it was there – her whole attitude implying 'Private Property. No Trespassers'.

'May I join you?' said Kate, who never had been able to resist the temptation of a Keep Off The Grass sign.

She put the tray down on a delicate, lacily carved side-table. Then, there being only the one (already occupied) chair in the room, Kate sat on the polished wood floor.

As if nothing had occurred, girl-talk during a scheduled break in filming, she poured two cups of tea and said, 'God, what a day! And we haven't even made it to lunchtime yet. You wouldn't believe what I have to put up with trying to keep those . . . "men" for want of a better word, under some kind of control. Honestly . . .' She paused to add the milk. 'Julian's not normally like this, really. But I'm afraid he got a bit carried away last night, one – or five or six I shouldn't wonder – too many rum punches. And when Julian gets a hangover, boy, does he get a hangover. Makes the mother of hangovers look like a virgin. Do you take sugar?'

'Three please.'

A look of surprise. 'How on earth do you stay so slim?'

The tiniest self-congratulatory smirk.

Kate looked her full in the face. 'And so beautiful?' she asked. 'I must admit, with all the things that've been written about you over the years and the paparazzi never getting past your big hats and dark glasses and veils and things, I was half-expecting to find a cross between Quasimodo and the Phantom of the Opera.' Subtlety had never been Kate's trademark.

'And that's what brought you here?'

Kate shrugged. 'Yes, partly.'

Tamsin Coe laughed. 'My God! Well, I'll say one thing for you, Kate. At least you're honest. I'm sorry to have disappointed you.'

'Oh, I'm not disappointed. Quite the contrary. But I am curious. I mean, what really happened after the car crash? Were all the rumours true? And why do you bury yourself away, why don't you show your face? It's beautiful, you've got nothing to hide.'

'After years of surgery, pain, convalescence, more surgery . . . when you're recovering from another bout of that you don't expose your face to the Barbados sun – or, if you're considerate, to other people. It gets to be a habit.'

'And it's all over now?'

'My dear, you're looking at the original bionic woman.'

Kate smiled. 'No, I meant the habit. Why now?' She changed position, the hard floor reminding her that there were bones under the fleshy padding of her buttocks, then looked up at the woman in the chair. 'And don't give me any more of that rubbish about people finally letting you be because I just don't believe it.'

Tamsin put her cup down. 'You're an incisive little thing, aren't you?' Her hand was shaking slightly and there was a little 'chink' of china on china. She studied Kate and then, as if she'd made a decision based on what she saw in the younger woman's face, she suddenly rose from the chair, crossed the room, opened a bureau and took out a weighty-looking box file. She put it on the floor next to Kate and then knelt down herself.

'You're quite right,' she said. 'There's a lot more to it than that.' She fingered the lid of the file, a caressing, protective gesture, then she slid it to Kate. 'It's an autobiography. Sort of.'

So much for valuing privacy above all things, thought Kate. 'You've got a publisher?'

'I'm still negotiating.'

'No agent?'

A little smile. 'And give away ten percent?'

Ah. The coming out of the closet conundrum was beginning to make sense.

'You see, it's either sell this,' Tamsin tapped the box lid, 'or sell up.' She looked at Kate almost as if she were making an appeal. 'I love this house, Kate. And I love this island and its people. This is my home. I don't want to lose it. So I thought . . .'

'You thought, get a TV show together, get the book together, hit the screens and the publishers and bingo?'

'Something like that.'

Kate drew the box closer. She was itching to see inside it. 'Any photographs in here?' she asked, all business now, practical, down to earth.

Tamsin pulled a face. 'Plenty. They're not all a pretty sight.'

'Well, if you're talking about money, that's all to the good. Can we use some of them as stills? For the programme?'

'If you must.'

Kate opened the lid. She explored the box's contents with little expression and just the occasional quiet 'hm' noise. Tamsin was right. The earlier photos, filched from her medical records, were fairly stomach churning. But beneath Kate's professional exterior she was jumping with glee. Talk about bonanza! Talk about compulsive viewing, even if some of it was going to be through gaps in fingers held over eyes. But one thing still puzzled her. Being Kate, she asked. 'Why me, Tamsin? You could have had Brad Marvin, Johnny Carson – any of that lot would have snapped you up. And they reach a far bigger audience. So why me?'

'To be honest, because you were the only one who had the temerity to ask. And because you're a woman. And you're British. And because you have something of a reputation for . . .' she paused to search for the right phrase.

Kate supplied one. 'Cutting through the crap?'

Tamsin grinned. 'Exactly. I can't bear sensationalism, or sentimentality or the thought of being put on exhibition as some kind of freak show. And I don't think you'd do that. Would you?'

'Of course not,' said Kate, not entirely sure. She got to her feet with a little 'ouch' at a painful tingle of pins and needles. 'Let's get to work then, shall we?'

With a truce declared between Ms Coe and the TV7 team, cosmic forces took the hint and ceased their hostilities too, the weather settling into a muggy, overcast brightness that was perfect for outdoor filming, though lethal to unwary white skins.

Kate was wary and armoured herself in sun-oil. Julian was dismissive and didn't. 'And either wash that muck off or wear something over your shoulders,' he declared as she and Tamsin settled into the first shots beside an unpretentious, small, rectangular swimming pool. 'Your oil's flaring.'

'I'll cover up. And so should you, my love. Or at least wear a hat.' She glanced at his bald patch. 'You don't look right as a redhead.'

'It's throbbing so much I don't think it would take the pressure.' He raised the back of a limp hand to his forehead and said, 'Petal?' in a voice that was a cross between a wheedle and a whinge, 'Have you got any aspirin?'

It was a good sign. He was progressing from abrasive to pathetic. With any luck, she thought, the next stage would be brave little soldier and they'd whizz through the rest of the day without too much hassle.

Tamsin said helpfully, 'Ask Milda. She'll have you fixed up in no time. Actually, she does this wonderful little voodoo recipe with egg yolks and peppers . . .'

They shot the next half hour without Julian's help.

From Barbados they took a direct flight to Miami, tourist class.

Somewhere between the drinks trolley and the plastic-wrapped, plastic-tasting food Kate suddenly said, 'What do you think we've got, Julian? Cinderella with a plastic surgeon playing the fairy godmother? Or a story of inspiration and courage against all the odds?'

'Either, petal. It's entirely up to you and what happens in the editing and dubbing channels. Which do you want?'

'What I *don't* want is a cliché. Lonely woman surrounded by memorabilia and beautiful possessions. Yet after everything she's gone through, all the personal achievements and whatever, when you come right down to it, that's what she is.'

Julian shrugged. 'So?'

'Oh, nothing. I was just thinking.'

'Well, don't. It's not good for you.' Out came an avuncular hand to pat her arm. 'Anyway, we can relax now. The hard part's over with. Whatever the next two throw at us it's going to seem like a doddle compared with these last few days. It was that Milda woman. I could feel the evil eye, I tell you.' He shuddered and Kate told him not to be silly, the gods were on their side and all was right with the world.

The O'Connell Encounter with Barbra Streisand did nothing to alter Kate's confidence. Having worked on both sides of the camera herself, the star had a professionalism and an understanding which made her a programme maker's dream. She and Kate took an instant liking to one another, which wasn't hard for Kate as Streisand topped her personal 'women I have always admired' list. And by the time they left Miami, with a promise of a 'white label' of the new album as soon as it came off the presses, Kate felt as though the thousand-piece jigsaw puzzle of a few months ago – the boxful of seemingly unrelated little pieces that all had to be fitted together to make up a new television series – was finally beginning to show a picture.

They took the flight to New York.

Chapter Seventeen

It was dark when Jeff arrived in New York but he wasn't tired. The BMW had done all the work for him, driving him back to the city on auto-pilot. He put the car to bed in the lock-up down the street for which he paid an exorbitant rent then walked the hundred yards along West End Avenue to the co-op building where he'd lived for the last eleven years – just by West 86th and lucky to have the address. At first it was a sub-let, sharing it with two other guys who'd been in his fraternity at college, then they'd moved out, he'd taken over the lease and Jennifer moved in. Then about eight years ago the landlords, sick of the maintenance and the fuel costs and the real-estate taxes had decided to let the building go co-op. He and Jen talked about it, worked out the finances from every angle and then some, and with their pooled salaries, pooled savings and a mortgage from a loan society they scraped together just enough to cover the insider price. Things had looked rosy back in those days.

He let himself in to the dark and silent apartment, turned on the lights and walked through to his bedroom aware of his footsteps, his breathing, the rustle of his coat as he took it off and threw it on the bed next to his bag. It was always like this for the first day or so without Danny. You get so used to having a child around, a kind of extension of yourself, that when you're on your own again although there's a sense of freedom, release, a letting go of responsibilities, you also feel a little . . . amputated. He left the light on, went through to the kitchen, took a can of beer from the refrigerator, left the kitchen light on, went back into the living room and switched on a couple of floor lamps then sat behind his desk, chair tilted back and feet up on the desktop. He pulled off the ringtab and the escaping froth made a brief electrical fizzing noise. The metal was cold against his lips as he took a long drink straight from the can. Then he picked up the phone with his free hand, rested it in his lap, nestled the earpiece into his neck and punched out the number for Gilberts Pond. Just to check, and to let them know he'd arrived okay.

The goodbyes had gone pretty smoothly till the moment Jeff was in the car and ready to go. They'd had a good afternoon, taken a walk together after a hefty midday meal of store-bought chicken, (the fresh-caught fish had yet again stubbornly refused to be caught) then Jeff and Danny had read a chunk of *Huck Finn* together until it was time for Jeff to go. Then, 'Dad, why can't I come with you?'

He could hardly say, 'Because you'll be in the way.'

'I wouldn't get in the way, I promise.'

So he had a mindreader for a son. 'I'm sure you wouldn't,' he said. 'But you'd be bored out of your mind.'

'But I want to see Kate. And if they're making a film about you, that ought to include me. I'm part of your life. You said.'

'I know. And you are. And we've been *through* all this already. I'll be back in three or four days or so, okay? So come on, cheer up. Send me off with a smile, huh?'

But all he got was a glare before Danny shuffled off with his hands in his pockets muttering, 'Yeah. Well. I'm going over to the Strakers'.'

Jeff frowned, promised himself that as soon as the filming was over he'd devote himself entirely to Danny for a few days and the writing could go hang, then as soon as he was on the road his thoughts turned to Kate.

And they stayed there. Through the drive, through the night in his dreams and through the long day, the day he'd come to think of as 'K-Day', when he was cooped up in the city again, waiting. The hours seemed longer than any waiting hours had any right to be, even for a Sunday, which it was.

The flight was due to arrive early evening. He filled the intervening hours at his desk, working. Or trying to.

Forgetting about hardware and software and getting to know his typewriter again. He was more keyed up than *it* was. He got a few dozen words on paper. Then he x-ed them all out. He sharpened up a handful of pencils, hoping that the act might somehow sharpen his mind too, then he tested one and the point broke off. He stood up, went into the kitchen, came back with a spray can and a cloth and proceeded to polish around the clutter on his desk. He re-typed word for word the paragraph he'd just obliterated. Decided a fresh ribbon might help so he put a new one in the machine then had to go scrub his fingers, get the cloth again and polish away the inky fingermarks from the typewriter casing. The whole exercise had taken care of twenty-five lousy minutes. It must be time for another coffee break. Or a walk. Or a drive. Or maybe a phone call to Des Lakerman, he had his home number somewhere. 'Hi, well, what do you think of it?' Because apart from a printed card acknowledging receipt of typescript the only reaction he'd had from his editor was no reaction. Silence.

Jeff kept telling himself that no news is good news. That alternated with, 'No news means he hates it and doesn't know how to tell me.' Either way, the last thing he needed at this stage was silence. He needed to hear someone say, 'Yes, this is good, you're a good writer, *Losing Time* wasn't a fluke.' (The words he really wanted were more like, 'Wonderful!' 'Incredible!' 'Marvellous!' But he'd settle for 'good'. Please, let them think it's good.)

He didn't pick up the phone. He picked up doorkeys and carkeys instead.

'Good Lord, he's come to meet us. C. J. Warren.' She'd worked hard at thinking of him as Warren. 'That's him, over there. Isn't that nice?' The words were quite ordinary, the voice normal. She gave a quick wave of acknowledgement to the figure in the waiting crowds.

'Ver-ree nice,' said Julian appreciatively. 'I'd forgotten just *how* nice. This could turn out to be an interesting trip. Is he your type or mine, Kate? I don't recall you ever saying.'

A short, sharp shock of possessive jealousy. Ridiculous. 'Down boy,' said Kate. '*Not* your type. Straight as a ruler.'

'Sure? No chance of a quick conversion job?'

'No chance. You're incorrigible, Julian. Behave yourself.'

There was a quickly muttered, 'Spoilsport,' followed by a speculative sideways glance and, 'You sound very certain. You haven't been testing the waters yourself, have you, petal?'

She neither admitted nor denied, just said dismissively, 'Julian Howard, can't you think of anything but sex?'

He grinned. 'Not when I'm confronted with a nice juicy plum like that!'

Maybe Kate wouldn't have used those exact words herself but she was in full agreement with their meaning. After all these weeks of pushing the holiday affair into a little cubbyhole wrapped up in a mixture of wistful regret and, latterly, as the professional encounter drew ever closer, an awkward embarrassment, she'd forgotten how sexually attractive she found him. Suddenly she was remembering. Down, girl! she told herself. This is business, purely business, dammit.

Pete and Lorne, pushing luggage carts loaded with the TV7 equipment, caught up with them and Kate led the little entourage briskly towards the waiting figure with her heart ridiculously pounding and her stomach muscles ridiculously clenched. She was really angry at her own body that it should dare to deny her hard-won objectivity. She walked. She repeated to herself: business trip. *O'Connell Encounter.* Subject, bestselling new author. Come up with the goods or else. She walked. And she had this sneaky feeling in the pit of her stomach that she might just be about to walk off the edge of a bloody great cliff.

Quite ridiculous.

She was within three feet of him. He looked different.

He looked the same. He looked ... 'Ver-ree nice,' her mind echoed. She held out her hand. 'Hello, Jeff. C. J. Good to see you again. You remember Julian, the series producer? And this is Lorne – take a good look at Lorne because you won't see much of his face after this, he'll be hiding it behind his minicam. And this is Pete, specialist in invisible microphones.' It was well done. No meeting of ex-lovers here. No cliff-fall, just a businesslike but friendly greeting. Perfect. She was pleased with the way she handled it. And annoyed because there was anything to be pleased about – like how come she felt as if she deserved an award or something?

Jeff gave them all an equally businesslike and friendly greeting. Then to Kate he said, 'You're looking well.'

She knew it. She'd spent the twenty minutes before arriving at La Guardia in the privacy of the plane's toilet cubicle making damned sure of it. 'Thank you. And how's Danny, your family?'

All the mandatory polite exchanges were performed successfully and Jeff led the group through the arrivals area. Then Julian said, 'Did you bring a car? Could we load our gear in it, do you think? I'd rather not trust it to a taxi if I don't have to. You wouldn't believe how much this stuff costs. Lorne and Pete are replaceable but the equipment ...'

'Cheek,' said Pete.

'No problem,' said Jeff. 'Just tell me where we're heading.'

'Good-oh. Me and the hard stuff will go with Mr Warren then,' he said, turning to Kate and the boys. 'You three can share a cab. See you all at the hotel, children,' and he and Jeff pushed the luggage carts off towards the parking lot leaving Kate looking after them and wondering why she felt Julian had scored some sort of point over her.

'He's quick off the mark,' said Lorne. 'Hope he's not going to balls things up for us.'

'He won't. You know he behaves himself where work

is concerned.' As we all should, she thought. 'Besides, I've already told him the man's straight.'

Pete grunted. 'So was Julian once upon a time. You never can tell.'

Oh, yes you can, thought Kate smugly. Rapidly followed by – I hope. Cancelled immediately by – what do I care?

'Was that dinner, supper or breakfast?' groaned Julian later when they were all seated in the hotel's dining room. 'My body clock's confused.'

Kate smiled indulgently and pointed out, 'It's ten o'clock. In the evening. Sunday.'

'My delicate constitution can't take much more of this jet-setting,' he said, delicately.

'Rubbish,' said Kate. 'You're about as delicate as a brick. You'll be right as rain in the morning.'

'Don't mention that word!' said Lorne.

'Which word?' asked Pete. 'Rain?'

'No. Morning. You shouldn't swear with a lady present,' the cameraman replied. He was indicating Julian, not Kate.

'Bitch,' said Julian with a little pout.

Jeff sat through the banter silently, looking a little bemused.

'Don't let them get to you,' Kate turned to him. 'They're not always like this. Just put it down to an excess of in-flight hospitality. They're quite sane and normal once they start working. Well, almost.'

And that was the cue for Julian to key in his efficient producer mode and run through the proposed filming schedule. 'And speaking of work,' he said, 'one man and his writing desk is hardly going to make scintillating viewing so we won't want too much of you slaving over a hot pencil and chewing the end of your typewriter, C. J. Basically it'll be fly on the wall stuff – all you have to do is go about your normal day and ignore us. So long as your normal day can include a meeting with your agent for an inside view of her selling you, then a visit

281

to the publicity department at the publisher's to see how they plug the book, a stopover at your old advertising agency to kind of link the two and show what you've given up for the sake of your art, some shots of you in your dusty garret, a bit of soul-searching, maybe a walk around the neighbourhood, call in on the neighbours . . . you know the sort of thing. A couple of days should do it, no problem.'

Jeff looked from Julian to Kate and back to Julian again, then checked on Pete and Lorne. Their faces told him the schedule was nothing out of the ordinary.

'And all with me tagging along to put the occasional pithy question and make incredibly astute observations,' added Kate, smiling. 'That's the framework. And somewhere along the way we'll try to fill in the picture of the man who lurks behind the pen-name. Nothing to it.'

'I was hoping you wouldn't need to get to that last part,' said Jeff, who could feel an acute attack of privacy phobia coming on.

'Why? Something to hide?' Julian's face lit up with a kind of greedy hopefulness.

Jeff shook his head. 'Sorry. I'm just an ordinary normal sort of person with a cupboard full of dust, not skeletons. None that I know of, at least.'

Julian sighed. 'Oh well, never mind. Maybe the doorman or the neighbours will be able to come up with something.' He put an appealing hand on Jeff's arm. 'You haven't changed your mind about us filming up at your country place? Kate tells me it would make a gem of a location.'

'Backwoods America?' said Jeff. He shook his head. 'Very dull. And very private. Sorry.'

'Oh well, it was worth a try,' said Julian, wistfully thinking of the 'apple-pie parents and a kid straight out of Captain America' (Kate's description). He gave a somewhat flamboyant stretch with the words, 'Well, children, it's beddy-bies for me. G'night all. See you in the morning, C. J. Your place, eight o'clock sharp, all right?'

Pete and Lorne picked up the cue and made their goodnights along with Julian.

Kate drained her coffee cup then looked at her watch and said, 'They've got the right idea. We've a hard couple of days ahead of us. We could all use an early night.' There was no invitation in her voice, not the slightest intimation that they might spend that night together. And Kate hadn't picked up any signals at all, not a hint of a look, touch, tone of voice, to suggest that Jeff had anything other than business on his mind. He was sticking to the rules exactly as agreed and as reinforced in her letter. Just as she wanted it. (Dammit to hell – not one lousy little spark.)

And then he reached across and put his hand over her wrist, hiding the watch face. 'Not yet, Kate.' Very soft. 'Isn't this the part where one of us is supposed to say, "At last we are alone"?'

His fingers lightly touching the back of her hand. Fingers that had an inside knowledge of her.

'We've hardly had a chance to talk. I mean really talk,' he was saying. 'God, it's so good to see you . . .'

Eyes looking right into her. Smokey grey eyes which had seen her face in moments of total abandonment.

'. . . so how are you really, what's been happening in your life . . .'

Lips moving, forming quiet words. Lips that had kissed and sucked and tasted her ultimate nakedness.

'Hey, lady, are you listening to me? Say something. Try, "Hello, it's good to see you too".'

No armour of professionalism could protect Kate from his knowledge of her.

She donned it anyway.

'Yes, it's good to see you,' she said, removing her hand from beneath his. 'I'm sorry, I'm just very, very tired. We've been working non-stop for . . . I can't even think. And there's hardly a bed of roses waiting for me at home . . .'

'Want to tell me about it?'

The trace of a frown skittered across her forehead. The

temptation was strong, very strong. But what she said was, 'Much as I'd love to talk the night away, I really must get some sleep.'

'But it's not even ten-thirty.'

'And Julian's not the only one with a worn-out body clock. Mine's pointing to bedtime. Eight o'clock sharp, he said, and he meant it.' The voice was firm. Kate O'Connell triumphed.

'You're right,' he said. Then he spoiled her victory by adding, 'Business first, huh?'

Like in save dessert for later? What happened to the strict diet? 'Not "first", Jeff. *Just* business. Do we have to go through it all again? Look,' she said wearily, 'what happened before was . . . was great. We had a good time together, it's a nice memory. But that's all it is now. Leave it be. Let's not make any complications. This is business. We're here because we have a job to do . . .'

'Okay.'

What? Just like that? She was supposed to be letting him down gently. He was supposed to be devastated. What *happened*?

'You're right,' he went on. 'So. If I'm going to be a TV star tomorrow I guess I'd better get some beauty sleep myself.'

That's one thing you'll never need, she thought, looking at him. It was an objective judgement, of course. 'Right,' she said. 'Well, goodnight then.' She pushed back her chair and stood up. 'See you in the morning.'

But Jeff wasn't quite ready to give in yet. 'May I walk you to your room, ma'am?'

And neither was she. 'No, thank you. But I'll walk you to the lobby.'

Lady Bickerdyke had had a very busy Sunday – the kind of day when she positively shone, even if the sun didn't. The flat, grey, drizzly skies were but a minor annoyance and she had no intention of allowing them to dampen the day's formal celebrations.

The caterers had performed magnificently – she

expected no less – and she cast a final glance over the long, white-damasked table with the huge christening cake (white, with *Edward Alexander Arnold* in delicate silver piping) forming a raised centrepiece surrounded by a tumbling arrangement of guelder roses, stocks and larkspur – white, cream and the palest blue. She gave a little nod of satisfaction before checking on progress in the kitchen.

Four women in black dresses and white aprons were putting the finishing garnishes to bite-sized canapés on silver platters. Translucently thin slices of smoked salmon were waiting to be stuffed and rolled. A basket of golden goujons of plaice were at that moment being drained and shaken and tipped on to absorbent paper.

'Hurry up, Grandma, we're all ready.' The younger of Lady Bickerdyke's two granddaughters came excitedly into the kitchen, took one look at the food, jumped up and down and said, 'Oh, goody, fish fingers!'

Lady Bickerdyke despaired of the child sometimes. This was one of those times. She ushered the little girl quickly out again to find her husband, her daughter, her grand-children and their father waiting for her in the hallway.

She had to admit it, they were a handsome family. Arnold, stockily built and just a little stout these days but still distinguished in the grey suit he'd worn to the garden party at the Palace earlier this summer. Elizabeth, so ripely pretty in cornflower blue, cradling little Edward in her arms. And the baby, unconcerned about his day of stardom, a chubby sleeping bundle in the flowing hand-knit white lace shawl in which Elizabeth and the girls had all been christened. The little girls looked demure and beautiful, careful curls escaping below berib-boned boater hats – one in pink and one in yellow and both with light wool coats to match. Fresh and innocent as summer flowers. Her daughter's daughters.

Lady Bickerdyke smiled with approval as she inspected her loved ones and the smile stiffened only slightly as it passed over the figure of her son-in-law. She was going to allow nothing to spoil this day. Not even Alex. 'All ready then?' she asked brightly. 'Elizabeth, darling, I think you'll be more comfortable with Edward if you come with Daddy and me in the Bentley. The girls can go with their father . . .'

The church service went exactly as it should – the baby cried (but not too much) when the vicar wetted his forehead with the cold font water, the godparents repeated their vows clearly without mumbling, and everybody knew the hymns and sang as if they were regular churchgoers – even if 'regular' was defined as 'hatchings, matchings and despatchings only'.

Mr and Mrs Ed Franklin drove slowly past the banks of rhododendrons which flanked the driveway to the Bickerdyke home. There was a Rolls-Royce in front of them and a Bentley behind. Mrs Franklin quickly checked her face and hat in the vanity mirror on the back of the passenger sun flap then picked a solitary fleck of dandruff from her husband's shoulder. She couldn't help a little exclamation of awe as the Tudor farmhouse, with centuries of add-ons, came into view.

'Careful, Moira, your roots are showing,' he said astringently, though he too was impressed. The Bickerdykes weren't just money or big business – they were class, the real thing, going back generations. The gracious, weathered, large but unpretentious house in the little Kent village emphasised it.

Moira Franklin had been delighted, if a little surprised, when the invitation to the Pritchard christening had dropped through their 'four bed, exec. detached' letterbox in Magnolia Dene, Woosehill, Wokingham. There was no way they could refuse although Ed, still prevaricating over 'the little problem' Sir Arnold had lumbered him with, had almost wanted to. Moira, in mounting indecision as to what she should wear and what would be an appropriate gift for a baby of such illustrious grandparentage (not to mention a Cabinet Minister for a father), had almost agreed that a refusal might be the easier option.

They were both glad, now, that they'd accepted. Ed

parked his Ford Sierra next to the Home Secretary's car – he'd recognised many of the guests in church, from senior politicians to the seriously privileged – and decided he could get used to this sort of lifestyle, no problem.

Indoors, the light buffet luncheon was enjoyed by all as red-jacketed waiters relentlessly poured Veuve Cliquot into any glass whose level fell below two-thirds full. The cake was cut, speeches were made, toasts were drunk, and the gifts – many of them in solid silver, not just plate, were displayed, exclaimed over and admired.

If you didn't know differently, nobody would have guessed that Alex and Elizabeth Pritchard were anything other than the happily married, proud parents of three beautiful children. They certainly showed a united front to the world and its we-know-otherwise glances. Alex kissed his wife's cheek, crooned proudly over his son and heir, hugged his daughters, circulated with an easy confidence among the guests, none of whom betrayed the slightest hint that they'd read the gossip (*helped* spread the gossip) and were eager for confirmation, denial, or at the very least a little detail.

The afternoon was a resounding success for family solidarity, tradition and propriety. The last guest had duly departed just before four, the caterers had cleared up and were on their way by five and Lady Bickerdyke didn't know whether to be dismayed or delighted when Elizabeth took her to one side and asked quietly, 'Mummy, would you mind if Alex stayed the night?'

Lady Bickerdyke settled for both options. Her son-in-law wasn't the only politician in the family. 'Of course not, darling, if you're sure that's what you want,' she said with delight to her daughter. 'Alex is staying overnight,' she said with dismay to her husband.

'Splendid, splendid,' said Sir Arnold.

'Is it?' she replied.

'Don't you worry, my dear,' said Sir Arnold, who'd earlier taken a few moments away from the festivities to have a private word with Franklin in the conservatory. 'I'm sure Elizabeth knows what she's doing,' he went on

287

to his wife. 'And as for the other little matter . . . Ed Franklin's quite an agreeable sort of chap, don't you think? Very accommodating. All in all, I think the after-noon went off very well, don't you, old girl?'

Lady Bickerdyke smiled. 'If you say so, Arnold.'

Chapter Eighteen

The first day's shooting went well. Too well, thought Jeff. At this rate they'd be over and done with before he knew it and she'd be gone again, back across to the other side of the ocean and then how long before it would be his turn to visit her world?

He wondered what that world of hers was really like. He'd had a taste of it once, seemed a long time ago, but that was different - that was before he knew her. What was it like for *her*? He'd imagined it as some kind of cosy amalgam of Brad Marvin glamour and Katy-ish ... what? 'Katy-ish', he repeated to himself impatiently, what the hell did that mean? It was nothing to do with the woman he'd seen today. Brilliant Kate. Whirlwind Kate, hard Kate, funny Kate, perceptive Kate. Beautiful Kate. She took his breath away.

'Okay, petal, boys, let's call it a wrap for now. We're getting nowhere fast and I'm bleeding knackered.'

The producer called *this* nowhere fast? Jeff shrugged. Kate sighed. Pete grunted. Lorne grinned and laid his camera gently on a couch. Minicam it might be but, unlike people, the more exercise it gets the more weight it gains, and his shoulder was in wholehearted agreement with Julian.

It was early evening and they were back in Jeff's apartment having done the home interiors, the meetings with Laura and Pam and some exteriors of the Matteson Building. All that was left was inside at Sherman Whitney (no problem getting their agreement – an ad agency refusing free airtime? Never!) – then a walk in Riverside Park and a few shots of New York as a place to live as opposed to New York, tourist attraction.

'It's called the Big Apple, isn't it?' Kate had said earlier.

'So show us some of the wormy bits you have to deal with. And don't try and kid us that there aren't any.'

'What did you have in mind? I could arrange to go out and get mugged if you like,' teased Jeff.

'Would you?' said Julian.

'No way,' said Kate protectively. 'We need him in one piece for the studio session.'

'Oh yes. Pity, though,' acknowledged Julian, not entirely joking.

'So what now?' asked Jeff as he watched them gather up their equipment. 'Can I treat you all to a meal? We could go out somewhere—if there's one thing you can say about this city it's that it has great places to eat. You name it, you can get it somewhere, from straight Italian to ethnic Eskimo. Or if you have the courage we could eat here – I do a great tuna salad?' And how in hell do I get you alone, lady? He tried to look the question at her but her receiver was switched off. And it was one night and one day gone already.

'Thanks,' said Julian, 'but it's a quiet night for me. I've got to go over my notes on today's shoot, get my head together for tomorrow. I'll duck out if you don't mind. Kate? You coming back with me or are you going to grasp the opportunity of a night on the town without it getting back to Ed Franklin?'

'Tell you what I could do with,' said Pete. 'A decent pint of draught bitter, a Cornish pasty and a bag of crisps. Anybody fancy a pub crawl?'

Jeff grinned. 'Ask again in English and I might be able to answer.'

So Julian bowed out, Pete and Lorne decided on a tour of the more (and later the less) salubrious drinking establishments in the area and Kate had not yet answered. There were plenty of things she could, should do – make notes for tomorrow, script the commentary she would be dubbing later, do some serious thinking about the studio interview sessions which were looming on her horizon. More mundanely, she ought to eat a light sensible meal, wash her hair, get a good night's sleep.

'Tuna salad sounds lovely,' she heard herself say.

She listened to the voices of Julian, Lorne and Pete recede along the corridor outside the apartment. There were water noises coming from the kitchen. The fridge door. Cutlery. Chopping. It was all slightly distanced, as if she were inside a thick-skinned bubble which let her see and hear but kept her insulated, isolated.

'Onions?' he called out.

'Why not? Let's live a little.' Even her own voice sounded slightly distanced from her. She moved around the room lethargically, energy all gone. It was often like this at the end of a day's shoot. Flat, like a used-up battery. Occupying a sort of no man's land that was the bridge between frenetic activity and the ordinary business of just being alive. She looked at his possessions. Mainly books. Books everywhere. Wherever the room had a recess or an alcove the space had been fitted with floor to ceiling shelves and the shelves were filled with books. From Wilkie Collins to Stephen King. *Pride and Prejudice* nestling flirtatiously up to *Kane and Abel*. Steinbeck and Tolkien, Tolstoy and Mark Twain, Jonathan Swift leaning rather heavily against John D. McDonald.

'Garlic? Or is that living a little too dangerously?' he called out.

'In for a penny,' she said from inside the bubble.

While Jeff was keeping himself occupied in the kitchen she took the opportunity to use his bathroom. It was neat and tidy and gleaming. She wondered if it was always like this or if he'd expected them to be filming him in there as well. Her trained eyes automatically noted only one bathtowel hanging on the rail, the shelf above the wash-basin containing man-sized electric shaver but no telltale tubes of depilatory cream or choice of toothpaste or stray cans of hairspray. Single occupancy, then, confirmed by this most indiscreet of rooms. Something in the back of her mind registered satisfaction. She washed hands, checked on reflection then decided it was time she offered to de-bug a lettuce or something.

'Need any help?' she asked, leaning against the kitchen

doorframe. His shirtsleeves were rolled up and he seemed enviably in control of his domestic environment, slicing at a cucumber with an easy speed and transparent-fine precision. Almost as efficient as Mrs Pickles, she thought. And much prettier than Milda.

'Yes,' he said, slicing away. 'But not with this.' He put down the knife, wiped his hands on a sheet of paper towel and turned to face her.

'What then?' She genuinely wished to make herself useful.

'You,' he said. 'I need help with you. I've been putting it off for as long as I can but there's only so much you can do to a tuna salad.' A little shrug, like someone admitting defeat.

She followed his glance. The salad bowl was overflowing. Literally. Lettuce leaves, endives, cucumber, celery, carrots, tomatoes, onions, cascading from bowl to tabletop. Kate stared at it. Then she put a hand to her mouth to smother a laugh. Then Jeff laughed too. The skin of her bubble thinned out and burst and she sent all her resolutions along with it. You want something? Then take it.

'Come here, Katy,' he said. It was a demand, a question, a plea.

She took the necessary steps. And in those three quick steps across the space which divided them Kate threw 'ought not' and 'shouldn't' and especially 'mustn't', out of the window. She leaned her body into his while his arms slid around her back enclosing her. Her cheek against his shoulder, his face burying itself in her hair, the warmth of his body pulsing into her, flowing through her.

'Oh Katy, I've missed you.' His voice was low, a little broken.

She answered by taking his face in her hands and covering it with kisses. She'd forgotten she could feel like this, wanting to pour him over her, bathe in him, breathe him into the very centre of herself. Utterly, totally ridiculous. And reckless, she told herself. But it's what she wanted.

She smiled.

'What's funny?' he asked, holding her away from him for a moment so he could see her face.

'We are,' she said. 'Standing here in the kitchen, necking like a couple of teenagers. I'm hungry. So would you mind terribly if we saved the salad for later?'

A grin. 'What? And let it go *cold*?'

'We could take it with us.'

He said, 'Know something?'

'What?'

'I've never done it in front of a tunafish before.'

But there was a strangeness, a tension. In spite of the private joke and shared memories it was impossible to just step back into being Jeff and Katy of the woodlands again.

She stood by his bed, a small, erect figure dressed in the working coveralls of an executive woman – loose fitting shirt in creamy crêpe de Chine tucked into waistband of classic Jaeger skirt of taupe linen – clothing carefully chosen to flatter but not distract attention from the subject of her work.

Jeff watched as, with her back to him, she began to unfasten the buttons of her shirt. The movement was slow – not sensual, but a sort of controlled fatigue, as if afraid or unable to let go of whatever had sustained her through the gruelling schedule of her last few weeks.

But the impression he had was one of fragility. He reached out to her, put his hands on her shoulders, felt the tension there.

Kate felt it too, but couldn't let it go.

Gently, he began to knead the base of her neck. 'Tired, Katy?'

She turned her face to him. A nod, an apologetic smile. 'A little.'

His fingers stilled. He kissed the top of her head and carefully pushed her towards the bed, sat her down on it. Kneeling in front of her, he took off her shoes and put them to one side. Wordlessly, he unfastened the remaining buttons of her shirt then pulled it free of the skirt and slid the soft fabric from her shoulders.

She reached for the skirt zip. He stilled her hand and said, 'No, don't do a thing. This one's for you. Just lie back and close your eyes.'

She wasn't about to protest. But she warned him, 'I might fall asleep.'

'No, you won't,' he promised quietly and eased her backwards so she was lying full length on the bed. He slipped the skirt down over her hips, undressing her with practised skill (being a parent gives you all sorts of useful expertise) and she settled herself face down, the quilt making a soft nest of warmth beneath her nakedness.

Once she was comfortable he rested his hand briefly on her shoulder. 'Don't go away.' Then he removed his own clothes, picked up the bottle of olive oil from the tray of salad things on the dresser, and knelt on top of the bed beside her. With a light touch he moved the soft strands of her hair away from her shoulders and began.

He let the oil rest in his palms a moment to warm it and then with firm fingers, smooth strokes, slow and methodical, deep yet gentle, he massaged the oil into her skin, probing around her neck and shoulders until he felt the knotted muscles soften.

A little more oil. The flat of his hands anointing the smoothly perfect skin, little circular thumb-movements working up and down her spine then hands working outwards, fingers slipping beneath her arms, skimming over the soft sideswell of her breasts.

He felt her move beneath him, stretching a little, settling, a tiny sigh of satisfaction. Again, she reminded him of a cat – sleek, sinuous, giving herself totally to the simple pleasure of being stroked.

He was straddling her legs now and working steadily downwards. More oil, a little trickle of it between her buttocks, which he caught and gently smoothed into her skin, palms and fingers massaging the soft roundness of her bottom while his thumbs insinuated into the cleft between the cheeks. The downward movement continued, hesitantly at first then with more confidence.

She felt his thumb slide delicately over that most private part of her, caressing around the tight back opening, smoothing across it, a gentle pressure which rested there for a moment. Involuntarily she moved, her legs parting, offering access to that other entrance which she could feel hot and wet and throbbing for want of him. But his hands moved on and downwards still.

Warm oil smoothed into the channel between top of thigh and outer lips, carefully avoiding contact with the silky soft interior. Down, down the oily massage continued, warm hands, warm fingers, diligently probing, easing tension from thigh muscles, the back of her knees, ankle tendons, concluding with firm but careful squeezes between both hands, first one foot, then the other.

He gave a light pat to her bottom. 'Okay. Turn over.'

Kate felt heavy, languorous, as though it would be a crime to demand action from muscles so totally relaxed. She murmured into the soft pillow, 'Your quilt, the covers. All this oil, they'll be ruined.'

'I can buy new ones. Do as you're told.'

She looked at him through half-closed eyes. With a lazy, teasing smile she whispered, 'God, you're so masterful!' and complied.

Again he warmed the oil in his hands before touching her. And again his ministrations were methodical, measured, deliberate – almost those of a professional masseur, expert and impersonal.

He smoothed the oil on to her skin, first between and around her breasts. The touch was easy, confident, as his hands then moved up, across, down – smooth stroking arcs sliding firmly over the dark pink circles of areolae, giving no special attention to the soft nipples sprouting into hard buds beneath his palms.

Kate lay there, naked and acquiescent, receiving all he offered, Jeff demanding nothing from her in return.

The therapy continued in its relentless path downwards. He followed the contours of her body, skimming her navel, reaching the hard roundness of hipbones and the pliant slope of abdomen where he took more oil to massage into the triangle of darker hair which crowned her sex.

He was kneeling between her legs now, fingers working gently through the springy hair, thumbs almost casually slipping into the cleft at its point and sliding smoothly down the inside of her labia, exerting the lightest of sideways pressure on the small, swollen nub of clitoris. He watched as he worked, sliding his hands quickly along her thighs and then under her knees, lifting her legs and spreading them apart so that she was totally open to him, to his fingers and his gaze. Not turning his eyes from her he edged his body further down the bed to bring his face between her legs. Then carefully he spread her glistening lips, stroking between the folds of outer and inner with slippery, oily fingers.

Very slowly and deliberately, as if he were savouring the first taste of an icecream on a sultry day, he began to lick at her soft, moist, secret flesh. Slow and easy caresses with the flat of his tongue. All her hidden places, long wet sweeps from back to front then lapping and sucking at the little, swollen bud before pushing his tongue inside her, giving circling caresses to her inner-most nakedness.

She moaned, none too quietly, her body tensing and giving little shudders as the slow burning built into a pulsing heat obliterating all other senses. Her hands came down, slim fingers reaching into his hair, grasping his head and guiding it so that his tongue was on her clitoris again, intensifying the centre of her pleasure.

Tenderly he licked and sucked and lapped and teased. He reached upwards, fingering and squeezing one hard nipple while his other hand slid beneath her, three fingers thrusting deep inside the wet warm tunnel of her female-ness, until her body arched and she cried out.

He didn't move then. He waited, quite still, until the pulses ebbed away under his motionless tongue and his fingers could no longer feel the spasmodic contractions of her inner sex. Then, very gently, he eased out of her, kissed her moist tangle of hair and edged himself upwards until his face was beside hers.

Taking her in his arms he drew her mouth to his own. He held her for a long time, her warm body relaxing into his, her skin smooth and sheening like satin in the aftermath of the massage oil. Tenderly he pushed a damp tendril of hair away from her eyes. The gesture turned into a caress, one fingertip lightly stroking down the side of her cheek, tracing the delicate curve of her jaw.

Her eyes opened and she looked up at him, shining pupils big and dark. A little smile teased at the edges of her mouth.

'Happy?' he asked softly.

She nodded.

He gave her three kisses: nose, forehead, chin. 'Anything else I can do for my lady?'

'I'll think of something,' she said and her hand confidently closed around his hot, hard cock to guide it home.

It wasn't until much later that, finally sated but still playful, they turned their attention to the tuna salad – nibbling at it from some very interesting and imaginative surfaces.

Jeff played 'mine host' to the last, clearing salad remnants on to a tray, coming back to the bed for a quick kiss, a stray celery stalk and the now empty olive oil bottle.

Kate lay back on the pillows watching him – the way he moved, his easy nudity. She delighted in the sight of him. And in the fact that he was hers. Totally. Exclusively. Neither borrowed nor guiltily stolen. Hers. Albeit temporarily.

He paused at the bedroom door, looked back at her, gave an exaggerated sigh. 'And I suppose you want a cup of tea or something now?'

'I'd practically kill for one.'

He left, muttering.

When he returned with tea things a few minutes later

he found Kate standing at the foot of the bed, already partially dressed in bra and underslip and slithering into the elegant skirt which earlier in the day had signalled: efficient, smart, cool. The clothes were the same – only the signals had been changed. He drew in a long breath between his teeth. 'If you intend to stay dressed, beautiful lady, you shouldn't be allowed to *get* dressed like that. It's asking for trouble.'

'What? And let the tea go *cold*?'

'It didn't do the salad any harm.'

Her answer was to tuck in her blouse and do up the skirt zip with finality, then she relieved him of the tea-tray and headed for the living room. When Jeff joined her, he too was fully dressed. She took one look at him and complained, 'What did you have to go and do that for? I rather liked having you mooch around with no clothes on. Besides, I'm the one who has to go out into the dark night looking halfway respectable, not you.'

'A guy feels kind of vulnerable when he's the only one without pants on. And anyway, who said anything about you leaving?'

'I did. There's a producer and a film crew expecting me at the breakfast table in case you'd forgotten.'

'So? You got a morals clause in your contract or something?'

She grunted and dropped into the arms of an easy chair. 'Many a true word spoken in jest. Julian and the boys may be part of the team and are hardly what you'd call shockable but honestly, Jeff, the way things are going at work these days the last thing I need right now is accusations of nepotism. Or whatever the word is for doing a programme on your lover.'

'The way things are going?' he repeated. 'Do you want to tell me about it?'

She looked at him silently for a moment, pondering. Then she said, 'Yes. I do. But I warn you, it sounds pretty squalid in parts.'

The juxtaposition of 'squalid' and 'Kate O'Connell' struck him as so ludicrous that he almost laughed. But the sight of her sitting there looking small and vulnerable stopped him.

'There's one condition though,' she said, and already there was a little spark back in her eyes.

'Yes?'

'You have to promise you won't ever write a novel based on the confessions of a TV star.'

It was close on midnight by the time she finished. It all came out. TV7's cutbacks. And the whole Pritchard mess. Then the press grubbing around and the Board of Management coming down heavy on Ed Franklin and him shifting it on down to her. 'No publicity is bad publicity?' she finished bitterly. 'Don't you believe it. And here I am, compromising my professional integrity again like there was no tomorrow. Some terrific, impartial, unbiased *O'Connell Encounter* this is going to be. Will I never learn?'

He kissed her fingertips one by one. 'I hope not. So long as it's me you're doing the compromising with. And don't worry, I don't kiss and tell. Besides, I have a sneaky feeling that whatever you and I do in our own time it's not going to influence your work one bit.' Then he grinned. 'More's the pity. I can but try!'

He tried beautifully, for about ten minutes, until she started muttering about the time again and going back to the hotel. 'I'm disappointed in you,' he said.

'I warned you you might be.'

'No, not any of that business. I mean why the hell didn't you call me through any of this? Just to talk? Anything? Why didn't you call me, period? What are friends for?'

She smiled at him and ruffled his already tousled hair affectionately. 'That's what we are, is it?'

'Amongst other things. So why didn't you call?'

She hesitated then hedged. 'Lots of reasons. You know the main one – we've been through it over and over.'

'Sure. Don't play games with me, Katy. Give me the real reason.' He finished quietly, 'It matters.'

He was right. It did matter. He deserved the truth. 'I

299

'didn't phone you,' she said slowly, 'because I thought . . .
hoped, that if I ignored it for long enough it might go
away.'

'And did it?'

'Yes. Sort of. Almost.'

'I see.'

'Lucky you. I wish I did.'

'So what now?' he asked. 'Where do we go from here?'

'I go back to my hotel,' she said. 'Then we get this
filming over with. Then I go back home, face the music
– or bury my head – and see what happens.' She spoke
as though she were checking off a shopping list. 'And if
I'm going to manage any of that,' she said, having neatly
sidestepped his real question, 'then the first thing I've got
to do is get back to that hotel and get some sleep. Do
you have a number for a taxi firm?'

He let it rest. They still had tomorrow. 'I'll drive you,'
he said.

'It's all right, honestly, I can get a cab.'

'It's *not* all right. For once in your life, woman, can
you stop being so bloody independent and let somebody
else take the driving seat? *I'll* take you back to the hotel.'

'Okay,' said Kate. 'Who am I to argue?'

At which Jeff merely raised his eyes heavenwards and
muttered, 'Women!'

She slept like a baby – woke up every half hour wanting
a cuddle. Bloody men! she thought, and wrapped her
arms around a spare pillow.

In spite of that she was bright as a button when she
appeared at the breakfast table. 'Morning, fellas. Everybody have a good night?' she said cheerfully.

'A bit too good,' Lorne said, with every word sounding
like an effort. A painful one. Pete only managed a half-
grunt.

'Well, *I* feel fresh as a daisy,' declared Julian. 'Amazing
what an early night can do for one's constitution. And
you, petal? You look well rested.'

She replied truthfully, 'As you say, Julian, early to bed . . .'

'Very sensible,' he said, pouring maple syrup liberally over a plateful of pancakes. Kate looked at the plate with a mixture of disgust and longing. The disgust won. She ordered herself a round of toast. Julian dug in without the slightest regard for yesterday's delicate constitution and mumbled through full mouth, 'So how's our pigeon feeling, would you guess? Happy with the way things went yesterday?'

'You could say that,' she said casually, wishing she were sharing this breakfast with Mo. In private. She could do with a good friend to talk to right now and even if Pete and Lorne weren't cluttering up the table Julian could hardly fill the bill. He wasn't that kind of friend. She thought, oddly, that whatever happened from hereon in, Jeff Coolidge probably would be. But seeing as he was the topic she had an urgent need to talk about right now, the question was hardly relevant.

'Message for Miss O'Connell. Message for Kate O'Connell,' an elderly bellboy paged through the restaurant.

Kate signalled her identity and was handed a note. Julian watched her face as she read. Curiosity, knowledge, disbelief, concern, all in about five seconds flat. 'Oh shit,' she said quietly and handed the note over to Julian.

He wasn't so quiet about it. 'What the *fuck*!? . . .'

Faces turned.

'What's up?' They were the first words Pete had managed to articulate that day.

But Kate didn't hear them. She was already on her way to a telephone.

Chapter Nineteen

Just one word, 'Hello?' but Emily's voice was tight, anxious, eager.

'It's Kate. Kate O'Connell. Emily, what on earth's happened? Is Jeff there yet? What's wrong?'

'Oh, it's you.' Naked disappointment. Flat. Hopes dashed, not the time to think about being polite. 'Have you heard anything?' A faint revival.

'What about? What's going on? All I've had is a note saying "*Family emergency. Gone to the lake. Sorry.*" And we're in the middle of filming!'

'He's on his way then. Please God he'll be here soon.' If a voice could wring its hands, Emily's was doing it.

Kate waited, but nothing, so she prompted again, impatiently. 'Whatever's wrong, Emily? Look, can I help at all?'

'Danny's gone. Disappeared.'

Just like that. Words to send a stone plummeting through the stomach. 'What do you mean, disappeared? Run away? Just gone? No note, nothing?'

'Nothing. Look Kate, thank you for your concern but would you mind getting off the line? He might, somebody might be trying to call us.'

'Of course. I'm sorry. Tell Jeff . . .' Tell him what? 'Never mind. I'll be in touch.' There was a faint 'goodbye', a click on the end of the line and the connection was broken. Kate replaced the handset very gently, as if not wanting to create further shock waves.

'So?' asked Julian when she came back into the dining room. 'What the hell's going on? What does the man think he's playing at just doing a bunk like that without so much as a by your leave? What does he think this is, some sort of toytown let's pretend we're going to be on the telly game? Of all the bloody . . .'

'Oh, Julian do be quiet,' she said. 'The little boy, Danny, he's missing. What the hell do you expect Jeff to do — stand around smiling at a minicam when his son might be injured or kidnapped or worse? God knows what's happened, I didn't get any details but . . . oh, let's just pray he turns up soon and everything's all right.'

'It'd bloody well better be soon. You realise what this means, don't you? If he's not back by tonight we'll just have to cancel the whole bloody thing and go home. I suppose we might *just* be able to scratch enough together from yesterday's footage and hope the studio session will fill in the gaps but . . .'

Kate looked at him aghast. 'You can't be serious. Just go home? Just like that? Tough luck Jeff baby, see you later in the year? No *way*, Julian. I've got to get up to Gilberts Pond. And fast.'

'Just a minute,' he said. 'Let me think.' He narrowed his eyes and you could almost see the thoughts dropping into place like he had a tumbler mechanism inside a fruit machine head. His eyes widened. Jackpot. 'You're right. Family drama, live in action! What a terrific *Encounter*. The gods have dropped it right in our lap.'

He meant it. She couldn't believe it. Not even Julian could be that callous. Wrong again, Kate.

'Right, boys and girls,' he said, dabbing decisively at his mouth with a napkin and making to stand up. 'Action. Let's get packed. And somebody call Renta-campa or Hertz or something, we've no time to waste.'

Kate pushed him back into the chair. 'Shut up and sit down,' she ordered. 'You're seriously suggesting that we go barging in on them with cameras rolling when Danny might be injured, or, or . . . something?'

'Do you suppose he *might* have been kidnapped?' said Julian. And yes, he asked it hopefully. 'The price of fame, that sort of thing? It could be, you know. Think of it — bloody marvellous television!'

And Kate caught herself in the act of agreeing with him. She caught herself and stopped herself. 'Julian. No.' It was a very firm 'no'. '*I*'m going to Gilberts Pond. By myself. It's only a few hours. You stay here till you hear from me. I'll call you as soon as I know anything definite.'

'She's right,' said Pete, slowly emerging from his hangover. 'It's probably all a storm in a teacup. The kid'll turn up and Warren will be back and filming before you know it. No point in us all chasing up there.'

But once Julian latched on to an idea he didn't like to let it go too easily. 'Oh, come on, petal. We'll all go. We can't pass up an opportunity like this. Besides, what the hell do you think you can do up there on your own without us? What were you planning? Just take a Uher? This is television, my darling, *pictures*. You and a tape recorder ain't going to be much cop.'

'Are you off your head? I'm not talking about the bloody programme, I'm talking about trying to *help*. Moral support. Man the phone. Make sandwiches. Anything.'

'What the hell for? Now who's barging in? Why should they want you there at a time like this? If you're not going to film it, stay out of it, I say. What business is it of yours, for Chrissake?'

'Of course it's my business. They're my friends. I love that child.' And Kate was even more surprised at the declaration than Julian or Pete or Lorne were. And they were pretty taken aback.

Jeff had been driving like an automaton, cursing the speed restrictions but sticking to them anyway. The scenario where the cops pull you over for speeding then offer you an escort with sirens wailing when they find out it's an emergency only happens in the movies. In real life it's questions, delays, and book him at the end of it. Couldn't risk the delay. Kingston was behind him. Interchange twenty next.

Approaching.

Gone.

The thruway had never seemed so long or so slow. Frustration. Impotence. Fear. Just drive, Jeff. Don't think, just keep on going. Another fifteen miles at a steady fifty-five, should reach interchange twenty-one in about . . . can't work it out, don't think, just drive. Drive and pray. Let Danny be there when I arrive. 'Hi Dad. Just went out for a walk.' Just let him be all right, let him be all right, let him not be . . .

Don't think. Drive.

The Interstate 87 was far behind now. Eight miles past Middleburgh take a left and head for Decatur then north into the country, a few miles and Danny will be there, safe and smiling and contrite.

Strike the last two. Settle for 'safe'. Please.

Jeff kept on driving.

The BMW screeched to a halt, sending the shingle spattering. Jeff flung open the door and leapt out of the car, engine still ticking over. He ran into the house.

Emily was sitting by the telephone. She was so still and grey she could have been sculpted from stone.

William was pacing the floor, four steps, pause, swing round and back along the same track. Like a polar bear Jeff had once seen in a zoo compound.

Emily turned. William stopped pacing. Jeff asked tightly, 'Any news?'

'Do you think we'll ever get him back?' asked Emily flatly. It took an awful lot of courage – or despair – to actually voice the question. It was early in the afternoon now. An insensitively bright, sunshiney afternoon. Emily and Mrs Straker were alone in the house. Jeff and William were out searching the woods. Along with every available adult from the township of Gilberts Hollow.

Mrs Straker had got the full story almost as soon as Danny's disappearance was discovered, when Emily had telephoned Jeff in New York just after six that morning. Not that the part-time postmistress had listened in intentionally, you understand, but at the note of panic in Emily's voice she had to check that there was nothing seriously wrong, didn't she? So now her husband was looking after the store and she was looking after Emily. And Emily had gone over the facts again. There weren't many. She'd looked in on Danny before going to bed the night before and he'd been sleeping normally. She'd tiptoed out of the room and closed the door softly behind her. She'd woken early this morning, decided to get up rather than try to go back to sleep, and had noticed his door was slightly ajar. She peeped in. The hump in the bed looked a little strange. She entered the room. Discovered the hump wasn't Danny, just a couple of pillows under the bedclothes. And that's about all there was to it. No Danny, no note, nothing.

'You've told the police?'

It was all Emily could do to stop herself from snapping Beth Straker's head off. 'Of course,' she said impatiently. 'But Chief Hollis said there's not much they can do at this point, short of telling the State Troopers to keep an eye out for a lonely-looking child. He reckons he's either gone off on some sort of adventure of his own or he's run away and he'll come back when he gets tired or hungry or scared. For now we just search where we can and wait. If he's not back by nightfall or if we haven't had a . . .' she hesitated then went on firmly, 'a ransom demand, then they'll put out a State alert.' Emily's voice sort of faded to a halt. She sounded and looked drained, deadened.

'Sweet Lord above, you don't really think he could have been kidnapped, do you? Danny? Here, at Gilberts Hollow? Why on earth would anybody . . . ?'

'It's possible,' said Emily. 'What with all the publicity over Jeff's book, it's entirely possible. Some sick person out there may have decided that Danny would provide rich pickings. I just pray that Chief Hollis is wrong.'

'Of course he is,' said Beth Straker with a lot more confidence than she was feeling.

'Yes, of course,' said Emily, determined to believe.

'And he wouldn't have run away,' Mrs Straker went on. 'Not your Danny. Now my Tom, I could believe it of him. But not your Danny. He's a good boy. I only wish some of his manners would rub off on my two. No, you'll see, Emily, he's probably just gone off on his own for a while and he'll walk in that door as if butter wouldn't melt, wondering what all the fuss is about.'

'He would have been home for lunch,' said Emily flatly. 'He could be lying out there injured somewhere, or fallen in the lake and banged his head and . . .' The tears came. At last.

'Emily, Emily, stop it, you mustn't think like that. He's probably taken a backpack full of cookies with him and he's just out in the woods somewhere having the time of his life. He can't have gone far. He'll be home before nightfall, just you wait and see.'

Emily wondered if Mrs Straker would feel so certain of it if it were her Tom or little Robert they were talking about. And she couldn't help wishing that it was. 'He can't have gone far,' she repeated. 'He can't have gone . . .' Suddenly she sat bolt upright. 'Unless . . . Oh my God. The bicycle. Jeff's old bicycle. Why didn't we think to . . . In the shed. The bike!'

The bicycle had been Jeff's pride and joy during his own childhood summers at the lake. But it had lain for years, forgotten and rusting, under the growing pile of detritus that all outbuildings have a voracious appetite for collecting. They'd never bothered bringing it out for Danny. It wasn't worth it, would probably be cheaper and certainly easier to buy him his own spanking new one. Except that as yet they'd done neither.

Emily and Beth hurried outside.

Jeff walked slowly along the track back to the house. He neither knew nor cared much what the time was. The sun was past the meridian. Bright hot sun outside. Dull cold cancer inside. A greedy cancer which had eaten away his capacity for hope, faith, belief – even feeling. He'd always thought that if anything ever happened to Danny, somehow he'd know about it. A primordial gut intuition would tell him if Danny was hurt, in danger, dead. Paternal instinct. He'd just *know*.

But it wasn't true. Even that had let him down. There was nothing.

Except for this heavy lump of coldness. With sharp edges.

Emily rushed out of the house. 'Jeff, oh Jeff, the bicycle! Your old bike in the shed, it's gone. Danny must have taken it . . .'

Danny had it all planned out. He was going to stick to the back roads. He was pretty sure he could make it on the bike as far as Middleburgh. Twenty, twenty-five miles, it should be good enough for that, just to get him well clear of Gilberts Hollow before they missed him. After that it would be safe to hitch a ride, little risk of being picked up by anybody who knew who he was.

So he'd dumped the bike outside Middleburgh somewhere and hitched in short stages. The short lifts were annoying but it was the only way he could think of to make his story believable. He might be only seven but he wasn't dumb. He knew as well as anyone that a kid on his own on the road is most likely a runaway. And an adult wasn't likely to offer much in the way of help except pick him up and take him straight back home again.

Danny's story went like this – that he *had* run away from home, but he'd thought better of it and was now hitching his way *back* again. He thought it was pretty watertight, so long as he kept his destination to a believable distance. He'd checked it all out on the map, thought fifteen mile stages should be about right, so his planned route was from Middleburgh back to his 'home' in Preston Hollow, then from there pick up another ride on to Cairo. A short hop from there into Leeds then he could get a Greyhound straight to New York. If it all went to plan he should be in the city before it came dark, no problem.

He'd considered the possibility that his father might not be at the apartment when he turned up but decided it was unlikely. Sure, he'd probably be on the phone to Grandma and Grandpa a lot when they found he was gone but he couldn't see his father walking out on a TV film. (And if he had left it all to go back to the lake to look for him, well, it would just serve him right, that's all. Let *him* see how it feels to have someone you love walk out on you. Do him good to stew a bit.) The more Danny thought about it, the more he hoped his father would indeed have gone back up to Gilberts Pond to look for him. At least that would prove it was true, all those things he'd said about Danny being more important than anything else.

So far his plans had worked out just fine. The hardest part was nearly over. A big bull of a man with gappy teeth and a farm truck which smelled bad had dropped him off just inside Cairo at around noon. Danny'd been worried for a moment when the man had said, 'Danny Peterson? Only Petersons I know around here live over on Kilhenny Street. You kin of theirs?'

'No,' he said quickly. 'John Peterson. John and Mary Peterson, they're my folks. We're new in town. Only moved here a couple of weeks ago. And I didn't like it much.'

'So you decided to take off, huh?'

Danny nodded.

'So where're you from originally?'

Better stick to the truth as much as possible, that way there's less chance of being caught out. 'New York.'

'Oh? So how come I picked you up coming from the other direction?' The man had looked over at him squarely, eyes narrowing in suspicion.

Danny thought fast. 'Guess I was lost. As I said, we're new around here. Don't know my way round too good.'

'Hm.' The man drove on in silence for a minute or two before saying conversationally, 'Sure you don't want me to take you straight to your door? What did you say the address was?'

'No, really, it's okay. This'll do fine. Anywhere around here will be just fine. Just put me down in the high street, we only live a couple of blocks away.'

'If you're sure.' The man didn't sound it.

But the truck slowed and stopped. Danny opened the

door and with a quick, 'Thanks a lot, mister,' he got out and started walking rapidly along the street, took the first turning left then waited for a full five minutes until he was sure the farmer would be well out of the way. Once he'd cautiously checked it was all clear – he didn't want to be handed over to the police force as a suspected runaway, not when he'd got so far – he set off again, looking this way and that until he found what he was looking for.

A big yellow 'M'. He went inside and ordered a Big Mac, large fries and a chocolate shake.

Fifteen minutes later, satisfactorily refuelled, he was walking determinedly along the main street again heading for the outskirts of Cairo and a suitable spot to thumb down the next ride into Leeds. After that it would be plain sailing.

Kate stood in her hotel room, overnight bag already packed, phone to her ear, and impatient toes tapping noiselessly on the thick carpet. 'Come on,' she mumbled on the second ring, 'answer, damn you.' The curse worked. The ringing stopped and an impersonal voice from the reception desk answered. Kate spoke quickly, gave her name and room number, feeling like a POW. 'I've got a problem. I need to be in the middle of nowhere by yesterday or quicker. It's a little place near . . . shit, I don't remember where it's near. It's about fifty or sixty miles due east of Albany. Should I take a shuttle flight to Albany then hire a car or a taxi, or would I be quicker on a train or even, God forbid, a bus? I have to get there fast. What do I do?'

Within half an hour Kate had the Avis keyring in her hand. She chucked the overnight case on to the back seat of the Ford Fairmont then familiarised herself with the controls. Automatic drive, of course. And steering wheel on the wrong side of the car. But basically, stop, reverse or go. She turned on the ignition and went.

Think, Kate. Think and drive. Logical, methodical, think all around it and think it through.

Up the ramp, slow down, wait for a gap, look over left shoulder not right, join the steady mainflow of unconcerned traffic.

Gone missing could just mean gone for a long walk. Even kids need to be on their own sometimes. In the middle of the night? Early in the morning? Keep on driving, keep on thinking.

Gone for a walk could mean had a fall, an injury. Or could have gone for a swim. Drowned? Logical, I said. Danny can swim like a fish. And fish don't drown. Do they?

She checked the road signs, glanced at the map that was lying open on the passenger seat, kept on driving, kept on thinking.

Run away, then? Why and where to? A seven year old hitch-hiker? God forbid. But maybe he had money. So could have taken a train or a bus. Again, where to? Think, Kate. Think and drive.

Junction 21 coming up. Get into the right hand lane ready to leave the Interstate. Kidnapping was a federal offence – have to be pretty damned sure the payoff would be worth the risk. Nationwide publicity. Father still in the top three on the bestseller list. In a country as big as the States that adds up to a lot of dollars. Worth the risk. She shuddered and took the exit ramp.

The longest, but fastest, stage of the journey was behind her now and God knew what use she was going to be when she got there. But she had to be with them. Him. Not logical at all. But a fact.

She cursed. Much as she wanted to keep on going, nature demanded she'd have to break the journey. And soon. She wriggled in the seat. The road sign promised another six miles to the next town. Cairo. Six whole miles. She prayed for a service station before then. And hoped the road wouldn't be too bumpy.

After all the dreadful scenarios that had been pelting across Jeff's mind, a missing bike and Danny planning to ride it probably the two hundred miles or so to New

York was kind of – not exactly laughable but definitely a relief. The ice began to melt a little round the edges as Emily explained what they thought must have happened.

Chief Hollis soon froze him up again. 'A boy his age,' he said, standing like a threat in the middle of their living room, 'and a good-looking little boy at that, out on the road alone – there are all kinds of freaks out there, sick people, violent people . . .' He finished the sentence by shaking his head.

'But the State troopers are on the lookout now, and the highway patrol. He can't have gone too far yet, they'll pick him up in no time, won't they, now they have a description and everything?' asked Emily.

The hope on her face was almost painful to see and the Chief of Police didn't want to crush it. He just said, 'Most likely, Mrs Coolidge, most likely.'

'And most likely if I'd gone with my gut feelings at the start we wouldn't be having this conversation now,' said Jeff bitterly. 'That damned publicity tour, Kate and the television people, me with my head stuck into my book instead of realising what was going on with Danny. Christ, he made it plain enough. He tried to. But I wasn't listening. Oh sure, I kidded myself I was. Thought I said all the right words. But I didn't, did I? He needed me and I wasn't there for him. And all I had to do was listen, I mean *listen*. But I got sucked in. Suckered. "Publicity, you've got to get publicity," they said. "Get your head down. Work. We need the follow up." And I listened to them. Instead of to what my son was trying to tell me." He spoke angrily, bitterly. Desperate to find someone or something to blame, he turned that blame on himself.

'Don't. What about us?' put in William. 'We were here too, you mustn't blame yourself.' But he was looking at the pipe in his fingers, not at Jeff. Emily had her arms wrapped across her chest as if she were hugging herself. Chief Hollis remained silent. They were all aware that there was an element of warped truth in what Jeff had said.

And that's when the telephone bell ripped across their silence.

If Kate had averaged just one mile an hour faster she would have been well past it before it happened. Or if she hadn't had to make the stop at the service station she might have actually seen it happen. Or if she hadn't spent those extra two minutes checking on her route with the attendant, it might have been herself, her own car.

At first she thought it was a breakdown. A car stopped in the middle of the highway, brake lights on and all four indicator lights winking. She slowed, prepared to overtake, then saw the other lane was blocked. Another car. Broken glass. Somebody's front fender lying in the road. A dazed looking man flapping his arms at her, signalling her to stop. She pulled over and leaned out of the window.

'There was a dog. I was trying not to hit the damned dog. I didn't see . . .' The man was obviously in shock but apart from that didn't appear to be injured. Just a small accident, vehicles damaged but no one hurt.

She opened the door and got out a little impatiently. At least somebody could have thought to move the offending bumper, let the rest of the traffic by while names and addresses were exchanged. It was only when she straightened that she saw. Realised.

Just lying there. At the side of the road. Unattended, as if it were a squashed cat. *Disregarded* while the man stood about, flapping at the air. But it wasn't a cat.

A child.

Looking like a little heap of discarded rags.

And still. So still.

And a shock of red instead of a face.

And a small hand, limp, palm upwards. And no one to hold it.

For a split second which felt like an eternity Kate was frozen into immobility. She fought back the urge to retch. Then she ran. 'An ambulance,' she cried, 'has anyone called an ambulance?'

The man nodded, flapped at the other car, the one with the lights blinking.

'They're on their way,' called another voice. A man hurrying towards them along the road.

Kate ran to the little body. Knelt over it. Reached out to feel for a pulse, clear the air passage, check the breathing, do what little she knew how to do. Gently, she smoothed the mat of bloody hair away from the child's face.

And that's when the tears started. 'Oh no,' she whispered. 'Dear God, no.'

His eyes were closed. There was no sound, no movement. The head wound was no longer bleeding but most of his face glistened red from where the blood had streamed over it. She leaned her cheek to his face, not breathing herself, praying she would feel the gentle flutter of breath on her skin.

She felt nothing.

Cautiously she pressed her fingertips against his neck, feeling for a pulse. And all the while she was whispering, 'It's all right, you're going to be all right. I'm here, I'm with you. Don't worry, Danny my darling, Kate will look after you . . .'

Cautious – terrified – she tilted his head back, eased down his jaw, gently pinched his nostrils closed then placed her mouth over his.

Chapter Twenty

Kate was sitting on a bench seat in a room opposite the nurses' station, waiting. Nurses with starched caps, smart trouser suits, white shoes. Looking busy. Looking professional. People whose job was to care, looking as if they didn't care at all.

She stared at a scuff on the white painted wall as nurses, doctors, anonymous people alternately hurried or strolled past the open door of the waiting room. Faces were grim or relaxed, silent or chattering in low voices. She heard someone laugh. The sound shocked through her. She wanted to scream at them, how dare they, when Danny was lying on an operating table fighting for his life, his brief life.

People had thrown questions at her about Blue Cross and names and next of kin and she'd answered automatically, as calm and efficient as the questioners. But she was not the patient's next of kin. Not even a relative. She was pointed towards a seat and told she could wait there.

And wait, she would. But there was no reason now for Julian, Lorne and Pete to do the same. She ignored the seat and found a telephone, called the New York hotel, spoke to Julian, told him calmly and concisely what had happened, ignored his histrionics and told him to get on a plane and go home, the Warren shoot was postponed.

And then she sat and waited. People passed by. She could see the elevator doors. She waited for Jeff. White. Sterile. Empty. Waiting. She waited for the surgeon to come. And stared at the scuff on the white painted wall.

The elevator doors opened again. A dishevelled man with a gaunt face elbowed his way out and then stood stock still, as if suddenly disorientated, afraid. He looked around, she went to the door, made a small movement of acknowledgement. Even though he could see that it was her, Jeff said, 'Kate?' Questioning, as if his eyes lied.

She ran towards him and held him tight. He looked like he needed something to hold on to. Let it be me, she thought.

He held on tight.

It was late in the afternoon then. Hope is supposed to be easier in the daylight. But it isn't. The minutes passed so slowly. Kate, Jeff, William, Emily, each sitting tightly in the prison of their own dread. They spoke rarely once Kate had told them what she could about what had happened. All their words were being used in silent pleas to their personal gods. They stood about, they paced, they sat. They stood again. And their faces were heavy with the weight of waiting.

'Mr Coolidge?'

Jeff had been leaning against the window frame staring unfocused at the world outside, locked in his own guilt. The voice jolted him back to the present and his body snapped to attention, faced the surgeon, waiting for the life or death sentence. It was all there in the doctor's eyes but Jeff wouldn't allow himself to read it. He had to wait, hear the words spoken out loud.

The words came gently.

There was an afternoon flight to Heathrow. Julian and the equipment and Kate's leftover luggage were going to be on it. That made it full. Pete and Lorne were on standby and complaining. Not because they were relegated to standby but because they had to be on any flight at all. They were supposed to be booked in at the hotel for two more nights. They'd had flight reservations for Thursday. As this was only Tuesday they'd seen the cancellation of the Warren profile as an unexpected bonus. They did *not* expect their producer to have an attack of punctilious parsimony and bundle them all off to Kennedy airport without so much as a, 'let's do the Empire State Building seeing as we're here'. The way Julian was going on about saving the cost of three rooms for two nights, they were amazed he hadn't insisted they all take the *bus* to London.

'Some freebie this turned out to be,' grumbled Lorne as they watched their producer disappear into the departure area.

'We might have a long wait,' said Pete. 'So where's the bloody bar?' Very philosophical.

Julian arrived at TV7 very late the next day with a face like a dollop of mortal sins. And as soon as he set foot in the production office he had a feeling that this was going to be one of those lousy days which, if he'd had any sense, he'd have written off as soon as he'd dragged his eyelids open a couple of painful hours earlier. It wasn't even as if he was expected till the end of the week. And it was still only Wednesday. And he was genuinely sick – if you count terminal jet-lag as 'sick', which Julian did. Kate was skiving off, so why shouldn't he? But he hadn't. He'd gone in to TV7, and within three minutes he knew it was going to be a lousy day.

He was greeted with a rapid fire question and answer session covering, yes he was back, why he was back, no Kate wasn't yet, why Kate wasn't yet and no, nobody, including Julian, had heard anything from her about when she thought she'd return.

He couldn't cope. He headed for the Club bar. Half a scotch later he wished he hadn't. The grapevine was busy dropping its fruits and leaving splodgy little messes all over the place. And Julian didn't like it, not one little bit. Every conversation he eavesdropped on concerned one subject and one subject only – O'Connell was for the push.

And by association, her producer along with her?

Julian, a great believer in the 'out of sight, out of mind' philosophy, buried himself in an editing channel for the afternoon with the rough-cut of the Stavros *Encounter* and a telephone with direct dial facilities. But the film ended up with a stubborn six whole minutes overrun which Julian couldn't for the life of him work out how to lose. And a variety of international telephone operators stubbornly kept on insisting that there was no reply from the number at Gilberts Hollow, New York State.

At six o'clock he gave in and called it a day. He couldn't decide whether to kill himself, run away to sea, or head for his favourite gay bar in Soho and pick up some temporary consolation. He was still undecided as he waited for the lift to take him down to TV7's reception lobby.

'Ah, Julian, glad I caught you. Mind if we have a little word? Over a drink p'raps?'

The Head of Programming sounded uncharacteristically jovial. Maybe the lousy day was going to redeem itself after all.

'In my office,' Franklin added.

And maybe it wasn't. Drinkie-poohs in the Club bar were one thing, and drinks in the privacy of a seventh floor executive suite were quite another. 'That'd be nice,' said Julian, trying to inject a smile into his voice. 'Can't stop long though, I've got an appointment in an hour.' He looked at his wristwatch to reinforce the lie.

'Don't worry, I won't keep you long,' said Ed.

That's what I'm afraid of, thought Julian as the lift carried him upwards instead of down.

Ed poured out a couple of large gins and added a cursory splash of tonic to each of them. He handed Julian a glass with the words, 'What it was, Julian . . . do sit down, man, relax, enjoy your drink . . .' Ed followed his own instructions and settled himself heavily on the couch, sighing with satisfaction as he swallowed a good proportion of his G and T in one go. 'Ah, nothing like it at the end of a long, hard day. I've been up to here going over the draft agenda for the quarterly Programme Planning Board.' He stopped there and looked across at Julian significantly, as if he'd said enough to make his point.

If he had, Julian missed it. 'Difficult, was it?' he asked casually.

'As a matter of fact, it was. Very.' Ed took another

drink. 'How far into production are you with the *Encounter*?'

'A fair way.' Perhaps that wasn't far enough. Julian hastily shoved the lousy day behind him and launched into hyperbolic drive. 'Going splendidly, in fact. Absolutely terrific. Fantastic. All set to sock 'em right between the eyes!' He wondered if it sounded as forced as it felt.

Ed made a play of lighting up a cigarette. As he exhaled the smoke he looked at Julian with narrowed eyes. 'I'll lay it on you straight, Julian. Item One on the agenda, proposed shelving of the O'Connell series.'

A silence filled with rapid thought. Then Julian said, 'Shelving? As in delay until later or as in cancel altogether?'

'Not my decision, old chap,' said Franklin with what was supposed to pass for a helpless shrug. 'That's the PPB's job.'

To his credit Julian came up fighting. 'Come on, Ed, don't give me that crap. You're the HP, you're the one who decides if it even *goes* to the meeting or not. Postpone it or cancel it? You can't! Not when we're all set to go. Bloody hell, Princess Anne'll be here next week for her studio session.' He took a drink to control his panic. Bewildered he asked, 'Why are you doing this?'

'There are reasons,' came the reply.

Julian waited for him to continue but the man just sat there. 'You could at least tell me what they are.' He struggled valiantly to keep the pleading note out of his voice. He almost succeeded. 'You've seen some of what we've done so far. The Stavros profile is brilliant, you said so yourself and that was just the rough cut.' (Actually, Ed's words had been, 'Mm. Nice work,' but this wasn't the time to haggle over minor details.) 'And Princess Anne's all done but for the interview. And Margaret Thatcher. You can't just ditch it, Ed. Not royalty. You can't!'

But the Head of Programming looked as though he certainly could if he wanted to.

Julian went for the jugular. 'Think of the money! All

that money down the drain if we pull out now. Can the company's finances stand it?'

Franklin sighed. 'You're quite right, Julian. But I have to ask myself, the Board has to ask, is it worth it? I mean, think of all the money down the drain if we go on with it and it turns out to be a ratings flop. You know the situation we're in. Financially, the future of the company is . . . well, shaky. We have to make cuts somewhere. Frankly, the *Encounter*'s the obvious choice − nothing ready for transmission yet and Kate's hardly the public's darling any more, is she? Not since all the Pritchard business . . .'

'No publicity is bad publicity,' said Julian weakly.

Ed finished his drink and put the empty glass back down on the table. He went on as if Julian hadn't spoken. 'So when it comes down to it the choice is between programme cuts or staff cuts. Or in some cases, both,' he added ominously. 'The meeting's on Monday afternoon and believe me, I'm not looking forward to it. Nobody likes having to be the hatchet man.' He sighed again. 'Jobs. Livelihoods. Redundancies.' He said the last word as if it had a heavy black line underneath it. With a little label attached, saying *Julian Howard*. 'So if you were in my − the Board's − position, which would you choose, Julian?'

Programme cuts, he thought. So long as it's not my programme. Staff cuts. So long as it's not me. 'Look,' he said, seeing no way he could commit himself without committing suicide, 'don't you think we should wait until Kate can be here before we discuss this? After all, it's her show.'

'A fair point. And where is the dear lady?'

Oops. 'Er, um, she's . . . a little tied up at the moment. A couple of loose ends over in the States. But she'll be back tomorrow. Or Friday. Yes, definitely by Friday.' It was a magnificent show of unfounded confidence.

Ed looked at Julian in silence for a moment before saying, 'Maybe it would be better if she stayed tied up. No more sex and scandal in the gutter press to worry about. Just quietly drop the *Encounter* and, well, there you are, problem solved. We'd have to pay her to the end of her contract I suppose, which is a pity but . . . then again, we might be able to find something in the small print. Yes, I'll get the legal department on to it.' He sounded very bright and businesslike all of a sudden.

'Just a minute.' Julian held up his hand. He heard it but he didn't believe it. He summarised for his own clarification. 'You're saying not only do we dump the *Encounter* but we dump Kate, too? You're mad. She's the hottest property this piddling little company's got. Okay, so maybe she's not all sweetness and light at the moment, but when was she ever? And it'll all blow over. The public has a very short memory. A few months, a few weeks, even . . . Don't do it, Ed.'

'Me?' All innocence. 'Not my decision. It's for the PPB to decide.' All Pontius Pilate.

'But where would that leave *me*?' asked Julian, selfless to the last.

Ed gave a cold-eyed smile. 'With a job,' he said. 'If you co-operate.'

The surgeon had addressed Jeff calmly and concisely. Jeff heard the words but they didn't sink in.

'I said,' repeated the surgeon, reinforcing his message with a gentle smile, 'he's going to pull through.' This was one of the good parts of his job. Watching the prayers answered, tears of joy not grief. 'Daniel is a very lucky little boy,' he went on. 'Someone at the scene of the accident knew what they were doing. If they'd waited for the paramedics it would probably have been too late, at the best brain damage from oxygen starvation, at the worst . . . well . . .' he shrugged. 'No need to worry about that. He's going to be just fine. Concussion, a hairline skull fracture, a couple of cracked ribs, broken radius, pretty extensive cuts and bruises. We set the arm, stitched and cleaned him up. All in all, nothing too serious. He looks a lot worse than he is. As I said,' he repeated, 'he's a very lucky little boy.'

'Oh God. Thank God. Can I see him?'

'Yes. He's still under the anaesthetic but you can sit with him. No more than two at a time, please.'

Emily went with Jeff, leaving Kate and William alone in the waiting room in the strange and quiet anticlimax of relief. William looked at the young Englishwoman, took her hands in both his and clasped them tightly. His voice was gruff with emotion when he spoke. 'You saved his life, Kate. How can we ever thank you?'

She shook her head. 'Please, William. Don't. Or I'll start crying. I'm just so glad that . . .' She couldn't say any more.

William put his arm around her shoulder. 'Come along, my dear. Let's see if we can find a decent cup of coffee in this place.'

Jeff stayed by Danny's side. Eventually Emily came out and William went in. And then, at last, it was Kate's turn.

Danny moaned quietly. No, it was more of a whimper than a moan. Jeff stroked the pale cheek and with tears of relief nearly choking back his voice he said, 'It's okay, Chief. Daddy's here. It's all right . . .' Eagerly he watched Danny's face. The lids fluttered, opened, drooped again.

'Daddy?'

'Yes, darling. You're all right. I'm here.'

Danny's eyes opened again, slowly focused. 'I hurt. It hurts, Daddy.' The voice was weak, puzzled.

Jeff kept on stroking his cheek, feeling he ought to be stroking back the hair but it was hidden away under the bandages across his forehead, wrapping round his head. 'I know, I know. But it'll be all right. Just sleep.'

'Don't want to sleep. Bad dream. It was . . . I was all by myself, Daddy. I was all by myself and everything was . . . I was hurting real bad. And this big dark thing was coming closer and closer and it was sort of dark and red and heavy and it hurt . . . and I was really scared and there was nobody there, nobody at all.' Tears slowly trickled from Danny's eyes.

Jeff kept on saying, 'Sssh. Don't talk. It's all right,

Chief, everything's all right now . . .' but he couldn't stop his own tears coming. Relief, joy, gratitude. And sharing Danny's pain like it was his own.

'Then I dreamed that Kate came.' The words were weak, sleep overtaking him again. 'That was the good part. She held my hand . . .'

'She did. That part wasn't a dream. She's here.'

But Danny's eyes were closed again, consciousness relinquished to healing sleep. And that was when Kate entered the room.

She saw more white walls, machinery going blip, blip, blip, suspended bottles feeding tubes into veins, going drip, drip, drip. And a broken and bandaged child in a tall bed. White bandages, white plaster cast, white face and Jeff sitting there gently holding the small white hand, the hand with the tubes being fed into it. Kate closed the door very quietly behind her.

Jeff looked round as she entered, dashed fingers to his eyes. Then carefully, as if not wanting to risk breaking it, he placed Danny's hand on the bedspread and stood. He waited for her to approach, looking at her as if every star in the sky had taken aim at his eyes. He said her name. Then he asked, 'Hold me. Please.'

They sat through the night at Danny's bedside in that state of quiet exhaustion which is beyond all thought of sleep. Danny drifted in and out of consciousness, Kate and Jeff drifted in and out of conversation, disposing of their questions and answers in voices barely more than a whisper: 'But you were there, how come you were there?'

'I was coming up to Gilberts Pond.'

'I thought you'd be on your way back to London.'

'Julian and the boys are. I couldn't.'

'Why?'

She settled for, 'Idiot. Did you really think I could just *go*, when Danny was missing and you were . . .' She shrugged. 'Hell, you're the one who said it, we're supposed to be friends, aren't we? What kind of friend would just call it a wrap and pack up the gear and go home at a time like that, just because the filming was ruined? Jesus, Coolidge, what kind of person do you think I am?'

He looked at her and slowly shook his head. 'Miraculous.'

Just about the time Julian was making the first of his many unsuccessful attempts to phone Kate from the security of his editing channel bolt-hole, William and Emily Coolidge were on their way back to the hospital. It was about seven-thirty on Wednesday morning Stateside of the Atlantic and they were eager to get back to their grandson, having spent the night in a local motel while Jeff and Kate stayed on bedside watch. Temporary base had been established, with rooms booked for Jeff and Kate as well, and now they left Jeff's car in the visitors' parking lot and hurried through the main entrance to the hospital building. A couple of minutes after, a dirty white TravelAll with a red and yellow logo emblazoned on its side, and with roof antennae swaying, pulled up just outside the doors.

After the grandparents' quick, eager questions – how is he, has he slept, what does the doctor say? – were satisfied, Emily gently ordered Jeff and Kate out of Danny's room. She and William were perfectly capable of sitting with him and of course they'd let Jeff know if there was anything at all . . . and so on and so forth.

'Go!' said Emily, pointing towards the door. 'Get some sleep. I don't want to end up having to nursemaid you as well as Danny when he's allowed home.'

Jeff kissed his son's cheek. 'Sleep well, Chief,' he whispered. 'I love you. Grandma and Grandpa are here with you. I won't be far away.' Then with a final, 'You'll call me *at once* if . . . ?' he was firmly and physically pointed to the doorway.

'Go!'

They left. They said nothing in the elevator, just two tired, very tired, people. They went through the main doors into the cool morning. 'I wonder where Dad left my car.'

'Mine's there.' Kate pointed. 'I'll drive.'

Then suddenly they heard a voice cry, 'That's him, C. J. Warren!' and there were people jostling around, a television camera aimed at them, a stranger carrying a clipboard rushed towards Jeff and a woman with a vaguely familiar face beckoned urgently at him with a hand microphone. The dulling lethargy surrounding Kate and Jeff splintered into shards of sharp-edged anger. 'What in *hell's* going on?'

'A TV crew.' Kate's voice was stony. 'Come on.' She grabbed Jeff's hand and waved the clipboard carrier aside like he was a marauding wasp.

'What *is* all this, get these goddamned people away from here!' Jeff yelled to nobody in particular.

The woman with the microphone chased after them as they ran through the parking lot. 'Please, Mr Warren, we only want three minutes live into the eight o'clock. I'm Dale Rainer, KMTV. Just a few straightforward questions on background and progress so far, like how's the kid, why did he run away . . .' Still on the run herself she thrust the microphone under his nose and went on, 'if you could just give me a few words for level, then we'll go over it once before . . .'

Kate stopped. She gripped the hand that was gripping the microphone then with an icy clarity she told the reporter, 'Go and shove this up your arse, lady.'

There followed a real live car chase to the motel – a fairly slow-motion car chase, not very box office. Driving after some twenty-four hours without sleep Kate was thankful for the car's automatic transmission.

They pulled up. The television OB truck trundled up behind them. They leapt out of the car and dashed through a door marked *Reception*. 'You have a room reserved for J. Coolidge?' she demanded of the clerk.

Two rooms reserved. Two keys handed over. Kate took a moment to smile at the morality, or maybe tact, of the elder Coolidges, then she dangled the keys at Jeff. 'Your place or mine?'

Jeff grimaced. 'Whichever's the closest.'

'Come on then. I'm good at this. All you have to do is keep on walking and say "no comment". Ready?'

He nodded.

So they strode, rather than ran, the gauntlet. Kate couldn't help partly sympathising with Dale Rainer who was hurrying beside them pleading, 'Just a few simple questions, Mr Warren, it's nearly time. How bad are his injuries, why did he run away, how did you feel when you heard about the accident?'

Kate wanted to wrench the microphone away and clobber the woman over the head with it. 'No comment,' she said, hustling Jeff along the walkway outside the concrete chalets.

But Jeff couldn't manage the no comment. 'What the fuck business is it of yours?' he lashed out.

'Like it or not, C. J., you're news,' said the reporter impatiently. 'The public has a right to know so . . .' Her sentence was punctuated by the slam of a motel room door in her face. She turned to her cameraman with a shrug and finished the sentence, '. . . so I guess we'll have to do a straight voice report.' She touched the earpiece which nestled unseen beneath her no longer perfect coiffure, nodded then said, 'Okay, yes, we're ready to go.' She looked wistfully at the closed door then turned back to the cameraman. 'Thirty seconds,' she said, switched her face into its serious news expression and waited for her cue.

Inside the motel room Jeff headed straight for the television. He switched it on, blatted through the channels till he found the right one, then watched unbelieving as the screen exposed his private nightmare. It was a violation.

' . . . *local celebrity Jeffrey Coolidge, better known to the public as bestselling author C. J. Warren, is too distraught to face the camera after the last harrowing hours in a life already scarred by tragedy. Six years ago his lovely young wife, Jennifer, died of cancer at the age of twenty-eight when Danny, who's now fighting for his own life, was little more than a babe in arms . . .'*

'This is appalling,' muttered Kate. 'News report? Soap opera, more like. What a load of bullshit.'

Jeff stared at the screen.

' . . . when attempting to hitch-hike the two hundred and thirty mile journey to New York City to be with his father who had yet again left him in the care of relatives . . .'

'I'll kill them. I'll sue. I'll . . .' His fists were tightly clenched, the knuckles showing white.

' . . . the child's physical condition is now described as stable . . .'

Kate switched off the set. 'Damn, damn, *damn* them to hell!'

'What are *you* so worked up about? It's not your life they just raped. Talk about vultures looking for the corpse, all that crap about fighting for his life and saying it as if they *wanted* him to die!'

She spun round. 'Stop it. Just shut up. Danny's going to be fine, you know that, you've seen him for yourself, you heard the surgeon. He's *all right*. Okay, so it was a crappy report, so what? Christ, why on earth didn't we just stand firm and give them what they wanted?' She shook her head, talking to herself now, rather than to Jeff. 'I should have taken that mike and done it myself. Properly. What the hell am *I* doing running from a camera?' She sat heavily on the edge of the bed. It creaked.

Jeff came to her, took her hands in his. 'Kate, I'm glad you did. I couldn't have faced it. Not even with you. Not right now.'

She looked up at him and smiled, her confused sense of anger and frustration fading as she looked into those dark grey eyes. 'No, of course you couldn't. Tact and timing. Not something TV reporters are much endowed with, I'm afraid. Present company excepted, of course,' she said modestly. 'Look, why don't you take a shower and a shave while I go outside and smooth Ms Whatser-name's rumpled feathers, then you can do a nice, factual, unsentimental, straightforward interview for the nine o'clock to put the record straight?'

'Uh-uh.' He shook his head. 'Dale Rainer already knows what she can do with her microphone. Somebody told her very clearly, very recently. And I think it was good advice. The shower and the shave can wait a while, too.' He spoke through a yawn and crawled on to the bed. It creaked again. 'The way I feel right now I'd probably drown.'

'In a *shower*?'

Another yawn. 'Or cut my throat with my electric shaver.' He closed his eyes. 'Imagine what she'd do with that in her precious nine o'clock . . .' His voice trailed off. He was already asleep.

It seemed to Kate that he had the right idea, but first things first. She felt tacky, dishevelled, like something an alleycat wouldn't even bother to drag in from a dustbin raid. She went into the bathroom and glanced in the mirror. A glance was about all she could take. Shiny patches down each side of her nose, mere remnants of yesterday's mascara, hair looking like a couple of rats had been having the time of their lives in it. Maybe it was just as well she hadn't attempted to usurp the KMTV woman . . .

They got back to the hospital after three or four hours' sleep to find Danny awake and fractious and complaining: 'I don't like it here. My head hurts. I want to go home.'

'Well, if you will try and argue with a ten-ton truck, what do you expect?' said Jeff, delighted by the grumbles of recovery.

'Was it really a ten-ton truck?' asked the boy, wide-eyed.

'No. It was just a car.'

'What sort?'

'What does it matter? Want to boast battle honours or something? I don't know. Ask Kate, she was there.'

'What make of car was it, Kate?'

'The same as your father's.'

'A BMW?'

'I don't know. A blue one.'

A hospital orderly wheeled in Danny's lunch on a trolley. Chicken. Mashed potato. A squodge of something vaguely green. They wound up the back of his bed so's he could eat. The intravenous drip was gone now. He took a fork in his one working hand and prodded at the food suspiciously. 'Dad? Couldn't you get me a Kentucky or something?'

The adults grinned at each other. There was nothing much wrong with this kid that time and junk food wouldn't cure.

The nurses threw them out after lunch so Danny could rest. Now that the crisis was over the adults felt like they could do with a rest, too. Emily and William retired to the motel with a sparkle in their eyes muttering something about old bones. Kate and Jeff remembered that they hadn't eaten for about a month and walked the nearby streets till they found a restaurant. It was the kind of place that calls itself a bistro and was small and unpretentious apart from the red gingham tablecloths decorated with chianti bottle candle-holders.

'So, a few more days and you'll be off back to Gilberts Pond, I suppose,' said Kate, once five minutes of concentrated eating had taken the edge off her immediate hunger.

'Yes. I've been thinking maybe I should sell up the apartment and move up there permanently. I'm not tied down to Sherman Whitney's any more, and New York City's hardly the place to bring up a child, not when you have a choice. And there's all that good old-fashioned fresh air and invigorating home cooking. Or is it supposed to be the other way round?' A little shrug. 'Whatever.'

'You sound like you're showing a layout to a client. And you're the client.'

'I know. I'm just trying to work out what's best for Danny, that's all. Danny, me, where our life is headed. I've got to be there for him. That's the only thing that matters now. Hell, none of this would have happened if . . .'

She reached for him. 'You mustn't blame yourself, Jeff.'

'No? Jesus, Kate, if he's only got one parent I could at least try to be a fulltime one.'

'What about your work?'

'I can do that evenings, after Danny's asleep. I managed to write *Losing Time* that way, didn't I? Then, when he's back in school, I can work during the day. As for the rest of it – publicity, interviews, all that bullshit – they can go hang. That Rainer woman was the last straw. I've decided. From now on, I'm a hermit.'

She grinned. 'I'm glad I'm not going to be around when you tell that to Laura Babski. Mind you,' she said, pausing for a sip of the somewhat rough red house wine they'd ordered, 'if the Coliseum publicity people play it right and make enough noise about it they could get quite a lot of mileage out of it. You could be to authors what Howard Hughes was to millionaires. Or Michael Jackson to pop stars. The famous recluse.'

'Just hold back on the Jackson if you please or I might be tempted to go for the plastic surgery as well.'

She shook her head, ran a finger down the bridge of his nose. 'You're pretty enough as it is, Coolidge.'

'Lady, you've got strange tastes.'

'This is true. So let's pay the bill and get back to the motel so I can indulge them.'

They locked the door. Closed the dingy curtains. Undressed silently and with haste, desperate to get to each other's nakedness.

There were no tender caresses, there was no gentle teasing out of pleasure. This was an animal desire – they fell on each other with an eager greed to have and to take. It was a primitive rite, male and female denying death, reaffirming life. Kate below, Jeff above, a basic coupling of gut instinct and bruising lust.

Urgent thrustings and tangled limbs, gutteral noises and jagged breathing, grasping fingers and hungry mouths, hot skin moist with sweat, the incessant, fervid straining for release. When it came it was sharp and burning and brief.

Afterwards they lay still for a little while, damp, heavy, spent, and Kate could feel the warm wetness of juices seeping from her, the softening and shrinking penis as it slipped out to nestle damply between her thighs. They were still wrapped around each other but each was wrapped up in their own thoughts, silent. It was a sweet, almost companionable silence now that passion, for the moment, was abated.

Kate loved the silences between them, the kind you never had to work at filling, free to indulge in your own thoughts with no pressure to share them. Which was just as well because she was having difficulty understanding them herself. They were running along these lines: two worlds collide. Bits splinter off each and get mixed up together so you can't separate the pieces any more. So you glue the worlds up again as best you can and then what? You can't just send them off on their different orbits again. It doesn't work like that. They'd wobble, or be pulled back together again. Another collision, more bits and pieces flying. Kate had too many bits of Jeff's world glued in to her own now. Superglued. They were part of her. And she wanted more.

Or less. Wanted never to have collided in the first place.

'Jeff?' Her voice was almost a whisper.

He nuzzled into her ear then smiled down at her before snuggling into her side. 'So who else did you think it was?' Little nibbles on her shoulder.

She ignored the distraction. 'When you said you were going to chuck in all the publicity and interviews and things . . . did that include me? *The O'Connell Encounter?*'

He didn't answer immediately. He marked time by pulling up a sheet to cover them both, plumping pillows, edging up the bed to lean back on them. 'Would it really drop you in the shit if I backed out?'

'Yes. Not that it's going to be all that easy as it is, with the filming only half done.' She looked at him long and hard while waiting for his reply. It didn't come. 'You *are* going to do it, aren't you? Finish off the *Encounter*, I mean, not drop me in the shit.'

It still took him a few seconds to reply. He wasn't hesitating over the answer, just over having to give it. 'No. I'm not risking any more publicity. No more interviews, nothing that's going to take me away from Danny. Not even you, Kate.'

'Well, thanks. Thanks a lot. And this is what I saved his life for.' She regretted it as soon as she said it. It was such a mean-spirited, horrible thing to say. But the closest she could bring herself to a retraction was, 'Please. You owe me.'

'Don't I know it. But it's still no.'

'You bastard.' She turned away from him, turning to anger. 'Okay. If that's the way you want it, you lock yourself away. Hide. Fine. And just see how short a memory the world has. And when you want to come out again, when nobody's buying your books because nobody can remember your name – whichever one you happen to be using at the time,' she added scathingly, 'don't turn to *me* to plug you and your flagging sales figures. In fact don't bother turning your face across the Atlantic because I can see to it that nobody'll want to touch you!'

He replied hotly, anger rising to match her own. 'If that's some kind of an ultimatum, lady, you can go shove it.'

She glared at him and leapt out of bed, grabbing bits of clothing from the floor. 'Oh, you've got it all worked out, haven't you? All tidied up into neat little boxes.

332

You'll have Danny and you'll have your work and the rest of the world can go screw itself? That's dreamland, Jeff. It'll never happen.'

'But I have to try and make it happen, Kate, don't you see?'

She started dressing. 'Frankly, no.'

He sighed. 'Why should you? The *Encounter*'s your baby. Danny's mine. Except *he*'s real.'

'Meaning that my work isn't?'

'Well, is it? Does it really matter? Is the world really going to come to an end if one lousy TV programme doesn't get shown?'

She answered by slamming into the bathroom the better to marshall her forces – attack or defence she wasn't quite sure. Both. The more the merrier.

When she emerged again, calmer, determined to handle this whole scene with dignity so they could at least part on good terms, she found that Jeff, too, was fully dressed. Both of them needed some kind of armour.

He was the first to say it. 'I'm sorry. I didn't mean . . .'

'I know. Me too.' She looked at her watch, peering at the figures in the dim light of the still curtained room. For some reason she switched on a lamp instead of letting the daylight in. 'I've got to phone Julian,' she said.

He put his hand on hers as it rested on the telephone. 'Do it later.'

She started to dial. 'That'll be too late. It's already around ten at night over there. And I have to let Julian know what's going on. And when I'll be back. There's not much point in me hanging around any . . .'

'Don't go, Katy.'

She didn't hear. 'Julian, hi, it's me. Look, we're going to have to cancel the Warren altogether . . .' She didn't get a chance to explain any further.

'Thank *God*! At *last*! Kate. My *darling* petal. Where on *earth* have you been? Come home. *Please*?' It was a theatrical and despairing plea. 'Where in hell have you been?' he repeated frantically. 'I've been phoning Gilberts Whatsit for an eternity! Where *are* you? Oh God, you haven't eloped or anything disgusting like that, have you?'

She smiled in spite of herself. 'No way. Now calm down and tell me what's the matter. You sound as if all hell's broken loose back there.'

'Hell has nothing on it, petal. Just get your little bum back here. Please. Franklin's lost his marbles. Totally off his rocker. He's threatening to write us off, the whole bloody series! I tell you, darling, I almost prostituted myself trying to persuade him to change his mind, but all I could get was . . . Oh, shit, I don't know how to tell you.'

'Say it with words, Julian.' Her voice was terse. She felt icy cold.

His pause was just long enough to be ominous. 'He's left it up to the PPB.'

'Left what?'

'The decision of course. To axe the *Encounter* . . . and you with it.'

'Pardon? *What*?'

'I'm sorry, petal. I tried. I did my damndest but . . .'

'Kate? What is it, what's happened?' said Jeff but she simply waved a silencing hand at him.

Her face was ashen. 'When is it? The PPB meeting?'

'Monday afternoon,' came the voice of doom. 'So are you coming home or not?'

'Kate, for Chrissake what's wrong?' Jeff mouthed at her.

'What isn't?' she said flatly, hand over the mouthpiece.

'Kate? *Kate*? Are you still there?' said the frantic transatlantic voice.

Her shoulders straightened and she spoke into the telephone briskly. 'Well, I could hardly be on my way *that* quickly, Julian, even for you. But yes, I'm on my way, lovey.' She replaced the telephone and turned to Jeff wordlessly.

He looked at her for a long moment before saying, 'This is it then? You're really going?'

'Yes.'

'But not just yet.'

She tried to inject a little humour. 'Well, I suppose I'll put my shoes on first.'

'You mean you're going *now*? Today? What's *happened*?'

'Nothing much. Seems that they've booked the end of the world for Monday afternoon, that's all. And I'm not sure I'll be able to find the escape clause. I'm not even sure there's any small print.' He hadn't a clue what she was talking about. She explained it for him, sounding totally poleaxed by it herself. 'It looks like I'm about to get the sack. Fired. The elbow. Just like that, no notice, nothing. The bastards. The fucking bastards! I'll . . .'

He put his hands on her shoulders, gripping tightly, grasping at chance. 'Kate. Leave it.' His voice was urgent. 'Turn your back on it.'

She gave a short, sharp laugh. 'Oh sure. Listen, you're the one who's playing run away from it and it'll all go away. Not me.'

'Why not? You could *stay*. I know your career's important to you but you could have that here. Hell, you've got the contacts and we've got thousands of TV stations . . . You *could* do it, Katy.'

'Just like that, huh? Easy, no problem. And what about my home, my family, my friends, all the years I've worked to get where I am today? It's not just a job in TV, Jeff. In England I'm at the *top*. And I like it.' Sarcasm touched her voice as she added, 'I don't expect *you* to understand that, but it's a fact. Over here . . . okay, I suppose I'd find work but I'd be just another little fish in a bloody big pond. And I like being a *big* fish. I like it a lot. I've worked hard for it, I deserve it and I'm damned if I'm going to give it all up without a fight. I have to see this through. Correction, I *want* to see it through. To *win*. To make them go down on their knees and beg me to stay.'

'What if *I* begged you to stay?'

She shook her head and turned away from him saying quietly just one word: 'Don't.'

335

She picked up the phone again. Called Kennedy airport. There was a seat on the night flight. Tonight. If she left now, she could be on it. Briskly she went round the room gathering up possessions and throwing them into her overnight bag. 'You'll say goodbye to Danny for me, won't you? Explain that I had to go, kiss him for me, tell him to keep well away from ten-ton trucks, blue cars?' It was an effort to sound light-hearted. She felt as though Danny were her own child. Jennifer wasn't the only one who'd given him life. Kate had, too.

He tried again. 'Don't go, Katy.'

'Please, Jeff, don't say any more. I have to go and there's an end of it.'

'Yes,' he said bitterly. 'That's exactly what I'm afraid of. You'll be so damned busy being the big fish in your precious little pond that you'll never come back.'

She shrugged. 'That was your decision. You're the one who just pulled out of the *Encounter*, not me.'

He considered her quiet statement and his eyes hardened. So did his voice. 'You mean that's all it was? One long charade just for the sake of your precious TV show? Oh, you're dedicated to your job all right. Was it hard for you, Kate? Or was it all just part of a day's work?'

She recoiled. Her cheeks burned as if he'd physically slapped her. But there was no fight left in her to hit back, she just turned away with a flat, 'If that's what you want to believe.'

He slumped on to the edge of the rumpled bed, the energy suddenly drained out of him. 'No, Katy, it isn't, you know it isn't. I'm sorry I said that. It's just that . . . oh hell, what are we going to do? When will we see you again? Next week? Next year? Or do we just have to stand by until next time you feel like playing Happy Families? Think you can just fly over and borrow mine for a few days?' He shook his head. 'No way, Kate. Danny and I deserve more than that.'

She dropped to her knees before him, reached out to touch but stopped, dropped her hands to her lap. 'Yes,' she said. 'You do. So maybe we'd better just call it a day.

Quit while we're ahead, before we spoil it any more than we already have.'

He touched her face, looked right into her. 'Is that what you want?'

'I don't think wanting comes into it. Just circumstances.'

'Bullshit. We make our own circumstances.' He stood then and brushed passed her, shoved her bag towards the door with almost a kick. 'Go then. Go fight your battle.' Very quietly, not looking at her, he finished, 'and I hope you lose it.'

'Thanks.' She rose and reached for her shoulder bag. 'Thanks for the moral support.' She took her coat, glanced round the room, eyes avoiding that place in it where Jeff stood. She donned the coat – and an air of practicality along with it. A direct question as she made for the door: 'How long will it take me to drive to JFK?'

'I love you, Kate,' was the direct statement that stopped her in her tracks.

She took a deep breath. Let it out again. Looked into his eyes not knowing anything any more. 'Damn you,' she said. 'What did you have to go and say that for?'

'Because I can't let you go.' He pulled her close to him and held on to her tightly, waiting for her, willing her, to fill the turmoil of silence between them. In vain. 'And I can't make you stay. Can I?' he finally said.

Mutely she pulled away from him, shaking her head, tears filling her eyes. She couldn't bring herself to say anything. Not even 'goodbye'. She left the motel room quickly, while she still could.

Chapter Twenty-One

Four and a half days to sort out the shambles and either clamber out on top or be buried under the débris. Subtract the time it takes to travel three and a half thousand miles or so, then lop off a bit more for the time stolen by moving from West to East and the inconvenient but unfortunately necessary requirement to spend some hours asleep.

Kate did the calculations and didn't much like what she came up with.

But sleep she must. Even before attacking the telephone or the answering machine or the pile of unopened mail stacked neatly on the kitchen table. She'd been through second wind, third wind, five-dozenth wind and there were none left, not even the whisper of a breeze. She'd managed to doze a little over the Atlantic but it was just enough to make her feel worse, not better. A proper eight hours' sleep was just an elusive memory from the dim and distant past. Her body clock firmly refused British Summer Time, stuck on Eastern Standard and totally confused. She couldn't think, let alone think straight. Could just about summon up enough brain power to signal muscles to drag herself upstairs and fall on to the bed. Get undressed? Who needs to?

She slept a straight thirteen hours. Which was just as well, she realised, once she'd talked to Julian – because it didn't look like she was going to get the chance again for quite some time.

'Right,' she said, as she swept into Julian's office that Friday morning. Not even a hello or a good morning just, 'Right. In a straightforward list from one to ten and in words of one syllable, what in hell's been going on?'

He didn't quite manage it – a few 'catastrophics' and 'bloody débâcles' crept into the telling here and there –

but she got the general drift. Plummeting to rock bottom. Her face set into the stony expression that always made Julian want to duck beneath the nearest solid object – preferably one made of carbon steel. She was already heading for the door. 'Kate, where are you going? You're not going to go storming off up to Franklin, are you?'

She turned. 'I never "storm", Julian. And Ed Franklin can wait. I'll save him for Monday when all the carrion crows are gathered together in one juicy little clutch.'

He was horrified. 'But you can't barge in on the Programme Planning Board!'

'Of course not,' she said. 'I shall knock first.' With that she left the room.

When everything else failed, Julian always had panic to fall back on. And that's what he did on this occasion, scurrying after her, out into the main production office. 'You've completely lost your marbles. You can't.'

Secretaries and researchers pricked up their ears. Kate disappeared into her own office. Julian rapidly followed.

'Come in,' she said. 'Do sit down. And close the door.'

He did as instructed, but not in that order, spluttering all the while, 'You can't do it. Nobody gatecrashes the Management meetings, Kate, not even you.'

Linda leaned forwards with her elbows on the desktop and watched the exchange with anticipation.

'And maybe that's why this whole TV company is in such a shambles,' replied Kate calmly. 'Maybe it's time someone did exactly that.'

'You'd be fired on the spot.'

It didn't happen often but in this instance Linda was inclined to agree with the producer. She waited for Kate's response.

It came with a smile. 'I thought that was first on the agenda anyway.'

Oh God, thought Julian, it's what she's angling for! Some wild, rash, kamikaze stunt so she can go down in a blaze of glory. God help the rest of us. Specifically me.

'Listen,' said Kate. 'Too much respect for authority never did much in the way of accomplishing things.

That's part of your trouble, Julian. Too much respect for authority.'

'She means arse-licking,' said Linda. 'Only she's in a ladylike mood. It won't last.'

Julian was shaking his head in despair. He looked at Kate with a sort of glazed expression, a bit like a cod on a fishmonger's slab.

'Faith, my darling. Have faith. We're not dead yet,' said Kate with confidence.

The cod twitched a little and prayed fervently for a bucketful of saltwater. 'What exactly are you planning to do?' The question was slow and despairing.

'Details, mere details, Julian,' said Kate with a dismissive wave of the hand. 'There's a whole weekend in front of us. It's amazing what one can accomplish when one sets one's mind to it. But I'm going to need a little help. Linda, how are you fixed for the next couple of days?'

'Oh, just a royal garden party and lunch with Dustin Hoffman – nothing I can't cancel.'

Kate grinned. 'Good. Cancel them. Now then, Plan A. Who's on drinking terms with anybody, anybody at all, who works at the BBC?'

Julian emerged from Kate's office about ten minutes later repeating a silent incantation to himself: 'Rules are there to be broken, strings are there to be pulled, rules are there to be broken, strings are there to be . . .' He just hoped they wouldn't end up with the strings wrapped around them, bluebottles struggling in the middle of a sticky little web. He threw a dirty look at the master programme plan board as he passed it, wishing he'd never even heard of the O'Connell bleeding Encounter, then beckoned to his secretary. 'Sue. I'm going to be busy for a little while. Have to go out. So any visitors, any phone calls, if anybody wants me, just take a message, okay?'

'But you have a meeting at ten-thirty with . . .'

'Cancel it. Say I'm dead.' He picked up his coat and left.

Sue shrugged, a sort of mine not to reason why gesture, and picked up her telephone.

Back in Kate's office Kate was saying, 'Okay, that's plan A underway. Now then, all set for plan B?'

A disgruntled sigh from Linda. 'If I must. Ready when you are.'

Julian was sitting in a taxi on his way to the BBC Television Centre at Shepherd's Bush wondering who was the craziest – Kate for suggesting it or himself for volunteering. He could pull it off, of course. Kate wasn't the only one around here who could play the flamboyant genuis. And Orson was an old friend. More than that. Orson's was the first cock he'd ever sucked. Literally speaking. Yes, Julian had always had a fondness for good old Orson, you always do with the first one, don't you? And Orson had always been game for a laugh or joke. A sense of humour. Just as well under present circumstances. But it would be good to see him again, even if it was only for purposes of espionage and grand larceny.

Julian closed his eyes and allowed himself a few moments of fond reminiscence while the taxi sped him along the Westway.

Meanwhile, Kate and Linda had accomplished the first part of plan B with surprisingly little trouble. The hardest part had been persuading Linda to do it in the first place.

'How pally are you with whatsername, Ed Franklin's assistant, Miss Routledge?' Kate had asked once Julian had been volunteered for the BBC duty.

'Not very. Not at all. Why?' Very suspicious.

'Well, if you took her to the Club bar this lunchtime and got her pissed you might be able to get something out of her, find out what's behind all this, find out something, anything.' She shrugged.

Linda grimaced. 'Yes, but that tight-lipped old cow, you must be joking. The only thing I'd get from her is indigestion. And we're hardly bosom buddies. Why on earth should I suddenly invite her out to lunch? She's not stupid, she'd be bound to know I was after something.'

Kate thought for a moment. Then, 'Tell her you're

thinking of joining the union. That should do it. You'd like to ask her advice, her being such a respected and senior pillar of the secretarial staff, you know the sort of guff.'

'But she *hates* anything to do with the union.'

'Exactly. So she'll do anything to prevent them getting their clutches on an innocent young girl like you, won't she? Even meet you for lunch?'

So Linda made the phone call and the appointment. When she finished, she grumbled, 'Maybe I *should* join the union. I think I missed something in the small print when I signed up to take this job.'

That was the first part of Plan B. What Linda didn't need to know was that there was a second part to it: that she wouldn't just be pumping for information, she'd be acting as a decoy as well — for Kate had to ensure the guard dog's absence from the seventh floor office suite.

So now Julian was on his way to the BBC, Linda was on her way to meet Miss Routledge in the Club bar and Kate was pacing the floor, watching the clock, confidence evaporating with every tick as she waited for the minute-hand to tell her that Ed Franklin himself must have gone for lunch by now.

It was time. She picked up the phone and rang the Head of Programming's extension just to check that no one was there. And if Ed answered she'd say . . . anything. The building's on fire, the Queen's down in Reception, the 'on-air' lunchtime newsreader's doing a striptease to camera . . . anything to get him out of the office for a few vital minutes.

She let it ring thirteen times. No reply. With a last glance at the clock she steeled herself for action then armed herself with an empty A4 internal envelope and walked quickly out of the room, through the production office, out into the corridor, heading for the back stairwell.

She emerged into the main seventh floor corridor feeling flushed and furtive as hell. She walked past the HP's door, marked with a little sign which said, *NO*

ENTRY – visitors and deliveries to Room 793, and stopped outside the door labelled, *793. Personal Assistant to Head of Programming – Miss P. M. Routledge.* The door was closed. She knocked on it just to make sure the office was still empty, half-hoping a voice would say 'come in' so she wouldn't have to go through with it. There was no response. She turned the handle, fully hoping to find the door locked, though it was unlikely to be so during office hours because of mail deliveries, fire regulations and suchlike. The door was sticking to the rules and opened for her without demur.

She went in quickly, closed it behind her and breathed a sigh of relief. She debated locking herself in but as there was neither key nor bolt in evidence she tried to persuade herself that she was actually safer with the door unlocked – nothing suspicious about Kate popping in to see if the boss was available. But her powers of self-persuasion had been severely depleted. She didn't bother rooting around Miss Routledge's desk, just went straight for the communicating door to the inner sanctum hoping that it, at least, might be locked against her so she could just go away again. It wasn't.

Go in. Close the door. Listen for footsteps on corridor. Scan room briefly. Wish, suddenly, that there were hours for a leisurely search, for what wonders might be disclosed behind *Confidential* and *Staff, Private* stickers? No time. Just find it.

Do desk. Not on desk top. Lots of other things, including a brass and walnut plaque stating that an untidy desk is a sign of genius, but not what she was looking for. Try drawers. Top drawer locked. Curses. Next drawer opens. Not there. Bottom drawer opens. Not there either. More curses. Look at the clock. Minutes passing, time running out, O'Connell wants to do the same.

HEAR FOOTSTEPS IN CORRIDOR! They approach. They slow down. HELP! Routledge office door opens. DON'T BREATHE.

Sound of door closing again and footsteps recede.

Breathe again. Hands trembling. One last frustrated tug at top drawer. *Not* locked after all, just sticky. It opens.

Eureka!

She grabbed for the booty, stuffed it into the envelope and got the hell out.

Which was just as well, had she known it, because seconds after Kate vanished into the stairwell, the lift bell went 'ting', the doors opened and Ed Franklin stepped out.

Kate's idea was to photocopy the contents of the stolen book, bung the original into the internal mail addressed to Lost Property and then spend a few hours over the weekend behind the closed doors of her own home going through the information with a fine-toothed comb. She knew she was clutching at straws, and pretty illegal ones at that, but right now, straws were all she had.

However, she didn't go straight back to the office. She headed for the nearest ladies' loo where she locked herself in a cubicle and smoked a cigarette to calm her nerves and give her hands a chance to stop shaking.

She expected the *Encounter* office to be empty. It wasn't. She found Sue, Julian's secretary, munching a sandwich at her desk and dialling a long number on the phone. The girl slammed it down guiltily at Kate's entrance. A personal call. No doubt to her boyfriend in China, Kate thought as she nonchalantly strolled past the photocopier without giving it a second hungry glance.

She opened the door to her own office and found Linda already ensconced and looking a cross between sheepish and defiant. 'Sorry,' she said before Kate had a chance to ask how come she was back already. 'Not my fault. Hadn't even got half a drink down her before she was bleeped. She went haring off back up to the seventh looking like there'd been rape, murder or robbery or something.'

'Oh dear, that's a shame,' said Kate casually, heart pounding fit to bust. She slid the envelope into her brief-case and spun the combinations. 'We'd best start on the editing channels then,' she went on. 'What's the state of play, do you reckon? Booked solid, I suppose, short notice like this.'

'Might be lucky with the channels,' Linda replied. 'It's the editors who'll be in short supply. It's POETS day.'

Kate, still preoccupied by Miss Routledge's bleeper, picturing herself being caught red-handed, convinced that her briefcase was emitting a supersonic signal saying, 'It's here, it's here, the stolen goods are here!' merely gazed at Linda without comprehension.

'POETS day,' the girl repeated. 'Piss Off Early Tomorrow's Saturday.'

Not a flicker.

'Kate, are you all right?'

She shook herself together. 'Me? All right? My programme's getting the chop, my job's on the line, my reputation's as pristine as mud, my whole career's down the plughole and there's only two days left to pull the bunny out of the hat and I haven't even got a clue where the bloody hat is, let alone the bunny. Of course I'm all right!'

Linda stared. Then she delved into her plastic shopping bag and came up with a little brown glass bottle. 'Here. Pop a couple of B6. Awfully good for the nerves.'

Kate stared back at her. And then she broke. Into laughter. 'I'm sorry, lovey, I didn't mean to snap at you. And thanks, but no thanks. God, why do you never have anything sensible in there? Like scotch?'

'I never touch the stuff.'

'It might be time you started.'

The discussion turned out to be academic. There was a jaunty rap on the door and Julian walked in clasping a large plain brown envelope to his pigeon chest.

'Thank goodness. We were beginning to think you'd been abducted.'

'Not yet,' he said with a broad grin. 'That comes later. It was Orson's condition for the deal, sweet old poofter that he is.'

'Julian, lovey, you haven't actually prostituted yourself

for this, have you?' Knowing him it would explain his long absence better than heavy traffic.

Again, a broad grin. 'Not yet, petal. As I said, that comes later!' He opened the envelope and withdrew its contents with a flourish and a poor vocal impersonation of a trumpet fanfare. 'Not only have I filched the appropriately-printed notepaper for you, my darlings – and there's only three sheets, Linda, so go easy on the Tippex – but you can tear up that fictional imitation of a BBC contract we were chewing our fingernails over. Don't ever say that I can't deliver the goods!' And with that he handed over his *pièce de résistance*. It was a photocopy, complete with salary details ('Look at all those zeroes! No wonder they're always going on about needing bigger licence fees,' said Kate,) and all the appropriate signatures, of Terry Wogan's last contract. 'So girls, am I wonderful or am I wonderful?' he said.

'How on earth . . . ?'

'Easy peasy one two threesy,' he said, then tapped the side of his nose and winked.

By ten o'clock that night they had the Mansell profile complete, edited down to time and ready for the studio interview. And it was good. And if the union ever found out they'd done it themselves without the services of a film editor, they'd be out on their ears. But as they were likely to be anyway, it didn't seem to matter much.

Kate sent Linda home as the girl was wilting severely. She and Julian carried on. By three in the morning they had the Coe down to a rough cut. It was shaping nicely. And the hot drinks vending machine in the corridor outside was richer by at least a dozen ten-pence pieces.

By four o'clock the canteen was open for breakfast and Julian was saying blearily, 'As sure as eggs is eggs, if I don't get one I'm going to crack.' Neither of them was alert enough to even notice the pun.

'Okay.' Kate yawned. 'I just want to clear up one or two things in the office then I'll see you up there.'

There's something especially eerie about an empty

office in the dark hours of early morning, even in a building which has a twenty-four hour production line. Parts of the TV7 Centre were always peopled but on night shift the activity is low. The Control Room – technicians in scruffy cords and baggy sweatshirts, comfort not smartness the priority, a computer game in the TM's cubbyhole, a snoring sound (not part of the new technology) emitting from behind a bank of switching gear, ashtrays overflowing beneath red *Please Do Not Smoke* signs. The Newsroom rejecting its daylight image – all hustle and an anxious sense of its own importance, reporters and editors striding, sometimes running, from one work station to another, clutching flimsy bits of print-out, GNS speakers crackling constantly with updates, the mad rush to get the kudos of being 'first with the news'. All Terribly Important. By night, the desks support feet, not copy. There's a somnolence in the voices – 'Oh, just re-write the two o'clock, nothing's changed.' Too-heavy waste paper bins which clink rather than rustle if you move them. The special night-time apathy, similar to Sundays – an unwritten rule broken only occasionally by inconsiderate hurricanes or air crashes, that big news stories don't break on the night shift. As for the rest of the building – mostly closed. Even the first aid station. So a VDU operator is spotting and threatening to miscarry? Tough. Wait till nine on Monday morning dear, we'll be open again then.

Kate switched on the office copier, unlocked her own room, retrieved the bulky envelope from her briefcase, went back to the photocopier – and did the lot in the dim orange light filtering up from the streetlamps. The red light on the machine turned to green. It seemed awfully bright. She was aware of the noise of her own breathing. She unclipped the contents of the fat little leather ring-binder and fed the first page into the machine along with a short prayer. It was one of the old-fashioned slot feed models, the type that had to eat up the original before regurgitating it along with the copy. Its digestive system seemed terribly loud. She jumped at every noise thinking, 'God, I could never be a burglar!' Thinking, 'Shit, I already am one!'

Page by page, careful to keep them in order, she replaced them in the book and took the copies from the machine, putting them straight into the envelope. It was taking an eternity.

She heard a noise. The overhead strip lights flickered and glared into brilliance. She spun round guiltily to face the doorway.

'I brought you a bacon butty,' said Julian.

She drooped with relief.

'What kept you, what are you doing?' he said, putting down the paper plate and picking up the partially-assembled original. Innocent puzzlement as he went on, 'Why on earth are you photocopying your Filofa . . . ? Good God!' His eye had caught the name on the personal information page. He looked at Kate then he looked down at the book in his hands. 'How on earth did you get hold of . . . what are you . . . ?' He put it down again quickly, as if it were some distasteful object riddled with infectious disease.

Kate continued to xerox. Calmly she said, 'You haven't seen this.'

'But what are you going to do with it?'

'With what?' she said innocently, feeding the last page into the photocopier.

'That . . . *thing*!' venturing to point at it with a forefinger.

She shrugged. 'I don't see anything.' The page slid out, she reclaimed it, put it back into the book and clicked the straining rings closed. 'There. Over and done.' She handed the Filofax to Julian while she put the last sheet of copy in the envelope with the others. Then she switched off the machine and went into her office.

Julian followed quickly, clutching the book. He closed the door behind them and whispered, 'How did you *get* it? What on earth do you want it for?'

She popped her copy of the boss's Filofax (addresses, contacts, diary, notes, appointments – his whole *life*) into her briefcase. Her voice was urgent, intense, desperate. 'We've *got* to find out why . . . if . . .' Then she stopped, as if suddenly struck by the stupidity of it all, the pathetic *futility*. She started to justify again but it was more to herself than to Julian. 'You never know, there might be something, something we can use. Every little helps, no knowledge is ever wasted and all that.'

'And a little knowledge is a dangerous thing,' added Julian dourly.

'Voice of experience, huh?' Still firing, even if not on all cylinders.

'Cow. I'm serious. How *did* you get it? On second thoughts, don't tell me.'

She did anyway. 'I stole it.'

'Oh . . . sh . . . it.' He tossed the Filofax on to her desk. 'Well, it's your baby. I'll work through the night for you, I'll play at MI5 for you, I'll lie through my teeth or on my back for you, but don't expect me to go along with you on this one. I wash my hands of it.'

'You'd better wash your fingerprints off it, as well, then,' she pointed out archly.

He grabbed for the book and started scrubbing at it frantically with the front of his jumper. 'Oh God. We've got to get rid of it. Quickly. Chuck it in the Thames or something. Burn it.'

'The thought did cross my mind,' she said. 'Serve the bastard right. But it'll be safer just to send it to Lost Property. After all, he could have dropped it somewhere. He'll be so relieved to get it back again that he won't think any more about it and no one will be any the wiser. Right?'

'If you say so,' said Julian doubtfully.

So she parcelled it up, stuck a label on it (in hand-written block capitals) and together they shut up their office, went two floors up for safety, tried various other office doorknobs till they found one that opened and slipped the envelope into the Internal Post Out Tray by the door.

'There,' she said, sounding almost as relieved as she

felt, 'now let's get some sleep and forget it ever happened.'

'What ever happened?' said Julian innocently.

'Quite.'

And back in the *Encounter* production office the only other witness curled up and died. The forgotten bacon sandwich cooled and congealed until the edges of the bread turned up into a rictus grin to greet the cleaners who arrived for the Saturday morning shift.

The weekend lurched onwards. Home in the dawnlight to snatch a couple of hours' sleep before delving into a year in the life of a television executive as revealed by a reliably informed source.

It made dull reading.

April 3rd. Flowers for M. That looked mildly hopeful until she discovered that his wife's first name was Moira. Flowers for his wife, how sweet.

She had a flash of hope that there might be grounds for blackmail in June and July with a series of meetings with Finchbury and Westbrook – stockbroker, merchant bank, insider dealing, some sort of financial intrigue? Sounded the right sort of firm. She ran her finger down the small print in the E to K section of the London telephone directory because she was at the stage where her eyes couldn't keep track unaided. Finchbury and Westbrook turned out to be tailors.

She ploughed on, the emerging picture more and more unenlightening. Franklin was either very, very careful, or did indeed live a life above suspicion. He remembered birthdays. He had his car serviced regularly. He paid his golf club subs on the due date . . . The Filofax yielded nothing, at least nothing of any earthly use to her. Disheartened, Kate yawned and snatched a half-hour catnap.

And so it was back to TV7 in the fading twilight for another all-night hijack of the editing channel with Julian operating the equipment, Linda manipulating two stopwatches and miraculously creating a 'ready for tx' script, cue sheets and camera scripts out of what looked like the aftermath of a paperchase. Kate watching the monitors minutely, piecing together a jigsaw puzzle: a bit from here, that bit from there then a bit from the first part and if we lose that wodge in the middle and go back to . . . , at the same time as jotting down rough notes for the commentary which they hadn't dubbed yet.

She scripted the voice-over commentaries properly on Sunday at home after a half-hearted brunch of zapped fish fingers. Tonight it was delete 'editing' channel and substitute 'dubbing'. When she finished she had a couple of hours to kill before meeting Julian and Linda back at TV7. It would have been no trouble to sleep them away. Almost as easy to while them away with the Sunday papers which she hadn't touched yet. She took the third option – ploughing through Franklin's engagements again – and there it was, staring her in the face except she hadn't had the wits about her to see it yesterday on the first go through.

A breakfast meeting with Sir Arnold Bickerdyke at the Atheneum Club (and no doubt as to which one of them was the member). A round of golf here, a weekend luncheon there, and what in hell was Franklin doing attending the christening of a Bickerdyke grandchild?

The more she thought about it, the more her reaction was 'curiouser and curiouser'. The Mr and Mrs Franklins were hardly the most socially acceptable match of the season with the Sir and Lady Bickerdykes. It didn't say much for the much-vaunted editorial independence of TV7's management team when their most senior member was ever so discreetly thick as thieves with the Chairman of the Board of Directors.

But Kate still couldn't work out what it had to do with her own little problem. What could Bickerdyke possibly have against *her*? She'd never even met the man. It was worth following up, though – any old straw to clutch at. As soon as she had the time. But, oh Christ, *when* – there was hardly any of that commodity left.

Around three on Monday morning, weary and bleary-eyed, Kate, Julian and Linda went through their check list one final time. As far as the *Encounter* was concerned they'd done everything they possibly could and there wasn't a single criticism that could be levelled at them. The weekend's work had put them way ahead of schedule, with filmed profiles on Costas Stavros, the Princess Royal, Barbra Streisand, Margaret Thatcher, Nigel Mansell and Tamsin Coe edited to time and voice-over commentaries complete, waiting only for the studio interviews – and transmission dates? It was an impressive record for this stage in production – and, they hoped, too impressive to be ditched at the whim of the Head of Programming. Or whoever.

'Linda,' said Kate as they collected their coats, 'you've been an absolute star this weekend.'

'Oh, that's all right,' came the yawning reply. 'You needn't bother to applaud. Just throw money.'

'Actually, I was thinking more on the lines of asking you to come in early tomorrow, I mean this morning . . .' She held her hands up in defence and ducked as she said it. 'You too, Julian.'

He groaned. 'Oh God, what did we forget?'

'Nothing. But we haven't finished yet. There's a little bit of private research I need your help with . . .'

By the time she got home Kate wondered if it was even worth bothering going to bed. But three hours are better than none at all. By the time the alarm pierced her unconsciousness what seemed like three minutes later, she decided maybe no sleep would have been less painful after all.

Nevertheless she dressed very carefully for her appearance at TV7. If you look like a winner you're halfway there, she kept telling herself.

Her reflection passed muster. Discreet make-up (tons of it), concealer for the under-eye purple, healthy glow added to the cheekbones, lashes heavily mascara'd and every one of them separate – she was going to exude vitality if it killed her. The effect cost her a full hour.

Today merited being one of those rare occasions when she piled her mass of hair upwards and back from her face. Unlike in all the movies she required more than two magic pins to keep it there. As for the clothes, her usual soft fabrics and subtle hues were pushed aside in favour of stark tailoring in black and white. Power dressing. Black cashmere suit with straight skirt and fitted jacket. White linen broderie Anglaise blouse pinned at the neck with an antique cameo brooch. Black leather court shoes with four-inch heels.

She looked like a woman to be reckoned with. She only wished she felt like one.

Once the morning was over, she did. Because she was.

Three pairs of eyes watched the second-hand on the wall clock climb, hit the meridian, begin the descent. Two o'clock.

'Look, petal,' said Julian soberly, 'I've gone along with you so far and we've all worked our little botties off but are you *sure* you know what you're doing? Wouldn't it be better just to let the *Encounter* stand on its own merits and keep our heads down . . .'

'Don't,' she interrupted tersely. 'Don't put me off now.' She checked over the fake BBC contract even though she'd already checked it twice, folded it, slid it into her handbag, gave a brisk little tug to the hem of her jacket and without giving Julian, Linda or herself any further opportunity for dissuasion, she strode through the outer office.

She was the flagship. The Ark Royal. Sailing forward into battle. A smattering of applause followed her.

Alone in the lift she felt more like the last surviving liferaft – with a slow puncture in the 'airtight' compartment where confidence and determination were supposed to hang out. The doors slid towards each other like a double guillotine. She pressed button seven. For once in its life the elevator made a non-stop journey.

The seventh-floor corridor was shorter than those on the other storeys. Office doors to the right and left, at wider intervals than those on the other storeys. And on the walls between them, framed paintings of good taste instead of the photographs and posters which decorated the other storeys. The management corridor was abbreviated by an imposing pair of highly polished mahogany doors upon which an equally highly polished brass plaque bore the inscription *Board Room*. It was like the entrance to a private gentlemen's club. It *is* the entrance to a private gentlemen's club, thought Kate as she approached.

So fuck you, gentlemen, and up yours!

Without even pausing for breath, she gave two firm raps, turned two brass doorknobs, and two doors opened before her. A split second pause to ensure her entrance was 'made', then she swept into the room.

Chapter Twenty-Two

Danny had been horrified when Jeff had tried to explain why Kate wouldn't be coming to see him again.

They kept him in the hospital for a couple more days' observation – the skull fracture, just to make sure – but after that there was nothing more they could do for him that couldn't be done just as well at home. Plenty of bed rest and tlc, no acrobatics and try not to make him laugh. Apart from that it was a case of child, heal thyself.

Emily and William went back to Gilberts Pond to prepare for the invalid's homecoming. Jeff stayed on at the motel. He was restless and irritable. Danny was bored and irritable. And Kate's sudden departure had helped neither of them.

'She can't have gone!' exclaimed Danny, forgetting his injuries and trying to sit up suddenly. 'Oww. Ouch.' He sank back on to his pillow mountain. 'I don't believe you,' he said, both voice and face sullen. 'She wouldn't have gone without saying goodbye, she just wouldn't.'

'She had to, Chief.'

'It's your fault. What did you say, what did you do to her?'

'Nothing. I wanted her to stay. You don't know how much I wanted her to stay, Danny. But she wanted me to kiss you for her, say goodbye for her. She was real sorry she had to go without seeing you.'

'Honest injun?'

'Cross my heart and hope to die.'

The sacred oath. It must be true then. But he still didn't understand. 'But why? You should have *made* her stay. I wanted her to stay. I love her.'

'Me too, Chief.' Small smile.

Small voice saying, 'Why do people always have to go away, Daddy?'

'Just part of growing up, finding out there are some things you have to let go of.'

'Well, I don't like it.'

'Me neither.'

A silence while Jeff remembered and Danny planned. Then, 'Dad? As soon as I'm better, why don't we just go and bring her home again?'

What do you say in the face of such clear cut logic? More clear cut logic. 'But this isn't Kate's home. She has her own. In London.'

'So we'll go visit. As soon as I'm better. Next week?'

Jeff wasn't quite so optimistic. 'I don't think we got an invite.'

'But I thought it was all fixed up. The TV show and everything. And she promised to show me round the dungeons.'

'She did? TV7 has dungeons?'

A scathing look. 'No, stupid. London has. And she said she'd show me around when we go there for you to be on her show.'

'But I'm not going to be on her show, Danny. Not anybody's.' He pushed some enthusiasm into his voice. 'No more interviews, no more going away on publicity tours! You've got yourself a full-time Daddy from now on. How's that grab you?'

Danny considered this new piece of information. Then with hopeful face he said, 'Well, maybe she'll invite us anyway. For a vacation or something.'

Nice to feel appreciated. 'Yeah. Maybe.'

That conversation had taken place Wednesday, just after Kate left. Now it was Monday and they were back at Gilberts Pond again, Danny milking the wounded soldier business for all it was worth and Emily and William (and Jeff, though not quite to such a degree) going along with it and spoiling him rotten.

And it was as if Kate O'Connell had dropped off the edge of the world. Not a word from her, not even a thirty-second phone call to ask after Danny. And the only thing Jeff knew about Kate for certain was that her telephone answering machine wasn't answering. Nobody was.

He'd spent the last few days trying not to calculate London time every time he looked at his watch but it had become an automatic response. Pacing the motel room had become pretty automatic as well. Would have worn a track in the carpet except it was already thread-bare. What a dump. Spartan and dingy. That such a place should have held such scenes between its walls.

Once Kate left he'd thought about checking out and commuting for the rest of Danny's stay in hospital but a hundred and fifty mile round trip at least twice a day was too much even for Jeff's restless energy. He'd thought about writing the rest of his novel. On Friday he'd even gone out and bought a yellow legal pad and sat on the bed with the pad in his lap and a ballpoint in his hand but the words weren't there. He did some more pacing instead. It wasn't exactly 'writer's block' – he'd never experienced that, didn't really believe in its existence, thought it was just a term used by those who were lazy or afraid or ineffectual, nothing that sitting down and *doing* it wouldn't cure. So he sat down again.

And called his agent. 'Laura? Hi. It's Jeff. Jeff Coolidge. I know it's early days yet but I haven't been able to get my mail recently and I wondered if you'd heard anything from Des Lakerman, any news, any reaction to the first part I sent off?'

What he wanted to hear, really needed to hear right then, was something on the lines of, 'Yes, it's terrific, keep on going just as you are, we love it.' Even if it was an exaggeration. Or a downright lie.

'Ah, Jeff honey, glad you called. I've been talking to Des and we both agree that, well, Des says it better than I can, that's his job, so he's put it all in a letter, it should be there by now, so you have a look at it and see what you think and then call me again and we'll have a little chat. Look, I'm in a meeting right now so I'll talk to you in a few days, okay honey?'

Laura must have read the wrong script. He dialled

357

another number, William answered and yes, there was some mail waiting for him, yes, one of the letters was from New York and had the publisher's name emblazoned on the envelope and was it urgent, did Jeff want him to open it and read it out to him?

'No, no, nothing urgent. It'll keep.'

Three hours later, after a quicker than usual visit with Danny, he was at Gilberts Pond.

He turned the envelope over in his hands, put his thumb under the flap and stopped. Sure, he could take the knocks and keep on coming back for more, just as well as the next guy. He could take the criticism. Once the work was finished.

But while it was in progress, that was a different thing altogether. When Jeff was still struggling with it – suffering the birth pangs of creation, as somebody somewhere *must* have said – then his ego was about as tough as a watered-down jello.

He ripped open the envelope. There was an introductory letter which summed up his editor's feelings about the work Jeff had done so far – that took a full page – then there followed three more pages of detailed textual criticism.

Jeff scanned Des's letter quickly but his heart and spirit began to sink even before he'd finished the first paragraph.

'*I hope you'll overlook the fact that I haven't attempted to dress up my remarks,*' he read.

Overlook it? Why the hell should I? And why *didn't* you make the attempt to dress up your remarks, Des?

He read on, '*If this is balder or brusquer than you would like, please forgive me.*'

If? What 'if?' And forgive you? Give me one good reason.

He scanned through the following pages. Key phrases leapt out at him. '*Brittle and artificial . . . you are right in trying to build up tension but this is* not *the way to do it*'; '*heavy handed . . . rings false*'; '*you must be more explicit . . . it's no use* telling *us, you've got to* show *us*';

'this sort of thing grates ... again, OTT'. It read like a really bad end of term report. The tone was irritable, belittling, scathing. And he was still only halfway down page two.

He refolded it and put it back in the envelope. Enough is enough. He hadn't found one word, not *one* word, that offered any encouragement or any reason to believe that any part of his work was any good. Good style, good writing, good characterisation, good plot – he wasn't picky, even good commercial crap would have sufficed. For if Jeff didn't believe that *something* about what he'd done so far was worthwhile then neither could he believe that there was any reason to continue.

That hitherto vague and shadowy threat called writer's block squatted darkly inside his head. It set like concrete. The jello went splattering beneath it.

'Was it important?' Emily asked the question as Jeff was getting back into his car, the letter crumpled any old how into his jacket pocket.

'I drove seventy-five miles to get it and now I'm driving seventy-five miles back again so I can see Danny before he settles down for the night. *Yes*,' he snapped, 'it was important.'

'Pardon me for breathing.'

'Sorry. It's not your fault. It just wasn't particularly encouraging news, that's all.'

'Well, are you going to tell me or not? It's about your book? What did they say?'

' "They" is a he. Des Lakerman. My editor.'

'So what does he think of it?'

'Basically, not a lot. It sucks. It's shit. Sorry, "sentimental" shit. All right? Can I go now? See my son, in the hospital?'

Emily tried desperately to find the right words. She really tried hard. But even as she said them, 'Oh Jeff. I'm sorry darling. But you mustn't let it get to you. What does *he* know?' she knew they were the wrong ones.

'What does *he* know? Christ, Mom, he's my *editor*! It's his *job* to know, God damn it!'

She gave up. Just put her hand on his shoulder and squeezed a little. 'Yes. Well. Put it out of your mind for now. You have a long drive. Don't drive angry, Jeff.' She felt the shoulder relax a little under her fingers as he took a deep breath. He looked up from the driver's seat and said, 'Yes. You're quite right. And I'm sorry I bit your head off.'

She smiled. 'All part of a mother's job, getting chewed out. Now off you go. And I'm sure it's not as bad as you think. Read it again when you're calmer and you'll see I'm right.'

He took her advice. He did read the criticisms again later when he was calmer. Much later, much calmer. He read the pages through, slowly and objectively and even dispassionately, word by word. And it read even worse that way.

The last dregs of the day were trickling into dusk but he didn't switch the lights on, he just lay back on the bed and let the deepening shadows wrap him up. The bed was like an island. He was the island. He remembered the last time he'd felt like this, the aloneness of not being able to share, to talk it out with somebody you could trust just to listen. Except last time it had been elation that he wanted to share. Jeff wasn't asking for sympathy or soothing words or consolation or even understanding. He just wanted to *talk*. Say it out loud. Make it acceptable. Say, 'Damnit to hell but Des is right. Now all I have to do is put it right. And I can do it.'

He tried saying it out loud, into the motel room. Unfortunately the room didn't know how to echo, 'Yes, you *can* do it,' when he'd finished.

That was when he'd made the first phone call to London. To apologise, to rescue the relationship, to work things out somehow. And yes, he knew it was pretty late, that in London tomorrow had already begun, but hell, it was Friday night and Saturday morning – the weekend – so it was okay. Wasn't it?

He never did find out, because her phone was never answered. Not that time, nor any of the other times he rang. He made all sorts of allowances but what started out as a mild 'I wonder how she is' when he rang from the motel room progressed through every varying stage until by Sunday night her time, early evening his, it reached 'Where the hell is she at this time of night and who the fuck is she spending the night with?' Jealousy and logic never did make good bedfellows.

He and Danny were back home at Gilberts Pond by then and Danny wasn't the only one of her menfolk Emily was worried about. Jeff was edgy, strained, putting on a bright face to Danny but the rest of the time he went around looking as though he was chewing over a mouthful of powdered glass . . .

Sunday afternoon. 'Will? You've got to do something about Jeff. I can't get through to him any more. Talk to him. See if you can get him to open up to you. He's tearing himself up inside and it's not just Danny, I don't know what it is. It might be his book. That letter from his publisher. Did you know he's gone right the way back to Chapter Two? Anyway, you're his father. Talk to him, Will.'

Sunday night. 'Dad? You okay?'

Bright smile for bedtime. 'Sure, Chief. Couldn't be better! Anyway, I'm the one who's supposed to be asking you that sort of thing. How're you feeling? How's the head?'

'Better.'

'Headache gone?'

The boy nodded, to prove it.

Monday morning. 'Jeff? Laura. Just calling to see how things are going. I gather Des hasn't heard from you. And Pam Mackenzie was on the line the other day wondering how you'd be fixed for a few more signing sessions, there's a big new bookstore opening up in Manhattan and . . .'

'Tell her she can shove her bookstore up her . . . just tell her to get someone else. I'm tied up. Head down and working hard, don't want to break the flow.' It was a downright lie. Head down and all bunged up was closer to the truth — big empty spaces where he used to eaves-drop for hours on the characters in his mind. 'I went back to the beginning. Re-writing the first part in line with Des's comments then the rest of it will pick up from there.' In theory.

'Fine. Good idea. If you think it's not going to hold you up too much. I could always renegotiate the deadline if necessary but obviously it would be better if we can leave it as it is. Well, just give me a call if you want to bounce any ideas off me . . .'

If only there were any ideas to bounce.

Monday afternoon. 'What do you say we drive into Decatur tonight, Jeff, just you and me. Knock back a beer or two at Joe's place like we used to, huh?'

'I don't know, Dad, I've got too much to do. I really ought to keep on working and once Danny's down for the night it's the best time for me. Mind if I take a rain check?'

'Yes. I do mind. I need the break and drinking on my own doesn't appeal.'

'So take Mom. She could do with the break, too.'

'Take your mother to Joe's Place?'

He was right. The picture didn't gel. 'Yes, I see what you mean. So take her someplace else.'

'I'm asking you, not Em. So come on Jeff, do it for me, make an old man happy. What do you say?'

'Well, maybe just for an hour or so.'

William left. Jeff turned back to his manuscript. He was still on Chapter Two.

Still Monday Afternoon. 'Did you do it? Are you going?'

'Yes. Joe's Place, tonight. Don't wait up for us, Em.'

'Ask him about Kate.'

Monday night. They were on their third beer before William judged it opportune to say, 'So how's Kate? You heard from her?' Very casual.

'No.' Very clipped.

'Oh?' Surprised. 'So you don't know what happened then, that work crisis she had to sort out?'

'No.'

'Well, aren't you going to call her, find out?'

A running out of patience sigh. 'Look. I've done nothing *but* try to call her since she left. I never got through. She's not there. I don't know what's happening or where she is. If there's something she wants me to know, she's got my number, okay?'

'Maybe she's just working hard.'

'Sure. So hard that she couldn't even take two minutes out to pick up a phone and ask about Danny? In five days? Look Dad, just leave it. She knows where I am. So she made her choice, so . . .' a shrug, 'I'll live.'

William cut in, 'Choice? What's choice got to do with it? Jeff,' a shake of the head, 'you're not telling me you were fool enough to give her some kind of ultimatum, are you?'

'No. All I said was . . .'

I'm not going to do your show.

If it drops you in it, tough.

I want you to stay here.

Your career problems don't matter to me.

What does matter is I love you.

Oh, and by the way, thanks for saving my son's life.

That's what he said. The great 'I'. Shit. No wonder she got the next flight out.

'. . . just leave it, Dad. Who cares?'

William finished his beer, put the glass down and said, 'You do.' A piercing look. 'And don't try and bullshit your way out of it. Not to me. I might be your ageing parent but I'm not senile.' He signalled to the barman when Jeff made no response. 'Two more over here, Floyd.' Then he turned back to Jeff. 'Well?'

'Well what?'

'*Don't* you care? And I'm not talking about loving her or wanting her or all of those other man-woman things that screw you up. Like pride, for instance.'

And Jeff thought, he might be my ageing parent but no, he's not senile.

'I'm talking about *caring*,' William went on. 'Caring

about what happens to her. Did her world come to an end? Did she win through? How does she feel about it either way? Do you care about all that? Because if you don't, Jeff, you're no son of mine.'

'Sure, Dad. I care. But what can I do about it?'

'Try getting off your ass. Stop moping about feeling sorry for yourself and making everyone else's life a misery into the bargain. What's your problem, boy? So she's in London and you're here, so what's a few miles between friends? She loves you, doesn't she?'

'No. How the hell should I know?'

William dismissed that with one of his hrmph's. 'Well, you know what they say. If the mountain won't come to Mohammed . . .' Sometimes, Will thought, clichés come in handy.

Jeff gave a short, sharp laugh, no amusement in it. 'Oh sure. Just leave everything and turn up on her doorstep out of the blue saying, "Take me, I'm yours"?'

William shrugged. A shrug can come in handy, too. 'Danny would be okay for a few days, just till you got yourselves sorted out. And if it's that important to you, I think they've got typewriters in England, might even be able to get hold of one of those word processor gadgets, too. As for me and your mother – I guess you'd let us have visiting rights. It's only half a day away.'

'You're talking as if I'm going to go live there or something.'

'Am I. Your insight is truly amazing.'

Sarcasm yet. Two can play. 'Don't you think I should at least talk about this with Danny first? It's his life too.'

'Kate's the one you should be talking to.'

'Chance would be a fine thing.' Jeff drained his glass and started on the fourth.

Chapter Twenty-Three

It was close on four in the morning when Kate finally got to bed. Tuesday morning. The morning after what Kate, Julian, Linda, Sue, (and definitely Ed Franklin) would for ever more think of as *the* O'Connell Encounter.

As she swept through those double mahogany doors nine heads had turned in her direction. The tenth, Ed Franklin's, merely looked up startled from his position opposite her at the Chairman's end of the long board-room table. The eleventh, the female one, from its suitably humble position to one side of the great white chief's, belonged to Miss Patricia Routledge, Personal Assistant to Head of Programming, personally responsible for taking confidential minutes of Very Important Meetings. She looked even more affronted than the men. Traitor, thought Kate, glancing at her.

No one spoke. Kate closed the doors behind her. Then, smiling graciously and nodding to vaguely familiar faces as she passed, she walked the length of the room to stand at the head of the table next to the Head of Programming. Not for her the position of supplicant. Not today. Not ever. 'Good afternoon, gentlemen,' she said confidently.

'Just exactly what is the meaning of this, Kate?' Ed's voice rang out clearly in a slightly delayed assertion of his authority.

Grumbles and whispers and nodding heads spread rapidly down the two lines before her. She almost felt pity as she looked down on them. Middle-aged or elderly men, a couple of them in biological terms only a few years older than herself, yet here they were, the so-called Management. 'Manage' as in 'get by'. Or was it, 'those who can, do, and those who can't, manage'? People whose names had to be followed by explanations because without them they might fade into the wallpaper.

This was a somewhat sweeping judgement. And it wasn't entirely accurate. But on that particular occasion Kate found it a help to think of her adversaries that way. 'I'm here because I have something to say which is pertinent to Item One on this meeting's agenda.' Papers shuffled as Item One was double-checked. She went on, 'Since this directly concerns my programme, myself and my future with this company, and since no one thought it necessary to issue me with an invitation – no doubt that was just an oversight on someone's part – I thought I'd better invite myself.'

Ed grunted. 'I see. Well?' The tone was impatient. 'We have a lot to get through so say what you have to say and let's be done with it.' He leaned back in the leather upholstered chair, folded his arms and began to drum his fingers on his bicep. The faces of his fellow Board members showed annoyance and indignation in about equal measure. This kind of intrusion was unheard of.

She would not be fazed. She took her time. She glanced at the empty chair between the Finance and Admin. Controller (who wore a pin-striped suit) and the Head of Drama (who was in pin-striped shirtsleeves), and wished someone would invite her to sit down so she could have the pleasure of telling them she preferred to stand. She also wished someone would offer her a cigarette. She wished most of all that she could accept one. But it would ruin the image. And image, face, bluff, was what this game was all about.

'Ratings,' she said. 'That's what you want, isn't it? Because ratings mean advertising revenue. And ratings mean kudos. Whichever one is most important to you, and sometimes I'm not so sure, it all boils down to the ratings. And that's what you're scared of losing. So you want to cut your losses and run, cut the *Encounter* before it ever gets a showing, rather than lose the advertisers – or lose face before the others. Thames? Yorkshire TV? Channel Four? Is it the independent companies you're competing with, all the other commercial stations? Or is it the BBC?'

'Miss O'Connell.' Head of Godspots. 'Ratings are important, yes. After all, the ratings get the advertising and the advertising pays our – your – salaries. But what really concerns us, and I'm sure I speak for my colleagues on this, is the moral aspect.' He laid heavy emphasis on the word 'moral'. 'The dignity and integrity of the image this company presents to its public. And this squalid – and regretfully most public – involvement of yours in the Pritchard business . . .'

'Particularly in a programme area such as yours,' put in another one, getting into the swing of it, 'where it's imperative, I repeat, imperative, that we be seen to be objective, impartial, above censure . . .' It was Hallam Mariot, of all people, the Advertising and Revenue Controller.

She cut him off with a laugh (the thought skittering across her mind: how's Routledge going to minute that?) and made her own note to come back to 'objective, impartial and above censure'. She said in scathing disbelief, 'A programme area such as mine? *The O'Connell Encounter* is nothing more than one long glorious snoop into the private lives behind public faces! Integrity? Or, what was it, the dignity? Do you really think the great viewing public gives a damn? So don't give me any of that morality bullshit.' Does your Pitmans cover that one, Miss Routledge?

She changed tack slightly – straight from the cuff, man to man, locker room honesty and all that – 'This is a confidential meeting, isn't it? So let's be honest about our motives here, even if we can't be honest outside this room. If you want big viewing figures and big advertising revenue and big salaries . . .' She paused there. Sod it. Let's really be honest. She opened her handbag and took out a packet of cigarettes. She lit one. Inhaled. Oh God, that was good. Exhaled. Continued. 'Hasn't it struck any of you that this squalid business, as you put it, that the gutter press has been feeding off recently, could be the one thing that will *guarantee* the *Encounter* shoots straight into the top five? You sit up here and shake your heads and mutter on about morality. This isn't McCarthy's America. And it's not Lord Reith's BBC. It's TV7.'

She was pacing up and down the room, the length of the polished walnut table, with only a slight pause every now and then to emphasise her points. This was stage one – try logic. Not much hope in the face of this lot but she gave it her all, bringing them up to date on what was in the can so far, interviews booked, the whole bit – without mentioning that she and Julian and Linda had practically killed themselves over the weekend to do it. She finished with, 'Axing the series at this late stage? Doesn't sound like good financial management to me.'

Ed could feel himself wavering. She was certainly putting on a show. He felt almost proud of her. Damnit, *was* proud of her. All this crap about integrity. He wished he had the guts to reclaim his own but he could still hear Sir Arnold's voice on the telephone last night: 'Just so long as you remember, old chap, it was my casting vote that put you where you are today. You want to stay there, don't you?'

He did indeed. 'But my dear girl,' he said, words and tone calculated to annoy her, to upset her composure so he could justify getting rid of her, 'there are other matters for us to take into consideration, matters that you neither know of nor which concern you . . .'

Nods of approval all round the table. Male management supremacy. Just go away, dear, and don't bother us or your pretty little head. So much for the direct attack.

'I know,' she said with what she hoped was a significant emphasis on the word 'know', 'more than you think.' She went on firmly, refusing to be needled. 'And there are matters that *you don't* know about. Which is why I'm here. So that when you come to a decision, at least it will be a fully informed one.'

Steady yourself, girl. Time for flanking manoeuvre,

change tack again. She went on almost conversationally now, like gossip over the garden fence. 'The editor of the *Sunday Mirror* was on the phone to me only this morning. And the *Express* . . .' It was a lie. But if she didn't pull this off she was damnwell going to make it true by tomorrow. She'd need the money. 'Funny how when one of them gets an idea the others follow,' she went on. 'Anyway, it seems my ten weeks of No Comment are about to pay off. I tell you, even I was surprised at the figures that were mentioned when the subject of a Kate O'Connell exclusive inside story came up. Ratings? Oh, I can get you the ratings all right. But.' She certainly had their interest now, and no mistake. 'But, you can't have ratings if you don't have a programme, can you?'

There were one or two throat-clearings and shuffling noises around the table. Somebody Kate didn't recognise, who might have been the mythical Head of Paperclips incarnate, opened his mouth for the first time since her entrance. 'I think perhaps you should leave us now, Miss O'Connell, so we can discuss this fully. We'll let you know our decision.'

'Well,' she said with a shrug, 'at least it's comforting to know that the decision is still yours to make. Can't think where I got the impression that it was the Board of *Directors* who were handling all the management decisions these days. Or to be specific, the Chairman, Sir Arnold Bickerdyke. I was beginning to wonder, what with Alex Pritchard being Sir Arnold's son-in-law, if personal grievances were perhaps being allowed to influence company policy decisions.' She waved it off. 'No, sorry, forget I mentioned it. Just me being paranoid. We'll just have to hope the papers don't latch on to it, though. You know how they like to make a fuss if the media's editorial independence is ever brought to question.'

'Patricia? Could you pour Miss O'Connell a cup of coffee, please,' said Franklin. Like butter wouldn't melt.

'I'd prefer tea,' replied Kate with an ambiguous little

nod of acknowledgement. 'White. No sugar.' The cigarettes had been indulgence enough for one day.

'What are we thinking of? Kate, do sit down . . .'

At last. It was Head of Current Affairs, positively bustling, leaping up to pull back an empty chair for her. 'I think an interesting point has been raised here which merits *full* discussion,' he said gravely.

Heads nodded in agreement. Except for the Head of Paperclips who merely watched the others as if his head didn't have the necessary weight.

'So, my dear,' Ed turned to her. 'To go back to your earlier point. You'd really consider splashing your private life all over the papers just to ensure public interest in the *Encounter*? You'd do that?'

'Yes,' she said. 'I *did* consider it. Briefly. But as you're intending to axe the programme and my contract along with it, there'd hardly be much point. Besides,' she took a sip of tea, placed the cup delicately back in its saucer before going for the big one, 'it's no longer necessary.'

'Don't be too sure, young lady. It's our decision. We haven't made it yet in case you hadn't noticed.' Head of Finance's feathers were decidedly ruffled.

Now, she thought. This is the moment. The Grand Bluff. 'There is just one more thing you ought to be aware of . . .' She took the folded sheet of paper out of her handbag and dropped it on to the table.

Franklin snapped finger and thumb together with a curt, 'Let me see.' It was handed along to him. He read it rapidly. Gave Kate a very searching look. She kept her face poker straight. He slid the paper along to the man on his left who scanned it. It was passed around the table with assorted looks of surprise, horror, disbelief, grunts and more throat clearing before she had it safely back in her hands again.

She tucked it away in her handbag before it could receive any closer scrutiny. 'As you may have noticed,' she said, 'I haven't added my signature to it. Yet. I thought I'd discuss it with my – er – superiors, first.' She gave them a questioning smile. 'So it's up to you. Are you going to match their offer?' She'd almost said, 'better the offer' but the stakes were too high, this was gamble enough, bluff enough, for one day – one lifetime? She hoped. She finished confidently, 'Or do I sign it and let the BBC headhunter win yet again?'

Her question was directed at Ed Franklin and everyone looked for his reaction before deciding which way they ought to jump. Kate was watching him too, and suddenly Jeff's words began a relentless echo through her mind: *'I hope you lose, I hope you lose, I hope . . .'*

Franklin leaned back in his chair, a slow smile creeping across his face and Kate knew with a dulling sense of certainty that she'd played right into his hands.

They tried to carry on as if this were just another Monday, as though the series were to go on as planned, but it wasn't easy. Every time a phone rang or a door opened the whole office came to a momentary standstill like some Dali-esque party game of musical statues.

'What on earth's going on up there?' Julian asked of the room in general. They all instinctively looked at the wall clock. It was nearly four. Nearly two hours.

'She must really have put the cat among the pigeons,' volunteered Sue.

'More likely the pigeon amongst the cats,' muttered their producer gloomily. 'Talk about flying on a wing and a prayer. Except I've got this awful feeling that the feathers dropped off and God's gone out for the day.'

'Look on the bright side, Julian.' Linda wasn't looking very bright at all. 'At least nobody's sent a porter along to clear out her belongings yet.'

'Oh, God I can't stand it.'

'Then if I were you I'd sit down,' came a voice from the doorway.

'Kate!'

'Who did you expect?' She walked into the room and flopped on to the nearest empty chair. Now that it was all over she felt like a rag doll. With most of its stuffing missing.

Julian took one look at her and said, 'Shit. I knew it. I knew it would never work. They called your bluff, didn't they? We've got the chop. You're fired. We're all fired?'

She looked up at Julian with a heavy face. 'Somebody ought to break open the hospitality cupboard. I don't know about you lot but I could do with a drink. I think we should all have one. And then I'm going. I've had enough of this place to last me a lifetime.'

'Bloody Marys all round, huh?' said Julian grimly. He looked at his staff then said pointedly, 'Bloody Mary. Get the chop. Geddit?'

People groaned. Except for Kate. She just looked at him and said, 'Not funny, Julian.'

Had she but known it, Ed Franklin thought it was hilarious. Wonderful. The whole situation had a kind of ironic humour that would have had him jumping to his feet and hugging her if he didn't have his image to think about. A BBC contract, all but signed, sealed and delivered. Talk about being let off the hook!

'Sack her,' Sir Arnold had ordered. 'Get her off the screens!'

But sacking her, only to put her on the BBC screens? It rather seemed to defeat the object. So tough shit, Sir Arnold, old chap. Who runs this TV station anyway?

Ed Franklin leaned forward and addressed the meeting quietly. 'There's been a lot of claptrap bandied about this table this afternoon,' he said, while Miss Routledge scribbled furiously. 'Morality, decency, integrity. For God's sake, gentlemen, we're running, *we're* running,' he repeated, 'a television station here, not a church mission for fallen women – no offence, Kate. And it strikes me that Kate here is one of the few people I know whose integrity can*not* be called into question.'

Kate felt a twist of guilt but exercised her right to remain silent.

'Firstly,' he went on with all the gravity of a judge summing up for the jury, 'she presented a flawless economic argument. I don't think any of us had realised just how far into production *The O'Connell Encounter* is. Secondly, there's truth in the old adage that no publicity is bad publicity, so suffice it to say that the Pritchard business will probably have helped to switch on more sets than it turns off when the first *Encounter* goes on the air . . .'

When. Not if. And nobody was arguing with him. Kate hardly dared breathe.

'. . . and after that, it's up to the quality of the programme to make sure they stay switched on. I personally have no doubts on that score.' He looked up to see if anyone else had. Again, nobody argued.

'Thirdly, Kate did not accept the BBC offer without a backward glance, but she came here to talk to us about it first.'

If they ever found out that the contract was a fake . . .

'. . . even though she was fully aware that we were about to discuss the axing of her series and the termination of her contract.' He paused for another glance around the table. 'That, gentlemen, is what *I* call integrity. So. Far from terminating her contract, I suggest that somebody proposes the motion that it be renewed, as of today. At the same salary that our esteemed colleagues at the BBC suggested, of course. Do we have a proposer?'

Nine hands begged for the honour.

'We hardly need to put it to the vote, then. A majority decision.' He turned to Kate. 'Well? What do you say?'

She said 'yes' of course.

'You cow! You bitch! You . . . oh, I adore you!' shouted Julian as Kate finished relating the tale. With a whoop of joy he tossed the keys to the hospitality cupboard at his secretary. 'Catch. Open up and then throw away the key!' he exclaimed magnanimously. 'Now then, petal, come on, where are we going tonight? All of us, the whole team, out on the town to celebrate!'

Kate shook her head. 'Sorry, lovey, I haven't the

energy. What do you say we just drink a toast to...'
She smiled. 'Honesty and integrity?'

Julian raised his glass and winked. 'Not to forget
Orson.'

'Who's Orson?' somebody said.

Kate hadn't been lying when she'd said she wanted to
get out of there. She did. Wanted to escape, get out of
the building quick before anyone could come down from
the seventh floor and say they'd changed their minds.
The whole day had been too close to an Ealing film
plot for comfort. She wanted to be someplace where
'television' was defined as just another piece of furniture.
And she wanted to talk. About something terribly
mundane. Like, nice weather for the time of day, or, read
any good books lately, or what the hell is happening to
my life?

She rang Mo. 'Hi there, stranger. What would you say
if I invited myself round for tea?'

'I'd say you're a brave woman. But welcome.'

Brave indeed.

'Now you know how they invented egg shampoos,'
said Mo, bearing down on Becky with a damp cloth
concealed behind her back. 'It's called self-feeding in one
thousand and one not so easy lessons. Feeding? Ha! Take
a tip from me, Katy,' she went on, 'if ever you have kids
of your own, when it comes to eggs, make 'em scrambled
not boiled.'

Kate and her cashmere suit watched the mopping up
operation from a safe distance.

The baby was lifted from highchair to playpen, Sammy
was summoned to guard and entertain his sister for ten
minutes while Kate and Mo retired to the sitting room
to partake of a restorative glass of Tio Pepe. 'You look
dreadful,' said Mo. 'Been burning the candle in the
middle as well as at both ends?'

'If your make-up had been through what my make-
up's been through today,' said Kate, 'you wouldn't ask.
God, I'm knackered.'

'Put your feet up, have a drink and tell me all about it.'

'It'd take all night.'

'I wasn't planning on going anywhere,' said Mo with a slightly resentful nod towards her brood.

Kate settled herself comfortably into an armchair which had seen better days, eased off her shoes and wiggled her toes in an ecstasy of release. 'Whoever invented four-inch heels did not have size four feet,' she said inconsequentially. 'We were never meant to walk around with isosceles triangles on the ends of our legs.'

'So why do you?' said Mo in the superiority of comfy sheepskin slippers.

'Image,' she answered with a shrug. 'And believe me, sometimes it's bloody hard work.'

'Wouldn't I love the chance to try.' A rueful swipe at the egg yolk congealed on her jeans.

'Really? Shall I tell you the saga of my last two weeks?'

'Could I stop you?'

Not a chance. 'Well, it started in Barbados . . .' Kate began to check off a list on her fingers. She soon ran out of fingers, but not out of breath. '. . . and meanwhile Ed Franklin, our dearly beloved Head of Programming, was throwing wobblies all over the place rewriting *The Axeman Cometh* with my programme and my contract as the main target. So I leave all the family drama going on over in the States and drive like a lunatic to catch the next plane. I get home – where are we? This was Thursday – and spend the weekend . . . Hey, where's that refill I was supposed to be getting?'

Mo simply handed over the bottle.

'Thanks. Anyway, you get the picture. To put it in a nutshell, it's been a pretty crazy few days. And here I am.'

'Well?'

'What?'

'Well, go *on*. You can't stop there! Do I still brag about My Friend the Famous TV Person or do I start sending you food parcels?'

'It was the thought of your food parcels that spurred me on to victory. I don't like what you do to boiled eggs.'

'Thank you. Go on. The axeman. What did you do?'

'Well, I thought about running away to sea . . .'

'I'm being serious.'

'Believe me, so was I.' Kate attempted to summarise the day's machinations but Mo wouldn't let her. She wanted details. With details on them.

She got them. And eventually said, 'Some nutshell. Trust you to need a coconut.' She shook her head. 'Give me motherhood, I say. At least after all the hassle you can see the progress.'

'So a new contract and a safely scheduled TV series isn't progress?'

'If you call going in a complete circle progress. You're more or less in the same place you were months ago.' Mo sounded a little smug.

'Ah, but I got a raise.'

'Big deal. And suppose you hadn't? I mean, what if after everything else they'd still said sign up with the Beeb and good riddance? What would you have done then?'

Kate pondered the question. It was the first time she'd allowed herself the luxury. 'To be honest, I don't really know. Gone home and cried? Signed on at the Job Centre.' She smiled. 'Run away to sea.'

'Gone back to America?' asked Mo, zeroing right on target as usual.

She shrugged. 'I doubt it. That's all finished.'

'What!' It was nearly a screech. 'What happened? I thought you loved him.'

'Yes but.'

'But me no buts, O'Connell. This is Mo Levy you're talking to, remember. And that means straight talking.' She sounded exactly like a schoolteacher with a recalci-trant pupil. A role, of course, in which she'd had much experience. She called out, 'Sammy? Darling, precious boy? What are your overtime rates today? Mummy and Aunty Kate have a little more talking to do.'

That was something of an understatement. And it was much easier to plan that to put into practice. Ben came home. The children needed supper. An evening meal had to be prepared for the adults. The children had to be put to bed. Put to bed clean. Then the adults had to eat and the saga of the battle of the boardroom had to be repeated for Ben's benefit. Then he had to be banished so that Mo and Kate could — at last — pick up from where they'd left off.

And then — but by this time they were somewhat 'tired and emotional' as the newspapers so tactfully describe it — Mo had to struggle to regain her temper after losing it thoroughly. 'You really piss me off sometimes! You know? God, woman, will you never learn, never grow *up*? What do you mean, you never told him? This man, with his kid lying in the hospital and his woman halfway out the door, tells you he loves you and practically goes down on his knees to beg you to stay . . .'

'Romantic twaddle! It was nothing like that.'

Mo didn't even notice the interruption. '. . . and you didn't even give him *that* to hang on to! You love him. *You* know it. *I* know it. But you don't consider that the man in question has the right to know it too?' She gritted her teeth and clenched her fists and uttered a sort of strangulated shriek. Quietly, so's not to waken the children.

'Okay, okay, you've made your point so let's just forget it, shall we?'

'No.' It was very late now and the heat in the conversation didn't quite compensate for the chill in the air so Mo turned on the gas fire. 'What did you think was going to happen?' Whoosh, it went, as she pressed the ignition button. 'That he's going to leave everything and come running after you, that he's going to turn up panting on your doorstep? For goodness' sake, woman, you haven't even rung him up to ask about Danny!'

Kate's pause was confirmation of her guilt. 'I've been berry viz I mean very busy. I've been trying to save a

career here in case you hadn't noticed. *And* I did it.'
Discreet burp.

'I suppose it never occurs to you that the universe does
not revolve around you and your bloody job? And that's
all it is, you know, you're supposed to work in order to
live, not the other way round.' She paused to pour herself
another drink. She didn't offer the bottle to Kate. 'And
what about Danny?' she went on replenished, 'How do
you think he feels, you marching off like that without
even a word to him? Poor little boy.'

'Okay, okay, you've made your point, I'll bloody ring
them up all right? Tomorrow. First thing.' Kate snatched
at the sherry bottle and upturned it over her glass. It gave
up its last dribble with reluctance. Kate pulled a face at
it. 'Story of my life,' she muttered. 'My head hurts. Mo,
I think I want to go home now.'

Mo sighed. 'And I think you'd better have a cup of
coffee first. Better still, take a taxi.'

Kate wrinkled her nose. 'Can't stand the taste. Too
crunchy. I'll have the coffee?'

Still friends.

As Kate soaked herself in a hot bath of perfumed bubbles
after a very slow and very careful drive home, she
contemplated the meaning of, the value of, friendship.
Still a little woozy, she contemplated lots of things. The
way bubbles cling to each other. The way a bar of soap
will destroy the bubbles. She thought she might be close
to some deep and meaningful philosophical revelation
there, but her mind drifted on its way before she could
catch hold of it. It was on to boardroom tables now. Pity
they couldn't be run as efficiently as Mo's kitchen table
(boiled eggs excepted). Now there's *real* management
material if ever I saw it, she thought in admiration of her
friend. She giggled quietly and wondered if Ben had ever
told his wife, 'My God, you're beautiful when you're
angry!'

She gave her alarm clock the night off, decided she
deserved the luxury of sleeping until she woke naturally,

then a long and objective scrutiny of her face in the magnifying mirror confirmed that it wasn't so much a luxury as a necessity. She screwed her face up and pulled and prodded at the skin. The term 'laugh lines' was getting closer and closer to euphemism than truth. She yawned and turned away, snuggled herself into bed and was asleep within minutes.

And within a few more minutes, it seemed, she was drifting back up into consciousness. She tried to stop it but was defenceless. And her head was throbbing. She reached for the clock. It *had* only been a few minutes. So it was still Monday evening at Gilberts Pond. So do it now. She put down the clock and picked up the bedside telephone extension.

It was Emily who answered. Sounded delighted to hear from her. How was she, was everything okay and yes, Danny was fine, much better, home now and convalescing. No, Jeff wasn't there, he'd gone out for a drink with William but she didn't expect they'd be too long, could she get Jeff to call her back?

'No, don't bother him, I just wanted to see how Danny was doing.'

'A message then?'

'Yes. Would you tell him . . . just tell him I won.'

In the morning she wasn't sure whether the phone call had been a dream or not. Either way, a fat lot of good it did her. The phone call or the sleep. She woke up hungover, snarled at her reflection which was the only thing that had changed – for the worse – decided she deserved the morning off and headed, gingerly, for the Sanctuary health club and a five-thousand mile service.

She expected to find a message from Jeff on her answering machine when she got back, looking and feeling almost human again, but it wasn't switched on. Hadn't been, she realised, for days. Oh well, what you never had you never miss. She expected to receive a phone call from the States at any minute. Saying what, she wasn't quite sure. Nor was she clear about what she *wanted* him to say. But it turned out to be a moot point because the phone call never came, not even to update her on Danny's recovery.

Tuesday passed.

Wednesday sprouted, flourished, faded.

Thursday and Friday copied.

Saturday she was back in TV7's studios, back to being Kate O'Connell, *the* Kate O'Connell. Looking good and looking forward and let's get this show back on the road, people.

Chapter Twenty-Four

She stood behind the hessian-covered screens looking coolly unruffled while a sound assistant fumbled beneath her skirt making final adjustments to the radio mike pack which was strapped to her left thigh, and the make-up girl dabbed a powdery wad of cotton wool at her nose and teased at her hair again with the tail spike of a comb. Inside she was icy with nerves. She listened to Julian getting his front-man rush as he did the audience warm up and she thought: all right for him, no unseen millions to think about, just play to the crowd then disappear up to the safety of the gallery. She breathed slow and deep – IN one two three, OUT one two three – and hoped that the Princess Royal was in position at the other side of the set – Kate couldn't see her yet.

It was always like this before she stepped out in front of an audience. These last few seconds. Every time. 'I can't do this. I'm going to quit,' were the words which always ran through her mind.

And then the floor manager cued GO! and she gave herself up to that heady rush of adrenalin and walked out into a wall of light, a wall of applause, and this time, like every time, she thought: oh, I could never give this up, *never!*

Julian edged himself into the gallery, a dark and noisy air-conditioned box of a room upstairs at the back of the studio. This evening it was more crowded than usual. The 'pull' of the Windsors. Producer, Studio Director, PA, Vision Mixer, Sound Mixer in her cupboard in the corner, two secretaries (including Linda looking unrecognisably well-groomed) and an extraneous researcher. And Julian's visitor. Julian stuffed him into a corner and told him to be quiet then fixed his eyes on the monitors.

'Cut to camera five.'

'Standby to cue telecine.'

'Run telecine.'

Beep.

'. . . four, three, two, one.'

'Now close up on the Princess. On three.'

'Right, cut to three.'

'What did she say? That's never on the cueboard.'

'Since when did Kate use the cueboards?'

Impromptu burst of laughter and applause from the loudspeakers.

'Quick. Audience shot. Cut to four.'

'Great. Lovely. Now back to one.'

Julian watched the big transmission monitor while Kate and HRH performed an exquisite verbal ballet and the technical team translated concept into actuality. He felt that rising sense of excitement in the pit of his stomach – it was going to work. It *was* working. She'd done it! He glanced across at his guest, who was smiling and enjoying it all thoroughly.

After the recording it was big smiles, all round. 'We've got a luverly bottle of bubbly down in hostility. You coming?' asked Julian.

'You bet,' said his visitor, so Julian gleefully led the way down stairwells and along gloomy corridors to the hospitality suite down in the basement next to make-up and wardrobe, relishing the surprise he was about to spring on Kate.

'Sorry you won't get to meet the Princess,' said Julian. 'She's got an official dinner or something or other tonight so she couldn't hang around. God, these royals, I wouldn't swop places, not in a million years.'

'Fine words from an old queen,' teased the other man.

'Now you wait there. Don't move. Don't come in till I tell you.' With that, Julian popped his head round the door and said, 'Kate, petal? Surprise, surprise!'

She had this stupid, wild hope that it was going to be Jeff. Stupid. Wild. Totally irrational. Wasn't it?

She looked up eagerly as Julian opened the door with a flourish. She managed to keep her face eager and pleased as Julian said, 'Kate, I'm proud to present my dear friend, *our* dear friend, all things considered, without whose contribution none of this would have been possible. Well, it might, but it would have been a damned sight more difficult . . .'

'Oh, stop blathering darling, *do* get on with it, never mind I'll do it myself,' said the man who grasped her hand and shook it warmly. 'Kate. I'm *so* glad I could be of help. I'm Orson.'

'No wonder he's been going round like a puppy with two tails all week,' Kate said to Mo the next afternoon.

A proper day off. For both women. Sammy had dragged Ben off to the Museum of Natural History to look at the dinosaurs and Mo had taken Becky off to spend the afternoon with Kate. Becky was now sleeping peacefully upstairs, like a little pimple in the middle of Kate's double bed. ('Are you *sure* that nappy won't leak?' Kate had asked.) Kate and Mo were sitting outside in the garden making the most of the late English summer which was struggling valiantly to rescue its reputation but was losing the fight, and it was the first conversation they'd had since the night they'd murdered the Tio Pepe.

'Do I detect a note of sour grapes there?' Mo teased. 'A touch of envy perhaps? Surely you don't begrudge Julian a little romance at his time of life?'

'Less of the "his time of life" if you don't mind. He's not much older than me. Or you, for that matter. And no, of course I don't begrudge it. In fact Orson's sweet. I hope they'll be very happy.'

'So what's needling you, as if I didn't know? You haven't heard from him, eh?'

Kate shrugged. 'Not a peep.'

'Never mind,' said Mo philosophically, 'plenty of time yet. You have to remember, Katy, that although you're pretty central to your own drama you're quite possibly just a minor character in other people's.'

'Thanks. You really know how to cheer a girl up.'

'Not me,' said Mo with a grin. 'Somebody else said

that. Or something like it. But I can't remember who. Good, isn't it? I've been trying to work it into an actual conversation for weeks.'

Kate just grunted and stared at the river.

Mo went along with the silence for a while – all of half a minute, which was practically a record for her – then burst out with, 'Well, what did you expect? That it'd be like pressing a magic button and he'd leave everything, including an injured kid, and come running? Just because you talked to his mother!'

'He wasn't there!'

'Couldn't you have said for him to ring you back?' pointed out Mo reasonably.

'It was four in the morning. I needed my sleep.' It sounded pretty lame, even to Kate.

Mo just said, 'I despair of you.'

'Me too.'

'So that's *it*, is it?' No way was Mo going to let it rest. 'The ball's in his court, it's his turn and you'll be damned if you'll make the next move. Katy, we're not talking about tit-for-tat dinner party invitations here.'

'I know that. But I'm a bit tied down in case you hadn't noticed. I can't just hop on a plane and pop in for tea on the off-chance. He's the one who has that kind of freedom if only he'd see it. Anyway,' she said by way of closing the subject, 'he knows where I am if he wants me.'

Mo opened it again. 'Does he? You could be dallying with Clint Eastwood on the other side of America for all he knows. Lucky cow.'

A moment's pause then, 'Does Ben ever complain about the way you nag?'

'Frequently.' Said with a tinge of pride?

'So how does he get you off his back?'

Mo smiled. 'Simple. There *is* only one way. He gives in. Hey, where are you going?'

Kate was marching into the house. She called over her shoulder, 'To get you off my back!'

Danny was sitting on the edge of the landing stage staring wistfully and wanly out over the water. It was one of those grey mornings, damp and misty, a presage of approaching Fall. It wasn't all that cold but he was all wrapped up snug in a parka, felt bundled and uncomfortable with one arm zipped inside the body because the plaster cast made it too big to go down the sleeve. But Grandma had insisted. She'd taken one look at the mist and first insisted he couldn't go out at all, not till it cleared, second (and it had taken some whining) that all right, he could, so long as he was all wrapped up.

And was he all wrapped up! He was hot and sweaty and irritable and he wanted to go fishing or climb a tree or run round the Strakers' yard with Tom and Robert and a baseball, *anything*. The novelty of being the invalid, the focus of concerned attention had worn so thin you could see right through it. He just wanted them all to stop fussing and let him alone. Wanted to be *doing* things. Even going back to New York and school was beginning to look mildly attractive – not that he was certain that was ever going to happen, not with his Dad thinking of selling up and moving away someplace. Here? To live with Grandma and Grandpa? It was okay for the summers. Great for the summer and for weekends sometimes. But *all the time?*

He picked up a round, flat stone with his good arm and skimmed it half-heartedly over the water. It bounced once and then sank. Great, just great.

'Hey, Chief?'

He looked round. His Dad wasn't all wrapped up. *He* was just in shirtsleeves. Bet *he* didn't have to whine for ten whole minutes just to get permission to come out at all.

'You busy?'

Did it look like it?

'Can we talk?'

He sounded cheerful enough. Big grin. Even looked like a real grin for once instead of that peculiar, too-bright grimace that he'd been putting on a lot recently. 'Sure,' said Danny with a lopsided shrug.

His dad sat down next to him on the wooden boards. For somebody who wanted to talk, he took his time about it. Eventually he said, 'Looks kind of pretty on a day like this.'

''S okay, I guess.'

'Would you be . . . sorry to leave it all, would you miss it?' It came after another long pause.

He was getting at something. Danny wondered when he was going to reach it. 'I said. It's okay.'

'The thing is . . . What I mean is . . . Look, do you remember a while back I promised that sometime before the summer was through you and me would go on a long vacation somewhere, a real one, do Europe maybe?'

Danny'd thought his dad was the one who didn't remember. He pricked up his ears. The slouching back straightened. 'Sure I remember. Gee, Dad, are we going? Where? When? Just you and me?'

'Well, not exactly . . .'

The spine sagged a little.

'How much of Europe would you like to see, Chief? Athens, Venice, Rome, Paris, Vienna, all those places? I mean, would you be real disappointed if we gave them a miss? And just went to London instead?'

This time it was Danny who took his time in speaking. And then it wasn't words, it was a high, piercing 'whoop' of delight accompanied by a one-armed hug and then an 'ouch' as his ribs twinged. 'You mean we're really going? To see Kate. We got our invite?'

Jeff nodded.

When he'd answered the phone just now, Kate's voice had been the last he'd expected to hear. He'd got her message. 'Tell him I won.' Oh, he'd got the message all right. But when he heard her voice (how can a disembodied, slightly distorted, thousands of miles away *voice* have such a powerful flipover effect on the gut muscles?) saying, 'Hello, Jeff, how are you, can we still be friends?'

he just gave in and said, 'How can we *not* be, Katy?' Friends. The best of. He could settle for that.

He grinned at Danny. 'Yup, we got our invite! So will London do? You want to go?'

'*Do* I!' Then Danny gave a dismissive little wave with his good hand. 'Paris, Rome, London, what's the difference?' he said with all the blasé casualness of a world-weary traveller. 'Seen one, see 'em all. Sure, let's just do London.'

They took their time over it. And they did it in style. A first-class double in the middle of three-deck on the QE2. For Danny it was a treat, a once in a lifetime experience. For Jeff it was an insurance policy. The ship had doctors and a fully-equipped hospital. With Danny he was taking no chances.

Southampton is hardly the best place to advertise the beauties of Britain. Especially on a grey early morning. The long, grey customs buildings. The long, grey dock. The long expanse of grey-brown water. And at the dock-side, that long, high ship. Massive. A city which floated.

Kate waited. Nervous as a teenager scared she'll be stood up outside the Odeon. She scanned the faces eagerly. Please, please don't let them be the last to disembark. She could see it, clear as day, her own solitary figure standing there, still waiting, hours after everyone was gone and the dock was deserted.

A cry. 'Kateeee!' A vigorous wave. A small boy pushing his way towards her and a man behind loaded with luggage trying to keep up. Danny bulleted himself into her open arms.

'Are you mended now, can I squeeze hard?' she asked, laughing.

'Not too hard,' said a voice to the side of them. 'He still creaks a little.'

Kate and Danny, still hugging, looked up at him.

'Hey, break it up you two. Don't I get my turn?' The embrace which followed sealed the tacit agreement to put their recent breakdown of communications behind them.

And it sealed a friendship: the greetings were warm, but not passionate, the standard pleasantries you'd expect from good friends who hadn't seen each other for a while.

'Which one's yours?' Danny asked, looking round bright-eyed and interested in everything as Kate led them to the car park.

'Over there.' She pointed to her orange Volkswagen.

'That's yours?' Surprise. 'A *bug*?'

'He thinks all TV stars should drive a Lamborghini or at the least a Ferrari,' explained Jeff.

'It's not a bug. It's a beetle. And his name's Albert,' she said with dignity.

A little later, approaching Winchester she couldn't help boasting, 'This road was built by the Romans, you know.' Her road atlas wasn't too specific so she assumed it was this one, it being very straight. It was her turn to play tourist guide and she played it to the full. She had a willing audience. 'We'll be coming into Winchester in a minute – it'll be worth a visit if you have the time while you're over here – there's the Cathedral and the Shire Hall, that's part of the old Castle and it's where King Arthur's round table lives. For two hundred years or so, up till the Norman Conquest in 1066, Winchester was the capital of England.' She glanced briefly at Jeff who was sitting in the front next to her.

'I'm impressed,' he said.

'You're supposed to be. I spent hours looking it all up for your benefit. We'll be joining the M3 before long then we'll go through Twickenham and Richmond.'

'What's in Richmond?' Danny was sitting forwards in the rear seat, his elbows resting on the backs of the two front ones, taking it all in.

'Mostly a park,' she said.

'Ah. Like Central Park.'

'Not exactly. Richmond Park has wild deer roaming round in it.'

'On the *loose*?'

Jeff looked round at Danny and pulled a face at him. 'Guess that puts us brash Americans in our place, huh?'

'Then it'll be Kew,' said Kate, ignoring them.

'As in Kew Gardens?' asked Jeff.

'Now I'm the one who's impressed,' she said.

It was about a two-hour drive.

She hesitated as she put the key in the lock. It meant a lot to her that Jeff and Danny should like her house. Her home. She turned it and ushered them in.

Jeff put the suitcases down. On polished floorboards and an Aubusson rug. It looked genuine. He stood for a moment looking round, taking it in. A large, square hallway full of light and elegance. The staircase was directly ahead and it turned on itself at a half-landing where there was a tall window with delicate stained glass insets. Danny was already halfway up the stairs, exploring. 'Hey look, Dad, there's a river! With a little island in it!'

Kate smiled. '*The* river. The Thames.'

'Guess you have quite a view,' said Jeff. 'Nice.'

'Yes. Except when the view floods into the garden. Which it has been known to do. Come on. You must be longing for a cup of tea or something. Don't stand on ceremony, for goodness' sake. Have a look round, make yourselves at home, while I go and put the kettle on. I thought Danny would like the little room over the sitting room,' she pointed vaguely ceilingwards, 'so he can watch the river. Yours is the one next to it, Jeff.' She went through into the kitchen, still talking. 'Are you hungry? Mrs Pickles – you'll meet her tomorrow – she's done us a chicken casserole we can heat up when we want lunch so just sing out when you're ready. Then I'm afraid I'll have to go in to the office. Sorry, it being your first day and everything but there's no help for it. It's the Stavros *Encounter*, we're recording the studio show tonight. You will come, won't you? I've got tickets for you both. Of course, if you'd rather not, if you just want a quiet evening, that's . . .'

'Kate.'

She turned, teapot in one hand, milk bottle in the other.

'Stop fussing.'

'I'm not!' Then she gave a tight little laugh. 'I am. Sorry, it's just . . .'

'I know. Me too.' He called out, 'Danny! Hey, come and help out in the kitchen.'

They both needed it.

It wasn't the first time in her career that Kate was thankful the show was being recorded and not going out live. And it probably wouldn't be the last. But tonight of all nights, with Jeff sitting there in the front row. And Danny, who still thought she was the bees' knees. Seven years old. She just hoped he didn't understand the innuendoes. The rest of the audience did, though. Thought it was a hoot.

Things had been going wrong since the moment she got to the studios. Linda was late, for a start. When she finally turned up it was obvious why. Talk about dolled up to the nines, she must have been at it all day. Should have expected something like that, though, her being the Stavros Chief Groupie. But at least she'd finally got here so Kate let it pass.

Julian took one look at Linda and said, 'Darling, is it really you? You look absolutely gorgeous! Good enough to eat. If it weren't for Orson I could . . .' He filled in the dots with a series of little lip-smacks.

Jeff and Danny were settled in their seats, the rest of them were filling nicely, Julian was doing the warm up, Linda had disappeared up to the gallery, Kate was made up and miked up and ready to go . . .

And Stavros was scowling at her from the other side of the set. And all because she'd turned down his dinner invitation for after the show. Except it hadn't been so much an invitation as an expectation – and Stavros had made it pretty clear that dinner wasn't the only thing he was expecting to eat. 'A little repayment of my hospitality on Hydra,' he'd called it. Insufferable man.

She went on. The audience applauded. She made her introductions and Stavros walked on. The audience applauded. He settled into the armchair and she started on the pre-profile chat up and he interrupted her first sentence with, 'Have dinner with me tonight.' Right there in front of the fucking cameras and the fucking audience and Jeff and Danny!

The audience laughed. Ha ha very funny.

She charmed her way out of it with a smooth, 'Much as I'd love to, I never mix business with pleasure,' then started to carry on as if there'd been no interruption when, clear as day, loud as thunder (it seemed) Stavros said, 'Really? That's not what I've heard.'

Nudge nudge, wink wink, oh shit, and Pritchard rears his ugly head yet again. Kate smiled. 'Ah, but I'm choosy,' she said. 'So it's still no.'

Then she made a big mistake, the kind of mistake she'd never normally have made but tonight, because she wanted it more than ever to go well, she blew it. She patted his knee and said, 'No hard feelings?'

Stavros clamped his hand on top of hers and replied, 'Plenty. But not in my knee.'

Ho ho ho. The thought of editing it out was no consolation. The packed studio audience was still witness. Jeff was still witness. Kate the professional kept on going but somewhere deep inside she felt cheapened, soiled by the smutty responses, the automatic assumption that the proposition would be accepted. Just another piece of meat, an easy lay, everybody knows that Pritchard has been there so Stavros would have his share, too.

After the recording the hospitality suite was filled with artificial geniality and the Greek was still being terribly greasy. He stood too close. He touched unnecessarily. She wished no ill on Linda but longed for her assistant to come and take him away.

'I didn't spoil the show for you?' he said over the rim of his glass of specially bought-in Ouzo.

'On the contrary,' she replied. 'It made good television. That's all that matters.' That's when Linda and the others

391

came in and Kate turned to the newcomers with relief to perform the introductions. 'Costas, this is C.J. Warren, the author. His son, Danny. Julian you've already met, of course. And this is Linda Ross, my assistant . . .'

Linda was already at the forefront holding out her hand.

Stavros took it and held on to it for much longer than necessary while saying, 'Lin – da! What a beautiful name. For such a beautiful girl. And what magnificent hair,' he said, skimming his hand over her frizzy ginger halo.

Kate only just prevented herself from wincing out loud but Linda was lapping it up.

'Maybe you'd care to accompany this poor, lonely stranger on a tour of your beautiful city's nightspots?'

Hardly poor, thought Kate. And hardly a stranger, with his business tentacles clutching half the world. And hardly lonely with three undisguisable bodyguards clinging to him like mutated limpets. She watched Linda's response with relieved interest.

Linda did what any self-respecting girl being propositioned by the multi-millionaire man of her dreams would do. She said, 'I'd love to.'

It was two in the morning and Danny was fast asleep.

Linda probably wasn't.

Kate and Jeff weren't either. They weren't even in bed yet.

And Kate still had her O'Connell persona firmly in place. It hadn't slipped all evening. Through the graciously granted autographs, through the personally guided tour of TV7, through the meal afterwards at Lacey's where the best table had automatically been reserved for 'Miss O'Connell's party'. And now just the two of them sipping coffee in her living room and she was still doing it. Katy wasn't home.

'That's some story,' said Jeff as she came to the end of a blow by blow account of her boardroom victory. 'Want to plot out my next novel for me? You provide the storyline, I'll put the words around it. We'd make a great team.'

'I'm sure we would,' she said. 'So why don't you put your money where your mouth is and finish your *Encounter*? We could complete the filming while you're here, even. An American in London. It makes sense. We'd make a great team, Jeff,' she said, lobbing his own words back to him.

'I wondered when you'd get round to that,' he said.

She was sitting in an armchair, her legs elegantly crossed, Jeff was on the sofa wondering when, if ever, she might join him there. Not tonight, he decided, so he spread himself out a bit more. 'It's about the only work-oriented thing you haven't touched on yet. Don't you ever go off duty?'

'You're not answering my question.'

'Tell me something first,' he said. 'Satisfy my curiosity.'

'Go on.'

'Is that the reason you invited us over to stay with you?'

It wasn't a very big question but it had a very big effect. She slammed her coffee mug down so hard that its dregs bounced. 'Christ! Of all the . . .' She stood with an angry, jerky movement. 'For God's sake, let's not go through all *that* again. Do you really believe I'm that devious? We've *had* that routine, Jeff, and I didn't think much of it the first time either.' She paced the carpet, pausing every now and then to punctuate her words with a direct glare. 'No. I did not ask you over here simply for the sake of my programme. And just for the record, in spite of any mistaken impression you or anybody else might have, I do not go to bed with people for the sake of my work, either.' The anger that had been stewing all evening because of Stavros finally spilled over on to Jeff. 'Okay? Got that? It probably hasn't occurred to you that there are much easier ways of getting people to do my show. Like asking them, for instance. But you're so bloody egocentric . . .'

'*Me* egocentric!'

'. . . that you think I'd do anything just to have an *O'Connell Encounter* on C.J. Bloody Warren.'

'Okay, okay, keep your voice down you'll wake Danny,' he said, hands raised in not altogether mock defence.

'Well, maybe Danny ought to hear this. Let him find out the sort of father he has. Suspicious, devious, egocentric . . .'

'You said that already.'

'And anyway, if that's what you thought then why did you come?'

He grabbed hold of her hand as it flapped the air in front of him. 'Because I was going to make the offer anyway. To finish the programme.'

That stopped her. 'What? Then what was . . . ?' She sat heavily onto the sofa next to him, energy spent. 'Then what the hell was all this about?' she asked wearily.

'I had to do something to get behind your defences,' he shrugged. 'You've been so smooth, so charming, so carefully *The* Miss Kate O'Connell all day I was beginning to think I'd imagined the Katy I knew at Gilberts Pond.'

'Bullshit,' she said. 'Here, there, Katy, Kate O'Connell, it's all the one package, Jeff. Take it or leave it.'

He grinned. 'If that's meant to be an ultimatum, lady, I'll take it. But you still haven't answered my question. Why did you invite us over here?'

'No ulterior motives. I just wanted us to stay friends, that's all.'

He considered the statement. Carefully and slowly he said, 'Well, I don't.' And then he kissed her pretty damned quickly before she could summon up the energy for further argument.

Kate had no intention of arguing. She managed to summon up a little energy, though.

Sometime in the middle of the night. Jeff and Kate in her bed, naked and totally spent. Jeff asleep, lying on his stomach, face turned towards her, a heavy arm resting across her ribs. Kate, not asleep, lying on her back, face turned towards him, watching him with a kind of surprised wonderment that he was there, wondering what the hell she was going to do when he wasn't any more.

Lightly she rested her hand upon his shoulder blade, loving the feel of his cool skin under her fingers. He didn't move. Very softly she whispered, 'I love you too, Jeff.'

His eyes opened and he smiled at her lazily. 'Thank God for that.'

'Hey, I thought you were asleep.'

'Ah, but I'm devious, remember.'

Kate arrived late at the office the next morning. Linda didn't arrive at all. She'd phoned in sick. Kate made no comment. She merely went to the wallboard, rubbed out the CANCELLED that was written across the C. J. Warren slot and replaced it with a beautiful, brilliant green CONFIRMED. Julian, also looking a little bedraggled (bed-raggled?) round the edges, made no comment save for the smallest of smirks.

And for the first time ever, Kate's workday dragged. She was eager to get home again, to a home with love inside it. She loved it. She loved them. She loved the thought of going home.

Jeff and Danny busily started on all the things that were expected of them – Kate had dropped them off in town on her way in to TV7 and when at last she was home again she was regailed with enthusiastic descrip-tions of the Science Museum and plans for Tower Bridge and the Crown Jewels and the Changing of the Guard and the thousand and one other things that Kate, as someone who lived in the capital, had never got round to investigating.

They celebrated a rainy Saturday with a 'first' for all three of them, a riverboat trip down the Thames all the way to Hampton Court Palace and back again.

Sunday was lunch with the Levys. The men were washing the dishes, Becky was asleep, Sammy had taken

Danny off to his bedroom where the contents of the toy cupboard were systematically being spread over every available inch of floor space. Kate and Mo took a moment alone together in the garden.

'Well?' asked Kate.

Mo looked at her very seriously and said, 'Grab him. Chain him up. Lock him in your cellar. Whatever. But don't let this one escape. He's . . . well, if it weren't for the fact that I'm a happily married woman and you're my best friend . . .' She glanced at the kitchen window. Then she muttered, 'What am I saying? To hell with you and Ben!' and headed back to the house with Kate following quickly.

Kate was tempted to follow Mo's advice. She even had a cellar of sorts though she wasn't too well-stocked on the chain front. And if the essential dilemma in their relationship could have been resolved by a simple, captivating action, she'd have done it. But it wasn't that kind of problem. Working on it through the night (though fun) wasn't going to help much, either. Magical as it all was in the here and now, nothing had really changed. Only the location. Kate had her world, Jeff and Danny had theirs, and everybody was carefully avoiding the topic of when they were going to go back to it.

Until that evening.

Danny had finally agreed to go to bed only on condition he could have a repeat telling of Prince Daniel and the Space Dragons. Kate had been hard pushed to remember it but Danny proved an able prompter. Jeff was allowed to listen in from the beginning this time seeing as he'd missed it first time round, then it was goodnight hugs and lights out and just as they closed the door Danny said, 'Kate, can I have another hug please?'

He got it. Kate suspected that she needed it even more than Danny did. 'Now go to sleep,' she ordered softly, unclasping his arms from her neck. 'You've got a busy day tomorrow, remember, and your dad's not going to want you dozing off on him in the middle of the London Dungeons.'

'Okay. Kate?'

'Mm?'

'Are you going to come home with us?'

She sighed. This time she was the one who instigated the extra hug. 'Oh Danny. I would if I could, my precious. But I can't. I'm sorry.'

Jeff, who was hovering by the door, said, 'Come on, Chief. Off to sleep. Now. It's late.'

Instant sleep isn't always so easy. Before the two adults were halfway down the stairs they heard, 'Dad? Da-ad?' so Jeff went up again as Kate continued down.

'More dragons?' she said, handing him a glass of bourbon when he finally joined her in the living room.

'Sort of.' He took the drink. 'Kate, we've got to talk.'

'I know.'

And then neither of them said anything for quite a while. Kate eventually broke the silence with, 'We just go round in circles, don't we? I can't leave.'

'I know. I'm not arguing with you any more. I can see that.'

'And I know that you can't stay. Danny needs security, stability, you. He needs you there. Full time. I couldn't argue against that, Jeff. I love him too, you know. He's got to come first in all this. For a few more years at any rate.' A long drink. 'So. Where do we go from here?'

'Airports?' said Jeff with a wry smile 'We're going to be seeing a lot of airports.'

'I'm not sure,' she said. 'I thought we'd agreed you deserve more than that.'

'So whoever said we get what we deserve? I'm not going to give up on us, Katy. Not now. You're not going to get rid of us that easily.'

'Why does she want to get rid of us?' said Danny from the doorway.

'What are you doing out of bed?'

'Couldn't sleep.' And the very sleepy-looking pyjama clad figure headed for Kate's lap and climbed straight into it without so much as an invitation. 'Don't you like us any more?'

How to twang the heartstrings in one easy lesson. 'I love you very much, Danny. And I love your father very much, too.'

'So we can stay here?'

'Well, of course . . . no . . . I mean . . . Jeff, help.'

Jeff came across and knelt next to their chair. 'We can't stay, Danny.'

'Why not?'

'Your schooling, Grandma and Grandpa, your friends, my work, home . . .'

'But you just said I came first.'

'How long have you been listening at the door?'

'Ages. And that's what you said, I heard you. And *I* want to stay *here*.'

Jeff took hold of his hand and stroked it. 'I know. But it isn't as easy as that.'

'Why?'

Kate, who'd kept silent during this last exchange, put her hand on Jeff's shoulder and said, 'Why, Jeff? Out of the mouths of babes and sucklings . . .'

'Who are you calling a baby?' Danny turned to her aggrieved. 'I'm seven. Nearly eight.'

'Nothing personal, Chief,' she said. 'Now scoot. Back up to bed.' She underlined her order by tipping him off her lap and escorting him to the door. She watched to make sure he went upstairs. As he reached the half-landing she stage-whispered up to him, 'Go on. Don't worry. I'll deal with your father.'

'Promise?'

She crossed her heart.

She went back into the living room with the words, 'Now shut up and listen,' before Jeff had the chance to utter a sound. 'You've both had your say and now it's my turn. So to summarise: I'm not giving up my job and I can't base myself anywhere else but here and don't you dare say one word about me leaving it all behind and finding a job in some piddling little American TV station because . . .'

398

And Jeff had no intention of saying any such thing but Kate didn't pause long enough to find out.

'. . . that's not going to happen, not now, probably not ever. Like it or not, I stay here. In London.'

'I worked that one out already.'

'You, on the other hand, could work here as well as anywhere, all you need is a desk and some paper . . .'

'Hey, lady.'

'. . . Danny likes it here, he's made one friend already, there are good schools, and this is the twentieth century, they've invented the aeroplane and New York's only hours away . . .'

'Kate.'

'. . . and damn it all, even if you don't come up with another bestseller I make enough money for both of us, all three of us. And you want to be a hermit anyway so . . .'

'*Katy!*'

'What?'

'Cool it, lady. Who's arguing?'

'What?' She looked at him long and hard, searching for confirmation that his words had meant what she hoped they meant. She found none. The face that was so dear to her, so necessary, looked back at her with all the deadpan guilelessness of a Laurel to her Hardy.

'If all that was meant to be some sort of proposal,' he said in a very matter-of-fact voice, 'then you could at least get down on one knee and do it properly.'

She gave a long, slow smile as she shook her head. 'I've got a better idea.'

He sighed. 'You would have.'

'Fancy a tuna salad for supper?' Whereupon she took his hand and led him firmly from the room. They did not head for the kitchen.

Kate was in an extremely good mood at work on Monday. Which was just as well because Linda was very late in.

She arrived just before lunch looking exactly like the

Linda they all knew from B.C. days (Before Costas) – baggy dungarees, knitting needles poking out from the plastic supermarket carrier bag – but she smiled, oh how she smiled.

'I hope you're not going to make a habit of this sort of thing,' said Kate, half joking, half serious. 'I must admit you surprised us all, waltzing off into the wild blue yonder with Stavros like that.'

Linda smiled.

'Well?'

Linda smiled.

'Did you have a nice time?'

Linda smiled and nodded.

By now Kate was smiling to match. 'Did you, er . . . ?'

Linda finally spoke, still smiling. 'I'll never tell. Kate?'

'Hm?'

'Can we book an *Encounter* with Don Johnson in the next series?'